THE DEVIL'S SEAL

By Peter Tremayne and featuring Sister Fidelma

Absolution by Murder
Shroud for the Archbishop
Suffer Little Children
The Subtle Serpent
The Spider's Web
Valley of the Shadow
The Monk who Vanished
Act of Mercy
Hemlock at Vespers
Our Lady of Darkness
Smoke in the Wind
The Haunted Abbot
Badger's Moon
Whispers of the Dead
The Leper's Bell
Master of Souls
A Prayer for the Damned
Dancing with Demons
The Council of the Cursed
The Dove of Death
The Chalice of Blood
Behold a Pale Horse
The Seventh Trumpet
Atonement of Blood
The Devil's Seal

THE DEVIL'S SEAL

PETER TREMAYNE

headline

First published in 2014 by
HEADLINE PUBLISHING GROUP

1

Cataloguing in Publication Data is available from the British Library

ISBN 978 1 4722 0831 6

Typeset in Times New Roman PS by Palimpsest Book Production Limited,
Falkirk, Stirlingshire

Printed and bound in Great Britain by
Clays Ltd, St Ives plc

Headline's policy is to use papers that are natural, renewable and recyclable products
and made from wood grown in sustainable forests. The logging and manufacturing
processes are expected to conform to the environmental regulations of the
country of origin.

HEADLINE PUBLISHING GROUP
An Hachette UK Company
338 Euston Road
London NW1 3BH

www.headline.co.uk
www.hachette.co.uk

This one is for

Kate and Dave Clayton

with deep appreciation;

and may good fortune always follow the clan Clayton

Dan, James, William and Matthew

. . . affuit inter eos etiam Satan. Cui dixit Dominus: Unde venis?
Qui respondens, ait: Circuivi terram, et perambulavi eam.

. . . and Satan came also among them. The Lord said unto him:
Where do you come from? Answering, he said: I have circled the
Earth, and walked around on it.

Job 1:6–7

Vulgate Latin translation of Jerome 4th century

pRINCIPAL chARACTERS

Sister Fidelma of Cashel, a *dálaigh* or advocate of the law courts of seventh-century Ireland

Brother Eadulf of Seaxmund's Ham, in the land of the South Folk, her companion

At Cill Siolán, by the River Siúr

Gormán, commander of the Nasc Niadh, bodyguards to the King

Enda, a warrior of the guard

Dego, a warrior of the guard

Brother Siolán

Brother Egric

At Cashel

Colgú, King of Muman and brother to Fidelma

Beccan, *rechtaire* or steward to the King

Dar Luga, *airnbertach* or housekeeper of the palace

Ségdae, Abbot of Imleach and Chief Bishop of Muman

Brother Madagan, his steward

Aillín, Chief Brehon of Muman

Luan, a warrior of the guard

Aidan, a warrior of the guard

Alchú, son of Fidelma and Eadulf

Muirgen, nurse to Alchú

Brother Conchobhar, an apothecary

Visitors to Cashel

Deogaire of Sliabh Luachra, Brother Conchobhar's nephew
Abbess Líoch of Cill Náile
Sister Dianaimh, her *bann-mhaor* or female steward
Cummasach, Prince of the Déisi
Furudán, his Brehon
Rudgal, an outlaw of the Déisi
The Venerable Verax of Segni
Bishop Arwald of Magonsaete
Brother Bosa, a Saxon scribe
Brother Cerdic, a Saxon emissary
Brehon Fíthel, from the Council of Brehons

In Cashel township

Rumann, tavern-keeper
Della, mother of Gormán
Aibell, friend of Della and Gormán
Muiredach, a warrior of Clan Baiscne

At Eatharlach

Brother Berrihert, a Saxon religieux settled in Ireland
Brother Pecanum, his brother
Brother Naovan, his brother
Maon, of the Déisi

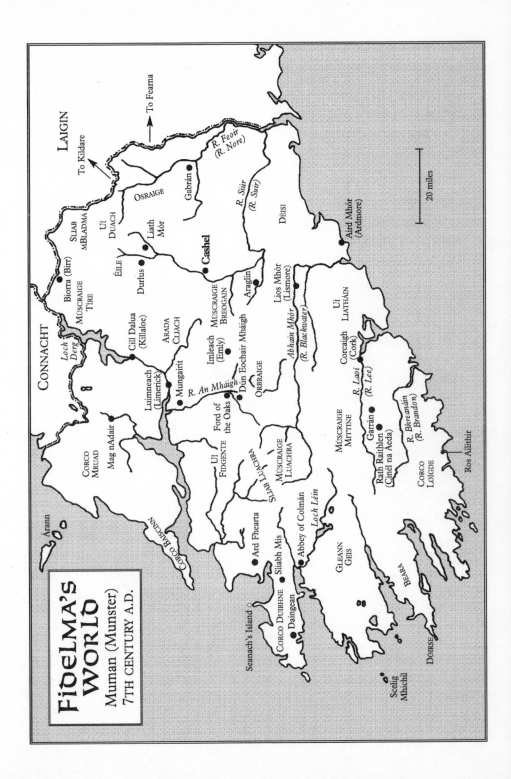

FIDELMA'S WORLD
Muman (Munster)
7TH CENTURY A.D.

LAIGIN

CONNACHT

To Fearna

To Kildare

R. Feoir
(R. Nore)

OSRAIGE

Gabrán

R. Siúr
(R. Suir)

DÉISI

Aird Mhór
(Ardmore)

20 miles

SLIAB
MBLADMA

ÚI
DUACH

Liath
Mór

Cashel

Biorra (Birr)
MÚSCRAIGE
TÍRE

Éile

Durlus

MÚSCRAIGE
BREOGAIN

Araglin

Lios Mhór
(Lismore)

Úi
LIATHÁIN

Cill Dalua
(Killaloe)

ARADA
CLIACH

Imleach
(Emly)

Dún Eochair Mháigh

Abhain Mhór
(R. Blackwater)

Corcaigh
(Cork)

Loch
Derg

Luimneach
(Limerick)

Mungairit

R. An Mháigh

ORBRAIGE

R. Laoi
(R. Lee)

CORCO
MRUAD

Mag nAdair

Úi
FIDGENTE

Ford of
the Oaks

MÚSCRAIGE
LUACHRA

MÚSCRAIGE
MITTINE

Garrán

R. Bhreanáin
(R. Brandon)

SLIAB LUACHRA

Rath Raithlen
(Cinél na Áeda)

CORCO
LOÍGDE

Ros Ailithir

Arann

CORCO
BAISCINN

Ard Fhearta

Sliabh Mis

Abbey of Colmán

Loch Léin

GLEANN
GEIS

BEARA

DOIRSE

Seanach's Island

CORCO DUIBHNE

Daingean

Scelig
Mhichil

AUTHOR'S NOTE

I intend to follow the Irish spelling of the River Siúr (pronounced 'shure') in this book and not the Anglicised spelling, River Suir. It is thought that this spelling came about by the mistaken transposition of the 'i' and 'u'. This explanation is to avoid letters from well intentioned partisans of either spelling who, in the past, have sought to correct previous spellings no matter which form was chosen.

The Siúr means the 'sister' river. It rises in the Devil's Bit Mountain north of Durlus Éile (Thurles) – see Chapter 16 of *The Seventh Trumpet* – and crosses south over the Tipperary Plain to swing east and, after its 185 kilometres journey, empty into the estuary by Port Láirge (Waterford). The actual Devil's Bit, or Bite, was anciently called Bearnán Éile (Gap of the Éile).

The events in this story follow in chronological order those related in *Atonement of Blood* and are set during the period known as *Dubh-Luacrann*, the darkest days, which now correspond to the months of January and February. The story begins just before the ancient feast of Imbolc, now fixed in the modern calendar as 1 February. This was the festival that marked the time when the ewes came into milk and when the days started to become perceptibly longer. It was associated with the Irish Goddess of Fertility, Brigit, but soon after the introduction of Christianity, it became the feast day of St Brigid of Kildare. The year is AD 671.

CHAPTER ONE

The three horsemen halted their mounts on the hillside and gazed down into the river valley. Below them, an expanse of trees formed a barrier between the hills and the broad, sedately flowing river to the south. The scene was a patchwork of greens, yellows and browns depending on the varied species and condition of the arboreal canopy and its foliage. The trees were mainly broad-trunk oaks, with their massive crooked branches and spreading crowns. Here and there were blackthorns, with tough yellow wood and long cruel thorns; and then appeared grey-brown rowans and even willows. They all crowded together, pressing towards the river as if seeking its nourishing waters.

The day was unusually warm for the time of year. Patches of blue with hazy sunlight appeared now and then behind the slow-moving grey-white clouds. For what was supposed to be the darkest days of the year, it was pleasantly light and mild.

The three riders were young men, warriors by their style of dress and weapons, and each wore the distinctive golden necklet that denoted that they were members of the élite bodyguard of the King of Muman, the most south-westerly and largest of the Five Kingdoms of Éireann. Their leader, Gormán, leaned forward and patted his horse on its neck. His eyes glanced quickly to the east and then, as if following the sun, which

had drifted behind the clouds, moved westwards. He finally gave a satisfied nod.

'We will be at the Field of Honey long before sundown,' he announced
to his companions. Cluain Meala, the Field of Honey, was a settlement
further to the west, on the northern bank of the river called the Siúr whose
waters lay before them. 'We'll stay there and ride on to Cashel tomorrow.'

'I shan't be sorry to get home,' sighed one of his companions. He
glanced nervously back in the direction from which they had come, back
to where the hills rose to a dark, impressive mountain.

The leader chuckled as he caught the young man's expression. 'Did
you expect to be enchanted by the women of the Otherworld while we
were crossing the mountain, Enda?'

'All very well for you, Gormán,' replied the other indignantly, 'but the old
stories are often true ones.'

'So you really believe that Fionn Mac Cumhaill and his warriors were
enchanted by women of the Otherworld as they crossed the mountain?'
enquired Gormán, his tone edged with derision.

'Is it not called Sliabh na mBan – the Mountain of Women?' protested
Enda. 'And the entrance to the underground sanctuary of the Otherworld
women is known to be located near its summit.'

The third member of the party interrupted with a snort of exasperation.
'Stories for the campfire! If we grew cautious when approaching the site
of every weird tale, we would never move from our own thresholds.
Anyway, we've crossed the mountain without problems, so there's no need
to worry about Otherworld entities now. Let us move on, for the sooner
we get to the Field of Honey, the sooner we can relax over a beaker of
corma, a good meal and a bright fire.'

'Dego is right,' agreed Gormán. He was about to nudge his horse forward
when a sudden cacophony of bird cries caused him to glance across the
tree-tops towards the river. His keen eyes caught a rising circle of alarmed
birds in the distance.

'Something has startled them,' muttered Enda, following his gaze.

'Birds are always being startled,' Dego said indifferently. 'Maybe a wolf or a fox has taken its prey.'

Gormán did not bother to comment further but led his companions down the hillside into the woods below. He knew the narrow track which descended towards the river. It was not long before the trees gave way to scrubland and then stretches of sedges and reeds which lined the banks of the broad river. They walked their horses westward, becoming aware, as they did so, of the still-wheeling birds ahead of them. Now and then, black-headed Reed Buntings went skimming by, barely above the level of the water, with a frightened repetitive cry. Gormán could pick out the hoarse, laughing chatter of magpies, as they fluttered against the cloudy sky above them. Then his eyes narrowed. Among the wheeling birds were large black ones with diamond-shaped tails.

'Ravens!' he muttered. His tone indicated his dislike of the creatures, for ravens were the symbols of death and battle; evil carrion which were said to feed off the corpses of the slain.

'Some creature must have been killed, as Dego said,' Enda observed. 'That is probably why the birds were making such a noise. And now the eaters of dead flesh have come to claim their share of the kill.'

They had been moving at a walking pace along the northern bank of the river and now, as the water course made a slight bend, they could see what it was that had alarmed the birds.

Gormán was not alone in catching his breath and sharply drawing rein.

Four corpses lay sprawled on the river bank among scattered items of clothing, remains of burned papers and other detritus. Nearby, not even secured to the bank, was a *sercenn*, a river craft with a single sail which, if the wind and current were contrary, was hauled in so that *ramha* or oars could be used to propel it. Now the sail hung limp and torn, and one of the oars, smashed and splintered, was floating in the water beside the boat.

Misfortune had certainly overcome the occupants of the craft. Two of the corpses were clad in leather jerkins and had the appearance of boatmen. One had bloody wounds to the skull while the other, who lay face down, had an arrow still impaled between his shoulderblades.

Gormán's mouth tightened as he realised that the other two corpses were clad in the torn and bloody robes of religious.

Enda and Dego had already unsheathed their swords and were peering cautiously around them, ready to respond to any threatening danger.

Gormán shook his head. 'It must have happened when we first heard the noise of the birds. The attackers are long gone.'

The heavy black ravens had withdrawn a little at the men's approach but remained watching them with unblinking malignancy. As the three riders had made no aggressive moves towards them, they had begun to edge back towards the corpses. With a sudden shout, Gormán jumped from his horse and picked up a few loose stones, which he threw at the birds. They retreated with a flapping of their dark wings to a safe distance, and then stopped to stare back at the creatures that had come between them and their food. They were obviously not to be removed so easily from the prospect of a meal.

Enda joined Gormán in surveying the scene. Dego had descended and stood holding the horses' reins, watching as his companions examined the bodies.

'Robbers?' he asked morosely.

'It would seem so,' replied Gormán. 'If there was anything valuable in this boat, then they have taken it.' He dropped to one knee by the corpse of one of the two religious. 'The crucifix that this one was wearing has been removed by force.'

'How can you tell?'

'A little trick the lady Fidelma taught me. Observation. See that weal on the neck? That would have been caused when the thieves tore off the crucifix. What else would a religieux be wearing around the neck but a crucifix?'

'Who was he? Someone local?' asked Enda, staring down at the corpse.

The man lay face down, and they noticed that part of his garments had been ripped away, revealing a number of criss-cross scars on his back. But they were old and healed wounds, as if he had been scourged some years ago. Gormán turned the body over. The victim was an elderly man, with sallow skin. There was something foreign in his appearance that Gormán could not quite place. His tonsure was certainly cut in the manner of Rome rather than that of the Five Kingdoms. The other body was that of a younger man, who also wore the tonsure of Rome.

'Strangers, I would guess,' Gormán said. 'They were probably travelling upriver when they were attacked. Robbery appears to be the motive. I can't see any signs of personal valuables or even a cargo on the boat. And before you ask, Dego, the boat's bow is facing upriver. It is logical that they were moving in that direction.'

Enda grinned. 'You have indeed been taking lessons from the lady Fidelma.'

Dego, having tied the horses to a nearby bush, had come forward and started turning over the remains of the burned pieces of vellum or papyrus with his foot. 'Well, there are not enough of these pieces surviving to make sense of any of them. I wonder why they burned them? Vellum and papyrus are so hard to come by that a scribe would offer much merely to re-use them; to clean and write over the old text. I've seen it done. And . . .'

He suddenly bent down and picked up something. He came to his feet squinting at a small round object between his thumb and finger.

'What is it?' Gormán asked.

'I thought it was a silver coin,' replied the other in disgust. 'But it is just a round piece of lead. There are some letters on it as if it was a coin, but no one would use lead as currency.' He squinted at it more closely. 'V . . . I . . . T . . . A . . .' he read aloud. 'I can't make out any more.'

'*Vita* is Latin for life,' declared Gormán knowledgeably.

'Well, it's not worth anything.' Dego tossed it in the air and caught it deftly. 'I can use it as a weight for my line when I go fishing.'

'But who do you think was responsible for this?' Enda demanded.

'I heard that there was a band of Déisi youths who are in rebellion against Prince Cummasach,' Gormán replied. 'It might be their work.'

The Déisi comprised a small principality south of the river whose princes owed allegiance to the King of Muman.

'Could rebellious youths have committed such butchery?' Enda asked dubiously.

'I have heard that there was bloodshed over a cattle raid these youths carried out near Garbhán's fort. They have been proclaimed *elúdaig*, absconders before the law, outlaws, losing their rights in society. This is why they have probably taken to murder and brigandage,' replied Gormán.

Enda glanced round and noticed some lengths of rope still coiled on the boat.

'The best thing to do is get these corpses onto the boat and cover them as decently as we can. That way, we can protect their bodies from the ravens. Then, if I am not mistaken, we are only a short ride from the chapel of Brother Siolán. We can use the rope to tow the boat along the river with our horses from the bank. I am sure that the good Brother Siolán will offer these men a Christian burial.'

Gormán agreed and waded to the boat to pull it closer to the bank. Enda and Dega lifted the first corpse, the elderly religieux, and placed it in the vessel while Gormán was securing one end of the rope to the bow.

'It's a light craft, therefore I think we can get away with one horse pulling it,' he said with satisfaction, stepping back onto the river bank.

It was while his companions were lifting the next corpse, that of one of the boatmen, that a movement caught the corner of Gormán's eye. At first he thought it was one of the intimidating ravens and turned to meet the threat. Then his eyes widened. It was coming from the body of the younger religieux.

6

In a moment, he had fallen to one knee beside the man and was feeling for a pulse point in the neck.

'By the powers!' he exclaimed in a shocked voice. 'This one is still alive.'

Enda brought the goatskin water bag immediately from his horse and poured some of the liquid across the lips and face of the man. He was a handsome fellow with dark hair. There was bruising on the side of his head, but Gormán's trained eye observed that there were no other deep cuts or abrasions.

The trickle of the water brought momentary consciousness, and suddenly the young man was striking out and moaning as if in the belief that he was still under attack. But he had no strength and Gormán was easily able to contain his threshing arms.

'It's all right, all right.' His voice was calm and reassuring. 'You are among friends.'

The young man coughed, muttered something in a harsh-sounding language that Gormán felt was familiar but did not understand, then he relapsed into unconsciousness.

'Will he survive?' demanded Enda, peering over Gormán's shoulder.

'We must get him to Brother Siolán,' replied Gormán. 'He has the knowledge of healing.'

Enda was frowning at the face of the young religieux.

'He is a stranger to me and yet . . . yet I swear those features are familiar. What language was it he spoke?'

Gormán shrugged, disclaiming knowledge. Then: 'Help me place him in the boat. It will be an easier way of transporting him than trying to put him on a horse.'

The young man did not recover consciousness while he was settled in the boat away from the three corpses that had been his companions.

Enda volunteered to stay on the boat with one of the oars to help guide it while Gormán, having had one last look at the debris on the bank, to make sure that they had left nothing of importance behind, took the other end of the rope and secured it to his saddle. Enda, using the oar, and with the help of Dego on the bank, pushed the craft away from the muddy bank. Gormán then began to walk his horse along the water's edge. It was difficult at first, and now and then Enda had to use the oar to keep the boat from embedding itself into the mud. It was not long, however, before Gormán and Enda achieved a means of hauling the boat along at a reasonable pace. Behind Gormán rode Dego, leading Enda's horse and ready to help should difficulties arise. All were uncomfortably aware that behind them, the dark ravens seemed to be following as if reluctant to part with their intended meal – the corpses in the boat.

Cill Siolán, the little chapel of Brother Siolán, was situated on a straight stretch of the river and marked by a wooden quay from which a path led to the nearby chapel and the cabin where Brother Siolán lived. As well as the path from the river, there was a track which led to the large settlement called the Field of Honey, which lay further to the west. Set apart from the river and track, Siolán's hut was nestled in the surrounding forests that spread over the hills towards the distant prominence of the Sliabh na mBan.

The three warriors guided the boat, with its grisly cargo, to the quay. As Gormán secured the craft, Enda looked up at the sky.

'We have no hope of reaching the Field of Honey before nightfall now.'

'At least we don't have to camp in the open,' Dego said. 'I've heard Brother Siolán is quite hospitable.'

A voice hailed them and a stocky figure in religious robes came trotting down the path to the quayside. He was a fleshy-faced man with bright blue eyes and a mass of sandy hair. By his side moved a large wolfhound, with wary eyes.

'Gormán! It is good to see you again. What brings . . .?' The greeting stopped short as his eyes fell on the contents of the boat. 'In God's name, what has happened?'

'Brigands,' explained Gormán succinctly. 'Probably those Déisi outlaws that there has been talk about. But one of the victims still lives and so we need your immediate aid.'

Brother Siolán did not waste time with further questions.

'Bring him up to the cabin so that I may examine him.' He turned and gave staccato orders to his hound; the beast loped off back to the cabin porch and lay down, ever-watchful.

Gormán turned to Enda. 'We two shall carry him. Dego, you see to the horses. We'll help you later with the burial of the corpses,' he added to Brother Siolán.

Gormán and Enda lifted the unconscious young religieux from the boat and, between them, carried his inert body up the pathway to Brother Siolán's cabin. He let them in and pointed to the bed, asking, 'How long ago did this happen?'

'We are not sure, Brother,' Gormán said breathlessly. 'But it can't have been that long ago. Will the man live?'

Brother Siolán was bending over the young religieux, examining him.

'The only wound seems to be the abrasion on the side of his head. Has he regained consciousness at all?'

'Only momentarily,' Gormán replied.

'A good sign anyway. It seems that the blow rendered him unconscious, which probably saved his life as the attackers may have thought they had killed him. Let us hope that the blow has caused no internal injuries. However, he will doubtless suffer headaches when he recovers consciousness.'

He turned to a cupboard. 'I have a paste of crushed flowers of a plant that grows nearby. That will cleanse and soothe the wound. Then when he comes round, I will try him with an infusion from the bark of the white willow. That should take away the headache. Then you can tell me in detail what has happened.'

'We ought to bury the poor man's companions before we sit down to recount our story,' suggested Gormán. 'The ravens have been following the boat since we discovered it and the corpses.'

Brother Siolán was apologetic. 'Of course. But do you have any idea of who these people are?'

'Only that they are two religious and two boatmen. We think the religious are strangers to this country. Maybe they came all the way upriver from Láirge's harbour.'

The harbour lay close to the mouth of the River Siúr and was a place where many ocean-going vessels made landfall.

'I see this one has the tonsure of Rome,' noted Brother Siolán. 'Well, time enough for speculation. I'll tend to him. Go, take the corpses to the back of the chapel here, secure the boat and you'll find an enclosure and fodder for your horses behind this hut.'

'What about your hound?' asked Enda, with a nervous glance at the dog, which seemed to be suspiciously watching their every move.

'Figleóir? What? Oh, I see.' Brother Siolán grinned. 'Don't worry about him. He won't bother you now that he sees we are friends.'

'Figleóir, that's a good name for a watch-dog,' Enda observed dryly. The name meant 'a watcher'.

It was well after dark when all the tasks had been accomplished. The corpses had been buried and the graves marked. The boat had been searched again for any clues of its origin, and now the three warriors had crowded into the cabin of Brother Siolán to relax in front of a warm log fire. The rescued religieux still lay on Brother Siolán's bed but was now breathing more easily.

'He's fallen into a natural sleep,' Brother Siolán explained, as he served a meal to the hungry warriors. He had already provided a jug of home-brewed ale, which they sipped appreciatively.

'Is that a good sign?' asked Enda. 'Sleeping so long?'

'It is. So now, what brings members of the Nasc Niadh, the élite bodyguard of our King, along the banks of the Siúr? What is the news from Cashel?'

Gormán stretched himself before the comforting fire. 'We can tell you little enough of recent news from Cashel as we have been away over a week, on an errand to investigate some dispute at the Ford of Fire.'

Áth Thine, Ford of Fire, was a crossing point between the Kingdoms of Muman and neighbouring Laighin – which often proved a cause for skirmishes and conflict.

'Then we came south-west by means of the Mountain of Women and hence to the river. Our plan was to ride to the Field of Honey before turning north back to Cashel.'

'I heard a rumour that Caol is no longer the Commander of the King's Bodyguard,' remarked Brother Siolán.

Gormán hesitated a moment before replying: 'That is so.'

Enda was grinning and there was pride in his voice when he said, 'Gormán is being too modest. He neglects to tell you that he is the newly appointed commander.'

Brother Siolán's eyes widened. 'Then congratulations are in order.'

Gormán seemed embarrassed. 'Colgú has placed a great trust in me,' he admitted. 'I shall do my best to fulfil his expectations.'

'Yet Caol was surely too young to retire from the command?' mused the religieux.

'Caol decided that he wanted to become a farmer,' put in Enda, ignoring the disapproving glance from Gormán. 'He has gone to farm somewhere west of the River Mháigh, on the borders of the Luachra territory.'

Brother Siolán looked surprised and was about to make a comment when Gormán said hurriedly, 'You may have heard that King Colgú has recovered from his wound and is well.'

Only a few months had passed since there had been an attempt to assassinate the King.

'I heard Caol slew the assassin. I suppose he had earned the right to be able to retire to follow a more peaceful calling,' reflected Brother Siolán. 'And how is the King's sister, the lady Fidelma? Is she well?'

'When we left Cashel, she was very well.'

There was a sudden groan from the figure on the bed and Brother Siolán moved swiftly across to him. It was clear the young religieux was regaining consciousness and becoming aware of his surrounding. Brother Siolán gave him a few sips of liquid from a beaker which Gormán presumed was some herbal concoction to help him.

The young man sat up, massaging his head. He seemed to be asking a question in a language that none of them understood.

When Brother Siolán asked how he was, the man hesitantly replied in the same language but with a curious accent. 'What happened?' he asked groggily.

'You were attacked by brigands and left for dead. Unfortunately, your companions were all killed in the attack. Luckily, these warriors found you and brought you here.'

The young man groaned again, partly in his discomfiture and partly from the confirmation of the news he must have expected.

'Do you remember what happened?' asked Gormán, rising from his seat to come closer. 'Do you recall your name?'

The young man licked his lips for a moment. 'I am called Brother Egric. We were being transported upriver when our vessel was approached by a larger vessel manned by half-a-dozen men. They greeted us in friend-ship and we thought they were just passing by, but all of a sudden they attacked us. I saw one of our boatmen fall with an arrow in his back. Our craft was driven into the bank. I was travelling with the Venerable Victricius. He tried to remonstrate with the attackers, who were all young men, but they laughed and then one of them hit him about the head with a war axe. I turned to flee, and something hit me on the side of the head. I had a passing thought that I was dead. I am not sure what happened next. I seemed to be in some dream until I woke just a moment ago.'

Brother Siolán nodded sympathetically. 'You are safe now, my friend. I am Brother Siolán. My little chapel is not far upriver from where you were attacked and where these good warriors found and brought you here. Alas, as I said, your companion and the boatmen are all dead. We have buried them behind the chapel.'

A look of pain crossed the young man's features.

'The Venerable Victricius is dead?' he repeated as if he could not believe it.

'He is dead, indeed,' confirmed Gormán.

Brother Egric sighed. 'And our belongings? Has everything been stolen?'

'Only a few items remain. That which was not destroyed was carried away by them. It looks as though you were attacked by robbers.'

'Did you retrieve anything?' There was a curious eagerness in his tone.

'We did, mainly items of clothing. They are piled in that corner.' Gormán nodded in that direction. 'But first some questions. You have told us your name and that of your dead companion. Where have you come from? Where were you going?'

The young man rubbed his forehead. 'We – that is, the Venerable Victricius and I – came to this country five days ago. We landed at a place called Láirge's harbour and arranged for two boatmen to take us upriver. Is this river still called the Siúr? It is? Then we were to land at a place called Cluain Meala where we were told we would find a guide.'

'A guide? To go where?'

'To a place called Cashel.'

'Cashel . . .' Gormán was surprised. He had expected any foreign religious to be travelling to Imleach, the oldest and largest abbey in all Muman.

'We were to meet a Brother Docgan in Cluain Meala.'

'Brother Docgan?' Gormán glanced at Brother Siolán who looked bemused. 'The name is unfamiliar to us. It sounds Saxon. Indeed, your own name and accent make you a Saxon.'

The young man shook his head and winced from the pain. 'I am an Angle; but perhaps you would not know the difference,' he said weakly.

Gormán chuckled. 'That is where you are wrong. I have a good friend who makes a point of correcting people when he is called a Saxon.'

'I don't understand.'

'Our King's sister, the lady Fidelma, is married to an Angle.'

'Then I must surely meet with him,' the young man replied gravely. 'From which kingdom of the Angles does he come?'

'From the Kingdom of the East Angles, he says,' replied Gormán.

The young man turned to regard him with an expression of astonishment.

'But so do I!' he announced. 'I am from the Land of the South Folk in the Kingdom of the East Angles.'

'Tell me,' Gormán asked excitedly, 'have you heard of Eadulf of Seaxmund's Ham?'

'Eadulf?' The name was issued as a strangled gasp by the religieux. There was a silence during which he seemed to be gathering his thoughts before he answered slowly. 'My name is Egric of Seaxmund's Ham: I am brother to Eadulf, who was our hereditary *gerefa*, as was our father before him.'

CHAPTER TWO

❧

'Brother Eadulf of Seaxmund's Ham, in the Land of the South Folk of the Kingdom of the East Angles, is summoned to the presence of Colgú, King of Muman.'

For a moment, Eadulf stared in amusement at the solemn face of the steward of the palace of Cashel, comptroller of the King's household. Then he assumed an equally solemn expression, for he knew that the rotund Beccan, who had served only months in his office of *rechtaire*, or steward, was a stickler for protocol. Eadulf had been told by Gormán that the steward's punctiliousness was affected because he was a comparative stranger to the palace. He came from the southern part of the kingdom, south of the Siúr, and had come to oversee the kitchens. A few months later the previous steward had retired to his family and farm, and Beccan was suddenly elevated to this new position.

'Eadulf, husband to Fidelma of Cashel, sister of King Colgú, will obey this summons,' Eadulf answered with equal gravity. Then he could not help relaxing his features in a smile. 'So what does Colgú want of me? Why summon me, and not Fidelma?'

Beccan's fleshy features assumed a disapproving look.

'It is not my place to guess the desires of the King, only to relay his orders.'

Eadulf sighed at the steward's uncompromising tone. 'I'll come immediately.'

Fidelma and Alchú, their four-year-old son, were out riding with Aidan, one of the King's bodyguards, as escort. Therefore there was no one to whom to explain his absence. Eadulf set off after the steward who led him from the chambers they occupied, across the courtyard to the main building of the palace complex which contained the private chambers of the King.

'I wonder if this summons has anything to do with the arrival of Abbot Ségdae and his companions last night?' he mused aloud as they proceeded.

Ségdae, Abbot of Imleach and Chief Bishop of Muman, had arrived at dusk the previous evening with his steward, Brother Madagan, and a foreign religieux. They had immediately retired to the guest quarters. As a regular visitor to Cashel, both as spiritual adviser and member of the King's council, Ségdae's arrival did not usually arouse any comment. But it was unusual that the abbot had not joined them for the evening meal.

'There is always some matter of church policy to be discussed,' Beccan replied shortly.

'Is the King's *tánaiste* with him?' Eadulf asked.

'Finguine, the heir apparent, left early this morning to visit the Prince of the Eóghanacht Glendamnach.'

'I expect he is late with the tribute again.' Eadulf spoke lightly.

A stony expression confronted him. 'I would not know,' said Beccan, 'and even if I did, it is not my place to discuss the policies of the King.'

Eadulf suppressed a sigh. There was no humour in the man. He fell silent while the steward moved into the passage to where a member of the King's bodyguard stood outside the red yew-tree doors which led to the private chambers. Beccan raised his staff of office and rapped it three times against the wooden panels before throwing it open. He stood framed in the door.

'Eadulf of Seaxmund's Ham . . .' he began to announce loudly.

He was interrupted by the tired voice of Colgú from beyond. 'I know well who it is. You may leave us, Beccan; make sure that we are not disturbed until I send for you. Come in, Eadulf.'

Beccan swallowed uncomfortably. He was always exasperated by the fact that Colgú liked to circumvent the protocols of court. He registered his irritation by assuming an expression of longsuffering resignation and stood aside to allow Eadulf to enter and then closed the doors softly behind him.

'I swear that Beccan is so pedantic that he even takes to writing the names of guests down so that he can announce them in the right order.' It was Colgú who made the comment as Eadulf moved forward into the room. 'I have a suspicion that he finds it hard to remember names unless he does so.'

Eadulf saw Abbot Ségdae seated by the fire opposite Colgú. The King waved Eadulf to a seat with a quick smile of welcome. Eadulf exchanged a greeting with the abbot before sitting. The man looked somewhat distracted. There were furrows on his brow as if he were wrestling with some problem.

'We need your help,' Colgú began without preamble.

'Whatever help I can give is yours to command,' Eadulf replied, settling down in a chair and looking expectantly from Colgú to Ségdae.

Colgú made a motion with his hand as if inviting the abbot to explain. Abbot Ségdae hesitated a moment and then spoke.

'We have received word that an embassy of your countrymen will soon arrive here in Cashel.'

'An embassy of my countrymen?' Such news was unusual. 'Who are they, and for what purpose do they come here?'

'No doubt the same purpose that is behind the many councils that have been held between our religious and those who follow the dictates of Rome,' Abbot Ségdae said, barely concealing the irritation in his voice. 'Those who waste time attempting to make us turn from the path of the Faith that we have chosen.'

Eadulf waited for the abbot to continue and, when he did not, he felt obliged to comment. 'You may have forgotten that I was an adherent to the ways of Rome before . . .' Eadulf paused as he was about to say before he had met Fidelma at the Great Council in Hilda's Abbey at Streonshalh.

'That is precisely why we need your advice,' Colgú interrupted quickly. 'I am hoping that you may tell us something about these people and their ideas.'

'I still don't understand. Are you saying that some religious are coming here to argue the merits of the practices of their Church? But who arranged this? Such councils have to be proposed, accepted and arranged well in advance – and why are they coming here and not to the Abbey of Imleach?'

'They have simply announced that they are coming here.' Abbot Ségdae was angry. 'The first we knew of this was the arrival of two messengers at my abbey. One was a Brother Cerdic, a Saxon. He was accompanied by Brother Rónán from Fearna who came with him merely as a guide. Brother Cerdic stated that an embassy would arrive at Cashel within a week, and demanded that this council be presided over by the King and no other.'

Eadulf shook his head slowly. 'And that was all? No other explanation?'

'It was enough,' fumed the abbot. 'It was sheer arrogance. In fact, I found their emissary, this Brother Cerdic, arrogant in his manner of relaying his message to me.'

'They came from Fearna?' pressed Eadulf. 'Is this some new evil scheme from Laighin?'

Fearna was the main abbey of the neighbouring Kingdom of Laighin, whose kings had long plotted against Muman.

'That was my thought at first,' Colgú confided. 'Yet Abbot Ségdae has had private assurance from Brother Rónán that Abbot Moling of Fearna was to emphasise that Laighin are not involved. Brother Rónán said the delegation had arrived at Fearna without prior warning. They had some inconsequential discussions and then asked whether Abbot Moling could supply a guide and interpreter for Brother Cerdic to come here. Abbot Moling also gave an assurance that King Fianamail has no interest in this matter.'

'Do we trust Abbot Moling?' asked Eadulf, adding, 'I heard that he was born and raised in Sliabh Luachra. My recent experiences prejudice me against people from that territory.'

'That is true,' agreed the abbot, 'but I think we can trust his word. Brother Rónán has fulfilled his task and returned straightway to Fearna. So Fearna are not represented here.'

'It sounds very strange,' Eadulf reflected.

'Certainly the attitude of the Saxon religieux is unwarranted,' the abbot grumbled. 'My steward, Brother Madagan, and this Brother Cerdic very nearly came to blows.'

Eadulf's eyes widened. 'Knowing Brother Madagan, I find it hard to believe he would be in danger of losing his temper.'

'Then you will gauge the conceit of this Brother Cerdic. And how arrogant he is to bring such a message to this Kingdom! Brother Rónán had tried to modify the language as he interpreted him, but Brother Madagan knows some of the Saxon tongue and immediately understood the high-handed nature of his words.'

Eadulf was reflective. 'Are you sure that there was no mistaken emphasis in the translation? Perhaps this group are merely coming to make arrangements for some bigger council in the future. There may be some misunderstanding of the intention of their embassy.'

Abbot Ségdae snorted with indignation. 'The message was perfectly clear. I was thankful that Brother Madagan had arrived back at the abbey to receive Brother Cerdic. The intention needed no interpretation. Besides which, Brother Madagan exchanged some words with Brother Rónán, who confirmed that even the King of Laighin felt that the Saxons were disrespectful.'

Eadulf was surprised to hear that Brother Madagan had some fluency in Saxon. During the times he had met the steward of Imleach, they had never conversed in Eadulf's own language.

'Yes, the message was clear enough, friend Eadulf,' Colgú said in support of the abbot.

Eadulf was still puzzled. 'But a council on religious affairs would best be held at the abbey, with scholars on hand to give advice. So why are they coming to your palace? Why insist that you, the King, preside over it?'

'I agree that this is the point of curiosity, Eadulf,' Colgú said. 'This is why we are consulting you.'

'There have surely been enough councils at which delegates from many strange lands have attended and tried to change our laws and ways of proceeding!' Abbot Ségdae was obviously irritated by the affair. 'Only the laws of hospitality require that we receive them, otherwise I would advise the King to turn them away.'

'You say that this deputation is currently staying at the Abbey of Fearna?' Eadulf enquired.

'I am told that while the leaders of the deputation stayed with King Fianamail at his fortress at Dinn Ríg before commencing their journey here, Brother Cerdic was sent to give us advance warning. They have probably already crossed into the Land of the Osraige and could be with us any day now,' sighed Abbot Ségdae, relapsing into gloom.

'Brother Cerdic says this deputation is from my people?' Eadulf frowned. 'East Anglia is but a small kingdom, and one which many of the other Kingdoms of the Angles and the Saxons have claimed jurisdiction over. Its abbots are not so influential as to lead deputations outside their own domains. Why, it was only in my childhood that it was converted from the Old Faith of my people and . . .'

Abbot Ségdae stopped him with an impatient gesture of his hand. 'When I said "your people", I meant that they have come from one or other of the Kingdoms of the Angles and Saxons,' he explained, as if the difference was a trifle. 'Whoever they are, Brother Cerdic says that they come with the authority of the Bishop of Rome, Vitalian. The Roman faction has made many attempts to force our churches to follow their rules. They should give up their endless councils and arguments, and leave us to proceed according to our beliefs.'

Colgú stirred uncomfortably and glanced at his Chief Bishop.

'Except, as I have heard it, several of our abbots and bishops, especially in the Northern Kingdoms, seem to have already accepted the rituals of Rome,' he said. 'Apparently, many are now following the teachings of Cumméne Fota of Connacht.' Catching Eadulf's perplexed expression, he added by way of explanation: 'He died not so long ago and was bishop and lector at Cluain Ferta. He became converted to the Roman liturgy and propagated their doctrine.'

Abbot Ségdae sniffed. 'I'll grant Cumméne was an intelligent man and a diligent scholar, but he was misled. We should abide by our own doctrines.'

Eadulf did not want to become embroiled in an argument on liturgy. 'I still cannot see what role you expect me to play in this matter,' he said, raising his hands in a hopeless gesture. 'What is it that you wish of me?'

'Do not the ancient philosophers have a saying – *nam et ipsa scientia potestas est*?' Abbot Ségdae asked dryly.

Eadulf nodded. 'I'll grant you that knowledge is power. But knowledge of what, exactly?'

'Brother Cerdic has told us that the name of the man who leads this deputation is a Bishop Arwald. Perhaps you might know something of him so that we can assess how best to treat him. He comes, we are told, in the company of a Roman cleric named Verax and they are under the authority and blessing of Vitalian, Bishop of Rome, and that of Theodore, the Archbishop of Canterbury, whom I believe you know.'

'Theodore? Indeed I do,' affirmed Eadulf. 'I was in Rome when he was appointed Chief Bishop to the Anglo-Saxon Kingdoms in place of Wighard, who was murdered in Rome. Fidelma and I solved the mystery of his murder. As Theodore was a Greek from Tarsus, it was requested that I should instruct him in the ways of the Angles and Saxons before he took office. Later, it was Theodore who sent me into this kingdom as an emissary. And here I have chosen to remain.'

Colgú smiled softly. 'We know your story, Eadulf. So now we are hoping you will be able to provide us with information. As we said, we hope that you may know something of the leader of this deputation so that we can learn something of his purpose. Have you encountered this Bishop Arwald of Magonsaete?'

'Of Magonsaete?' Eadulf raised his head sharply in surprise.

Colgú caught the movement. 'Then you do know this man?'

'I do not know *him*,' Eadulf said quickly, 'but I do know Magonsaete. I would have thought it the last place to be able to appoint a bishop to discuss church matters with this kingdom or, indeed, any other kingdom.'

Colgú was intrigued. 'Tell us what you know. Where is this place?'

'It has recently come into being; a hybrid kingdom, neither of the Angles nor of the Britons. It is situated betwixt and between the two peoples. It came into existence when Penda of Mercia – Mercia is one of the major kingdoms of the Angles – joined forces with some of the Britons to extend his western borders. Among the Britons fighting for Penda was a warrior called Merewalh – the name means "illustrious foreigner". I am afraid I do not know his real British name. Twenty years ago, Penda made him sub-King over this newly acquired territory which was called Magonsaete. That was in reward for his services.'

Colgú rubbed his chin thoughtfully. 'Are you telling us that this is a kingdom of Britons which owes its allegiance to a kingdom of Angles? I am confused.'

'That is not exactly the situation. The Angles from Mercia began to settle in this new kingdom, displacing the native Britons who fled westward. Merewalh is a Briton, but he rules over the new settlers. Merewalh married one of Penda's daughters. He has forsaken his own people.'

Colgú struggled to understand the politics of the situation. 'So you are saying that this Briton has the authority of Rome and Canterbury to send his bishop to debate with us?'

'It seems scarcely credible,' agreed Eadulf solemnly. 'It was only ten years ago that Merewalh was converted to the faith of Christ.'

'But surely all the Britons were Christian?'

'Maybe Merewalh had originally been of the Faith but changed it when he made his alliance with the Mercia King. Penda was no Christian. He believed in the ancient gods of our people, like Woden.'

'You seem to know a lot about his kingdom. Yet it is not connected with your own. How is this?'

'Penda was an Angle but he was the most ruthless and ambitious of the kings,' explained Eadulf. 'He sought to subdue my own Kingdom of the East Angles and slew our great King Anna when I was only a lad. Even after Penda died – I was about twenty years of age then – Penda's son, Wulfhere, continued to exert his will over our small kingdom. So we were always aware of the Mercian threat.'

Colgú shook his head in frustration. 'With due respect to you, Eadulf, I find all these foreign names very confusing. I have no understanding of any of these kingdoms of the Angles and the Saxons. Have they no High King governing them as we have here?'

'Such an idea is growing among my people,' Eadulf conceded. 'But there are eleven major kingdoms of Angles and Saxons, and all their rulers are often at war with one another. I doubt whether we will ever see unity among them. Anyway, the conflict among them is not even about uniting the kingdoms – but about claiming the title to be conqueror and ruler over the Britons.'

'I don't understand.'

'The title that is claimed is *Bretwalda* – wielder or ruler over the Britons. Don't forget that the kingdoms of the Angles and Saxons were carved out of the lands of the Britons when our ancestors first landed on the island of Britain two centuries ago. But the title is meaningless for the Britons have not submitted.'

Colgú remarked sadly, 'Your people seem to be very warlike, always intent on conquest.'

'I regret that it is so, Colgú,' nodded Eadulf. 'But perhaps, as the New Faith takes firmer hold, we may become calmer and more content. Our kingdoms were born in bloodshed and conquest. Therefore it may take us some time to recover from those years.'

'So what are we to make of this Bishop Arwald of Magonsaete?'

'It is hard to make anything of him until we know him. You say he comes here on the authority of the Bishops Vitalian and Theodore?'

'So far as we are told.'

'Then I have little understanding of it,' Eadulf said. 'Why would Rome and Canterbury send any delegation to Cashel, even if it was to discuss matters of the Faith?'

'It is a mystery which we were hoping you could enlighten us on before this delegation arrives,' sighed Abbot Ségdae.

'I can only tell you what I know. What did you say were the names of the other members of the delegation?'

'There is this Roman cleric named Verax,' offered the abbot.

'The name is common enough among clerics,' Eadulf shrugged. 'It means "the truthful one".'

'And, of course, this Brother Cerdic.'

'Well, it does sound as if Cerdic comes from Magonsaete,' mused Eadulf. Then, seeing their baffled looks, he told them: 'Cerdic comes originally from a name popular among Britons – Ceretic. With the mixture of Britons and Angles in Magonsaete, it is not unusual to see such a name. It is now adopted by the Angles.'

'So it seems that we can do nothing except wait for the arrival of this deputation before we can discover their intention,' commented Colgú.

And then, to Eadulf's surprise, Colgú suddenly grinned. It was the mischievous smile that he shared with his sister when a humorous thought came to his mind. 'Unless, Abbot Ségdae, you want to consult with Deogaire?'

Abbot Ségdae's brow gathered in an angry frown before he saw the smile on the King's lips.

'I certainly do not,' he replied tightly.

'Excuse me?' asked Eadulf. 'Who is Deogaire?'

'A person to avoid,' snapped Abbot Ségdae. 'Especially with your prejudice against Sliabh Luachra.'

'I referred to Deogaire of Sliabh Luachra,' Colgú explained. 'Unfortunately, if we did not have concerns enough, he has chosen this time to make one of his infrequent visits to Cashel. He claims to have a gift of prophecy.'

It was only a short time before that Eadulf had found himself on the borders of Sliabh Luachra, the territory of the Luachair Deaghaidh, and witnessed the killing of their chieftain, Fidaig, by the chieftain's own son! Eadulf suppressed a shiver, remembering the forbidding mountains that made the territory a fortress against outsiders. It was a grim and frightening land.

'This Deogaire,' Eadulf went on after a moment or two, 'is he of the chieftain's family? Why would *he* be able to answer your questions?'

It was Abbot Ségdae who responded. 'It is the King's humour. Deogaire is a wild man, a man of the hills and mountains. As the King says, Deogaire claims to be able to foretell the future; he calls himself a wizard, a sooth-sayer. Every so often, he comes out of his mountain fastness and sells his prophecies to the gullible – credulous people who do not trust the Faith.'

'Deogaire has a talent for creating arguments, especially among the brethren,' added Colgú.

'Then why is he allowed in the palace?'

Colgú sighed. 'It is hard to refuse him. He is the nephew of old Brother Conchobhar; the son of his sister.'

There was little need to explain further because Eadulf knew that Brother Conchobhar was the physician and apothecary who had tended and been mentor to both Colgú and Fidelma since childhood. Even before they were born, he had served their father Failbhe Flann. If there was one person in

Cashel that Eadulf had come to trust implicitly, it was this bright-eyed old man.

However, Colgú was moving on. 'Eadulf, I will want you to attend this coming council as my adviser, for you will be valuable in that role.'

'Surely Fidelma will make a better adviser?' he protested.

Colgú shook his head. 'You are from the land of these people; you know their language and the way their minds work. I need that knowledge. As for Fidelma, Aillín is my Chief Brehon and it will be his role to advise on legal matters as it is Abbot Ségdae's role to advise on matters of the Faith.'

'Speaking of which,' intervened the abbot, 'I was surprised to learn that Brother Cerdic insisted on visiting Abbess Líoch of Cill Náile and suggesting it was in her interests to attend here.'

'I recall that the abbess is an old friend of Fidelma,' Eadulf said. 'Now I am completely in the dark as to the intention of this deputation, as there are more senior religious in the kingdom than Abbess Líoch who should attend any council.'

'It could be that Brother Cerdic was asked to invite her because of her knowledge of your people – I mean, the Angles,' Colgú suggested. 'Some years ago, Abbess Líoch joined a party of missionaries to the Kingdom of Northumbria and spent time at an abbey called Laestingau. So she knows something of your people and their ways.'

Abbot Ségdae nodded. 'It would be good to have her expertise at this meeting as well as your own.'

'I have no objection,' Eadulf agreed, knowing full well that the abbot was not asking him if he objected or not. 'I have not met the abbess before.'

Cill Náile, he knew, was an easy ride east of Cashel, but he had never visited the small religious community there. Líoch, so Fidelma had told him, had been one of her companions when she set out to join the group of Irish delegates journeying to the Great Council of Streonshalh. As far as he recalled, Líoch had not attended the council. She remained at Laestingau, some days' ride west of Streonshalh.

'Where is Brother Cerdic now?' he asked the abbot. 'I understand that he came with you to Cashel.'

Abbot Ségdae's face became glum. 'He did. He is here awaiting the arrival of the rest of his deputation.'

'Then perhaps I should go and speak with him? I might be able to pick up some further information.'

'I was hoping you would,' Colgú said. 'It is hard to get any understanding of what is going on. This whole matter makes me uneasy.'

'You should find him in the chapel,' offered the abbot. 'He is someone who appears to prefer to keep himself to himself.'

Eadulf was crossing the courtyard towards the chapel building when Fidelma came riding in through the main gates on her short-necked grey stallion, which she had called Aonbharr after the horse ridden by the old God of the Oceans, Mannanán Mac Lir. Alongside her, smiling broadly astride his piebald pony, was their four-year-old son, Alchú, with his mop of bright red hair. Behind, keeping careful watch, rode Aidan, one of the élite warriors of Cashel.

Eadulf paused for a moment to admire his wife. After the years during which she had been Sister Fidelma, clad in the robes of a religieuse, he had not fully become used to seeing her as 'Fidelma, Princess of the Eóghanacht'. Her red hair was plaited in three braids, held in place with silver circlets on her head. She wore a tunic that fitted tightly to the waist and then billowed over her upper legs, which were encased in tight-fitting *triubhas*, or trousers, that fitted into leather boots that came just above the ankles and were of a matching blue. From her shoulders hung a short cloak, with a beaver-skin collar, clasped together by a silver brooch. Each garment was patterned in designs picked out in gold and silver needlework.

Although Fidelma had quit the religious, Eadulf had not and so still kept to his Roman tonsure and robes, though at times he felt a little drab standing at his wife's side.

He stirred himself and hurried forward to help his son from his horse, a fraction of a second before the *echaire*, who looked after the stables, had reached the group.

'Hello, little hound,' Eadulf greeted the child. 'Have you had a good ride?' He used the literal meaning of the boy's name as a term of endearment.

The boy fell into his arms with a laugh of greeting.

'We had a wonderful time, *athair*,' he replied. 'We were riding through the forest and surprised some deer. They ran away from us. Then we were coming home and saw a lot of men putting up a new building.'

'A new building?' Eadulf frowned for a moment.

'He means the repairs to the south-western wall,' explained Fidelma. 'They are putting up a temporary wooden framework to support the workmen and their materials while they repair the wall.'

Eadulf recalled that there had been a rockfall under the wall of the King's fortress during the winter, which had caused damage to that extremity of the fortifications. The Rock of Cashel, on which the great fortress of the Eóghanacht Kings of Muman was built, rose from the surrounding plain with almost inaccessible limestone faces to a height of sixty-two metres from its immediate base. On top, nearly a thousand square metres were enclosed by the fortifications that the Eóghanacht had erected since they chose the site as their principal fortress nearly four centuries before.

Eadulf was about to warn the little boy of the dangers of going near a building site but Alchú was continuing, 'And we saw two strange women and we saw . . .'

Smiling, Fidelma had dismounted and handed her horse to the care of the stable-master, while dismissing the warrior Aidan with a wave of her hand.

'You'll be able to tell your father all about it as soon as you have cleaned yourself up,' she told the boy. 'See? Here is Muirgen come to take you for a wash and something nice to eat afterwards.'

Muirgen, the nurse, had appeared and the boy went to take her outstretched hand without any sign of reluctance. Eadulf was mildly surprised at Fidelma halting the boy's enthusiastic recital of his morning adventures, but then he caught something in her eye and knew she wanted to speak to him privately.

'I'll come along soon, little hound,' Eadulf called after his son, as the nurse led him away. 'You can tell me all your adventures then.'

Alchú's mind was clearly on the promised snack so he barely acknowledged his father but trotted off happily with the nurse.

The horses had been led off to the stables and the courtyard had emptied when Eadulf turned back to Fidelma.

'Is something wrong?' he asked softly.

'I am not sure,' she replied. 'I met someone I knew on the way to Cashel. We stopped for a chat.'

Eadulf raised an eyebrow in query. 'The strange women of Alchú's story?'

Fidelma grimaced. 'I suppose Abbess Líoch would seem strange to a little boy. As you know, in this land we love bright colours in our dress and the religious are no exception. But since Líoch has returned from the Saxon lands, she has affected black in all her garments; even her *cenn-barr* or head veil is black, as well as all the fasteners for her upper garments. There is not a precious stone to be seen unless it be a black stone in dark metal.'

'Abbess Líoch?' Eadulf did not conceal his surprise. 'Has she arrived already?'

'Already?' Fidelma stared at him, puzzled. 'You knew that she was expected in Cashel?'

'I know that she had been asked to come here,' he confirmed. 'But you tell your story first. I'll keep quiet and then I'll tell you what I know.'

'Well, we were on our way back from our ride, joining the main track to Cashel,' Fidelma said. 'That was when we saw the abbess and her *bann-mhaor*, her female steward – I forget her name, but it was one of the sisters of her community. As I know Líoch, we stopped to speak. She told me that she had been asked to come here as there was to be a council. A deputation from one of the kingdoms of the Saxons was expected. It sounded very mysterious.'

'Where is Abbess Líoch now?' asked Eadulf, looking expectantly towards the gates.

'She would ride only as far as the township with us. She and her companion have gone to seek hospitality in the town, although I pointed out that my brother's palace has room enough to extend food and shelter to them both. The point is, Eadulf, it seems as if she has some trepidation about this gathering. What is it all about?'

Eadulf exhaled softly. 'I wish I knew. It is beginning to sound like a mystery.' He held up his hand as Fidelma was about to question him further, saying, 'Let me tell you what I know.'

He quickly described his meeting with her brother, Colgú, and Abbot Ségdae.

She was perplexed. 'I see no logic for a council. But there is an interesting point. You said Abbess Líoch was asked to attend?'

'I did. That also seemed curious to me, although Abbot Ségdae seemed to think it was because she had been in Northumbria for some time.'

'Líoch told me that two religieux called at her abbey several days ago. One of them was the Saxon religious you mentioned, called Brother Cerdic. The other was someone from the Abbey of Fearna. She said it was Brother Cerdic who told her that she should attend. Rather, her words were that he said it was "in her interest" to attend. I had the impression that she was troubled by his request.'

'In her interest to attend? That is surely a strange phraseology.'

'Those are the words she used. Do you know this Brother Cerdic?'

'No,' Eadulf said. 'I only know what I have just been told.'

'Where is he now? Here in Cashel?'

'He accompanied Abbot Ségdae and his steward, Brother Madagan, to Cashel. In fact, I was just on my way to find him in order to see if I could discover anything further about this strange deputation.'

'And Brother Rónán?'

'He has already returned to Fearna, having accomplished his role as guide. Abbot Ségdae says that Brother Cerdic maintains he acts merely as a messenger to announce the coming of the deputation.'

Fidelma's features bore a sceptical expression. 'Did Abbot Ségdae believe him?'

'I doubt it,' Eadulf replied cynically. 'It is a long journey to make across the sea to a strange land without knowing something of the intention of the group in which you are travelling. And if he suggested to Abbess Líoch that it was in her interest to attend, then he must surely know more of the matter.'

'I agree,' said Fidelma. 'She seems to be nervous of Brother Cerdic. That surely means she knows him or, at least, he has told her why she should come here.'

'I shall contrive to speak with this Brother Cerdic alone,' Eadulf decided. 'He might be more forthcoming to a fellow countryman.'

'But first you must keep your promise to Alchú,' Fidelma said sternly. 'He wants to tell his father about the adventures he had on his ride. You do that, and I will go and see my brother as I want to hear his thoughts about this strange deputation.'

A short time later, Eadulf re-emerged in the courtyard on the way to fulfil his errand. He passed Beccan, the steward, crossing the courtyard and asked if he had seen Brother Cerdic. The solemn-faced steward indicated the chapel behind him.

'I think I saw the Saxon entering the chapel,' he replied. 'A very unfriendly man,' he added with a sniff of disdain.

Eadulf was almost resigned to the fact that whether one was an Angle, a Saxon or even Jute, in the minds of the people of the Five Kingdoms of Éireann, they were all regarded as Saxons. Eadulf entered the chapel discreetly, waited a moment for his eyes to adjust, then peered about in the gloomy interior.

A figure was kneeling before the altar in a position of supplication.

Eadulf coughed softly to draw attention to himself. The figure made no motion. It seemed so still: knees and legs drawn up beneath the bent body, the forehead resting on the cold stone floor. Something glinted on the ground beside the figure, and it took some moments before Eadulf realised it was the flickering light of the candle reflecting in a pool of liquid. It was blood!

With a suppressed exclamation, he went hurrying over and knelt beside the body. He reached out a hand to touch the shoulder of the figure, and no sooner had he exerted a slight pressure than it rolled onto its side. The face was white, the dead eyes wide and staring.

There was no sign of a weapon but it was clear from the blood both on the floor and across the man's throat how he had come by his death. The fact that there was no weapon to hand also indicated that he had not died of his own choice.

CHAPTER THREE

⁊

E adulf had seen the dead and slain before, but there was something curiously pathetic about this body that had been crouched in a praying
position with its throat cut.

The flickering candles illuminated a man of similar age to Eadulf: thin,
almost gaunt-looking, with fair, lanky hair and the tonsure of Rome. He
was clad in nondescript woollen robes that were midway between white
and grey – the dirty colour of undyed wool. In Eadulf's eye, this identified
him as an adherent to the Rule of the Blessed Benedict, which Rome,
at the recent Council of Autun, had decreed all religious should follow.
Those adhering to it believed they should use only what they found in
nature without adornment in their clothing, and that they should follow
the simple life of work and prayer.

There was no doubt that this was Brother Cerdic – and now he would
no longer be able to answer any questions.

Eadulf reached forward and touch the man's neck. It was still warm.
He sprang up, suddenly alert, because he now realised that Brother Cerdic
must have come by his death only moments before he himself had entered
the chapel. He peered quickly round into the dark recesses of the interior.
There was no sound save the drip of tallow falling on the stone floor from
one of the tall candles.

Eadulf moved swiftly to the chapel door and, opening it, saw the aged Brother Conchobhar, together with a younger man, at the far side of the courtyard. He glanced around but no one else was about.

'Brother, a moment of your time,' he called.

Brother Conchobhar raised his hand and then made his way to the chapel door with his companion following. The latter was a stranger to Eadulf – a fellow clad in a bright multi-coloured cloak. He had well-formed, handsome features, a pale skin and long black hair that held a shimmer of blue when the pale sun glinted on it. Yet it was the eyes that held Eadulf's attention: they were of a curious light blue that seemed restless, like the waters of some ocean which threatened to draw Eadulf into their fathomless depths. It was almost an effort to draw his gaze away.

'You look worried, my friend,' the stranger said. When he spoke, the timbre and cadence of his voice were such that Eadulf knew that others would fall silent on hearing its haunting quality. It was not often that he had such a reaction to people.

Brother Conchobhar introduced him, saying, 'This is Deogaire, a relative of mine. He is right. Something *is* worrying you, friend Eadulf.'

'Have you seen anyone emerge from the chapel while you have been in the courtyard?' Eadulf asked.

'I saw no one,' answered the old apothecary. The young man also shook his head. 'Who are you looking for?'

Eadulf simply beckoned the two of them to follow him inside the chapel. Without a word, he pointed to the body lying before the altar.

Brother Conchobhar went directly to the corpse and bent down. His experienced gaze took in the injury and the mottling of the skin tone now visible even in the flickering light.

'What happened?' he asked.

'Frankly, I do not know,' Eadulf replied. 'I came into the chapel moments ago in the hope of speaking with this man. I found him crouched here and touched him on the shoulder, thus causing him to slip on his side.'

'There is no sign of a weapon,' Deogaire said, gazing about thought-fully. It was a statement, not a question.

'I saw none,' agreed Eadulf.

'Yet death was caused almost instantly,' Brother Conchobhar announced, rising to his feet. 'I would say a slash across the throat which prevented him from crying out, and then a single blow to the heart which caused immediate death.'

Eadulf's lips compressed a moment. 'It indicates that whoever did this was skilled in the use of weapons.'

'With knowledge of anatomy,' Deogaire added dryly.

'He is not long dead,' Brother Conchobhar said. 'Is that why you asked if we had seen anyone leave the chapel just now?'

'It was.'

'Well, there is hardly a place to hide in the chapel,' Deogaire said, looking around. 'They must have left just moments before you came here.'

'This bodes ill for Cashel, my friend,' Brother Conchobhar said heavily. 'You obviously know that this was a Saxon religieux, newly arrived here?'

'Colgú and Abbot Ségdae have told me all about him. Apparently we are expecting a deputation of Saxon clerics to arrive soon, to take part in some council. That is why I was asked to have a word with him.'

Brother Conchobhar grimaced sadly. 'I was told that this man, Brother Cerdic, was causing some upset here with his attitude.'

'Who told you that?' asked Eadulf.

'Brother Madagan, the abbot's steward.'

'Upset enough for someone to kill him?' Eadulf mused.

Deogaire was shaking his head. 'There are bad times coming to Cashel – evil times. I feel it.'

Eadulf found himself averting his gaze from those bright, deep-set eyes. 'I must inform Colgú about this,' he murmured.

Brother Conchobhar was nodding. 'We shall take care of the body.' The apothecary usually took charge of the bodies of anyone who died within the confines of the fortress and prepared them in his rooms for the rites of burial.

Eadulf left him and his relative, Deogaire, with the body of Brother Cerdic. He was making his way towards the King's chambers when Fidelma came hurrying towards him.

'What news?' she demanded without preamble. 'Did you get anything out of your compatriot?'

Eadulf's expression was grim. 'He is dead. Murdered.'

Her fiery green eyes widened as Eadulf told her briefly what had happened.

'That bodes ill for Cashel,' she said, almost repeating Brother Conchobhar's words. 'You saw no one in or around the chapel? No, I know,' she went on before he could reply. 'A stupid question to ask since you have already answered it.'

'We must inform Colgú and Abbot Ségdae about this.' Eadulf hesitated. 'By the way, do you know much about Deogaire? I have never heard him mentioned before today.'

'Deogaire?' Fidelma was dismissive. 'He has always been a strange one. Strange but harmless, unless one really believes he has the power of prophecy. Now and then he comes to Cashel to visit his uncle, old Conchobhar, but he likes to be among people who believe in his predictions.'

'Such as those in Sliabh Luachra?'

'Exactly so.'

'He has a powerful personality,' Eadulf admitted. 'Even I felt that he has some kind of magnetism.'

'That, I will not deny. If it were otherwise, he would not be able to fool the people that he does. Oh dear . . .'

Eadulf had barely wondered at the reason for her comment when he caught sight of the elderly and sharp-featured figure of Colgú's Chief Brehon, Aillín, hurrying from the direction of the chapel. His features were drawn into a belligerent scowl as he came up and halted before them.

'I have just seen Brother Conchobhar,' he snapped at Eadulf. 'I am on my way to inform the King.'

'So were we,' rejoined Fidelma – and received only a glance of irritation in response.

'I am told Brother Eadulf was a witness to the murder of his fellow countryman,' the elderly judge replied. 'I shall need to know what the Saxon said to you before he died.'

Eadulf's eyes widened with astonishment. 'He said nothing to me,' he protested. 'He was dead when I found him, so I was *not* witness to his murder. I did not even know the fellow.'

'Then why did you seek him out? You are both Saxons. What was he to you?' The older man almost spat out his questions.

Eadulf exhaled slowly to calm his rising temper. He knew that Brehon Aillín had always resented Fidelma, especially when she had offered herself before the Council of Brehons of Muman for the role that Aillín now held. He seemed to have taken a personal dislike to Eadulf – probably because of his relationship to Fidelma.

'I am from the Kingdom of the East Angles, while Brother Cerdic was from the Kingdom of Magonsaete. So, if you wish to be accurate, we are *not* Saxons,' Eadulf replied, his voice slow but with emphasis.

'Angle! Saxon! What does it matter?' Aillín replied aggressively.

Before Eadulf could respond, Fidelma had intervened.

'Eadulf went to see this religieux on behalf of my brother, in order to discover his purpose in coming to this place. My brother specifically invited Eadulf to meet with him and Abbot Ségdae this morning in order to ask his advice about the matter. It was the King himself who suggested Eadulf seek him out. So if this does not answer your question, any further information on the matter should be addressed to my brother, the King.'

Brehon Aillín blinked; the muscles in his face tightened a little.

'I am your brother's Chief Brehon,' he said slowly. His voice seemed to be propelled like a harsh breath through an almost closed mouth. 'It is my task to investigate this death. I will *not* have my rôle usurped.'

Fidelma actually smiled, albeit without humour. 'I know of no one who is seeking to usurp your rôle, Aillín. Therefore I suggest you accompany us to consult my brother, who would be anxious to hear what has transpired from Eadulf's own lips. My brother will be most anxious about this entire matter.'

With a quick glance at Eadulf, she turned and led the way towards her brother's council chamber. Eadulf immediately fell in step with her and, after hesitating a moment, Brehon Aillín scurried after them.

Colgú greeted the news glumly. 'We must inform Abbot Ségdae. Now we know nothing of this Brother Cerdic. How do we begin to cast around for suspects?'

Brehon Aillín cleared his throat. 'There is one person of his nation in the palace . . .' he began.

Colgú turned to him expectantly and then realised what the man was about to say.

'Oh, you mean Eadulf here? Well, that doesn't help, does it? I am talking about the person responsible for his death. We have no suspects.'

'But Brother Eadulf was with him when he died,' Brehon Aillín persisted. 'Therefore . . .'

'Don't be ridiculous, Aillín,' Colgú said irritably. 'It's no joking matter. We must think sensibly about it.'

Brehon Aillín's mouth closed in a thin, bloodless line. Colgú had interpreted the man's words as a joke. However, Eadulf knew that the elderly, prejudiced Brehon was far from saying it for amusement. He would have to be careful of the man.

Fidelma had moved on rapidly. 'Brother Cerdic and Brother Rónán called on Abbess Líoch and invited her to this council. She has apparently decided to stay in the township instead of coming to the palace. As I know her, I shall ask her if she was already acquainted with this Brother Cerdic and whether he said anything specific when he called at her abbey at Cill Náile.'

Colgú shrugged. 'If you think it worthwhile, then by all means do so. You should also persuade her that we have better guest facilities here than any lodging down in the township.'

Brehon Aillín intervened with another dry cough: 'May I remind you that as your Chief Brehon, it is *my* duty to conduct all these enquiries.'

Colgú turned to the man with a look of irritation. 'I was not overlooking that fact. But now you will be faced with more important tasks, for I wish you to liaise with Abbot Ségdae over the matter of this forthcoming deputation. That is a priority. The death of this religieux can be handled by Fidelma, as she is used to such matters.'

'But . . .' Brehon Aillín began to object.

Colgú held up his hand to silence him. 'I suggest that the sooner you consult with Abbot Ségdae, the better. Of course, if you hear anything that you think pertinent to Fidelma's enquiry about Brother Cerdic, you will naturally inform her.'

The Brehon stared sullenly at the King for a moment and then, with a brief inclination of his head, turned and left.

There was a palpable relaxation between them as the door closed behind him.

'I swear that man is getting more irascible each passing week,' muttered Colgú, surprising them by his comment. It was not protocol for a King to criticise his Chief Brehon to others.

'He is your Chief Brehon,' Fidelma pointed out gently.

'Yet not by choice,' her brother reminded her.

It was true that Aillín had assumed the position by default when Áedo, the elected Chief Brehon of Muman, had been slain protecting King Colgú from an assassin only some months before. Aillín had been his Deputy only by reason of age and experience, and it had been felt, by the Council of Brehons, that he would soon retire and so being appointed Deputy

Chief Brehon was a suitable acknowledgement for his service. Then Áedo had been killed. Aillín's automatic appointment had been accepted in spite of his known prejudices, fastidious attitudes and pedantry. The delays caused by his concentration on unimportant details drove even Colgú to distraction.

The King now turned to Eadulf. 'Do you have any ideas – about Brother Cerdic's death, I mean?'

'Only that I agree with Fidelma's suggestion of having a further word with Abbess Líoch. It seems the only logical path now. Obviously, there must have been someone here in the palace who knew him well enough to have the motive to kill him.'

'Why do you say that? Couldn't a stranger have done this – someone who had a grudge to bear against the man's race, or way of keeping the Faith? Don't forget, many of our churchmen and their followers have recently been chased out of the kingdoms of the Angles and Saxons after the decision at Streonshalh to follow the ways of Rome . . . Why, even some of the Angles and Saxons have sought liberty to follow their Faith by coming here – for example, Brother Berrihert and his companions who have settled in Eatharlach.'

'A good point,' agreed Eadulf. 'But Brother Cerdic knew his attacker. I don't think it was random.'

'What is your reason for saying so?' queried Colgú.

'Because Brother Cerdic was not suspicious of his attacker. He allowed whoever it was to come close enough in order to inflict those two mortal wounds. The victim did not suspect what was going to happen. He died without a sound or protest.'

'That's a reasonable deduction,' Fidelma commented.

Colgú suppressed a sigh. 'Then follow your thoughts by all means. It would be good if we could resolve this matter before Bishop Arwald and his companions arrive. I do not want other distractions clouding whatever is behind the reason of their coming.'

'We'll do our best to resolve things. Don't worry,' Eadulf replied, rising.

Fidelma rose with Eadulf and moved towards the door. She was opening it when Colgú called after them: '*Post equitem sedet atra cura.*'

Outside, Eadulf said: 'I didn't catch the meaning of that.'

'It was from an ode by Horace,' Fidelma explained with a brief smile. 'Behind the horseman sits black care.'

'Even a king is not free from worry,' Eadulf re-interpreted philosophically. 'I must confess, there seems much to concern him.'

They collected their horses from the stables, rode across the courtyard and approached the main gates. The commander of the guard, a warrior called Luan, greeted them with a respectful salute.

'We are just going into the township, Luan,' Fidelma said. 'If anyone enquires, we shall not be long.'

'Where will you be, lady?'

'We are going to find the lodgings of Abbess Líoch.'

'But you have just missed her, lady.'

Fidelma exchanged a quick glance of surprise with Eadulf. 'What do you mean, just missed her?' she asked.

The warrior shrugged. 'She and her companion have only just left the palace. Why, you will overtake her on her way back to the township as they are both on foot.'

Fidelma knew Luan had been at the gates when she had arrived after her morning ride with little Alchú. But she had left her friend, Líoch, and the abbess' companion at the track leading into the township which sprawled on the southern side of the great limestone rock on whose top the palace of her brother rose. She restrained herself from asking Luan if he was sure. He would not have said so, otherwise.

'When did the abbess arrive?' she asked.

'Shortly after you did, lady,' replied the man. 'You were talking with friend Eadulf in the courtyard and then you parted. It was just after that they arrived.'

Fidelma said thoughtfully, 'She must have changed her mind about going into the town and followed us.'

'But Luan has just said that she and her companion were on foot,' Eadulf reminded her. 'Didn't you say that they were on horseback?'

Fidelma turned back to Luan. 'You did say that the abbess and her companion arrived on foot?'

'I did, lady,' confirmed the warrior.

'Another mystery,' Eadulf muttered, almost to himself.

'But one we can easily resolve,' replied Fidelma, urging her horse forward through the gates.

They overtook Abbess Líoch and her companion as the women were crossing the market square of the township. They were not on foot but on horseback. As Fidelma called to her friend, the abbess turned her head and then drew rein while her companion followed suit.

'Líoch!' greeted Fidelma, as they rode up. 'We missed you at the palace.'

Eadulf wondered if he had mistaken a nervous exchange of glances between the abbess and her companion, but nothing was said.

'My brother insists that you accept the hospitality of our guest quarters and will take "no" as a personal insult,' went on Fidelma pleasantly. Then, before the abbess could respond, Fidelma indicated Eadulf. 'By the way, this is Eadulf, of whom you have heard me speak. Eadulf, this is Abbess Líoch of Cill Náile.'

Eadulf inclined his head in greeting. 'I have often heard Fidelma speak of you, Abbess.'

Abbess Líoch returned his greeting with a quick scrutiny but said nothing. Eadulf could see why little Alchú had described her as 'strange'. She was not much older than Fidelma but with dark eyebrows and deep-set, dark eyes. The features were attractive although plump; the cheeks rosy, the lips full and red without the necessity for highlighting them with berry juice. However, as Fidelma had described her, the abbess was clad in black robes from poll to feet. It was unusual dress for the country, although he had seen similar costumes worn among the elderly in Rome.

'I am sorry. I have forgotten your name, Sister.' Fidelma turned brightly to Abbess Líoch's companion, ignoring the silence which greeted them.

'This is my *bann-mhaor*,' the abbess answered for her. 'Sister Dianaimh.'

The abbess' companion was, by contrast, dressed in the usual colourful robes affected by the people of the Five Kingdoms. Her fair hair showed in wisps under the *caille* – the hood or veil worn by those who entered the religious – and her features were sharply moulded but otherwise attractive and youthful. She regarded them with suspicion from bright blue eyes.

'As I said, my brother insists that you stay in our guest quarters, especially during the visit by these foreign clerics. You cannot refuse.'

The abbess seemed to reflect for a moment and then gave a shrug. 'If it is the King's order, then it must be obeyed.'

Eadulf noted the reluctance in her voice.

'We missed you when you came to the abbey,' Fidelma persisted, a slight inflection in her voice. 'When I left you, I thought that you were coming straight to the township.'

The abbess cleared her throat. 'After you left, I realised that I should at least report my presence to Abbot Ségdae, for you told me that he was at the palace.'

'Of course. The guard mentioned that you came up on foot,' Fidelma said, with an air of innocence. 'It is surely tiring to do so when you could have ridden up?'

'The horses were fatigued.' There was a sudden edge to the abbess' tone, which was unexpected. Seeing their expressions, she added less abruptly, 'We thought to rest them and saw a youth by the track. We asked him to remain with our horses while we climbed up to the palace.'

'Ah, so you saw the abbot?' Eadulf asked.

Abbess Líoch shook her head quickly. 'He was nowhere to be found, and so we returned to get our mounts and look for somewhere to stay in the town.'

'A wasted journey, then?' commented Fidelma.

'Just so,' replied the abbess dryly.

'Come,' Fidelma said, turning her horse back towards the palace. 'Let us get you settled at our guest quarters. At least we can offer you better food than you might otherwise find in the township.'

After a moment or two, during which Eadulf wondered whether the abbess might refuse, she and her companion also turned their horses. Eadulf also wondered whether Fidelma was going to neglect the purpose of their seeking out of Abbess Líoch until later, but Fidelma suddenly said: 'My brother and, indeed, Abbot Ségdae, are perplexed about this deputation. You said that the Saxon emissary, Brother Cerdic, came to your abbey and suggested you attend?'

'I did,' frowned the abbess.

'We have no understanding of why this Bishop Arwald should be coming here. Did Brother Cerdic mention the reason for this visit?'

'Only that they came with some ecclesiastical authority.'

'Interesting that he stopped at your abbey before he journeyed on to Imleach to see Abbot Ségdae.'

The abbess was keeping her gaze firmly on the track before her, as if concentrating on guiding her horse.

'He came from Laighin, therefore Cill Náile lies on the road before Imleach,' she pointed out. 'It is natural he and Brother Rónán would pass it before they went on to Imleach.'

'Of course,' agreed Fidelma lightly. 'However, why would he have come to you with this request? You gave me the impression earlier this morning that it was a specific request for you to attend.'

Abbess Líoch tutted in annoyance and Fidelma gave her an apologetic smile. 'You must forgive me, my friend,' she said soothingly. 'You know that I am a *dálaigh*, and isn't it a lawyer's manner to ask silly questions?

Questions are now second nature to me but I have no wish to pry in matters that are not my affair.'

'I have no wish to give the impression that I resent your questions,' Abbess Líoch said.

'So, apart from geography, why would Brother Cerdic call at Cill Náile and ask you specifically to attend this council?'

Abbess Líoch thought for a moment. 'I can only presume that he had heard that I had lived and worked in the Kingdom of Oswy of Northumbria. Perhaps he thought I could be useful, for I have some knowledge of the tongue of his people.'

'Indeed. So you had not met Brother Cerdic during your time in Oswy's Kingdom? I remember that you were in our party when we crossed to I-Shona and came with us on the journey to Streonshalh. As I recall, you did not accompany us to Hilda's abbey and attend the council. Didn't you decide to stay and work in a place . . .?'

'Laestingau,' supplied the abbess. Her voice was sharp. 'The Abbey of Laestingau. In answer to your first query, no, I had not met Brother Cerdic before he arrived at Cill Náile. Why do you ask these questions, Fidelma?'

Fidelma turned and looked at her. She said quietly: 'I do not want to cause you alarm but I must tell you that Brother Cerdic has been found murdered.'

Abbess Líoch pulled on her horse's reins so roughly that the animal whinnied in protest and its forelegs kicked at the air in front of it before returning to a standstill. Her face was white, and she looked in the direction of Sister Dianaimh, who remained silent although it was clear from her expression that she was troubled.

'I presume that you did not see Brother Cerdic when you came to the palace to look for Abbot Ségdae?' Fidelma went on, apparently ignoring their reaction.

'We did not,' replied the abbess immediately. 'Are you saying he has only recently been found?'

'He was found dead in the chapel,' Eadulf confirmed. 'I found him.'

'And he was murdered, you say?'

'Stabbed to death,' confirmed Eadulf, deciding to leave aside the fact that his throat had been cut.

'That will cast a blight over this visit,' muttered Abbess Líoch.

'Whatever this visit is about,' Fidelma said, adding, 'I was hoping that you might be able to shed some light on it, as no one else seems able to do so.'

'I can tell you no more than I have already. All I know is that this deputation is coming to discuss some matters with the King and our Chief Bishop, Abbot Ségdae of Imleach. The rest is beyond my understanding.'

'I hoped that you might know more. No matter. I presume you saw nothing while you were looking for Abbot Ségdae?'

'What, for instance?'

'Perhaps you went near the chapel?' Fidelma suggested. 'You might have seen someone nearby; someone entering or leaving?'

'We saw no one,' the woman replied firmly.

They had reached the gates of the palace and Luan, still on guard duty, came forward.

'Get the *echaire*, the stable-master, to take our guests' horses,' instructed Fidelma. 'Then send someone to find Beccan so that he may arrange accommodation for the abbess and her steward.'

A few moments later, Fidelma and Eadulf watched as Beccan conducted the abbess and her companion away towards the guest quarters.

'Do you believe her?' Eadulf asked.

Fidelma sighed. 'It will not help us at this stage to confront her. What should we confront her with, anyway? Something is definitely not right here . . . yet the Líoch I knew was never given to subterfuge. However, I have not seen much of her since she returned from Oswy's Kingdom and became Abbess of Cill Náile. She appears to have changed considerably. The carefree young girl I knew has gone. She seems so morose! You noted the black mantle she now wears, and her manner of speaking to me as if she is speaking to a stranger?'

'And was that how she greeted you earlier when she met you and Alchú on the track here?'

'It was, although I did not set any store by it then.'

'And now?'

'There is little we can do until we obtain some more information.'

'We can question her companion,' Eadulf suggested. 'If Abbess Líoch is not forthcoming, perhaps she will be.'

'Sister Dianaimh? The *bann-mhaor* is so quiet, it's as if she is but a shadow. You would almost think that she did not exist. She has a strange name – one that I have not encountered before.' Fidelma grimaced without humour. 'It's a Laighin name, and means "Flawless One". She should have been named "Silent One". Well, I suppose there is little we can do but find out if anyone was seen lurking around the chapel when you were in there. You said that Brother Conchobhar didn't see anything?'

'Nothing. You know – Aillín is right,' Eadulf suddenly declared.

Fidelma turned to him. 'Right about what?'

'If I were in his place, I would suspect me.'

'Don't be ridiculous,' she snapped.

'You forget that I am an Angle. I could easily have known Brother Cerdic before. I know something of the kingdom from which his bishop comes. Who is to say that I did not know him or anything about this curious deputation?'

Fidelma suddenly chuckled, causing Eadulf to look puzzled.

'It's the first time I have heard someone *demanding* to be a suspect in a murder.'

Eadulf grinned. 'All I am saying is that Aillín has a point.'

'Aillín is a bitter old man who was not talented enough to be endorsed as Chief Brehon by the Council of Brehons. Only Áedo's death caused him to reach the position he has, as my brother said. Unfortunately, he has no breadth of vision, no imagination to see beyond literal fact. Anyway, enough of Aillín. Let us go and speak with Brother Conchobhar and see if he has anything more to tell us, now that he has examined the body.'

But Brother Conchobhar could tell them nothing more than to confirm the manner of Brother Cerdic's death, which they already knew. With a feeling of frustration the couple left the apothecary. A call arrested their attention and they turned to see Gormán hurrying after them.

'Gormán!' Fidelma smiled at the newly appointed commander of her brother's bodyguard. 'It is good to see that you have returned safely. Did you resolve the dispute at Áth Thine? Is all well?'

Gormán returned the greeting with a big smile. 'Áth Thine was nothing more complicated than an argument that a local Brehon could have resolved, lady. It was a simple dispute over cattle straying across the border. However, there seems to be a more serious dispute brewing among the Déisi.'

'More serious?' queried Eadulf.

'Some travellers were attacked on the river east of the Field of Honey, and two boatmen and one of the travellers, an elderly religieux, were killed. It occurred on the river just beyond Brother Siolán's little chapel,' confirmed Gormán. 'We were just crossing the Mountain of Women, heading for the Field of Honey in the late afternoon, when we came across the scene.'

Fidelma was shocked. 'Who attacked these travellers?'

'We heard that Prince Cummasach of the Déisi has been having trouble with some of his young men of late. We reported the matter to the Brehon at the Field of Honey and he will investigate. One of the travellers survived and said they had arranged to meet a Brother Docgan there. We asked around, but no one had heard of such a man.'

'Docgan is a Saxon name,' Eadulf told them. 'It means "a little dog".'

'You say there was a survivor?' Fidelma asked.

'Yes. We brought him here with us. I think you should speak with him, friend Eadulf. I have taken him to your chamber.'

Eadulf gazed at the young warrior for a moment, waiting for him to explain further.

'You are being very mysterious, Gormán.' It was Fidelma who made the comment.

The warrior shrugged diffidently. 'I just need to make sure that the man I have escorted here *is* who he says he is. Friend Eadulf needs to see the man first.'

Eadulf was puzzled, but quickly realising that he would get no more information from Gormán, he said: 'Then the sooner I see this survivor, the better.'

He turned and led the way to the chambers that he shared with Fidelma.

Entering, they were aware that Gormán had apparently left Enda to watch over the guest. The warrior greeted them with a quick nod and smile before they turned to examine the figure on the far side of the chamber, standing with its back towards them, gazing out of the window. Hearing their entrance, it slowly turned. It was a young man.

Eadulf moved involuntarily backwards with a gasp. 'You!' was all he said.

chapter four

The young man simply stood with arms held out.

'It is indeed myself, Eadulf,' he replied with a chuckle. The words were exchanged in their own language but Fidelma knew enough of it to understand.

'I believed you to be dead, these many years,' Eadulf said with emotion.

'Far be it for me to shatter your beliefs, dear brother,' replied the other, still smiling. 'Yet, in this matter, I am glad that I can do so.'

'Egric, it is truly you?' Eadulf was still shaking his head in disbelief.

'And ten years older, brother.'

Eadulf suddenly moved, crossing the distance between them, and flung his arms around the young man. A torrent of his native language poured from him that Fidelma had no hope of following, so rapid and inflected was it.

The newcomer laughingly disengaged himself, replying in the same language. Then he looked towards Fidelma and seemed to ask a question. Eadulf turned with an apology.

'This is my younger brother, Egric.' The introduction was almost unnecessary. With the two of them, side by side, the likeness was obvious.

'He said as much,' Gormán told them. 'But I had to make sure. Now we shall leave you to your family reunion.' He motioned to Enda to follow him from the room.

After Eadulf had introduced Fidelma, Muirgen was summoned to bring drinks and refreshment as they seated themselves before the fire.

'There is obviously much to catch up on,' Eadulf said, first in his own tongue and then he lapsed into Latin, knowing that Fidelma was fluent in that. 'Do you know enough of the tongue to follow?' he asked his brother.

Egric chuckled. 'I spent some time among the followers of the New Faith, but I also speak a dialect of the tongue of this country. I was converted to the Faith by teachers from this land, just as you were. Not only that, I spent some years among the Cruthin of the north as a missionary after Oswy defeated them in battle. There were many from Dál Riada who had settled among them and speaking a similar tongue, so I was able to extend my knowledge.'

'You and Eadulf will have much to talk about.' Fidelma reverted to her own language, deciding to test Egric's knowledge. The thought had struck her that he must have had a sufficient command of the language to have communicated to Gormán and the others. 'But first things first: what purpose brought you here?'

'It is a long story but I shall make it short,' replied Egric. 'I don't know whether Eadulf has told you of my past?'

Fidelma frowned for a moment and then decided that she could only speak the truth. 'I am afraid that he has never mentioned his brother.'

Eadulf appeared uncomfortable for a moment. 'It was because I thought him dead. As young men we were converted to the New Faith by Fursa and his brothers. They were missionaries from this land who came to preach in the Kingdom of the East Angles. Fursa inspired me to study at Tuam Brecain and so I left Seaxmund's Ham. I had thought young Egric had gone to join Athelwold's warriors at Rendel's Ham. Egric was always dreaming about becoming a warrior. At the time, our land was threatened by Wulfhere of Mercia and an army was being raised. When I returned to Seaxmund's Ham, no one had news of Egric. I never heard from him again until this moment. I truly thought he had perished in a battle.'

'A boy may grow to maturity,' shrugged Egric. 'I decided to follow the Faith and not the army.'

'But it is amazing to meet up after all these years – and to meet here, of all places in the world!' Eadulf exclaimed.

'Our paths never seemed to cross after you left Seaxmund's Ham, brother. I found myself among a band of brethren at the court of Oswy at Streonshalh. It was there I heard your name spoken of in connection with the Great Debate that had been held there. But it was said that you had gone on to Rome.'

'True enough,' agreed Eadulf. 'That was my second journey to Rome.'

'Oswy had accepted the Rule of Rome, even though there were still some among his priests and bishops who favoured the ways of the missionaries of Aidan of Iona, who brought the Faith to Northumbria,' explained Fidelma. 'Eadulf and I made the journey to Rome together. So what abbey did you join when you were in Streonshalh?'

'I did not,' Egric replied. 'Oswy wanted new missionaries to preach the Faith among the Cruthin over whose kingdom he ruled as lord. Thus I went to that land and spent some years preaching among them as well as learning their language.' He paused and then went on: 'Last year, before spring was on us, Oswy died. The Cruthin were then ruled by Drust, son of Donal, who had been a client king under Oswy. The Cruthin had long chafed under what they saw as rule by foreigners, and now they rose up in rebellion. I had to flee for my life. I managed to make my way back to Streonshalh.

'Things were also changing in Oswy's kingdom. There was a confusion of sub-kings of Deira and Northumbria, each vying for power. Wilfrid, who had led the pro-Roman faction at the Great Debate at Streonshalh, had obtained almost a king-like power. He began ensuring the removal of many of those who were of the old Columban Church, like Bishop

Chad. Presumably he wanted them removed from any position where they might harm his Roman party. Even Oswy's wife, Eanfleda, and her daughter had fled for safety into the abbey of the dead King's relative, Hilda, who also still favours the teachings of Colmcille. Apparently, Wilfrid had full permission of Theodore of Canterbury to pursue these policies, and now Theodore had designated Wilfrid as Bishop of Northumbria.'

He paused to sip thoughtfully at his drink.

'Anyway, Oswy's Kingdom was not mine and so I was thinking of going south. I made my way to the town of the people of Kent. It was there I met an aging cleric from Rome, the Venerable Victricius of Palestrina. He told me that he had been given a mission from Theodore, Archbishop of Canterbury, to journey to this kingdom and contact some people here. The Venerable Victricius knew little of the tongue therefore asked me to accompany him as translator and companion.'

'So it was Theodore who sent you hither?' Eadulf was regarding him in surprise. 'This is a curious tale, brother, for I myself was adviser to Theodore during my short time in Rome and accompanied him to the Kingdom of Kent. Then it was as his emissary that I came here – and here I have remained.'

'Understand that I did not meet with Theodore, but all my dealings were with the Venerable Victricius,' Egric said hurriedly.

'Why did Theodore of Canterbury send this Venerable Victricius hither to this corner of the world?' asked Eadulf. 'Is it the same mission that brings Bishop Arwald of Magonsaete to this kingdom?'

Egric sat up, suddenly alert. 'Is Bishop Arwald here?'

'He is expected to arrive any day soon. So, there is some connection?'

Egric seemed to relax with a slight shrug. 'Perhaps. Alas, Victricius never shared the objective of his mission with me; I was merely asked to act as companion and interpreter on his journey here.'

Fidelma and Eadulf glanced at one another in surprise.

'He never gave a single hint of his purpose during the long journey here?' demanded Fidelma. 'Did he mention Bishop Arwald?'

Egric shook his head. 'Bishop Arwald was known at Canterbury, but I have never met him.'

'Then, by the holy rood, this is a curious tale,' Eadulf declared in astonishment.

'The Venerable Victricius did not explain anything,' insisted Egric. 'He had a box with him and was very careful of it. When we were attacked, the contents were destroyed or carried off by the raiders. I never found out what was in it.'

'So never once, on the long journey between Canterbury and here, did your companion take you into his confidence about the purpose of your journey,' clarified Fidelma.

'That is the truth, lady. The Venerable Victricius was the type of person who keeps his own counsel. I know it is hard to believe that I could journey with him under those conditions, but I did so – and willingly. My allegiance was to Venerable Victricius; his was to Theodore of Canterbury; and Theodore's allegiance was to Vitalian of Rome. It was as simple as that. I accepted that I would be told the purpose, when the time was right for me to be told.'

Fidelma bowed her head. Her voice was slightly cynical when she responded: 'In such blind faith and obedience, you certainly differ from your brother. But now the Venerable Victricius is dead and his papers disappeared, how then will you be able to fulfil his purpose if you do not know it?'

'I cannot,' replied Egric simply. 'All his papers seem lost.'

'I suppose you will be told when Bishop Arwald arrives with his companions,' Fidelma said.

'His companions?' There seemed uneasiness in the way Egric asked the question.

'A Roman cleric named Verax.'

Egric sighed. 'I do not know him.'

'What about Brother Cerdic – do you know him?' Fidelma asked suddenly.

Egric turned to her, startled. 'What name do you say?'

'Brother Cerdic,' she repeated carefully.

This time, Egric tried to assume a blank expression but it was clear the name had registered. 'Brother Cerdic? I don't think so. Who is he?'

'An emissary sent here to announce the imminent arrival of a deputation from Theodore of Canterbury.'

There was an awkward silence and then Egric said: 'Are you saying that Brother Cerdic is here already? Perhaps he could explain everything.'

'He can't,' Eadulf replied shortly.

'I don't understand,' his brother returned with a puzzled glance.

'He is dead.'

Egric paled. 'Dead? Cerdic is dead?'

'He was murdered this morning in the chapel here. We don't know by whom or why.' Eadulf went on: 'You seem disturbed, Egric, yet you said that you don't know him.'

Egric passed a hand slowly across his brow. 'Nor do I,' he maintained. 'But a Saxon visitor to this place . . . I may be in some danger. I have already survived one attack that killed my companion.'

'It is true there is a mystery here,' Fidelma said patiently. 'So that is why we require all the information we can get in order to resolve it.'

'Of course,' Egric nodded. 'I am but newly arrived here and my first encounter with any animosity was the attack on my companion and myself on the river.'

'We will do our best to bring the culprits to justice.' Fidelma rose. 'Meanwhile, the news of your coming will have spread through the palace. It will be a breach of protocol and manners to keep you to ourselves any longer. First, we will take you to meet the King. You must also meet with Abbot Ségdae who is the Chief Bishop of the Kingdom.'

'Is it really necessary for me to meet the King and his bishop?' Egric seemed reluctant. 'My journey has been long and not without incident. I feel quite exhausted.'

'You are Eadulf's brother,' Fidelma said. 'Eadulf is my husband. The King is my brother. Thus your arrival becomes a family matter. The King will want to meet the brother of my husband, especially in view of the circumstances.'

Egric caught the word and said sharply, 'What circumstances?'

'The imminent arrival of this deputation, the death of Brother Cerdic, this emissary – not to mention the attack on yourself and your companion. Obviously, the Venerable Victricius of Palestrina must have been a man of authority from Rome. There is already an atmosphere of menace spreading through Cashel.'

'We'll present Egric to Colgú at once,' agreed Eadulf. 'Or perhaps Egric would like to see his nephew first?'

Egric looked startled.

'Our son, little Alchú,' Fidelma explained. Then she turned to Eadulf and reminded him: 'You forget the lateness of the hour, Eadulf. I cannot wake Alchú up even to meet his new uncle. Muirgen would never allow it. There will be plenty of time for that tomorrow. First, we must take you to meet the King.'

As they rose, Egric cast a nervous glance at Fidelma and then turned to his brother, speaking in their own language.

'I would like to . . . er, visit the privy before being conducted into the King's presence,' he said awkwardly.

'Come, I'll take you there.' Eadulf glanced at Fidelma, not wishing to embarrass his brother by pointing out that Fidelma had a knowledge of their language. 'We will rejoin you in a moment.'

Outside the chamber, Egric seemed embarrassed. 'I am sorry, I don't remember any polite words for a privy in the language of this land.'

'Polite?' Eadulf smiled. 'Well, you can call it a *fialtech* or veil house.

A urinal is called a *fúatech*.' He pointed to a nearby door and added: 'I'll wait here for you. It is the custom here to wash your hands in a basin in the corner,' he added. The people of the Five Kingdoms were fastidious about washing rituals. There was the full bath at night and then the morning wash. He knew that this was unusual among his own people, so felt it necessary to point it out to Egric.

His brother nodded and pushed inside. It was not long before he came out. Noticing his brother's frown, Egric asked: 'Is there something wrong?'

'Not really. I just thought it was the custom among all religious to perform the Sign of the Cross on entering and leaving the privy.'

Egric chuckled. 'What use would that be?'

'Oh, it is the belief that the privy is the abode of demons, and whoever enters is enjoined to bless the demons and themselves. Similarly a blessing is usual on leaving it.'

'A quaint custom,' Egric replied, amused. 'But now, do you think that your wife, Fidelma, is right in that the people here are afraid of this recent murder?'

'I am not sure that she used the word "afraid",' replied Eadulf. 'The murder of a foreign emissary – a religious emissary – in the King's own palace, is certainly disturbing. Then you arrive and tell us that you have been attacked and that your companion, an eminent religious from Rome, has been killed. That is enough to cause consternation anywhere.'

'Eminent?'

'The title Venerable is not lightly obtained.'

'True enough, I suppose.'

Fidelma was right about the atmosphere in Cashel. By the time they conducted Egric to the King's chambers, the whole of the palace was abounding with wild speculation.

Egric was greeted with due politeness by Colgú and Abbot Ségdae, yet Fidelma noticed that he seemed very ill at ease. Many pressed him for details about the attack on the river, especially Brehon Aillín, who was inclined to a sharpness of tongue and obvious suspicion when he questioned the young man.

'The Brehon at Cluain Meala is investigating,' said Gormán, who was in attendance and apparently felt sorry for the deluge of questions Egric was facing. 'He shares my suspicions about the Déisi outlaws.'

'Then we will leave the matter for him to resolve,' Colgú agreed glumly. 'We have enough problems here with the death of Brother Cerdic. What of the obsequies?' His question was directed at Abbot Ségdae. Then he peered round. 'Shouldn't your steward, Brother Madagan, be here to take charge of such details?'

'He had some urgent business to attend to but he will be here to oversee the arrangements,' the abbot confirmed. 'Brother Cerdic will be buried outside the walls at midnight, as is the custom. Perhaps, as a fellow Saxon, Brother Egric might like to conduct the internment and blessing?'

Eadulf's brother stirred uncomfortably. 'I have just arrived here and do not know your customs. It would be better if Eadulf took on this task.'

'I have no objection to you performing them with your own rites,' encouraged Abbot Ségdae.

It was clear that Egric was not keen and so Eadulf agreed to accept the task.

'We have come to no conclusion as to who might be responsible for Cerdic's death?' Colgú asked his sister.

Fidelma could not help an automatic glance at Abbess Líoch, seated on the other side of the council chamber, before responding: 'No, not yet. It seems there were no immediate witnesses and we have yet to find anyone who even saw any suspicious figure enter or leave the chapel. However, we will widen the search and the questioning. I am sure something will develop.'

There was a moment's silence before Colgú sighed in resignation. 'So, then we must await the arrival of this mysterious Bishop Arwald. Only then will we know the purpose of this deputation.'

Beccan, his steward, coughed and took a step forward. 'There is the matter of tonight's meal to be arranged, lord, now that we have some extra guests.'

The King frowned. 'What needs to be arranged?'

'There is the list of guests to be considered,' the steward answered sheepishly.

'Guests? Oh yes. Abbot Ségdae, Brother Madagan, Brehon Aillín, Abbess Líoch and her *bann-mhaor* will join us and, of course, Eadulf's brother, with my sister and Eadulf. That is all.'

'So the meal will end before midnight?'

Colgú looked crossly at his punctilious steward. Even Fidelma wished that Beccan would act on his own accord from time to time and not seek her brother's approval for every matter.

'After the meal we will gather in the courtyard *just before midnight* to escort the body down to the old burial ground below,' the King snapped. 'Surely these procedures can be sorted out with Brother Madagan?'

Beccan flushed. 'But we are speaking of events that impinge on the King's household and therefore, before agreeing to any proposals, protocol dictates that I must seek permission of the King himself.'

Colgú was firm. 'I do not wish to hear any more. Make the arrangements with Brother Madagan and we will meet the funeral cortège in the courtyard just before midnight.'

Beccan bowed his head for a moment before raising it to meet the King's gaze. He began to open his mouth again – but Colgú interrupted.

'Nor do I expect to be consulted on the dishes that are to be served up this evening. Dar Luga, my *airnbertach*, can sort out the choices. If my housekeeper does not know what my favourite dishes are by now, then perhaps some changes need to be made in my personal household.'

Beccan flushed. Everyone knew that he was very pedantic about following protocol and doubtless, had Colgú not made the jibe, he would have gone on to voice the precise request that the King had anticipated.

Despite the choice dishes, however, the meal that evening was not one of the most enjoyable, for there was a strange atmosphere at the table. Brehon Aillín was in a scowling, suspicious mood, speaking tersely; Abbess Líoch clearly did not wish to be there and was almost as quiet as Sister Dianaimh. Everyone invited had attended, with the exception of Brother Madagan whose urgent business had turned into an indisposition. 'A chill that afflicts his chest. Our friend, Brother Conchobhar, has prescribed some wild garlic and other herbs that should help him,' explained Abbot Ségdae. 'But he insists he will attend the obsequies later.'

The conversation would have become stilted had it not been for Eadulf persuading his brother to speak about his previous adventures. Egric had not really wanted to attend the meal, but as it progressed, he grew more relaxed. Indeed, he seemed to dominate the conversation – not that his stories were boring or repetitive. He spoke mainly of his time among the Cruthin, a strange people who dwelled in the north of the island of Britain. It seemed their progenitor was a chieftain called Cruthine, who had seven sons. The Cruthin were a fierce warrior race who painted themselves before going into battle. The Romans had called them 'the painted people' – the *Pictii*.

Oswy of Northumbria had ruled the Cruthin through puppet kings, but Egric explained that when he arrived among them, there was growing resentment between them and the Angles of Northumbria. The Dál Riadans, who had started to settle in the west three centuries earlier, were also growing in strength. It was a year before, when Oswy had died, that the Cruthin rose up.

'It was a difficult time,' Egric admitted to his rapt audience. 'We had been sent to serve Oswy and now even Oswy's client king, Drust, turned against us.'

'Sent to serve Oswy?' intervened Abbot Ségdae with a frown. 'Surely you were sent among the Cruthin to serve Christ!'

Egric turned and smiled apologetically. 'You are right. A slip of the tongue.

But Oswy was then the legitimate ruler and protector of the Church. The rebels were burning and destroying without distinction.'

'So how did you escape this carnage?' Colgú asked.

'Many of us managed to get to the coast; to a port at the mouth of a river called Deathan. We took a ship back to Streonshalh in Northumbria.'

'Surely, at such a time, the people you left behind were in need of the Faith?' Abbot Ségdae remarked. 'It is against the law that religious be attacked and killed. So this attack was an outrage.'

'It is difficult to make that argument to a man wielding a sword and shield,' Egric said sombrely. 'The company that I was in barely escaped with their lives from the devastating attack of the Cruthín.'

'Were they not Christian?' asked Brehon Aillín curiously.

'They are.' They were surprised because it was Abbess Líoch who broke her silence. 'Over two centuries ago a man called Ninnian established his mission to what was then the land of the Cruthin. Many other religious went to that country – even our own Colmcille who took the Faith to the Dál Riada on the seaboard of the Gael.' She raised her head suddenly and looked at Egric. 'It is hard to believe that such a people would rise up and attack the holy communities without provocation.'

Egric said indifferently, 'I can only relay what I saw.'

'And thankfully, you came safely out of that land,' Colgú said warmly. 'And with the even greater support of Providence, you have come safely to Cashel and found your long-lost brother.'

'Yet at the loss of your companion the Venerable Victricius,' pointed out Brehon Aillín. 'And, of course, your two boatmen. Presumably you did not know their names – the names of the boatmen, I mean?'

Eadulf glared at the old Brehon, hearing the derisive note in his voice.

'I regret that I cannot remember their names,' he said.

'And you have no idea of the purpose of your journey?' Brehon Aillín had asked the question more than once.

Colgú bent forward. 'Brother Egric has already answered that question.

He has stated that he was not taken into the Venerable Victricius' confidence on that matter.'

Brehon Aillín sniffed as he lowered his head, indicating suspicion on the one hand and acquiescence on the other.

Brother Egric had turned to Abbess Líoch. 'Mother Abbess, you seem to know something of the Cruthin. Were you ever in their territory? There were a lot of travellers from the Five Kingdoms when I was there, especially from the Kingdom of Ulaidh. The Cruthin spoke a strange mixture of your language and that of their southern neighbours, the Britons.'

Abbess Líoch's expression was uneasy. 'Many of us, like my friend Fidelma there, had to travel north to Ulaidh and cross the narrow sea to the seaboard of the Gael where Colmcille set up his abbey on I-Shona. We would then travel through the territories of the Cruthin, as did our countrymen Aidan, Finan, Colmán and Tuda and their companions before us. We went to bring the word of the Faith to the Angles of Northumbria. A Faith rejected by Oswy after his Great Council at Streonshalh.'

Fidelma heard a note of bitterness in Abbess Líoch's voice and looked nervously at Eadulf.

'I met Eadulf at that council,' she reminded her quietly.

'As we recall, the council ended on amicable terms, and those who wished to maintain the liturgies and rites of the Five Kingdoms did so,' Eadulf stated. 'Even Abbess Hilda in the abbey called Witebia did so. So did Cuthbert, Chad and many others. Those who felt they could not live alongside the Roman rites, such as Bishop Colmán, decided to return to this land with those who wanted to do so. There was no discrimination against those who wished to retain their own interpretation of the Faith.'

'Not while Oswy was alive,' Abbess Líoch replied curtly. 'Since I returned from that land, I have heard that the main advocate of the Roman Church at that council has now contrived to make himself Chief Bishop of Northumbria, deposing Chad, who remained sympathetic to our rituals and Faith. I have heard that he and Theodore of Canterbury plan to eliminate all who remain true to the teachings of Colmcille in the kingdoms of the Saxons.'

Colgú intervened with a diplomatic cough. 'My friends,' he said, 'we are here, sharing a meal together. We are not re-enacting some religious council. It is not time for a new subject?'

There was an embarrassed pause, and then Fidelma began to tell the story of how the ancestors of the Eóghanacht had been led to set up their capital and main fortress on the Rock of Cashel. This was for the benefit of Egric. The change of conversation was unnatural but she persevered. There was a general feeling of relief when the chapel bell rang and they moved from the feasting hall to join the small funeral procession gathering in the courtyard.

The body had been washed and wrapped in the traditional *racholl* or winding sheet. Four members of the religious carried it on a *fuat* or bier of broom. There were a dozen or so attendants, each carrying flaming brand torches, ready to accompany the body to its last resting place. The apothecary, old Brother Conchobhar, who had laid out the body, was chief among them. Brother Eadulf, having volunteered to conduct the obsequies, took his place at the head of the procession.

Another figure joined them in the darkness, well wrapped and hooded from the chill night air. Abbot Ségdae peered forward in surprise.

'Brother Madagan? Should you be abroad with your chill?'

'The wild garlic is soothing,' the steward replied, suppressing a cough. 'And I should not be neglecting my duties.'

'All is arranged and is well,' the abbot assured him.

Colgú glanced round with a shiver, pulling his cloak more tightly round his shoulders. He bent forward to Fidelma and said softly, 'When this Bishop Arwald arrives, at least he cannot accuse us of treating his emissary with disrespect.'

'Is that likely?' she asked.

'Better that we find the person who slew him,' her brother replied. 'To find the culprit would show a greater respect.' He raised his voice: 'Let us proceed.'

Before the cortège could move forward, however, a commanding voice rang out, halting them by its very power.

'Be warned, people of Cashel! The Son of Chaos will reclaim this place!'

A figure stood on the steps of the chapel in the darkness. They could see that his arms were flung out as if to encompass them; his cloak had fallen behind him, making his silhouette grotesque. Those in the procession turned uncertainly towards the speaker.

'The *Antikos* approaches from the east,' the voice went on, firm, almost melodious. 'Your adversary will arrive as the Morning Star, the Light Bringer. And death and destruction will follow.'

Abbot Ségdae crossed himself, staring in horror at the figure. '*Quod avertat Deus!*' he muttered.

'It is only Deogaire,' Fidelma sighed as Eadulf moved to her side as if to protect her.

Colgú made an angry, inarticulate sound and turned to seek out the commander of his guard. 'Gormán, take Deogaire to a place where he cannot insult the dead.'

Gormán was about to obey the order when old Brother Conchobhar hurried forward. 'Forgive him, lord,' he wailed. 'Let me take him back to my house and swear surety for his good behaviour. He did not mean to insult the dead.'

Deogaire moved slightly so that a brand torch illuminated his features. He gazed on them all with an expression that was hard to define, something akin to exhilaration and anxiety. 'I do not insult the dead but merely warn the living. Soon the Tempter, the Father of Lies, will approach this place and then – be warned! I feel it in the cold breath of the air from the east. It is written in the dark skies and the paleness of the moon. Take heed, Ségdae of Imleach, over those you claim to protect. That is all I have to say.'

With that, Deogaire disappeared into the darkness. Gormán and Brother Conchobhar made to hurry after him, but Colgú held up a hand to restrain them.

'Let him go. Words do not harm us. We shall continue with the funeral.'

Abbot Ségdae said grimly to his steward, Brother Madagan, 'Be warned about prophesying and digging up tombs. Such things could mark you as beyond redemption, like that poor fool.'

Fidelma proceeded with the cortège through the gates and down the hill towards the cemetery, where a grave had already been dug. Since no one knew Brother Cerdic, there was no *amrath*, or elegy, to be recited. Instead, Eadulf stepped forward to give the *nuall-guba*, the recitation of the Lamentation of Sorrow. The abbot pronounced the blessing, and the mourners returned to the palace in silence, leaving the grave-diggers to fill in the earth.

Later that night, Fidelma spoke into the darkness. 'A curious day, Eadulf. You never mentioned that you had a brother before.'

Her words clearly implied the question: 'why?' Eadulf turned slightly. He had been unable to sleep, thinking about the events. The arrival of his brother had been almost as unnerving as the mystery surrounding the murder of Brother Cerdic. Then had come Deogaire and the curious spectacle of his warning.

'I thought I had explained,' he replied quietly. 'As I said, I had presumed Egric was dead. The last time I was in Seaxmund's Ham, I was told that he had gone off to be a warrior and, frankly, the rumour was that he had perished. I felt that there was little gain in conjuring ghosts.'

'I can understand that,' she replied. 'You did tell me that your father was a magistrate among your people.'

'A *gerefa*,' affirmed Eadulf. 'Indeed, he was. So was my grandfather. Our family tradition has it that he was so learned in law that he went to

Canterbury as King Athelberht's adviser when he drew up the first great law texts written in our language.'

'Was there just yourself and your brother in the family? You make no mention of your mother. I thought you had no relatives.'

'My mother died of poison when I was fifteen years old and my father was taken by the Yellow Plague when I was eighteen.'

Fidelma's voice was shocked in the gloom. 'You told me about your father, but not your mother. How was she poisoned?'

Eadulf found it difficult to tell the story. 'One day she went to a neighbour's house and they had just baked fresh bread. They all sat and ate it. When she returned home, my mother fell ill; soon she had convulsions and her skin began to turn gangrenous. The neighbours also fell ill with the same condition. Thankfully, our apothecary was a knowledgeable man and forbade the eating of the bread. But it was too late. Our neighbours died within a few days . . . as did my mother.'

Fidelma clicked her tongue and reached out a hand in the darkness to find his in sympathy.

'What was it?' she pressed gently.

'The apothecary searched the neighbour's barn for the rye that had been threshed to make the bread. There was a fungus growing on it, which sometimes happens during cold or damp conditions. If unnoticed and it is ground to make the flour, and then baked in the bread, it produces a poison – and if the bread is consumed . . .' Eadulf's voice trailed off.

'I am sorry,' Fidelma whispered.

'I told you, I see little to gain in conjuring ghosts.'

'It must have affected you and, of course, your brother. How old was he at the time?'

'He was five years old.'

'And so, you were only eighteen when your father perished? It is sad to be without parents, Eadulf. I know. I vaguely recall my father but did not know my mother – she died giving me birth.'

Eadulf sighed heavily. 'As I have said, there is little gain in conjuring ghosts. He cleared his throat. 'Anyway, by that time, Fursa had arrived in our kingdom and was preaching the word of the New Faith. Although I had inherited my father's role as *gerefa*, I was more attracted to the world Fursa opened for me. As you know, on his advice I went to study not only the Faith but, having long been interested in the apothecary's art, I chose to continue those studies at Tuaim Brecain. The rest you know.'

'Was that because of what happened to your mother?' Fidelma asked. But her question was met with silence and she felt the answer was obvious. 'What made you think your brother Egric had been killed? Just gossip?' she continued after a few moments.

'Oh, he was keen to be a warrior when he was younger. I knew we both attended the discourses given by Fursa but I had thought that the New Faith made little impression on him. When I left to follow the path Fursa had suggested for my studies, young Egric was talking about joining the army of our King Athelwold. Years later, when I went back to my home, I was told that he had gone away and no one knew what had happened to him. I presumed he had joined Athelwold and must have perished in some battle.'

'And now he is alive and following in your footsteps. You must be pleased to see him, Eadulf.'

Eadulf sighed in the darkness. 'It is hard to express what I feel. Having lived without a brother all these years, it is difficult to suddenly meet that lost brother again and in such circumstances. Also . . .'

Fidelma waited and finally felt she had to prompt him.

'I find some of the things Egric says curious, like his experiences among the Cruthin, even his reactions to the customs on entering the *fialtech*.'

'I don't understand.'

'It's as if he has no religious background at all. Ah well – we have been apart too long. I am no longer used to having a brother.'

'I assume there are no more of your brothers or sisters that will suddenly appear on our doorstep?' Fidelma asked.

'If they do, they will be as unknown to me as they are to you,' Eadulf replied stiffly.

'Well, it is interesting that little Alchú has a new uncle.'

Eadulf smiled slightly in the darkness. 'I suppose he'll have to learn a new word, then. And so will I.'

'I don't understand,' yawned Fidelma.

'Well, *amnair* is your word for a maternal uncle. Alchú addresses your brother as King Am-Nar, not being able to pronounce it properly yet. So what will he call Egric?'

'Bratháir-athar.'

Eadulf pulled a face. 'How will he ever get his tongue around that?'

Fidelma chuckled. 'He'll probably wind up calling him "Braw-her".'

They were silent again and then Eadulf said sleepily, 'It is certainly strange that the Fates have guided Egric to Cashel of all places. But I wonder what the purpose of this deputation is? It seems obvious that this Venerable Victricius was supposed to join them. What has that to do with Brother Cerdic's death?'

'That is the perplexing thing,' sighed Fidelma.

'What is, exactly?'

'That someone was able to kill this Brother Cerdic in the chapel of this palace and that we have not been able to discover them. There is a murderer on the loose here tonight.'

Eadulf was silent for a while, thinking about this. Then he said: 'I find your friend, Abbess Líoch, to be an odd sort of woman.'

'I certainly find her changed from the person I knew,' Fidelma agreed. 'I need to speak with her further, yet I am not sure how to approach her. If I accuse her of the crime, she will simply deny it. She did not become an abbess without having a firm resolve and strength of character to support it. I need to find a way to challenge her.'

'What do we know? Brother Cerdic called on her before he went to see Abbot Ségdae,' Eadulf mused. 'Why did he do that? Because he must have known her beforehand. Why did he tell her that it was in her interest to come to Cashel if she did not even know him, and if he did not tell her what this deputation was about?'

'All good points, Eadulf. And if we knew the answers to those questions, there would be no mystery.'

'And what do you make of poor old Brother Conchobhar's soothsaying relative? I am inclined to think that he is not quite right in the head. That performance this evening – all that prophesying that there is some evil about to descend on Cashel!'

Fidelma was silent and for a moment or two Eadulf wondered whether she had fallen asleep. Then she said, 'I would not be inclined to completely dismiss Deogaire as mad. Eccentric, indeed, but there is a something about him . . .'

Eadulf chuckled. 'I know he is supposed to have some reputation for prophecy, but . . . well, what about all those fanciful titles he gave to this person who is supposed to arrive here out of the east and whom we must be warned about.'

'Fanciful titles?' Fidelma echoed, surprised. 'All I noticed was that, for one who dwells in the mountain fastnesses of Sliabh Luachra, who claims to worship the old gods and goddesses and shuns more general contact, Deogaire has quite a knowledge of Christian Scripture.'

'I don't understand.'

'Son of Chaos, the Adversary, the Tempter, the Father of Lies, coming as the Morning Star which is the Light Bringer . . .'

'It sounds like nonsense to me.'

'*Antikos* means the adversary, and even our Christian Fathers, Origen and Jerome, knew that the Morning Star was the Light Bringer – Lucifer.'

Eadulf gasped in the gloom. 'What are you saying?'

'Deogaire was using names that the Scriptures employ to identify what the Greek texts call *ho diabolos* and *ho satanos* – the Devil or Satan.'

CHAPTER FIVE

ॐ

T he morning sky was dark and it had started to rain long before dawn. There was no wind to promise the dispersal of low-hanging clouds and yet it was not exceptionally cold. The rain swept the fertile plains around Cashel, falling so thickly that anyone looking from The Rock, on which the palace of Colgú stood, could barely see the town nestling beneath. Even the pall of smoke of the numerous domestic fires was obscured by the downpour.

It was a day which was cursed by farmers and travellers alike. The farmers cursed it because the soil became a quagmire, thus delaying the planting of oats and barley. The travellers cursed it because the tracks and roads were turned to muddy stretches, the streams became turbulent rivers, while rivers became impassable. It was a day when no one felt like venturing out unless they had no alternative; a day when any outside task that could be delayed was ignored. It was the same within the buildings of the King's palace at Cashel. Those warriors of the Golden Collar, the King's élite bodyguards, who were not on duty, remained in the *Laochtech*, the Hall of Heroes as their accommodation was known. Even the horse-master and his stable lads remained cosseted inside by the fire.

Fidelma and Eadulf had decided that Eadulf should introduce his brother to their son Alchú, and then conduct him around the palace.

70

While he was doing this, Fidelma would take the opportunity to seek out her friend Abbess Líoch and diplomatically question her about their suspicions.

Fidelma found the abbess in the *Tech-screptra*, the House of Manuscripts. She was alone in the library apart from *leabhar coimedach*, the Keeper of the Books, who sat in a corner working on a wax tablet, which was often employed to make notes, after which the wax could be smoothed out for further use. The man started to rise as Fidelma entered, but she placed a finger to her lips and nodded towards the figure of the abbess sitting engrossed in a manuscript in a distant corner of the library. Cashel was proud of its library; although it was smaller than most abbey libraries, it possessed several treasures in Greek, Latin and Hebrew, as well as the language of the Five Kingdoms. These were hung in leather book-satchels on pegs or racks along the walls. The books were greatly valued and often brought as gifts to the King.

Abbess Líoch glanced up as Fidelma approached. There was a slight frown on her features.

'Are you busy, Líoch?' Fidelma asked pleasantly, seating herself without being invited.

The abbess tapped the top of her desk with a forefinger. 'I am reading the latest work of Tirechán of the Uí Amolngid of Connacht.'

Fidelma was surprised. 'Tirechán? I heard that he had died recently. Wasn't he a great propagandist for the claim of Armagh to be considered the principal seat of the Faith in the Five Kingdoms?'

'So he was. But there have been many counter-claims from abbeys older and more important than Armagh.'

'I didn't realise this library had the work of Tirechán,' Fidelma said. 'Abbot Ségdae would doubtless be horrified. As I recall, Tirechán also claimed that Patricius built each and every church and abbey in the Five Kingdoms.'

'Tirechán calls everyone who does not agree that Ard Macha should be the first city of the Faith "deserters, thieves and robbers, and merely war-lords",' agreed Abbess Líoch.

'As Abbot of Imleach and Chief Bishop of Muman, Ségdae would be the first to dispute that Ard Macha held any authority over all the churches and abbeys,' rejoined Fidelma.

'I am intrigued to hear you take so much interest in matters of ecclesiastical authority, Fidelma. As far as I knew, you were always more interested in law than in religion.'

Fidelma was not offended. 'Sometimes the religious insist on having an impact on law. You yourself are known as standing against the adoption of the Penitentials – the laws that are to the detriment of our own laws. Several abbots have adopted these Penitentials, especially those who believe we should move in closer alliance with the teachings of Rome.'

'You are a clever advocate, I'll not gainsay that. Indeed, I stand for both our Faith *and* our native laws,' replied the abbess. 'I was not surprised to hear that you had formally left the religious. Yet you are still known widely as Sister Fidelma. However, you were always better suited to law than the religious life.'

'I'll take that as a compliment.'

'It is meant as such. I had not met your husband, Eadulf, before yesterday. He still wears the tonsure of Rome. How does he regard himself?'

'In respect to the Faith? He accepts the teachings of the Faith but he always had a mind for justice which transcends other matters. He was converted by missionaries from Connacht who went to the Kingdom of the East Angles where he comes from. Then he came to study here.'

'Although he wears the tonsure of Rome?'

'He left here and went to Rome. I met him at the Great Debate at Streonshalh where he supported the Roman side.'

Abbess Líoch's austere features broke into a rueful smile.

'That was not so many years ago. What is it – six or seven? Do you remember our little band of pilgrims? We all met together at the Abbey of the Blessed Machaoi on the island of Oen Druim to take ship across the narrow sea to I-Shona.'

'I remember it well,' nodded Fidelma. 'It was the first time I had travelled so far north among the Five Kingdoms, north to the country of the Dál Riada of Ulaidh. We were all afraid of the wild tempest, for the passage across the narrow sea from Oen Druim to I-Shona was a turbulent one.'

'I was sick most of the way,' recalled Abbess Líoch. 'However, with God's grace, we arrived safe on the island of Colmcille.'

'A beautiful little island,' Fidelma agreed. 'Then came the journey onwards and through the Land of the Cruthin and into the Kingdom of Oswy. What excitement we felt as we followed the steps of Aidan and the others to Hilda's Abbey. It was to be our first great clash with those who wanted to impose these new ideas from Rome.'

Abbess Líoch gave a sidelong glance at Fidelma. 'Even then you went there, not to advocate religion, but to advise our delegation on law.'

'I have not denied it. But why did you take that journey, and what made you halt before we reached the Abbey of Hilda?'

'If you recall, I was travelling with a young scholar. He was . . . he was a good friend of mine.'

'I remember. Olcán was his name. What happened?'

'We left your group and made our way south-west to a place called Laestingau; it was a small abbey which one of the kings of the area had set up because he had chosen it as the place where he wanted to be buried. It was only a full day's ride from Hilda's Abbey and we had originally meant to rejoin you after a few days.'

'But why did you go there?'

'Cedd was the abbot at Laestingau at that time.'

'Cedd was one of the main interpreters at the Great Council,' Fidelma remarked, but could not see where her story was going.

'Cedd was adept at several languages,' the abbess continued. 'He had asked Cummène, the abbot of I-Shona, to send him a copy of the *Computus* of Mo Sinu maccu Min of Beannchoir as he wished to study it before the council began. Cummène entrusted the manuscript to the care of Olcán and myself. We were told to take it directly to Cedd's abbey at Laestingau. And that was the reason why we left you on your way to Streonshalh.'

'But Cedd came to Streonshalh and took a lively part in the debate. Why didn't you and Olcán join him?'

'When we reached Laestingau, Cedd had already gone on to Streonshalh. We needed to rest so we stayed there that night. And that night . . .' She paused and there was a curious expression on her face. 'We were prevented from joining you.'

Fidelma was frowning. 'Prevented? How so?'

'The abbey was only a small group of wooden buildings without any defensive walls. As we lay in bed, it was attacked. Olcán was killed. Others were killed as well, including some of the women.'

'I didn't know. I am sorry.'

'As you say, it was years ago now.'

'How did you escape?'

Abbess Líoch made a sound that was closer to a moan than anything else.

'Escape? I did not escape. I was used and left for dead. When Cedd returned after the council, he found the survivors huddling in the ruins. I was one of them. It took me several weeks to recover.'

'Who were the perpetrators?'

'Raiders from the neighbouring Kingdom of Mercia.'

Fidelma breathed out softly. She was recalling how raids from Mercia had threatened the peace during the Council at Streonshalh.

'Were the raiders ever caught and punished?'

'All I knew was that it was not long after Cedd returned to his abbey that he sickened. It was the autumn of that year that he fell ill with the Yellow Plague and died. We buried him in the burned-out ruins of the abbey at

Laestingau. I spent some time trying to repay those people for looking after me when I was beside myself with grief and shame. Without their support, I would surely have died. But after a while, I made my way back here to my own land, my own people, and buried myself in the work of my little abbey at Cill Náile. Within a short time I found myself risen to lead my small community and was appointed Abbess.' Abbess Líoch sat back and smiled ruefully at Fidelma. 'That is my sad story. Since my return, all has been well.'

'Until now?'

The abbess started and for a moment she stared at Fidelma before dropping her gaze.

'I don't understand.'

'Until the appearance of Brother Cerdic at your abbey. I find it curious that he calls on you and tells you that it is in your interest to attend at Cashel. He comes to you before he has even consulted Abbot Ségdae or my brother. I am told by Eadulf that the leader of the deputation coming here is led by a Bishop Arwald of Magonsaete and that is a sub-Kingdom of Mercia.'

'My response to your question has not altered since yesterday,' replied the abbess tightly.

'You told me that you did not know Brother Cerdic.'

'It is true. I never saw him before he came to Cill Náile.'

'Eadulf says that his name would indicate that he too was from Magonsaete.'

'Which implies?' The abbess glared at her.

'After your experience at Laestingau, I would expect you to have some antipathy towards people from that land,' pointed out Fidelma.

The abbess' mouth formed into a thin line. 'I would hope, even after my experience, that I could differentiate between an entire people and individuals.'

'That would be a laudable quality. But I have to ask you . . . did you kill Brother Cerdic?'

'I did not!' came the sharp reply.

'You had the opportunity,' went on Fidelma. 'You left your horse at the bottom of the hill and came up here on foot. You told me that you wanted to rest your horse.'

'It is the truth. Sister Dianaimh thought her mount was going lame.'

'So you both came into the palace on foot. Why?'

'I came to see Abbot Ségdae.'

'But you did not find him. You did not find him and so returned without speaking to anyone. Only the guard saw you come and then depart. Where did you look for the abbot? In the chapel?'

Abbess Líoch's face was a pale mask without expression.

'You have already made up your mind, is that it?' she said slowly. 'I thought you were only interested in truth. It seems you are more interested in finding a sacrifice to explain this man's death.'

Fidelma gazed into her eyes, long and hard. 'Tell me, by all you hold sacred, by our friendship when we were young, Líoch . . . that you did not have anything to do with the death of Brother Cerdic.'

Abbess Líoch pushed her head towards Fidelma so that their faces were scarcely a hand's width apart. Her expression was intense.

'I tell you by all I hold sacred, on the grave of poor Olcán, far away in a foreign land, that I raised no hand against this man Cerdic.'

Fidelma waited for a few moments and then said: 'I have accepted your word, Líoch. You, I hope, will understand why I had to pursue this path. Unless we find out who killed Brother Cerdic, Colgú will have much to answer for when Bishop Arwald and his deputation arrive here.'

Abbess Líoch stared bleakly at her friend.

'We have known the days, Fidelma of Cashel. We were both young and, perhaps, innocent. Now we have grown to know that there is much evil in the world and that it must be challenged. You have chosen your method of challenging it and I have chosen mine. When I depart from here, I will have no wish to see you as a friend again. Now, if you will excuse me, I shall return to my studies.'

'I am sad to hear that,' Fidelma said. 'But friendship does not cancel out the search for truth.'

Fidelma left the library feeling dissatisfied. She had made no progress at all. If anything, she had simply gathered more suspicions. The story of what had happened at Laestingau could well have provided Líoch with a motive. Fidelma thought she knew the abbess well enough to accept her oath, and yet there was a conflict of emotions within her; she was not entirely at ease with the woman's denial.

She paused in the covered entrance outside the library door. A figure was hurrying through the driving rain, across the courtyard, head down. It was the abbess' young female steward, Sister Dianaimh. She halted before Fidelma in the cover of the porch and wiped the rain from her pale face, then gave a nervous smile.

'I am looking for the abbess – have you seen her?'

'She is inside,' confirmed Fidelma, but as the girl moved to open the library door, Fidelma stayed her. 'A word with you first.'

The bright blue eyes of the girl turned enquiringly on her.

'I wondered how long you have served Abbess Líoch?'

'Since last summer.'

'You are young to be a *bann-mhaor*.'

'Before joining the abbess, I served in the Abbey of Sléibhte in Laighin, lady. I joined Abbot Aéd's community there when I was at the age of choice.'

'When Brother Cerdic called at Cill Náile a few days ago to see Abbess Líoch, had she ever seen him before?'

Sister Dianaimh's chin came up defiantly. 'You should ask the abbess that question.'

'You see,' went on Fidelma, ignoring her reply, 'I have to ask questions when someone has been killed. You will recall that I rode with you into Cashel, having met you on the highway . . .'

'Riding with your son and a warrior,' the girl nodded. 'I remember.'

'And I left you and the abbess riding into the township to find lodgings while we went on to the palace here. Then you changed your minds, left your horses at the bottom of the hill and came up here on foot. I find that strange.'

'The abbess suddenly realised that she should let Abbot Ségdae know that we had arrived in the township. However, we thought the horses were tired – my horse was developing a limp – so we left them in the care of a boy and walked up the hill to the palace.'

'You did not find Abbot Ségdae.' It was a statement rather than a question.

'The abbess has already told you that we did not,' replied the *bann-mhaor* suspiciously.

'So where did you search for him?'

For the first time Sister Dianaith looked uncertain. 'I did not. I remained at the gate while the abbess went to find him.'

'Did she ask the guard at the gates where he might be found?' prompted Fidelma.

'I cannot remember – I presume so.'

'So the abbess went to look while you remained at the gate; was that by the gate or in the courtyard?'

'Just inside the gate. The abbess was not gone very long. She found a member of the brethren, an old man, who told her that the abbot was with the King. So she decided that we should continue to look for lodgings in the township. We had barely returned to our horses and set off when you and the Saxon, your husband, overtook us. And now, if that is all . . .?'

'A moment more.' Fidelma held up a hand. 'You said you remained inside the gate?'

'I did,' the girl replied impatiently.

'In that case, you could see across the main courtyard to the side of the chapel that faces it. Did anyone cross that courtyard while you were there?'

'A few people, as would be expected.'

'Such as? Describe them.'

Sister Dianaimh made a gesture with her shoulder as if dismissing the question. 'I would not know them. The *echaire* – that is, the stable-master, two warriors . . . oh, and a religieux.'

'A religieux? What did he look like?'

'He had his hood over his head. Even if he had been uncovered, I would not have recognised him. I have not been here before. Now, can I go?'

Fidelma nodded thoughtfully as the girl moved past and entered the library. She waited a few moments before pulling her cloak tightly around her and going out into the still driving rain, hurrying towards the smaller courtyard at the back of the chapel where, in a corner, Brother Conchobhar's apothecary was situated.

She entered the apothecary with its almost overpowering aromas that arose from the countless dried plants and herbs that hung from the ceiling or grew in pots on benches that crowded inside. Old Brother Conchobhar was bent over a bench at the far end, busily mixing a paste with a mortar in a pestle. He looked up as she entered and laid the work aside.

'I was expecting you,' he greeted her. His expression was serious.

'You were?' she frowned.

'I thought you would come to see me about Deogaire's outlandish behaviour last night.'

'Ah, that. Yes, it was extraordinary,' Fidelma admitted. 'But that was not my main purpose.'

'Then how can I help?' The old man was surprised.

'I was told Abbess Líoch might have been about here early yesterday. It was before Eadulf found the body of Brother Cerdic. I just wondered if you saw her then.'

Brother Conchobhar rubbed the side of his temple, as if it aided his memory. 'Yes, I saw her and she was enquiring for Abbot Ségdae,' he confirmed. 'That's right . . . I told her that the abbot was with the King.

She thanked me and left.' He paused and then added: 'Wait! That is in the wrong order. I was in here and happened to glance at that little door across the way which leads into the back of the chapel. She was trying the handle.'

'So you saw Abbess Líoch at the door of the chapel. Did anyone answer her?'

Brother Conchobhar shook his head. 'Not that I am aware. Certainly, when I saw her there, I went and told her that the door was kept bolted from the inside. Only the main doors were open. I asked if *I* could help her. When she said she was looking for Abbot Ségdae, that was when I was able to tell her that he had gone to see your brother.'

'And then she left?'

'She did. I was waiting for Deogaire to join me to help me carry some things to the blacksmith's forge.'

'But she might have gone into the chapel,' mused Fidelma.

Brother Conchobhar looked quizzically at her. 'Not unless someone came and opened the bolts when I turned my back. Surely you don't suspect Abbess Líoch of killing the Saxon – Brother Cerdic?'

'It is my nature to be suspicious, as you know well, old wolf-lover,' she replied, using the literal meaning of her mentor's name as a form of endearment.

'I know your nature well enough. Didn't I teach you something of the art of seeking answers when you were a child?' he replied with a smile.

'You especially taught me that one should ask the right questions to obtain the right answers. The trouble is, the answers to the questions that I have been asking do not make sense.'

'Which means that you are not asking the right questions,' rejoined the old man.

'That may well be so.' Then a thought occurred to her. 'It must have been only a short time after this encounter with the abbess that you were joined by Deogaire and you were walking around the front of the chapel, across the main square?'

'That is so. Deogaire had returned and he and I were taking some herbs to the smithy's forge when Eadulf appeared at the door on the other side of the chapel and called out to us. He asked if we had seen anyone leave the chapel, which we had not. There was no one about . . . well, I saw Brother Madagan on the far side of the courtyard, but he was going in the other direction. Then Eadulf showed us the body of Brother Cerdic.'

Fidelma shook her head in frustration. 'There is something that I am missing. Ah well, it will come back to me soon.'

'And Deogaire?' asked Brother Conchobhar. 'Is your brother thinking of punishing him for his outburst last night?'

'I would not think so, unless those present felt insulted,' replied Fidelma.

Brother Conchobhar was unhappy. 'As you know, Deogaire claims to have the *imbas forosnai* – the prophecy of the poets. It is not wise to boast of such things nowadays.'

'Abbot Ségdae says it is forbidden. He claims it is a denial of the New Faith.'

'True,' the old man sighed. 'But forbidden or not, it does not make it vanish as if it has never existed. Many things are forbidden but are none the less true because of it. Did not Fionn Mac Cumhaill often display that talent for such divination? Between us, I believe Deogaire has some gift. He has often proved a worthy sage.'

'Yet is it not said that a sage is not wise all the time?' Fidelma pointed out.

'True once again,' agreed the old man. 'And they say that there are times when the silent mouth sounds most melodious. Perhaps Deogaire should have pursued the most melodious course?'

'Did he ever explain to you what he means about his prophecy?'

'The prophecy never came to me before.' The voice cut through the pause before Brother Conchobhar could respond. Deogaire emerged from the back room into the apothecary.

'And in what form did your prophecy come to you, Deogaire?' asked Fidelma, undeterred by the sudden appearance of the young man.

'It came last night, when I was watching the queen of the night rise above the hills. Do we not often call her Aesca, the place where knowledge is found?'

'And watching the moon, you suddenly saw danger approaching my brother's palace?'

'I'll not deny it.'

'I know you have little time for the New Faith, Deogaire. But is it wise to boast of the possession of the *imbas forosnai*?'

'Not everyone has forsaken the old paths of knowledge for the new and unknown, lady. You have left the religious yourself in order to maintain our old laws.'

'I have left the religious – which does not mean that I have left the Faith, Deogaire. And what I was going to say is that while you reject the New Faith, yet your prophecy was laced with images of the New Faith.'

Deogaire chuckled. 'Should I have placed older images of our ancient faith and culture in my warning? How then would the interpretation of what I said have been made clear? Images, like words in a foreign language, have no meaning unless they are shared.'

'As a matter of fact, the images were lost on some until I pointed out the meanings of the terms you were using,' replied Fidelma, amused. 'Why did you give this warning that Satan was about to descend on Cashel?'

'I used the images of the Devil because it would have had little impact if I had warned that the messengers of the Fomorii were about to come and sup with the King.'

Fidelma's eyes widened a little. The Fomorii had been the ancient evil deities of her people; the name meant 'undersea dwellers'. From their caverns beneath the waves, led by Cichol, Balor of the Evil Eye and the goat-headed Gaborchend, they launched attack after attack on the good gods and goddesses, the Children of Danú. Finally, Lugh Lamhfada and Nuada of the Silver Hand drove them back into the sea.

'Well, in whatever image,' Fidelma replied, 'your prophecy is that evil is about to strike Cashel?'

'Has it not already done so?'

'You mean the murder of Brother Cerdic?'

'I will leave it to you to make your own interpretation, Fidelma of Cashel. All I say is that I feel a chill wind from the east. I would issue you with a warning. Two glances behind you are sometimes better than looking straight ahead. Death can come in many forms – even a winged demon out of the sky. You know that I am not given to idle speculation. I inherited the gift of the *imbas forosnai* from my mother's mother and back to her mother's mother and their line since the dawn of time.'

With that he turned and left the apothecary.

Brother Conchobhar stood a moment in silence and then he coughed nervously, extending his arms in a helpless gesture.

'I am sorry, Fidelma.'

She had been thinking and now she raised her head with a smile. 'You have no need to be, old wolf-lover. I have known some with the gift of prophecy – enough to know it would be silly to dismiss it lightly. If there is evil approaching from the east, then we must be prepared for it.'

chapter six

'This is my son, Alchú,' Eadulf declared, after giving the boy a hug. He had brought Egric into the chamber where Muirgen was looking after the child. 'His name means "little hound". Alchú, this is your Uncle Egric, my brother.'

Eadulf had taken Egric to meet Alchú as soon as Fidelma had left to pursue her enquiries. It was Muirgen's task to wash, dress and give their son breakfast and then entertain him until his parents were free. Now Muirgen withdrew to the side of the chamber and busied herself sorting clothes. The red-haired child, who had greeted his father with a smile, now stood gazing up solemnly at the newcomer. Egric seemed stiff and awkward as he stared down into the clear blue eyes that examined him.

'He looks more like your wife than you.' Egric spoke directly to Eadulf and made no effort to greet the boy.

'That is in his favour,' Eadulf joked. Then he seemed to realise that there was a silence between the two. 'Say hello to your uncle, Alchú,' he said encouragingly.

The boy did not reply directly but continued to survey the newcomer with curiosity. 'Is he truly my uncle, *athair*?' he asked, turning his gaze to Eadulf.

Eadulf felt embarrassed. 'Truly, he is,' he replied. 'And you must greet him nicely. It is . . .' he fought to find the word for 'ill-mannered' in his vocabulary. He settled on *dorrda*, which meant sulky or surly. 'It is ill-mannered not to do so.'

Alchú said reluctantly, 'Hello.'

Egric shifted his weight and merely jerked his head in response. 'I am not at my best with children, Eadulf,' he finally said.

'He does not greet me.' Alchú turned again to his father, speaking sharply. 'Is that not also *dorrda*?'

For a moment or two, Eadulf, with crimson face, was unsure what to do.

'I see and hear you, child,' Egric said irritably, clearly understanding the comment. 'Remember that a sweet voice does not injure the teeth.'

Eadulf compressed his lips as the old saying of his people tripped from his brother's tongue – a condemnation of the boy's manners. It was clear the meeting was not a success. He had never thought his brother would be so stiff and unfriendly towards his son. It was obvious that the child sensed it.

Muirgen suddenly came bustling forward. It was clear that she had heard the exchange and felt she should intervene.

'Time to take the little one to his morning game of *fidchell*,' she announced. *Fidchell*, or 'wooden wisdom', was a popular board game played throughout the Five Kingdoms. Alchú was proving himself very adept at it.

Eadulf gave her a glance of both relief and thanks then took his younger brother by the arm and guided him from the chamber. Egric was silent as they walked through the corridors of the fortress, avoiding the rainswept exteriors. It was curious how much of a stranger Eadulf now felt with his brother. The intervening years seemed to have severed them emotionally as well as by experience.

'Things have changed quite a lot over the years, Egric,' Eadulf finally said, in an attempt to break the awkward silence.

'No man remains the same as they grow older,' replied his brother.

'I never thought that you would enter the religious. You always wanted to be a warrior. Our father named you Egric after the Warrior King of our people.'

'I remember King Egric and his brother Sigebert. They were both killed in battle when the Mercians invaded our land. Sigebert was killed even though he had spent years in a monastery and went on the battlefield alongside his brother with only a staff in his hand.'

'I can hardly remember that, but I remember the years when Ana became King, and that was after Sigebert and Egric were killed.'

'I should say, then, that I do remember the stories,' explained Egric, a little on the defensive. 'I remember Ana driving the Mercians out of our land. We became powerful then. Why, even Cenwealh of the West Saxons sought asylum in our land when the Mercians threw him out of his own kingdom.'

'Surely you were too young to remember all that?' Eadulf was astonished.

Egric smiled thinly. 'I remember a lot, brother. I was old enough to remember when we received news that Ana, too, had been killed in battle against the Mercians. That was the day I decided that I should be a warrior.'

'You were only about thirteen years old.'

'I was. But I recall those dark days when the Mercian King, Penda, was overlord of the East Angles. He was a godless tyrant.'

'Penda lived and died a pagan,' agreed Eadulf. 'But we all, at that time, followed the old gods until the word of the New Faith came to us.'

'Oswy of Northumbria challenged Mercia in the rain and mud of Winwaed where Penda perished,' Egric continued enthusiastically. 'We were free again and Athelwold seized our kingdom back, driving out the remaining Mercians and their placemen. The God of Battles was with us! They were great days, Eadulf. Do you remember them?'

For a moment, Egric had become animated and the light of excitement glowed in his eyes. Eadulf wondered whether to point out that his tone hardly reflected a religious calling.

'Of course,' he replied quietly. 'I was older than you.'

'So you remember how we went with our father to the great court of King Athelwold at Rendel's Ham?'

Eadulf sighed at the memory. 'And how we ran off on our own to see the royal burial site nearby, a place where only members of the royal line were allowed to enter, to witness the ancient rituals?'

'They were thrilling times, Eadulf.'

'Soon after that, I left Seaxmund's Ham to pursue my studies. I came here to the Five Kingdoms as directed by Fursa.'

'You abandoned the role of *gerefa*, which should have been yours when our father perished.' Did Eadulf hear a rebuke in the voice of his younger brother?

Eadulf shrugged. 'Learning from him something of the role of a lawgiver has stood me in good stead. What he gave me has not been abandoned. But when I left Seaxmund's Ham to pursue the Faith, why didn't *you* take on the role?'

Egric laughed sharply. 'Me? A *gerefa*, a lawgiver? I was still pursuing the dream of being a warrior defending our people. You left our village – did you ever go back?'

'A few times. I was even a witness at Rendel's Ham when King Swithhelm of the East Saxons converted to the New Faith and was baptised at the royal court there, with Athelwold acting as his godfather. That was when I asked what had become of you. I attended the Council at Streonshalh and then I returned to Rome in the company of Wighard, the archbishop-designate of Canterbury. He had gone there to receive the blessing of the Bishop of Rome. He was murdered there and it was Fidelma and I who helped resolve that.'

'And you never returned to our home after that?'

'Once more. Do you remember my old friend, Botulf? He, too, converted to the Faith and went to serve at the Abbey of Aldred. Five years ago, Fidelma and I went to see Archbishop Theodore at Canterbury, and while there, we received a message from poor Botolf. He wanted to see me urgently. We went to the Abbey of Aldred, but arrived too late. Botulf had been murdered and we had to discover the culprit. Thankfully, the forest around Rendel's Ham proved a sanctuary for Fidelma and me when we were in danger of our lives. That was the last time I enquired for you.'

'And what were you told?'

'People who remembered you assumed that you had gone away to serve as a warrior in the King's army. A local farmer, Mul . . .'

'Mul? Mad Mul of Frig's Tun?' Egric chuckled. 'He never would convert to the New Faith! He swore that he had followed Woden all his life and would never change his allegiance.'

'That was he,' confirmed Eadulf. 'He remembered me, but didn't remember you converting to the Faith.'

Egric shrugged. 'I did not stay in Seaxmund's Ham after I decided to follow the Faith, nor did I return as you did. But you say that you have not been there for five years now?'

Eadulf shook his head. 'I am settled here and happy.'

Egric was cynical. 'Truly happy? A foreigner in a strange land?'

'I am accepted,' Eadulf replied defensively. 'My wife is here, my son is here. I have friends. Is that not enough?'

'There is no longing in you to see the places of your childhood and youth?'

'Those places remain in the memory only. It cannot be otherwise, for the motion of the days continue and things must change with them. Is it not said that there are no footsteps that go backwards?'

'Perhaps,' Egric said softly. 'But if that is what you want, brother, so be it. I mean no insult to your decision. It is just strange to meet up after so many years and find our life paths have diverged so widely. In spite of all, I trust you are happy.'

'It seems our paths have not diverged so widely. You have also become a religieux. Also, oddly, you seem to have grasped some of the tongue of these people in your travels and, indeed, here you are in Cashel. A curious coincidence.'

'It is a coincidence nevertheless,' his brother said curtly.

Eadulf paused to glance out of a window. The rain had ceased. It was still cloudy but the clouds were lighter in shade and beginning to move quickly as the wind gathered strength.

'Alas, I have matters to attend to, Egric. I will introduce you to one of the King's bodyguards, a warrior called Dego. He was one of those who found you on the river. He will show you the township below the palace and explain something about this place and its history since you are a newcomer.'

The truth was that Eadulf had no matters to attend to. He felt guilty that he had suddenly made the excuse to leave his brother's company and tried to reason why. Of course, it was easy to explain that the great changes in Egric since Eadulf had last seen him were a cause for the alien feelings that now caused him unease. The eager young man, who enjoyed life, had an ambition to be a warrior – albeit as all young men do at a certain age – who enjoyed the company of girls, feasts and dancing, seemed to have vanished. Eadulf was not sure he liked the surly self-contained man with his unfriendly look and his open condemnation of Eadulf's chosen lifestyle. Yesterday, Eadulf had been happy to find his long-lost brother. Now he was trying to avoid his company.

Later, Eadulf met Fidelma crossing the main courtyard.

'You look troubled,' she greeted him.

'And you look as though you have a problem,' he said in an attempt at a light-hearted deflection of his thoughts.

Fidelma decided the matter in hand should have priority. 'Yesterday, it seemed no one saw anyone near the chapel, yet now we have several sightings. I find that strange.'

'I told you that I saw old Brother Conchobhar and Deogaire,' Eadulf pointed out.

'But now we have Abbess Líoch and an unknown religieux, who might have been Brother Madagan, close to the chapel. Deogaire said he saw

Brother Madagan while Sister Dianaimh saw an unknown religieux while she was standing waiting for the abbess inside the gates. It might have been the same person.'

Eadulf raised his eyebrows slightly. 'I presume that you are still suspicious of the abbess?'

'I never discount anyone until all the facts are in, Eadulf,' she replied. 'I need a word with Brother Madagan. Maybe he can confirm that the unknown religieux was himself.'

'I saw him enter the main door of the chapel just now.'

'Excellent. Where is your brother, by the way? I thought you were introducing him to our little Alchú?'

'I don't think he is much good with children. I've left Alchú with Muirgen and have asked Dego to take Egric to see the township.'

'Something is wrong, I can tell. What is it?'

'Let's say Alchú did not seem too enamoured with his new uncle. Not that the boy was to blame. Egric just seemed awkward. That was all.' Eadulf did not want to go into his own inexplicable feelings.

'I wouldn't worry about it.' She tried to give him assurance. 'After all, it must be a shock for him – that is, arriving in the manner he did. His companion killed and then rediscovering his brother after all these years. A brother with a child . . .'

'And married to the sister of a foreign King,' Eadulf finished. 'You think this is why he seems so tense?'

'I am sure of it. When was the last time you said you saw him?'

'Over ten years ago.'

'There you are, then. You cannot expect to regain those lost years in one evening. Give him time. He has much to learn about you, and you about him.'

Eadulf was uncertain for a moment and then he grimaced dismissively. 'I suppose you are right. Maybe I was expecting too much, too soon.'

'Indeed,' she smiled. 'So, let us now go and find Brother Madagan.'

They made their way across the courtyard to the main entrance of the chapel.

It was dark inside and, of course, the weather did not help with its grey, shadowy clouds. A small lantern lit the entrance beyond the doorway and two candles spluttered on the altar although they did not give out any meaningful light.

Fidelma and Eadulf stood by the entrance waiting until their eyes grew accustomed to the gloom. At first there seemed no one in the chapel. Everything was so still that even the steady beat of raindrops came like the sound of noisy pebbles on the roof above.

'Brother Madagan?' called Fidelma softly, her voice echoing in the vaulted tranquillity of the chapel. Her voice came back to her as a soft sighing echo.

At once there came the sound of a throat being cleared. A shadow moved from behind a pillar at the far side of the dark interior.

'Sister Fidelma?'

The figure was still shrouded in the gloom but they recognised Brother Madagan, the *rechtaire* or steward of Abbot Ségdae, by his voice.

'But no longer a Sister of the Faith, as you should know,' replied Fidelma gravely.

'Forgive me, lady. I had heard that you left the religious to pursue the law more vigorously.'

'How is your chill, Brother Madagan?'

'Much improved, lady; though it was sad that I had to miss the meal last night.' He peered closer towards her. 'Is that Brother Eadulf with you?'

'Indeed, it is,' replied Eadulf, stepping forward.

'I was going to make myself known to your brother. Where is he?'

'He has gone to the township in the company of Dego.'

'I am anxious to hear what happened when he was attacked on the river. I hear a senior cleric of Rome was killed. Has he told you much about it?'

'Little enough. But didn't you see him at the funeral last night?'

'I missed him in the darkness, especially after the intervention of the mad nephew of Brother Conchobhar.'

'Do you think he is mad?' intervened Fidelma.

'It was certainly madness that spoke last night,' Brother Madagan declared.

'You mean Deogaire making his prophecy?' asked Fidelma.

'That is exactly what I mean,' confirmed the steward with some vehemence. 'Sacrilege. The young man should be punished. You know the old saying – woe to him who considers his opinion a certainty! Woe to the bringers of warnings and prophecies!'

'Is not the Holy Scripture full of warnings and prophecies?' replied Fidelma gently.

'Not with sacrilegious pagan nonsense,' the man snapped.

'You mean because he used terms from the Holy Scripture?'

'That he chose a funeral to utter his warning was blasphemous, as it was also disrespectful.'

'As I recall, discretion was not a virtue with Deogaire. But it is not of him that I wish to speak.'

Brother Madagan sniffed in disapproval. 'What is it?'

'Let us sit awhile.' Fidelma pointed to a bench by the pillar, where light from a window illuminated the area. When they were seated, she went on: 'I was told you were passing this chapel just before Brother Cerdic's body was found. Did you see anyone at that time – anyone emerging from the chapel?'

Brother Madagan paused for a moment, as if trying to recall. 'I saw no one. However, I did hear some shouting. I glanced back and saw Brother Eadulf calling to old Brother Conchobhair and Deogaire. Was that when the body . . .?'

'I had just found the body,' Eadulf explained unnecessarily. 'Brother Cerdic came to the Abbey of Imleach and then accompanied you and the abbot here. I was wondering whether, during that time, he said or did anything which might have indicated that he had made an enemy, or mentioned anything which could have suggested he would be victim to this lethal assault?'

Brother Madagan gave a derisive snort. 'He was a most arrogant fellow, who would have done well to remember that he was not among his own people and their customs!'

'I am told that you nearly lost your temper with him when he came to Imleach,' Eadulf said in a mild tone.

Brother Madagan was indifferent. 'That is true. He provoked me with his conceit.'

'I had not realised that you spoke my tongue, Brother Madagan,' Eadulf went on.

'Did you not? It is a matter of little importance except that Brother Cerdic had no word of our language. His Latin was indifferent and his Greek was non-existent. That was why Brother Rónán of Fearna had to act as his guide and interpreter.'

'Where did you learn the Saxon tongue?' It was Fidelma who posed the question this time.

'I spent some time in the town of Láirge, the harbour on the coast. Many travellers from foreign places, especially those who come to study at our colleges, make their landfall there. I spent two summers there teaching students from the kingdoms of the Saxons before they travelled on to colleges like Darú.'

'Let us return to Brother Cerdic,' Eadulf said. 'I understand you were in attendance when he and Brother Rónán told the abbot about the nature of their business.'

'Of course. As *rechtaire* it was my duty.'

'So tell me, exactly how did he explain the purpose of this deputation led by Bishop Arwald?'

Brother Madagan sighed. 'That was the problem. He did not. He simply said that this deputation was coming to Cashel and required the attendance of the abbot. It was nothing short of an order.'

'Did he mention that he had called at Cill Náile and requested the presence of Abbess Líoch?'

'That he did not mention. I later heard it from Brother Rónán.'

'And what did Brother Rónán have to say?'

'I think he was as frustrated as we were. He had not been privy to the discussions with Bishop Arwald when the deputation was at Fearna. So he could not even tell us what had been discussed. I think he was grateful when, having guided Brother Cerdic to Imleach, he was able to set out to return to Fearna.'

'And Brother Cerdic was not forthcoming at all on his journey with you and the abbot?'

'When he spoke, it was as if he were commanding servants to do his bidding. That was what caused my anger.'

'So he had the ability to anger people?' pressed Eadulf.

'Had he been killed anywhere outside of Cashel, I would not have been surprised.'

'What do you mean?' demanded Fidelma.

'Simply that some people might have taken offence at his manner, as did I.' Brother Madagan was gloomy. 'Let us pray that this bishop is not as hateful as his messenger.'

'Did Brother Cerdic have anything to say about Bishop Arwald?' Eadulf asked.

'Little enough. He was more concerned about some cleric who was accompanying the bishop.'

'Some cleric? Can you be more specific?'

'It was the cleric from Rome. He told us that it was some scholar.' He thought for a moment. 'Ah, I have the name now. His name was Verax. That's it – the Venerable Verax, son of Anastasius of Segni.'

Eadulf drew in his breath sharply, causing Fidelma to glance at him in surprise.

'Are you sure of the name?' he asked.

'Such a foreign name does stick in one's memory,' asserted Brother Madagan. 'Why?'

'I . . . It's just that I have heard the name spoken of when I was in Rome,' Eadulf replied lamely. 'That is all.'

Fidelma cast a thoughtful glance at him before turning back to the steward of Imleach.

'Why do you think Brother Cerdic was concerned with him?'

'Difficult to say, lady. His voice had a tone of respect when he mentioned Verax's name. I think he was in awe of this aged and renowned scholar. That's all.'

'Brother Cerdic gave you absolutely no idea of the purpose of the coming of this Venerable Verax and Bishop Arwald?'

'Only that it was to be an important discussion which Abbot Ségdae must attend in the presence of the King of Cashel.'

'I do not like it,' Eadulf commented.

Brother Madagan nodded. 'I agree with you, friend Eadulf. I feel there is something afoot. Something . . .'

Fidelma sniffed deprecatingly. 'In another moment, you will be echoing Deogaire's prophecy by saying that you believe that this is the devil's deputation.'

Brother Madagan flushed indignantly.

'Anyway,' Fidelma rose abruptly, 'all I needed to know was whether you had seen anything unusual as you passed the chapel yesterday. You have made it clear that you did not.'

'That is true,' the steward of Imleach confirmed, also rising to his feet, with Eadulf following his example.

'Then we will trouble you no more. Thank you, Brother Madagan.' Fidelma turned for the door of the chapel.

Outside, she halted and addressed Eadulf accusingly.

'The name of Verax meant something specific to you, didn't it?' she demanded.

'Not Verax on its own but the Venerable Verax, son of Anastasius of Segni,' corrected Eadulf carefully. 'That is the name that meant something to me. You will recall I spent some time in Rome after we had resolved the mystery of the death of Wighard, the Archbishop-designate of Canterbury? You had left on your return journey to Cashel. During the time I remained in Rome I was to counsel the new Archbishop of Canterbury, Theodore, because he was a Greek from Tarsus and knew nothing of my people.'

Fidelma restrained her impatience. 'I know all this. But what about the name?'

'I spent much time in the Lateran Palace . . .' Eadulf said reflectively.

'Eadulf!' Fidelma was becoming impatient.

'The Bishop of Rome is named Vitalian.'

Fidelma almost ground her teeth in exasperation. 'I know it. So?'

'Vitalian is son of Anastasius of Segni.'

It was a few moments before a startled expression crossed her features. 'Are you saying that this Venerable Verax is . . .?'

'He must be brother to Pope Vitalian himself and therefore a foremost prince of the Church.'

'Brother to the Bishop of Rome? Brother to the Pope of the Faithful?' Fidelma breathed.

It was only in recent times that the Bishop of Rome had adopted and been acknowledged by the Latin title of *Papa* – the child's name for 'father'. It was still unusual for members of the churches of the Five Kingdoms to use that title. Now Fidelma was using it as a means of emphasis. She focused her piercing green eyes on Eadulf.

'If a person of that rank is coming here, this makes the reason for this deputation even more mysterious.'

'And makes it even more essential for us to resolve the murder of Brother Cerdic before his arrival,' claimed Eadulf. 'Brother Cerdic would have been his emissary, not the messenger of Bishop Arwald.'

'Colgú must be told of the importance of this guest.'

'And I think I should question my brother further. Surely his companion, the Venerable Victricius, was coming here in connection with this deputation. He must have been a leading Roman cleric, judging by his senior form of address and will have known that he was meeting the Venerable Verax in this place.'

'But why wouldn't he tell your brother of his mission?' asked Fidelma.

'I do not know,' Eadulf said hesitantly. 'Perhaps Egric . . .' He left the thought unarticulated.

'Are you saying that your brother was not telling us the truth?' guessed Fidelma.

Eadulf admitted unwillingly, 'He does seem to be holding something back. I am thinking that there are possibilities. Firstly, that he was told not to say anything in view of the identity of the Venerable Verax. This could mean that if he found out that we have learned of that identity – and it was only by chance I knew, because of the time I spent in Rome – then he might now be more forthcoming.'

'And the other possibilities?'

'That he simply does not know. Or that he knows and will not say because of some ulterior reason. I still find some of the things he says to be strange for one in the religious.'

Fidelma was about to speak further when a rider came through the gates into the courtyard. It was the lean, saturnine figure of Aidan, one of the warriors of the King's bodyguard. He came to a halt hurriedly and had leaped from his horse almost before it had halted, shouting for one of the *echaire* to attend to it while he hurried purposefully across the flagstones towards the main doors that led to the King's chambers.

'Aidan!' called Fidelma. 'Where are you off to with such a serious expression?'

Aidan halted and turned, as if seeing them for the first time. He gave a quick smile of apology.

'News for your brother, lady.'

'Bad news?'

'Yesterday I was told to send lookouts along the eastern roads: your brother is expecting a group of visitors from the direction of Fearna.'

'I know all about that.'

'Well, I have learned that they crossed the River An Fheoir, and last night, I am told, they were resting at the church of Mogeanna.'

Fidelma raised her eyebrows. 'That is about forty kilometres from here, which means . . .'

'They could be here tomorrow,' Aidan finished for her and, with a quick salute, he turned and hurried on.

Fidelma gazed in concern at Eadulf. 'Tomorrow,' she repeated in a tone of dismay. 'Somehow I don't think that gives us enough time to resolve anything, before the brother of Pope Vitalian arrives in Cashel.'

CHAPTER SEVEN

❧

Eadulf spotted Dego's horse outside the tavern of Rumann on the western side of the town square. Dego was inside with Egric enjoying the local ale, which was a product of Rumann's own brewery at the back of the tavern. They looked up as Eadulf came across to join them. Rumann was already following him with another pottery mug of his ale.

'It is not often we see you in here, Brother Eadulf,' the big alehouse-keeper greeted him cheerfully. 'I suppose this is a special day with the arrival of your brother. How is the lady Fidelma? And your son?'

'They are both well, Rumann. And your own family?'

'My son is well and a great help to me.' With a smile at the company, Rumann turned towards his other customers, a couple of local shepherds seated in a corner.

Eadulf raised his drink towards his companions. Egric was regarding him with an odd expression – something like apprehension. Dego, however, did not seem to notice his companion's discomfiture.

'I have shown your brother around our town,' he reported. 'Not that it took long so I thought I should introduce him to the most important place.' He waved a hand to encompass his surroundings. 'Oh, I saw Della as we passed, and she asked me to pass on a message – that if

99

Fidelma calls by soon, she has some special herbs for her. It seems that now Aibell is living with her, Della is able to spend more time cultivating her land.'

Della was a longtime friend of Fidelma, who had successfully defended her from false accusations of murder. A few months ago, Della had begun to look after the wayward young girl, Aibell. Found near Della's home, it turned out that she had escaped to Cashel, having been illegally sold as a bondservant and mistreated in the country of the Sliabh Luachra. Fidelma had given the girl her protection.

'I'll pass the information on to her,' Eadulf assured him.

'Did you come here in search of me?' Egric wanted to know. He frowned. 'Is anything wrong?'

'Nothing is wrong that we did not know already,' replied Eadulf. 'I just wanted to ask you a few more questions.' He glanced at Dego apologetically. 'Would you give us a few moments?'

Dego rose. 'Old Nessán is over in the corner. I haven't seen him for a while. I need a few words with him.'

When they were alone, Egric challenged: 'What is this about?'

'The same matter,' Eadulf said with an easy smile. 'I just wanted to clarify that the Venerable Victricius gave you absolutely no hint about the purpose of his journey here.'

'I have told you that he did not.' There was irritation in his brother's tone.

'I just wanted confirmation. You had no idea that you would find Brother Cerdic here?'

There was a slight hesitation before Egric replied. 'I also told you that I did not know Brother Cerdic.'

'Very well.' Eadulf sat back, watching his brother keenly. 'Tell me again, when did you first meet the Venerable Victricius?'

Egric's eyes narrowed in suspicion. 'I met him in Canterbury.'

'How exactly did you come to meet him? It is important.'

'How exactly? I arrived there, having taken the sea route from Streonshalh with some other members of the religious.'

'You did not know him at Streonshalh?'

'I did not. Was he there?'

'So where and how in Canterbury did you meet him?' went on Eadulf without answering.

'I was going to find a band of religious or merchants heading to a new abbey that I had heard about in the east of the Kingdom of Kent and . . . I think I met him in a tavern.' He saw the expression on Eadulf's face and grimaced. 'Where else would one pick up news of a merchant band leaving Canterbury?' Eadulf was about to point out that there were plenty of religious houses and hostels in Canterbury, but Egric was continuing. 'I was despairing of finding such a band when I fell into conversation with the Venerable Victricius. He told me that no less a person than Archbishop Theodore had given him a special commission which would take him here. I mentioned that I had been in the land of the Cruthin; I knew something of the common tongue, though I had never been here before. All this I told you earlier.'

'And so he asked you to accompany him?'

'He needed my skill; also the fact was that he was old and I was young.'

'And you agreed without knowing the purpose of the trip, to come on a long and arduous journey into an unknown land? It seems strange.'

'How so, strange?' Egric challenged.

'That you set out from Canterbury to accompany the Venerable Victricius, without knowing him and without any idea of his purpose.'

'Strange but true, brother. I had no other urgent task to occupy me and the prospect of adventure seemed good. Did you never set out on a journey without knowing where it would lead you?'

Eadulf paused, for his brother had a point. 'I do not have to be convinced, Egric. But the fact that Brother Cerdic arrived here to tell us that there was a deputation coming from Canterbury and then was murdered . . .'

Egric frowned quickly. 'Are you accusing me?'

'Don't be so touchy, Egric. You did not arrive at Cashel until after Brother Cerdic was found murdered. What I am trying to find is some thread that would lead me into untangling this mystery.'

'You were always trying to resolve riddles when you were a boy.' Egric sounded disgusted.

Eadulf sighed. 'Isn't it curious that Brother Cerdic came here from Canterbury and was killed here? That you and the Venerable Victricius came here from Canterbury and were attacked here, leaving Victricius dead? Surely there is something more you can tell us.'

Egric was shaking his head firmly. 'All I know is what I have said. It might well have something to do with the Venerable Victricius' purpose in coming to this kingdom – I don't know.'

'Bishop Arwald will soon be here in the company of the Venerable Verax. You said that you had heard of Arwald – but what of Verax?'

Egric was silent and covered the silence by taking a sip of his drink.

'So you do not know the Venerable Verax?' pressed Eadulf.

'Eadulf, I am a lowly cleric – not one who mixes with highly placed members of the Faith.'

'Yet you were travelling as companion to the Venerable Victricius,' Eadulf said patiently.

'That is different.'

'How different?'

'When is this deputation due in Cashel?' asked Egric, without replying.

'They were reported as being about a day's ride away.'

Eadulf sat watching his brother for a moment. He knew instinctively that Egric was keeping something back. But what was it? He could hardly accuse him of complicity in the death of Brother Cerdic because, as he pointed out, Brother Cerdic had been murdered *before* Egric arrived at Cashel. But he was sure that his brother knew far more than he was telling him.

'I must get back to the palace,' Eadulf finally said, rising. He tried to conceal his exasperation. 'I have things to do before the Venerable Verax and his party arrive. I will see you later.'

Egric glanced up at his brother. 'I am sorry to give you such trouble.'

'Don't worry. As soon as this deputation has come and gone, we must get together properly and catch up on all that has happened to each of us. I'll take you fishing along the Siúr; the river circles to the west of us here and further north there is good fishing. I remember how you liked to fish in the Fromus where it passed by our father's house . . .'

'That was long ago.'

'Not so long that it has passed from memory. But there is good fishing here. Good hunting, too.'

Egric was suddenly looking thoughtful. 'You are right, brother. Maybe I should take time to relax.'

'That's the spirit.' Eadulf leaned forward and patted his brother's shoulder approvingly. 'You've had a bad time. Once we find out what the Venerable Verax wants, things should feel a lot easier.'

He turned. Raising a hand to Rumann, and to Dego and the others, he left the tavern.

Arriving back in the palace, Eadulf went to their chambers to see if Fidelma was there. Muirgen was actually tidying up while Alchú sat watching her.

'Hello, little hound,' Eadulf greeted him as he came in.

The boy looked up and peered around Eadulf as if expecting someone to be behind him.

'Where is that strange man, *athair*?' he asked.

'Strange man?' Eadulf was puzzled.

'He means your brother,' Muirgen offered sheepishly pausing from her work.

'That is no strange man, little hound.' Eadulf shook his head reprovingly. 'That is Egric, your uncle.'

The little boy pouted. 'I don't like him.'

Eadulf sat down opposite his son with a strained smile. 'So what makes you not like your uncle?'

The child stared intently at his hands then mumbled: 'I don't know. I just don't like him.'

Eadulf wondered how best to deal with the situation.

'You must have some reason,' he said gently. 'Why, you don't even know him. Tell me, what do you feel about your uncle?'

The little boy did not respond but stared stubbornly down, not meeting his father's eyes.

Eadulf raised his eyes in a helpless gesture to Muirgen. She motioned him with her head to come to the far side of the chamber and then spoke quietly.

'He seemed strangely silent after you had introduced your brother to him this morning. Some children – indeed, most children – have an intuitive feeling for certain things. To ask them to explain those feelings by means of logic is futile.'

'I have great respect for your abilities as a nurse, Muirgen. Indeed, that is why we brought you and your husband, Nessan, all the way from Sliabh Mís to look after our son. But I have no understanding of this.'

'Well, a child will suddenly say they don't like eggs, or some other food. You ask them why, and often they can't explain. The same goes with people. Sometimes, someone will come along and you will take an instant dislike to them. Why? You, being older and more mature, might try to find reasons but usually you fall back on instinct.'

'So you say I shouldn't force Algú to like him?'

'What I say is that it will be up to your brother to win the boy over.'

Eadulf grimaced. 'Easier said than done. Alas, Egric doesn't seem to have a way with children.'

'Well, from what I have picked up from gossip, he might be finding it hard to be open with people here at the moment. Having survived an attack, his companion killed, he finds himself a stranger in a strange land. Whom can he trust? No wonder he is awkward with everyone, not just our Alchú.'

Eadulf stared at the nurse for a moment, surprised at her understanding. 'I swear that you would make a good philosopher, Muirgen.'

She chuckled. 'Why, sir, I was raised in a family of country folk. Being close to nature, we are closer to all living creatures than most people who are raised in townships. Your brother keeps his thoughts and emotions to himself. That is all.'

'So you advise me to let matters take their natural course?'

'Yes, that is my advice.'

'And not try to challenge or correct the boy?'

'Exactly so.'

'So be it,' agreed Eadulf. Then: 'Have you seen Fidelma? It must be nearly time for the *eter-shod*.'

The *eter-shod* was the midday meal.

'There is food prepared in the adjacent chamber and the lady Fidelma has said she would return for it after she had finished speaking with her brother.'

'Is there a place laid for Egric?'

'Naturally.' Muirgen seemed slightly offended and Eadulf apologised immediately.

But Egric did not return to eat with them. Fidelma and Eadulf made no mention of the fact in front of Alchú as they ate the light meal which was usual at this time of day. Only after they had finished and Muirgen had removed the boy did Fidelma broach the subject. Eadulf described the stilted encounter between their son and his uncle, and then spoke of Alchú's dislike and Muirgen's views on the situation.

Fidelma sighed absently and asked: 'Egric knew he was to eat with us?'

'He did.'

'Perhaps you had better check on him. I want to have a further word with Brother Conchobhar.'

Eadulf did not really want to return to Rumann's tavern to remonstrate with his brother for not joining them for the midday meal. He was sure that Egric would resent the fact. However, as he made his way down to the courtyard he saw Gormán, and some instinct made him ask if the guard commander had seen Egric return to the palace.

'I think he is still in Rumann's tavern, friend Eadulf. I was on my way back from my mother's place and had cause to have a word with Rumann. He and Dego were still in there. They are as thick as thieves and talking about fishing or something.'

Eadulf said in bewilderment, 'I am surprised he is so interested that he has forgotten to come back for his meal.'

They were interrupted by a shout. It was from Enda, who was on watch-duty in the tower above the gate. 'Riders!'

'From the east?' called Gormán, having been warned to watch for the arrival of Bishop Arwald's deputation.

'No, from the south. Six men – four look like warriors. One of them carries a banner.'

'Whose banner?' demanded Gormán.

'I can't see it from here. They are crossing through the township and making for the palace.'

'Sing out when you can identify the banner,' Gormán replied, turning back to Eadulf. 'Well, at least they don't appear to be the visitors that the King expects. I have some men placed on the hill to the east, so they should give us ample warning of their approach.'

'There is certainly a lot of tension about their coming.'

Gormán was in agreement. 'To be honest, friend Eadulf, some people are a little unnerved by the pronouncements of Deogaire.'

'Evil from the east?' Eadulf feigned a laugh. It sounded hollow and he knew it. 'I would take little notice of that.'

'I am not personally concerned,' replied the warrior, 'but there are others who cleave to the old superstitions.'

'The riders are approaching!' Enda called down. 'I can see the banner now . . . yes, it's that of Cummasach.'

Gormán whistled softly. 'Whatever brings the Prince of the Déisi to Cashel? That's a rare occurrence.'

'Wouldn't it be because of the attack on my brother and his companion?' Eadulf asked, coming to the logical conclusion.

The warrior clicked his tongue in annoyance. 'Of course, that must be it! But even an event like that makes it unusual to get the Prince of the Déisi to stir himself north of the Siúr. They have a strange history, these Déisi.'

'What do you mean?'

'Time was when they were a wealthy and powerful people, living in the fertile lands of Midhe – the Middle Kingdom. Legend has it that an argument broke out and their chieftain cast a spear at the High King and took out his eye. The Brehons met and decided that one half of the Déisi, under that Prince, Aonghus of the Terrible Spear, should be banished across the water to the east. They settled and created a kingdom called Dyfed. The other half of the Déisi were sent south where the King of Cashel allowed them to settle south of the great River Siúr.'

Eadulf was startled. He recalled how he and Fidelma had been shipwrecked on the shores of Dyfed and realised that there was some close affinity with the people there and those of the Five Kingdoms.

'When were they sent into exile?' he enquired.

'Oh, that was centuries ago. Don't worry – the Déisi of Muman are peaceful enough and pay regular tribute to Cashel.'

'I realise that,' Eadulf replied, a little defensively, 'for have I not often accompanied Fidelma through their territory?'

A horn suddenly sounded from the path leading up to the palace gates. It was customary for armed strangers to announce their presence in such a fashion.

'Make the response,' called Gormán to Enda. 'I will greet them.'

Enda drew his hunting horn and gave an answering blast as Eadulf followed Gormán across the courtyard to the main gates. By the time they reached them, the band of horsemen were entering and Eadulf stood back in the shadows while the Commander of the King's Bodyguard went forward to formally greet them.

The leader was a broad-shouldered man, with wiry brown hair and beard and an expression of authority. His colourful clothes, the cloak and arms, proclaimed him as a man of rank. Next to him rode a warrior carrying a pole with a banner – the emblem of the Déisi. Behind them came a man of advancing years, his dress and insignia proclaiming him to be a Brehon. It was the youth who accompanied him who caught Eadulf's attention, for his hands were tied with rope before him. His clothes were torn and dirty. There was dirt and blood on his face and his mouse-coloured hair was ragged and askew. In spite of his appearance, the boy wore a smile of superiority and seemed to concentrate his gaze upon the middle distance. Bringing up the rear of the group were two warriors.

Gormán moved forward and greeted the leader.

'Welcome to Cashel, Cummasach. I am Gormán, Commander of the Nasc Niadh, Bodyguard to the King.'

Cummasach glanced down at the warrior, his glance neither friendly nor antagonistic. The ritual of greeting was a formality.

'I thank you for your welcome, warrior of the Golden Collar. I have come, with my Brehon, Furudán, to speak with Colgú.'

'I will have Colgú informed of your arrival, Cummasach. Your escort will be attended to, but who is it that accompanies you as a prisoner?'

'His name is Rudgal and he is, alas, a renegade of my people.'

Gormán glanced quickly at the indifferent prisoner. 'Is he . . .?'

Cummasach interrupted irritably, 'You were to inform your King, if you please. It has been a long and tiring ride and I do not wish to tarry longer than can be helped.'

Gormán remembered protocol and turned quickly to one of his warriors.

'Call the *echaire* and attend to the horses. Have the warriors conducted to the House of Heroes and offered refreshment.'

Eadulf stepped forward and said to Gormán: 'I will inform Colgú.'

He was aware of the sharp gaze of Cummasach directed at him as he turned and hurried off. As he left, he heard Cummasach telling Gormán that he wanted his prisoner taken to a secure place under guard. Eadulf bumped into Fidelma as he hurried along the corridor to the King's council chamber.

'I heard there are new arrivals,' she said breathlessly.

'Cummasach and his Brehon,' Eadulf informed her. 'They have a prisoner with them. I think it is one of the men who attacked Egric and his companion on the river. Cummasach has demanded to see your brother.'

Fidelma's eyes had grown wider. 'That is good news. At least one of the attackers has been caught. But why does Cummasach need to see Colgú?'

'We'd best not keep them waiting,' was all Eadulf said. She accompanied him to her brother's council chamber. Colgú was inside meeting with Abbot Ségdae and Beccan, the steward. The King looked up in surprise as they entered. Fidelma waited while Eadulf quickly explained the reason for the interruption.

'Cummasach has brought his prisoner here in person?' The King was puzzled. 'That is unusual behaviour for a Déisi prince.'

'I believe he must be one of those who attacked my brother and his companion, the Venerable Victricius,' Eadulf confirmed.

Colgú turned to Beccan. 'You had better inform Brehon Aillín that his presence is required, and find Eadulf's brother, Egric.' As an aside he said to Eadulf: 'If this is the man, your brother should be available to identify him. You and Fidelma should stay to hear what this is about.'

It was almost as if Brehon Aillín were waiting outside the door, for

Beccan had hardly left when the elderly judge came in. A few moments passed before there was a tap on the door and Beccan re-entered.

'Cummasach, Prince of the Déisi,' he began ponderously, only to be interrupted by an impatient Colgú.

'I know, I know. Bring them in.'

'Prince Cummasach and his Brehon, Furudán,' the steward announced, as they entered, followed by Gormán.

Eadulf could not help but notice that the greetings between Cummasach and Colgú were fairly stilted. Colgú resumed his chair of office but, while the others stood, a chair was placed for the Prince of the Déisi. The ceremonial drinks were offered and an attendant hurried round dispensing them.

'And now, lord Cummasach?' prompted Colgú.

'I will let my Brehon tell the story.' Cummasach made a motion with his hand in the direction of his companion. 'It will save time.'

There was silence for a moment until Colgú realised that the Brehon was waiting for his formal permission to speak. He gave it impatiently.

'I heard from the Brehon at Cluain Meala about the attack near Brother Siolán's chapel on the river. My lord, Cummasach, had been having trouble with a band of wild young men who refused to obey the elders of the clan and ignored the laws of the Brehons. My suspicions immediately fell on these troublemakers, for they had attacked several travellers passing through the mountains of the confluences, even as far as the church of Míodán.'

'Míodán's church?' interrupted Fidelma. 'That lies just south of the Siúr before you reach the harbour of Láirge?'

'That is so, lady,' Furudán agreed. He evidently knew Fidelma by sight. 'They attacked a merchant boat coming up the river some time ago. Therefore, when I heard of this attack, I felt it sounded like their work. It so happened that we had information about where they were hiding that very day. They had fled south from the river into their lair in the mountains. My lord Cummasach summoned a score of his warriors and we made our way there, attacking their camp just before dawn.'

As he paused, Cummasach put in: 'They were foolish young men. They chose to resist rather than give themselves to justice. They fought and were so determined that two managed to escape but the others fell to my men's swords.'

Brehon Furudán added softly, 'Except one.'

'The one you have brought here as a prisoner?' Eadulf asked.

Cummasach glanced at him with a frown.

Seeing the look, Colgú said immediately: 'You may speak freely to the husband of my sister, for he has our complete confidence.'

'The prisoner's name is Rudgal,' confirmed the Brehon.

'What of the two that escaped?' asked Eadulf.

'They have not been found. But they cannot hide forever.'

'If their companions fought to the death, why did your prisoner surrender?' Colgú mused.

'He did not appear to me to be in any apprehension of punishment when I saw him in the courtyard.' Eadulf could not help making the observation aloud. 'Yet he certainly seemed the sort who would fight rather than surrender.'

'I congratulate your sister's husband on having a sharp eye,' commented Cummasach with a grim smile. 'Indeed, he would have probably fought on, but seeing that his companions had fled or fallen, he decided to make a bargain.'

'What bargain could *he* make?' Fidelma asked.

'We still do not understand completely. He lowered his shield and sword and shouted – truce!' The word *essomon* which the Brehon used was one which Eadulf realised meant a cessation of conflict for a moment to speak.

'So I presume the fighting stopped and the young man was taken captive?' Colgú was clearly eager for the story to end and for his visitors to come to the point.

'Yes, the fighting stopped,' replied the Brehon gravely. 'Rudgal told us that he would bargain for his freedom with information that would be of benefit only to the Chief Bishop of the Kingdom.'

Abbot Ségdae was startled. 'What would a thief know that is of benefit to me?'

'I can only relate what he said. Furthermore, he said he would only reveal this knowledge if he were taken before Abbot Ségdae and the King. He would speak to no other person.'

'Have you questioned him further?' asked Colgú.

'We did, but he was firm in his resolve. He did, however, reveal one important fact. He said that he and his companions had been given a *cumal* each to attack the two foreign religious on the river and kill them. Whatever happened, they were to ensure that the elderly one was killed. As well as money, they were told they could help themselves to the goods that these religious carried.'

There was a shocked silence. 'Who would pay them to carry out such a deed?' whispered Abbot Ségdae.

'That he would not tell us. He said he would reveal this only to you, Abbot Ségdae and the King.'

'You searched the camp of these assassins, I presume?' Fidelma asked. 'Did you find any of the objects stolen from the victims?'

'We found a store of coins – several were bright *cumals* which seemed to support Rudgal's claim. There were various pieces of booty that they had taken at various times, some of which probably belonged to the religious who were attacked, but there was nothing specific. There were also signs of burned parchment and other materials – perhaps books and other items such as would be carried by religious, but nothing that was truly identifiable.'

Colgú beat a tattoo on the arm of his chair with his fingers. Then he sighed.

'So let us see what information this man has which he believes will buy him freedom from the punishment for these heinous crimes. Gormán, you and Eadulf will go and fetch this . . . what is his name?'

'Rudgal, lord,' Brehon Furudán repeated.

'Then go and bring this Rudgal here and we will listen to what he has to say. If his claim is true – that someone paid for the assassination of these religious visitors to our kingdom – then we must find the culprit at once.'

'Well, friend Eadulf,' Gormán remarked, as they left the King's council chamber and made their way down to the courtyard, 'these are strange times. I have no understanding of what this means.'

'Alas, you are not alone, Gormán,' muttered Eadulf. Aware that the King had asked for Egric to formally identify the man as one of his attackers he was hoping that his brother had returned to the palace. However, the guard at the gate reported that Egric and Dego were still in the township. The two men crossed the flagstones of the courtyard to the *Laochtech*, the House of Heroes, which housed the King's élite bodyguard. Enda was sitting in the anteroom to the barracks with another warrior called Luan. They were playing a board game with the warriors of the Déisi. It was called *brandubh*, Black Raven, which was popular among the warriors, though less skilful than *fidchell*, the Wooden Wisdom, at which all nobles aspired to become masters.

Enda looked up as they entered, and then he and Luan rose in the presence of their commander and Eadulf.

'We've come to collect the prisoner,' Gormán told them.

'He's in the storehouse at the back. We've kept his hands tethered, just in case.'

'No guard outside the barn?' Gormán asked in surprise.

Enda smiled complacently. 'With hands tethered and a bar on the door, what need was there? Anyway, the prisoner doesn't seem inclined to escape.'

Gormán nodded and motioned the warriors to reseat themselves and continue their game. 'We'll fetch him ourselves.'

He and Eadulf went around to the back of the building where there was a general storehouse, mainly used for storing weapons and equipment for the warriors. As they approached, Gormán came to an abrupt halt and swore. Eadulf glanced at him in surprise, for profanity was hardly ever used by the young warrior. Gormán pointed.

'Enda may have left his prisoner with hands tethered, but he is so sure of himself that he didn't bother to put the bar properly in place to secure the door. A slight push and it would swing open. Damn his eyes! He'll be doing extra guard duty for that omission.'

Eadulf saw that the heavy wooden bar should have been swung across the double doors, making them impossible to move. Instead, only a fraction of the bar had spanned the division, as if it had been hurriedly slotted into place.

Gormán pushed it aside and swung open the doors. Inside the storehouse it was gloomy. They stood for a moment at the open doors and heard a soft rhythmic creaking sound, like someone swinging a heavy object on the end of a piece of rope.

Eadulf was peering into the shadows beyond. Then, as his eyes grew used to the darkness, he exclaimed, '*Quod avertat Deus*! Gormán, get a light in here.'

Eadulf stood waiting at the door while Gormán ran back to the *Laochtech*. It was a moment before he returned, bearing a lantern and followed by Enda and Luan, with the latter carrying a second lantern.

'I tell you, the bar was pushed fully into position. It was completely secure,' Enda was protesting.

They came to a halt at the entrance behind Eadulf. Gormán and Enda raised their lanterns.

A body was swinging gently from a rope tied to one of the rafters. The dead man's feet were only a short distance from the ground, but far enough above it so that there could be no weight resting on it. The position of the rope around the neck, the odd angle of the head, was enough to show that he had been hanged. The body was that of Rudgal.

CHAPTER EIGHT

‍❧

Eadulf moved quickly and called upon one of his companions to hold the weight of the body while he loosened the rope. Luan put down his lantern, then he and Enda did as requested while Eadulf took a knife to sever the rope. The body was lowered to the floor. Eadulf did not need to examine the corpse to see that Rudgal had choked to death, for the face was blackened and the features distorted. There was something else that caught his attention; something protruding from the corner of the corpse's mouth. At first Eadulf thought it was his tongue, but when he carefully took it with thumb and forefinger and pulled, he found it was a piece of cloth.

Enda was peering at the corpse without emotion. 'So he preferred death to the rule of law?'

Eadulf glanced up at him cynically. 'So you think he hanged himself?'

Enda was puzzled at his response. 'Isn't it obvious? No wonder he was calm about being brought here as a prisoner. He knew he would never have to face the consequences of his actions.'

'He was calm because he thought he could bargain for his freedom,' Eadulf corrected.

'I don't understand.' Enda was still baffled.

Eadulf stood up impatiently. 'The facts are obvious. Look! His hands,

115

as you saw earlier, are still bound together. So you leave a man tethered in this place and, as you claim, you have secured the doors properly.'

'Doesn't the fact that the bar was in place, even though it was not done as correctly as it should have been, indicate that no one else was involved in this?' Gormán felt obliged to defend Enda.

'Are you asking me to believe that a man who has confidence that he can negotiate his way out of this situation resorts to hanging himself? Are you suggesting that a man with hands securely tied can, in the darkness of this place, find a length of rope, fashion a noose, throw the rope over that high beam, place the noose round his neck, tie the other end to that bar across there and . . . then what? Miraculously levitate himself so that the rope leaves him suspended in the air?'

'If he had tied that end of the rope it would have been secured, then he could have found something to stand on, place the noose round his neck and taken the plunge that ended his life,' Enda argued.

'So, if that were possible – which it is not – where would he have taken the plunge from? Where is the stool on which to climb or a wooden box? Are you saying that after he had hanged himself, he climbed down and hid them? And he did all this with his hands still tied together?' Eadulf tried to keep the derision out of his voice

'What conclusion is there, friend Eadulf?' Gormán asked patiently.

'While we have been speaking with the King, someone came to this shed, removed the bar, stuffed that cloth into Rudgal's mouth in the form of a gag, took the rope, put it in position and then hauled the victim up, choking him to death. The killer then secured the rope to the bar, and left the body. Perhaps he left in a hurry, for he did not properly secure the bar in its place at the door. Rudgal has been murdered – silenced to prevent him revealing the information with which he planned to barter for his freedom.'

Gormán was staring at him in amazement. 'But that means . . .'

'Yes. It means that someone in the palace is the killer. That same person who killed Brother Cerdic has now killed Rudgal, which proves that there must be a connection.'

'Well, we can eliminate some people from being suspected of the crime,' Gormán suggested brightly.

'Such as?'

'Well, everyone who was in Colgú's chamber. They are still there, waiting for us to take Rudgal before them.'

'That still leaves a lot of suspects,' Eadulf pointed out gloomily. 'You had better take charge here while I inform Colgú. Question anyone who had business in and around the *Laochtech* while Rudgal was incarcerated. Someone might have seen or heard something that could lead us to the killer.'

'I'll do my best, friend Eadulf.'

Eadulf was not prepared for the reception that he received from Colgú's Chief Brehon, Aillín, when he reported the death. Everyone had been shocked by the news, but Brehon Aillín stood forward aggressively.

'I should now take over this matter, lord,' he said stiffly. 'This is the second murder in your palace within days, and both remain without a resolution. I would argue that this is because I have not been allowed to follow the obvious suspect. I should have been permitted to investigate the killing of Brother Cerdic in the first place. Had I done so, perhaps this second murder would have been prevented.'

Fidelma's eyes narrowed dangerously; she already anticipated who the pugnacious Brehon would suggest as 'the obvious suspect'.

'You have a theory then which connects the murder of Brother Cerdic with this young outlaw?' Colgú invited, not being as perceptive as his sister in the matter.

Fidelma could not restrain herself. 'Yes – speak, Aillín. Share your insight with us and explain how the solution of the first murder might have prevented the second one?'

Brehon Aillín flushed angrily at her mocking tone. 'Am I to be questioned by a junior, a *dálaigh*?' he demanded.

'I presume you do have an explanation?' Colgú asked quietly. 'The investigation into the death of Brother Cerdic has been placed in the hands of my sister who, junior or not, is experienced in such matters. But if you have a theory . . .?'

Brehon Aillín drew himself up to his full height and his scowl deepened.

'*I* am more experienced in law, which is why I am your Chief Brehon.'

'By default!' exclaimed Abbot Ségdae, softly but audibly. He had no time for the elderly judge.

'I would at least be independent of undue influence,' retorted the Brehon heatedly, glancing at Eadulf, who now picked up what was being implied and coloured hotly.

'Independent?' Fidelma found it hard to control her irritation. 'By which I presume you imply that I am biased? As I recall, you wanted to blame the death of Brother Cerdic on Eadulf, based on the simple fact that he, too, was of the same nation. Is that so?'

Brehon Aillín would not back down. 'I would have used logic, not emotion. The fact that Brother Eadulf has now been shown to be in the proximity of both deaths would not be ignored by me.'

Eadulf took an involuntary step forward, his hands clenched at his sides, but Colgú raised his hand to stay him. His own scowl had deepened. His voice became cold and deliberate.

'You forget yourself, Brehon Aillín. In the matter of the death of this man, Rudgal, your *logic* may recall that Eadulf was here with us from the time Rudgal was brought into the palace until the time he went with Gormán to bring him before us and discovered the body. As for the death of Brother Cerdic, I thought you were joking when you claimed that Eadulf should be regarded as a suspect. Now I think I see some prejudice in your reasoning, for I see nothing else that needs to be responded to. You may now leave us.'

Brehon Aillín's figure was rigid as the King spoke. His lips were bloodless; it seemed he had difficulty in articulating. 'B-but the death of Rudgal,' he stammered. 'That has to be investigated.'

Colgú stared moodily at him for a moment. Then he said: 'I shall appoint someone to consider the matter. I suggest you now retire to consider your own position. You are impugning the character of my sister's husband without just cause and before witnesses.'

Brehon Aillín continued to stand absolutely still for a moment or two. His lips were still twitching, as if he were trying to respond. Then his jaw clenched, he swung round and strode out of the council chamber.

Fidelma's expression had softened from anger to sadness. 'Perhaps we were too hard on him, brother,' she ventured.

Colgú regarded her in surprise. 'You have a changeable temperament, sister.'

Fidelma shook her head. 'I admit my faults. Sometimes I allow my passion to control me. I am inclined to think that Aillín is an old man and old men are sometimes wont to foolishness.'

'He is Chief Brehon of Muman,' Colgú replied sternly. 'Even if he came to the position by the untimely death of poor Áedo, he is still the chief official of the law in my kingdom. He has standards to uphold.'

Eadulf cleared his throat awkwardly. 'I would not like to see the man suffer simply because he dislikes me,' he ventured.

'Dislike is one thing, Eadulf,' Colgú pointed out, 'but accusing you of murder on the basis of dislike only, places him beyond service to the law. We all take an oath to pursue the truth.'

'And to commit such a breach of etiquette in front of visitors . . .' It was the voice of Abbot Ségdae which brought them back to reality. Throughout the exchange Prince Cummasach had been sitting in silence with his Brehon standing at his side. They had been shocked by the exchange, and the news that had engendered it, but they had offered no comment. Now Cummasach rose from his chair.

'We are wasting time,' he announced distantly. 'I have done my duty in capturing the man who led the attack on the religious on the river. I brought him here and placed him in the custody of the King. Now he is dead. I shall return to the Land of the Déisi.'

'One thing remains, however.' It was the Déisi Brehon, Furudán, who demanded their attention. 'Although a confessed killer, Rudgal was killed unlawfully and in the palace of the High King. He was brought here under the protection of Cummasach, Prince of the Déisi. Therefore reparation must be given to Cummasach, whose reputation is thus impaired as being unable to extend his protection to those who have submitted to him.'

There was a silence before Colgú turned with a helpless glance to Fidelma.

'Is that true?' he asked.

Fidelma nodded slowly. 'It is so. However, an adequate time must be given for a Brehon to be able to investigate and consider who was responsible for the unlawful killing before reparation is offered.'

'An adequate time?' queried Colgú, looking relieved and turning back to Brehon Furudán.

'It is the law,' agreed the Brehon. 'Yet "adequate" is a word that can be debated.'

'That which is acceptable for the task to be undertaken?' suggested Fidelma softly.

'*Comchirte*,' replied the Brehon. It was the legal word for 'acceptable'.

'Then, as we are approaching the full of the moon,' Fidelma said, 'so let us wait until the next full of the moon. We will endeavour to complete the investigation by that time. Is that acceptable?'

Brehon Furudán and Cummasach exchanged a glance and both nodded at once.

'*Comchirte*,' repeated Furudán.

The rituals of the departure of Prince Cummasach and his Brehon were amiable enough. The laws of hospitality were adhered to. They had been pressed to stay and attend the evening meal, but politely declined. If the truth were known, Colgú was relieved.

After they had gone, he said to his sister, 'It's all very well, but what if you can't resolve this matter? Now we have that to deal with as well as the death of that emissary of the deputation from Canterbury.'

'There is no mystery without a solution, Colgú,' Fidelma said firmly. 'Leave it to us. A period between the full moons is adequate.'

The King did not look confident but accepted her optimism.

'Gormán is already questioning the members of the bodyguard to see if they noticed anything,' Eadulf told him.

'The body should be taken to Brother Conchobhar to prepare for a funeral,' Colgú declared. 'Where is Egric? Did he identify the man as his attacker?'

Eadulf was unhappy. 'My brother hasn't returned from Rumann's tavern since Cummasach brought his prisoner here. He's with Dego. I will fetch him now and take him to view the body.'

'Let us try to resolve this matter quickly,' Colgú urged. 'Now that Fidelma has informed me that this coming deputation includes none other than a brother of the Bishop of Rome, it becomes even more urgent.'

'Are we sure that this Venerable Verax is truly brother to the Bishop of Rome?' Abbot Segdae looked questioningly at Eadulf. 'Brother Madagan did not know.'

'If the man *is* the Venerable Verax, son of Anastasius of Segni, then that is the case. And he has great authority in the Church. There was no reason why Brother Madagan should know this. Only I recognised the name, having been in Rome for a while.'

'Well, it is known now,' Colgú said heavily. 'This means we are dealing with someone of importance, a prince among princes. It also means,' he turned with a scowl in search of his steward Beccan, 'that we will have to prepare a feast and entertainment fit for such a man.'

'What of Brehon Aillín, brother?' Fidelma asked, still feeling guilty about the departure of the disgraced elderly judge.

Colgú sat back with a look of resolution at Fidelma. 'I shall need a new legal adviser.'

'Aillín is still your Chief Brehon,' she demurred.

'The man is a liability. He has never liked you nor accepted Eadulf. Now he has gone beyond reasonable behaviour. He has dishonoured me in front of the Prince of the Déisi and his Brehon.'

'It will be up to the Council of Brehon to see if he has erred in any way and whether he needs to be replaced,' Fidelma reminded him. 'You cannot take his title from him before that happens.'

'I wish I could,' her brother sighed. 'However, I can appoint whoever I like to advise me, so long as they are qualified. We have two unexplained deaths on our hands. You have already been charged with investigating one, Fidelma. Now you must take on the investigation of the other. Also . . .' he paused for a moment. 'You and Eadulf will have to hold yourselves ready to advise me when this deputation arrives.'

Eadulf cleared his throat awkwardly.

'You have a problem with this, friend Eadulf?' the King wanted to know.

'Brehon Aillín should be at your side during the visit by this deputation. Won't it look strange if your Chief Brehon is absent?'

Colgú made a dismissive gesture. 'I want someone I can trust, someone without prejudice. Moreover, someone forward-looking rather than the pedant and conservative that Aillín is.'

'He will not take kindly to being dismissed,' Fidelma warned.

'I do not like doing it,' confessed her brother. 'But it is one of the responsibilities of kingship.'

'It is up to you who you appoint to advise you, but it is the Council of Brehons who must appoint their Chief Brehon,' repeated Fidelma.

'The Council appointed Áedo as Chief Brehon,' replied Colgú. 'When Áedo was killed a few months ago while trying to save me from that murderous assassin, Aillín took over the office because the Council had made him deputy out of respect for his age and service. They did it as an honour for his age, not expecting him to accede to the office. Now it is time they convened and a new Chief Brehon was appointed.'

Abbot Ségdae smiled meditatively at Fidelma. 'You stood against Áedo for the position last time.'

Fidelma replied, without amusement, 'That is true. But it taught me that being Chief Brehon was not the position I thought it would be. I need to be involved in administering the law. A Chief Brehon spends most of their time administering the work of judges and lawyers throughout the kingdom and dealing with complaints and appeals. They become removed from the people – and it is with the people that my strength lies. I am content to remain an advocate.'

Eadulf disguised the relief that he felt at her words. For a while he had wondered if Fidelma would seize the opportunity to apply again for election before the Council of the senior Brehons of the kingdom. If truth were told, he had been delighted when she was rejected in favour of Áedo.

'Well, we must ask the Brehons to convene their Council soon,' Colgú decided. 'I will send a messenger to let the leading Brehons know of my request.'

'What of Brehon Aillín? How is he to be told?' Fidelma asked, still concerned.

'I will have a private talk with him,' Colgú assured her. 'He is a widower but his daughter and her husband have a farmstead south of Rath na Drinne. He will be well looked after.'

'He might not accept this without protest,' Fidelma said anxiously.

'But accept it he must,' Colgú replied, his voice firm. 'Now we all have much work to do. Keep me informed of the events of your investigation.'

He rose, indicating their meeting was over.

Outside the King's chamber, Fidelma seemed dispirited. 'I wish there was some more pleasant way to end Aillín's career. After all, he was not always an aging curmudgeon. Many young lawyers learned from him.'

'It is out of our hands now,' Eadulf responded philosophically.

Fidelma did not reply for a moment. Then she said: 'Let us go in search of Gormán and see if has come up with anything. With luck, someone saw something around the storehouse.'

'First I must find Egric and get him to identify the body, if he can,' Eadulf reminded her.

As they entered the courtyard they found old Brother Conchobhar hurrying towards them.

'I was coming to find you,' he murmured, casting an almost conspiratorial look around him. 'There is something that you must see.'

He turned and led them to his apothecary. They asked no questions, for the physician seemed in a state of some agitation. They followed him to a small room at the back of his workshop – a place where he usually examined and prepared bodies ready for burial. The corpse of Rudgal was stretched out on the table, ready to be washed for the burial. A *racholl* or winding sheet loosely covered him.

'I was undressing the body,' explained Brother Conchobhar, 'when I found this object tied around the waist.' He turned, and from beneath a bundle of clothes on a nearby chair he picked up a piece of material and handed it to Fidelma.

It was a narrow band of woven lambswool, once white in colour, but stained and dirty now. It was a curious shape – a band some three fingers thick, made as if to loop through itself. Embroidered on it were six black crosses.

'In the old days,' Brother Conchobhar recalled, 'something like this was a ritual vestment worn by all bishops of the New Faith. Although this seems to be of a slightly different design.'

'But why would Rudgal be hiding it around his waist?' asked Fidelma. 'Was this what he thought was significant?'

'Do you think that Rudgal stole it from Victricius?' Eadulf wondered. 'Maybe Victricius was a bishop and this was his vestment?' He took the lambswool from her and examined it carefully.

'If so, he must have known something more about it,' Fidelma said sensibly.

'But what would someone like Rudgal know about the vestments of the ecclesiastics?' Eadulf was frowning. 'According to Brehon Furudán, Rudgal claimed that someone at Láirge's harbour had paid him and his thugs to attack and kill the Venerable Victricius and my brother. I suppose that person may have told him something about it.'

'That doesn't sound likely.' Fidelma was dubious. 'If they were just hired thugs, Rudgal and his gang of cut-throats would not be let into any secret which gave them additional power, surely.'

'Then if they weren't told, why did he take it and hide it on his person? Why did he come here confident we would make a bargain with him? And why was he killed?'

Fidelma returned his gaze thoughtfully. 'You are asking too many good questions, Eadulf. Anyway, I think we can be sure that he kept it as a means of bargaining for his freedom. But now I think we have another question to pursue.'

'Which is?' prompted Eadulf.

'We know that this used to be a symbol that was worn by bishops years ago. Perhaps that symbolism has changed?'

Brother Conchobhar intervened. 'I can make some discreet enquiries. Our Keeper of the Books is a man of great knowledge, and an enquiry from me would not give rise to any undue attention.'

'But don't show him this,' Fidelma warned, folding the band. 'Just describe it to him as if it was something you had once seen. In the meantime, I suggest you hide it somewhere safe.'

They emerged from Brother Conchobhar's apothecary more perplexed than they had entered it. They found Gormán looking for them.

'I just wanted to tell you that I have spoken to all the members of the bodyguard who were around the *Laochtech* while the prisoner was held there.' He sounded frustrated. 'None of them saw anything. Enda was in charge, since he and Luan secured the prisoner in the storehouse, as Eadulf will have told you. The Déisi warriors never left the *brandubh* game. Everyone else had their guard duties to perform and have been accounted for.'

'The trouble is that the storehouse is behind the *Laochtech*,' Fidelma observed. 'Anyone could have gone round it and entered it without being seen by the warriors in the *Laochtech*.'

'Well, there are other matters that I must proceed with,' Eadulf said. 'Has my brother returned yet? He needs to identify Rudgal's body to say whether he was one of the attackers. He can't still be in Rumman's tavern, surely?'

Gormán turned to him in surprise. 'He didn't tell you?'

Eadulf frowned. 'Tell me what? I haven't seen him since I asked you where he was earlier.'

The young warrior nervously cleared his throat at Eadulf's response. 'He has left with Dego. They will be gone for a few days.'

Eadulf was staring at Gormán in incomprehension. It was Fidelma who asked the question. 'Gone where for a few days, Gormán?' she asked softly.

'I told friend Eadulf here earlier that they were talking about fishing or hunting.'

'And?' snapped Eadulf, his voice dangerous. 'What are you saying now?'

'Well, Dego had permission from me to take some days' rest after our recent trip. He was going to spend a few days fishing and hunting. He has a cabin somewhere in the Sliabh na gCoille.'

Eadulf knew that the Mountains of the Forest was the name of the peaks to the south-west. It was a large area.

'When did you learn this?' he asked coldly.

'When you went to tell the King about the discovery of the body of the prisoner. Dego came back to the fortress at that moment to tell me he was leaving. As he had been in the township, the matter of questioning him about the death of the prisoner did not relate to him. I saw no objection to allowing him to leave.' The warrior looked embarrassed.

'That was not the problem.' Fidelma spoke quietly. 'This prisoner was supposed to be the man who attacked Egric, so Egric was needed as an official witness. Why did you not keep him here so that he could identify him?'

Gormán raised his arms in a helpless gesture.

'Egric did not come back with Dego. I presumed that he was waiting for him in Rumann's tavern. I thought that he had already told Eadulf his intention when Eadulf went to the tavern to see him earlier. In fact, I've just seen Beccan, who was asking whether Egric would be feasting with the King this evening. He was worrying about the arrangements as usual. I never saw a steward so worried about details. But . . . well, didn't you say that you were speaking about fishing to your brother?'

Eadulf shook his head in annoyance. 'He did not mention any intention of leaving immediately with Dego on a fishing or hunting trip.'

The warrior was looking unhappy. 'I did not realise that he had not told you, and it did not occur to me that you would disapprove.'

'It's not that I disapprove,' muttered Eadulf fiercely. 'However, the timing and circumstance are . . . are odd.'

'It's not your fault, Gormán,' Fidelma intervened. 'We just needed to ask if Egric could identify this Rudgal as his attacker. But it is no matter, since that was just a formality. We have evidence aplenty. But with this second murder and the fact that the arrival of the deputation from the east is imminent, it would be better had all the trusted members of the King's bodyguard remained in the palace.'

'Perhaps if I sent a fast rider after them?' Gormán offered.

'Just a moment. Were they both on horseback?'

'They had the horses they left with this morning. Dego only came back here to collect his belongings for the trip. Your brother had lost all his belongings in the attack on the Siúr, so I presume they would purchase some items in the town before they left.'

'Which way were they heading?'

'I am not sure. Dego's cabin is among the mountains south of the Valley of Eatharlach.'

Fidelma turned to Eadulf. 'A good rider might eventually be able to overtake them if he were sure of the direction they were taking.'

'Surely there is only one main track to the south-west?' he protested.

'I think Dego would know a dozen more,' she replied. 'One could hide an entire army among those mountains, searching for years without being able to discover them.'

Fidelma understood the real reason why Eadulf was upset. His brother had felt so little concern for Eadulf's feelings that he had left without a word, having only just been reunited with him.

'If Dego has promised to return in a few days then he is a man of his word. We will have to wait until then, as probably nothing will be resolved meanwhile,' Fidelma said soothingly. 'Anyway, twice now Egric has told you that he did not know the purpose of the Venerable Victricius' journey. Will he change his mind on a third questioning? He told you that Victricius carried papers. We now know from Cummasach, or rather his Brehon, that the papers had been destroyed by Rudgal and his companions. So there is not much help there.'

Eadulf breathed in deeply and then let the air out in a rush. It seemed to calm him a little. 'So you advocate that we wait for Egric and Dego to return?'

'There seems little else to do,' she said. 'There will be time to try to understand your brother's attitude later.'

Eadulf was still troubled. He addressed Gormán: 'You said that Dego's cabin is in the mountains of Sliabh na gCoillte. Has he ever told you where?'

'Dego likes to keep what he calls his "retreat" a secret from people.'

As Eadulf sighed, Fidelma asked: 'There is something else on your mind. What is it?'

'I was just thinking that, if what Victricius and Egric carried were part of this wider mystery – that they were attacked *because* of it, and now Rudgal has been killed *because* of it – then some danger may still attend Egric. After all, it was only by the smallest luck that my brother escaped from being killed alongside Victricius and the boatmen in the first place.'

Fidelma thought for a moment. 'It is a good point, Eadulf. Yet by going away with Dego, whom we know from our own experiences to be a good warrior and able bodyguard, Egric may be safer than staying here in Cashel.'

Eadulf had not considered the point before. After a few moments, he concluded, 'Perhaps you are right. He is safer being out of the way.'

CHAPTER NINE

C olgú decided to host the evening meal again as Abbot Ségdae and Abbess Líoch were still officially his guests. Their stewards were also invited, along with Fidelma and Eadulf as well as Gormán. Often the Commander of the Bodyguard was invited to feast with the King. Beccan the steward, bobbing and grinning, took the guests to their appointed places and then, as was protocol, announced the arrival of the King before withdrawing. Apparently, he had already told Colgú of Egric's absence with Dego, for when Eadulf started to apologise, the King smiled sadly.

'I wish *I* could join them over the next few days,' he said. 'I'd rather be hunting a wild boar than trying to deal with these matters.'

During the meal, Fidelma found herself seated next to Sister Dianaimh, the *bann-mhaor* of Cill Náile. After some inconsequential remarks, she asked the young woman if she had ever heard of the Venerable Victricius.

'The Venerable Victricius? I do not think I have ever heard that name. Why?' The young girl's expression was blank.

'It was just a thought,' replied Fidelma. 'That was the name of the cleric who was killed on the way to Imleach. Eadulf's brother was his companion, but he escaped with minor hurt.'

'I heard the story but the name did not register with me.'

After the meal ended the wine was still circulating, perhaps a little too freely. The tables were cleared and the musicians came in to entertain them. Fidelma saw her opportunity to have a word with Gormán as a matter had come to her mind that she wanted to clarify.

'When you found the bodies near Brother Siolán's church, did you examine that of the old religieux?'

'Of course.' Gormán regarded her in surprise for a moment. 'I first had to ascertain that he was dead and give authority to Brother Siolán to bury the corpse.'

'It is hard to form a picture of someone when you have not seen them. It was, of course, Egric who identified him as the Venerable Victricius?'

'He did.'

'The old man wore a Roman tonsure?'

'Yes, and his appearance was small and swarthy. It was clear that he was a stranger from beyond these shores.'

'And in physique – was he strong?'

'Not to my mind, for he was elderly. Nor was he well-endowed with good looks. Also . . .' Gormán hesitated. 'I think he was one of those strange ascetics that one hears of. There are some who think that mortification of the flesh brings them closer to God; those who deny themselves and who inflict punishment on their bodies to show what a godly person they are. Personally, I think they have a disorder of the brain.'

At once Fidelma was interested. 'What makes you say that?'

'I saw that his back had once been lacerated by a lash or scourge. The wounds had healed over, so they had been inflicted some time ago. But I have heard that some of the brothers flagellate themselves because, so it is said, they claim it shows God how willing they are to stand pain to assert His cause. Why such a thing as pain should be pleasing to God, I don't understand. Are we not told that He stands for peace and love?'

Fidelma smiled and patted the warrior on the arm.

'You are shrewd, Gormán. Don't say anything about this, though. You have been a great help.'

She turned to find Colgú approaching. He seemed relaxed for the first time that evening. 'A good meal and good wine,' he greeted her. 'At least we did not have to put up with Beccan banging his staff every few minutes and officiously announcing this and that.'

'Better someone who is punctilious when there is serious court work to be done, brother.' Fidelma knew how irritated Colgú became with his steward but she was practical. 'You remind me – where is Beccan? He disappeared the moment we sat down to the meal. He is not usually absent from these gatherings.'

Colgú said casually, 'Oh, he had something to do in the township and begged me to excuse him. I heard that Eadulf is rather annoyed that Egric has left to go hunting when they had only just been reunited. What do you make of that? Aren't they close?'

'They have not seen each other for ten years. I think the reunification was awkward. Egric has gone off for a few days to hunt and fish with Dego.'

'I know. Lucky fellow,' Colgú sighed. 'I said so earlier to Eadulf. I wish I could join them but now is hardly the time. I suppose that we will have to wait until the Venerable Verax and Bishop Arwald arrive before we know their purpose.'

'Which will probably be tomorrow, if the reports of their progress are correct.'

'I wish we had more time. I suppose that you have made no progress about the death of Brother Cerdic? No? Two deaths to be resolved and I am without a Chief Brehon that I can rely on.'

'Speaking of whom,' Fidelma glanced around the feasting hall, 'I do not see Brehon Aillín here tonight, brother. Wouldn't protocol dictate that he should attend?' And when Colgú looked indifferent: 'Did you speak with him again? You said that you were going to.'

'I did. It was right I should do so before Beccan finally sent out the messages to the members of the Council of Brehons suggesting they appoint a new chief among them.'

'I presume that he did not take your decision well and that is why he is not in attendance.'

'Take it well?' Colgú grimaced. 'He almost attacked me! He said he was going to bring legal action against poor Eadulf, even though Eadulf was the one who was insulted. He also had the temerity to remind me that a king is not above the law.'

'Well, that is true. A king is expected to obey the law even as the lowliest farmworker is expected to.'

'I know, I know. But to threaten me . . . It was difficult to act with restraint when the old man was yelling about the *gáu flathemon*.'

'The king's injustice and its consequences?' Fidelma sounded worried.

'The old fool started to threaten me with the *troscud*; said that he would sit before my door and ritually fast until I agree to withdraw and accept him in office.'

'What?' Fidelma was surprised, for the *troscud* or hunger strike was not a weapon easily used. 'Has he given you proper legal notice of that?'

'No, it was just a threat. Why?'

'There is a ritual to it. He must give proper legal form to it if he is serious.'

'Well, I hope it doesn't come to it, any more than his threat to take legal action against Eadulf.'

'I was going to ask, what charge does he level at Eadulf?' She was curious. 'It can't be an accusation of being behind the killing of Brother Cerdic, surely?'

'He said that he would demand compensation for the dishonour that Eadulf had put upon him.'

'*Deirmitiu*?' Fidelma supplied the legal term.

'That's it. He demanded that Eadulf should pay the fine of *enech rucce*, the compensation for his being dishonoured.'

Fidelma mentally worked it out. 'That would mean a compensation of eight *cumals*.' That was the value of twenty-four milch cows. It was half the honour price of a Chief Brehon as laid down by law. 'He wasn't serious, surely?'

'As serious as an angry man can be. But I dissuaded him.'

'How?'

'Merely by saying that I would stand as a witness for Eadulf and against him. That's when he threatened the ritual fast against me. He has turned into a bitter old man. I hope the Council of Brehons will act soon.' Colgú sighed and then dismissed the subject with a cutting motion of his hand. 'Anyway, if it helps you, Aillín was invited, as he is still a guest here and I have to obey the laws of hospitality. It seems he prefers his own company this evening.'

He turned away. Fidelma suddenly felt sorry for him as he had left her having returned to a more morose state than the one in which he had greeted her. She wished she had not brought up the subject of Brehon Aillín. She went to where Eadulf was sitting with Abbot Ségdae and Brother Madagan. The abbot looked up with a wan smile as she joined them.

'Brother Eadulf has been telling us that there has been little progress in your investigation.'

'Alas, that it were otherwise,' she confirmed.

'He was also telling us something about this Bishop Arwald of Magon-saete,' added Brother Madagan. 'It seems curious that such a person should be coming here in the company of the brother of the Bishop of Rome.'

'Believe me, we are just as intrigued as you are,' Eadulf asserted.

'Well, we won't be in suspense much longer,' Fidelma said. 'By tomorrow you should know the purpose of their coming. It does no good to speculate without knowledge.'

She caught Eadulf trying to hide a smile as she added her favourite saying.

'The saying is a true one,' he said swiftly in amelioration.

'Indeed, the old truths are none the less the truth, despite their age,' she told him.

The musicians had begun playing, a quick enthusiastic piece which silenced all conversation, for against its boisterous tones no one could speak. It was designed for that purpose, to draw attention to the musicians and it was usually called *corm-cheól*, or ale music. They employed drums, bells, pipes and stringed instruments. Then, using the quietness that had descended on their audience, the musicians moved into a softer melody, with the youngest boy among them coming forward to sing, accompanying himself on a small eight-stringed harp.

The entertainment continued on until Abbess Líoch placed a hand in front of her mouth and feigned a yawn. It was simply a diplomatic means to herald her standing up and expressing her sorrow that tiredness had overcome her. Colgú with a smile indicated that she could withdraw and the abbess, followed by her young steward, left the hall. Fidelma glanced meaningfully at Eadulf and he knew that after the next piece of music, she would repeat this method to retire and so was ready when she, too, made the same gesture.

In fact, when they rose to depart, Colgú also ordered the musicians to be dismissed, remarking that the following day would be a long one and they all needed rest.

Fidelma and Eadulf left the feasting hall and began to walk unhurriedly back to their own apartments.

'I keep wondering about this Venerable Victricius,' Fidelma remarked. She had told Eadulf what Gormán had noticed about the lacerations on the back of the corpse. 'I don't suppose you ever heard his name in Rome?'

'Victricius may not be common but it is certainly not unknown,' offered Eadulf. 'There was a bishop of that name in a town called Rotomagus in Gaul. He had served in the legions until he was converted.'

'How do you know about him?' asked Fidelma.

'Do you remember when we were in Menevia? Abbot Tryffin told me about him.'

'Our shipwreck on the shores of Dyfed is not one of my more pleasant memories,' Fidelma said stiffly. 'But why would Abbot Tryffin tell you about a former Roman soldier? I thought the Britons disliked them?'

'It seems that this Victricius endeared himself to the Britons and they invited him to settle a dispute between their bishops. Of course, that was many, many years before my people began to settle on the island of Britain. In fact, Abbot Tryffin showed me a book that this Victricius wrote – *De Laude Sanctorum.*'

'In Praise of Saints,' translated Fidelma.

'So,' concluded Eadulf, 'there are probably many people with that name – Victricius.'

Fidelma was quiet for a moment and then said: 'Gormán thought that Victricius might be one of those ascetics who ritually flagellate themselves. Yet the scars of the flogging showed that they had been made sometime in the past.'

They had been passing along a short passageway which ran between the King's quarters and the building which housed their own apartments. The passage was lit with two brand torches – one at either end – which threw shadows here and there on to the greystone walls.

It was Fidelma's sharp sense of hearing that saved them. A scraping noise came from somewhere above them. When a movement flickered on the gloomy walls that seemed out of place amid the shadows of the night, she did not hesitate but abruptly pushed Eadulf forward and leaped after him. They both tumbled in a heap on the cold stone flags just as a heavy piece of marble smashed into the ground behind them, splintering as it did so and sending fragments flying in all directions.

Fidelma was back on her feet in a second, peering cautiously upwards.

Eadulf stared at the remains of what had been a statue – one of several that stood on the roof of the King's apartments.

Figures came rushing out of the dark, alerted by the thunderous sound. Enda, holding a lantern, was leading them.

'What happened?' he demanded, and then he saw the fragmented statue and was shocked. 'Are you hurt?'

Fidelma shook her head while Eadulf, rubbing his forearm, muttered, 'A few scratches from the splintered marble.'

Fidelma stood gazing at the remains for a moment or two. There was something familiar about it. It was a statue of some grotesque Otherworld creature with wings. She shook herself, almost like a dog shakes itself after an immersion, and then seemed to spring into action.

'Enda, you and your men will follow me,' she commanded.

Eadulf was still in shock while the others were already moving, following Fidelma in through a side door in the building.

'What is it?' he demanded breathlessly, catching up with her.

'A statue the size of a small child does not fall of its own accord,' she flung back at him over her shoulder.

Eadulf almost halted as the implication struck him. But the warriors, with Enda and his lantern, were pushing by after Fidelma as she hurried towards the stairway which led up to the flat roof of the building. Then he was rushing after them. As they raced upwards, Enda's companions took two of the lighted lanterns from the walls.

They burst onto the roof with lanterns held high. It seemed deserted. On either side of the roof ran a broad parapet. There had been six statutes placed on these parapets – three along each side – except one was now missing on the side that had overlooked the narrow passage.

'Make a search,' Fidelma rapped out. 'Enda – bring your lantern over here.' She moved to the empty space where the statue had stood on the parapet and examined it.

Eadulf looked over her shoulder. He could see white scuff-marks on the stonework; pieces of stone seemed chipped, as if someone had been trying to dig something out. Fidelma sighed.

'What is it?' asked Enda.

'It is as I expected. You'll see where the statue was placed, like the others still are, in the middle of this broad parapet. It is not possible for it to fall of its own accord. So someone had to push it to the edge. They had to use a metal bar to do so. Hence the dents dug into the stone – there and there.' She pointed. 'See the scuff-marks as the statue moved? It was pushed to the edge, then whoever did this waited until they saw us enter the passage. They must have leaned over, looking down. As soon as they saw us, they made the final push. I heard the scraping sound. Had I not . . .' She shuddered.

Enda's men had rejoined them.

'No sign of anyone, lady. But we found this by the other door.'

It was an iron bar just over a metre in length, with both ends hammered flat.

'Well, that's what was used as a lever to push the statue over,' Fidelma said. 'What of the other door that gives access to this roof?'

'It is bolted on the other side.'

'If the assassin left by that means, then he must have thrown the bolt,' Enda offered.

'It is the only means by which he left,' Fidelma said grimly. 'No one passed us as we came up the other stairway, did they? So whoever did this has escaped.'

'Where does the other stairway lead?' asked Eadulf. The building was the King's apartments, and he was unfamiliar with parts of them.

'It gives access to the King's guest quarters,' explained Enda. 'From there, stairs lead to the quarters for the King's personal attendants, the King's quarters and the council chamber and feasting hall.'

'So the culprit would have easy means of leaving the building? That is a pity.'

'That is not so,' Fidelma interrupted quietly. 'At night, members of my brother's bodyguard are posted at all the entrances. The Nasc Niadh have become especially vigilant since the attempt to assassinate him.'

Enda was nodding in agreement. 'Moreover, we are also vigilant since the High King, Sechnussach, was assassinated in his own bedchamber at Tara.'

'Then . . .' Eadulf began but Fidelma was already moving and issuing orders.

'One of your men guard the bolted door, lest the assassin, thinking we have gone, comes back on the roof and tries to escape by other means.'

Enda had time to motion one of his men to follow her orders before Fidelma was racing back down the stairway, into the passageway. Followed by the others, she darted back into the main courtyard and to the guarded portals of the King's quarters.

A member of the King's bodyguard, standing at ease outside the wooden doors, straightened as he saw the party approaching. Fidelma did not give him a chance to challenge them but snapped: 'Has anyone left through this door recently?'

'None since you and Brother Eadulf left, lady.'

'Then ensure no one does without my authority,' she said, pushing by the surprised warrior and opening the doors.

The guard stared stupidly after her for a moment and his muttered acknowledgement came too late for her to hear.

Inside, they were met by an astonished-looking Gormán who apparently was in charge of the guard for the first third of the night.

'Lady, I thought you had retired?' he spluttered, but she cut him short and told him what had happened.

'Ensure all the guards are in place and no one has left the building.'

'It shall be done, lady.'

'Send Dar Luga to me.'

Gormán went hurrying away and as he did so, Fidelma's brother appeared from the council chamber to one side of the corridor, Abbot Ségdae by his side. They had clearly not yet retired for the night. Once more, Fidelma quickly explained matters.

'Remind me, brother, what access is there between the guest rooms and other parts of this building?' she asked.

'The guest rooms are on the fourth floor and so there is one stairwell which leads from that floor down to the third floor. Of course, there are stairs that lead up to the roof – and one can cross the roof easily to the other stairwell, which takes one all the way down to the passage. That was built by the *foirgnidh*, the architect, as an exit if there was a fire which prevented the main stairwell from being used.'

'So anyone coming from there would have to come down that stairwell?' clarified Eadulf.

'Indeed they would.'

'And it is now custom to have a member of the Nasc Niadh on each floor?' asked Fidelma.

'Yes. A superfluous custom,' Colgú told her, 'which I was going to abolish. It was introduced after the attempt to assassinate me.'

'Perhaps that is to our advantage now. It will mean that no one has been able to come and go from the guest quarters since we left, so our would-be assassin is still there. Enda, bring me the guard on duty at the entrance to the guests quarters. I need to ask him some questions. Oh and Enda,' she called after him, 'stay on guard in his place and let no one move beyond you.'

Colgú immediately suggested that they enter the council chamber. Moments later, Aidan followed them in.

'Have you been on guard at the stairwell since the guests retired?' Fidelma asked.

'I have, lady.'

'Since you have been on duty, has any guest needed assistance or passed your position on the stairwell?'

If Aidan was surprised at the question he merely made a negative motion of his head.

'So no one could have left any of the guest rooms since you have been on guard?'

'Not coming down the stairwell. They could have gone up onto the roof though.'

'We are only interested in anyone coming down the stairs. I mean not just guests, but anyone.'

'If they didn't go onto the roof and use the other stairway, then they would have had to pass me, lady,' confirmed Aidan. 'And no one did.'

'Therefore, anyone who had been on the roof a few moments ago, who had not used the second stair, must still be in the guest chambers,' Eadulf concluded.

'That is correct,' asserted the warrior.

'Very well. You can return to your position and tell Enda to come back here.'

Aidan hesitated at the door. 'Is anything wrong?' he asked.

'Nothing to worry about for the moment. Oh, and has Beccan returned to the palace yet?'

It was Colgú who answered. 'Remember, I gave him permission to leave Cashel.'

Fidelma swung round. 'I thought you meant just for the evening?'

'I have allowed him to be absent for two days. He said he had a relative who is sick in the township, and that he needed to visit them.'

Fidelma made a soft noise in her throat expressing displeasure and asked: 'Was that wise, now that we are expecting the deputation any day?'

'He should be back before they arrive. He is only in the township,' Colgú assured her.

Fidelma was still frowning. 'I didn't know he had a relative here. And what illness do they have? Should we not be alarmed in case it is a contagion that communicates itself to Beccan and thence to us?'

'I have thought of that.' Colgú bore Fidelma's irritation patiently. 'I am not as incompetent as you seem to think, little sister. I have his pledge that it is not contagious. And as for his duties, Dar Luga has served my house longer than Beccan has served as my steward. If she cannot see to the wants of my guests, then who else is more competent?'

As Aidan left, Gormán entered the council chamber, bringing with him the *airnbertach* or housekeeper, Dar Luga, whose rôle was to attend to the domestic chores of the palace and see to the comfort of the King's guests. The plump housekeeper came into the chamber, rubbing her eyes. It was obvious that she had been roused from her sleep.

'We are sorry to disturb you,' Fidelma reassured the elderly woman. 'Can you tell me if all the guests retired to their chambers tonight?'

The woman looked puzzled and took time to gather her thoughts. 'Only Abbot Segdae has not been in his chamber. Everyone else has retired for the night and there has been no call for any servant to be summoned. Is something wrong?'

'Abbot Ségdae has been with me in here since you left, Fidelma,' Colgú said immediately. 'So that's one suspect less.'

Fidelma did not respond to his humour. 'So now we must search the guests' rooms and ask whether they have left them since they retired,' she instructed Gormán. 'As far as I recall the layout of this building, there is the main door, which is always attended by a doorkeeper, one of my brother's bodyguards. There is the exit from the guest quarters, across the roof, and . . .'

'The door in the kitchen and storage quarters,' finished the plump housekeeper. 'That leads to the back.'

'Is it bolted?'

'There are no bolts on the door but it is locked.'

'Who usually locks it?'

'Why, the steward, of course.'

'But Beccan was not here tonight.'

'Indeed, lady. So I locked it.'

'So while Gormán checks the guests, Dar Luga and I will check the rear exit,' Fidelma declared.

With Dar Luga leading the way, Fidelma and Eadulf followed her along the passages that eventually led into the kitchen area of the King's quarters. The *cuchtar* or kitchen was a large room, full of cupboards and tables where all the food of the palace was prepared. There was a stone hearth with a spit at one end built onto an outside wall, but most of the heavy cooking was done in stone houses outside the palace, a little way removed from them in case of fire. There were two, in fact, one housing the *áith* or kiln for drying grain, and the other the ovens for cooking. A lamp had to be fetched now that the kitchen was in darkness. It did not take long to confirm that the great wooden door was securely fastened and that the metal *echuir* or key was hanging in its rightful place inside the door.

It was obvious that no one had left through the rear door. Fidelma finally instructed Dar Luga to return to her bed and herself went back to the council chamber. They had now been joined by Brother Madagan, Abbess Líoch, Sister Dianaimh and even a sour-looking Brehon Aillín. Colgú had already explained matters to them.

'I hardly think we can level suspicion on any of these guests,' Brehon Aillín said stiffly. Each had already protested that they had only just retired to their rooms and not moved since.

'Perhaps not,' Fidelma replied. 'But that statue did not topple by itself, nor did the iron lever—'

There was a sudden shouting outside and they turned to the door. It burst open and Enda came stumbling in. He had clearly emerged from a struggle and was breathing heavily.

'I have the culprit,' he announced in a triumphant gasp. 'After the guests were brought down, Aidan and I decided to examine the guest chambers that were not being used. We found an extra guest.'

He turned and motioned through the doorway. Three men entered the council chamber.

One of them was Aidan and the other was Luan. Between them, they held a writhing dishevelled figure. It was Deogaire of Sliabh Luachra, Brother Conchobhar's nephew.

CHAPTER TEN

'Hold still, Deogaire!' Fidelma commanded. 'You are in the presence of your King.'

Something about her cold command caused the man to stop struggling.

'Then tell these brainless idiots to release me,' he grunted.

'These are warriors of the Nasc Niadh, my bodyguard.' Colgú's voice was sharp. 'They will not let you go until you have calmed yourself and ceased fighting with them.'

'I am not the one who attacked them. I was asleep, when I was leaped upon and dragged from my bed. How else should I respond to physical violence but to protect myself?'

'No violence will be offered to you if you calm down,' Fidelma assured him.

'Do I have Colgú's word as King?' Deogaire sneered.

'You have *my* word as *dálaigh*,' snapped Fidelma.

'Then I will struggle no longer, providing the King's yelping dogs obey you.'

Fidelma glanced at Enda and his companion and motioned them to stand aside. They released their hold cautiously and stood back, ready to move forward again if Deogaire did not keep to the agreement. Deogaire drew himself up with a curious dignity and began to rub his wrists where

red marks were already showing from his handling. He bowed towards
Fidelma with a cynical smile.

'You will forgive me, lady, for appearing in this state of undress. I was
not allowed time enough to clothe myself before I was dragged into your
presence.'

'You say "your bed",' Fidelma replied, ignoring his disrespectful tone. 'Yet
there is no record of you having been invited to stay in the King's guest
quarters.'

The man actually smiled. 'When I say, "my bed" I did not, of course,
mean complete ownership of it. I have not slept in a bed that truly belonged
to me since I left Sliabh Luachra. But is it the law that I must now prove
ownership of the bed in which I sleep?'

'You take me too literally, Deogaire. To put it more clearly: what are you
doing in the guest chambers of the King?'

'Why, sleeping – until I was rudely awoken.' The man adhered to his
bantering tone.

'Matters are too serious to play semantics with us, my friend,' interposed
Colgú. 'You will answer the lady Fidelma's questions without prevarication.
There has been an attempt on my sister's life and that of her husband.
Any further show of levity must point to your guilt, even if we have not
proof enough.'

For a second Deogaire's eyelids fell like a bird of prey, hooding the
sharp blue of their intensity. Then he made a motion with his shoulders,
a kind of shrug, although those watching were unsure of its meaning. 'I
had a row with my uncle, the pious Brother Conchobhar, who told me
never to cast my shadow across his portal again. Therefore I was in search
of a comfortable bed.'

'And somehow you just happened to wander into the King's apartments,
in spite of the guard, find your way into the guest chambers to choose a
conveniently empty room and then climb into bed?' Gormán challenged.

'Not at all,' Deogaire replied. 'I told my story to Beccan earlier this evening. He said that not all the guest chambers were filled this night and that if I told no one, I could have the use of one.'

'So you blame Beccan, do you?' Gormán looked to Colgú and said: 'We are wasting our time, lord. It is clear that he did the deed and was hiding out, thinking we would not search all the rooms.'

Deogaire glanced round. 'Where was I supposed to have made this attempt on the lady Fidelma's life?' he demanded.

'A marble statue was pushed from the roof as Fidelma and Eadulf passed below. The culprit escaped through the door leading to the guest chambers, throwing the bolt behind him. There was, however, no way of getting from those chambers anywhere else because of the guards. We have accounted for all the known guests. So it seems that Enda was right to constrain anyone who had no authority to be in those chambers,' Gormán explained.

For the first time Deogaire seemed to appreciate the gravity of his situation.

'I have told you the truth,' he insisted, all blustering gone now. 'Ask Beccan. I met him at the side door of the building that leads to the store-rooms. He took me up the stairs and showed me into an empty chamber while everyone was in the feasting hall. He told me that I could rest there, but warned me that there was a guard who would be posted during the hours of darkness. He advised me not to emerge until after daylight, when I could hear movement.'

'Then it is a pity that Beccan is not here to corroborate your story,' Eadulf observed dryly.

'Not here?' An expression of apprehension crossed Deogaire's features. 'Where is he? He said he would not be long.'

'Tell me, how is it that Brother Conchobhar came to throw his own relative out of his house?' Fidelma asked without answering him. 'He is a great respecter of old custom and holds that the laws of hospitality, especially to a blood relative, are not easily dismissed.'

Deogaire had lost more of his confidence by now.

'You know that he and I do not see eye to eye on matters of religion,' he muttered. 'I maintain the old paths while he accepts this new mysticism from the east. It is not to be trusted! The ancients say – knowledge is found in the west, battle to the north, danger to the east and tranquillity to the south. Danger to the east! That danger is coming.'

'You threatened me once,' she replied, recalling. 'You said: "two glances behind would be better than one before".'

'A warning to some is seen as a threat by others. I foresee the danger from the east. That is no threat – that is a warning. Be afraid and you will be safe. That was all I said.'

Fidelma grimaced at the old saying. 'I am aware of what was said. You also mentioned that death could come in many forms – even a winged demon out of the sky.'

Eadulf breathed in sharply. 'And the statue was . . .' he began.

'Was it the statue of Aoife?' Colgú asked in a curiously strangled tone, his features suddenly pale.

When Fidelma silently nodded, there was an obvious unease among those present.

'Aoife? Who was she?' asked Eadulf, knowing there was some significance that was lost on him.

'Aoife was a wicked stepmother, and in punishment for her evil acts against the Children of Lir, the god Bodh Dearg changed her into a demon of the air.' It was Gormán who explained. 'The statues on the roof are representations of creatures from our ancient legends.'

Deogaire's eyes had widened slightly. Then he quickly recovered his poise. His chin thrust out defiantly. 'And what does that prove? The only thing it shows is that I am truly blessed with the gift of the *imbas forosnai*, of the prophecy of the poets.'

Fidelma reflected for a moment, then said: 'Foreknowledge of events is usually explained by involvement. I am no seer, as you claim to be,

Deogaire. I have to rely on facts and logic. That is the beginning of *my* wisdom.' She looked at him before continuing.

'Your claim to be in the guests chambers by invitation of Beccan cannot be confirmed until the King's steward returns. Do not worry, we will not condemn without seeking evidence. That is not our way. While we wait for his return, we will provide you with another bed for the rest of this night.' She turned to Gormán. 'Take Deogaire to the *Laochtech* and secure him there as a prisoner until I order otherwise. It will go badly for you, Deogaire, if you do not leave peacefully with these warriors.'

The young man looked anxious. 'The last person who was secured there was found hanged – and not by his own hand,' he protested.

'Do not be concerned,' Fidelma replied. 'You will be placed in one of the rooms within the *Laochtech* and a warrior will be within call at all times. You will see to that, Gormán,' she added.

'It shall be done, lady.' The warrior touched Deogaire on the shoulder. 'Are you going to cause trouble, or will you come with us peacefully?'

Deogaire, still rubbing his wrists, sighed and said, 'Peacefully, by all means, let us proceed peacefully.'

After Gormán had left with Aidan and the prisoner, Fidelma slumped uninvited into a chair.

'I don't suppose you have some *corma* left, brother?' she smiled faintly.

Colgú poured the fiery alcoholic drink for her before indicating that they should all be seated and take a drink. Everyone seemed shocked at the events of the evening. Only Brehon Aillín excused himself, somewhat stiffly, and retired to his chamber.

'So Deogaire is the guilty one?' Abbot Ségdae phrased the question with an air of satisfaction. 'Guilty of the other deaths as well . . . you think? And why? To have his prophecy fulfilled, no doubt.'

Fidelma stared, preoccupied, into her drink before telling them: 'I am not sure of his guilt.'

Everyone looked at her in surprise.

'Not sure that he is guilty of the other deaths?' Eadulf asked.

'It all sounds a little too plausible,' she replied.

'Sometimes things *are* simple and straightforward. Not everything is as complicated as many would have us believe,' pointed out her brother.

'It's true. And yet let us bear in mind what has happened here during the last few days. Is it so easy to say that Deogaire was guilty of Brother Cerdic's death? That he hanged Rudgal? Then what of the attack on the river and the—' She stopped suddenly, realising that she was about to say too much. The cloth that Rudgal had hidden had to remain secret for the time being. Yet Brother Conchobhar knew of it . . . did that mean that Deogaire knew of it too? She turned her gaze to Eadulf, hoping he would pick up the warning message from her eyes, without her having to speak it.

'What now?' Eadulf asked. 'Do we wait until Beccan comes back?'

Gormán had just returned to report that the prisoner was now locked up and under guard, and overheard him.

'I could go down to the township myself and search him out, if I knew where this sick relative lived,' he offered. He looked to the King. 'Does anyone know where his relative is to be found?'

Colgú turned to him, puzzled. 'You mean, Beccan's relative is not known here? But everyone knows who lives in the township of Cashel. There are surely no strangers here.'

'I have never heard Beccan speak of having a family member living nearby,' confirmed Gormán, 'but my mother knows everyone. It should be easy to find him.'

'While we wait for his return, I will have a word with Brother Conchobhar,' Fidelma said. 'At least that will confirm whether it is true that he threw Deogaire out.'

Abbot Ségdae emptied his goblet and set it down with a disapproving look. 'I would have thought Deogaire's guilt is clear. I don't understand you wanting further proof, Fidelma.'

'It is not clear to me – but then I am a *dálaigh*,' she replied. Then, realising that she had sounded rather curt, she added: 'He might well be telling the truth.'

'But if he *were* telling the truth, then it implies that the murderer, or attempted murderer, if you will, is someone else,' the abbot said. 'That someone has to be one of us in the guest chambers, and that—'

'That means,' Gormán continued with a grin at their sudden discomfiture, 'that you have quite a choice. There are four suspects: the abbot's steward, Brother Madagan; Brehon Aillín; Abbess Líoch and her *bann-mhaor* Sister Dianaimh.'

'Each accusation is as ridiculous as another,' Abbot Ségdae said impatiently. 'Why, I'd sooner believe in Deogaire's demon from hell springing into the statue of Aoife. Evil from the east, indeed!'

They sat quietly for a while and finally Fidelma rose.

'Come, Eadulf, the hour grows late.'

Gormán was on his feet. 'I will come with you to make sure you get to your apartments safely.'

Fidelma shook her head with a smile. 'I think we are safe now. Besides, I am told that lightning never strikes in the same place twice. We will be safe.'

They left the King's quarters but this time Fidelma took a slightly different path around the building to their chambers. When Eadulf commented on the longer route, he heard her chuckle in response.

'Because I realised after we left that it was a misconception,' she whispered.

'What was?' He frowned.

'Lightning *can* strike again in the same place. There was once a shepherd near where I studied at Brehon Morann's law school. He tended his sheep on the hills nearby and often refused to take shelter during the storms. He was struck four times on four different occasions by lightning and survived each time. However, I do not want to tempt fate.'

'I am glad that you told me,' Eadulf grumbled. 'But why are we going this way?'

Fidelma pointed through the darkness beyond the chapel. There was a light in the building. It was the apothecary.

'I think we should take the opportunity for a word with Brother Conchobhar.'

'It's going to be a late night,' Eadulf protested, 'and I promised to take Alchú riding first thing in the morning.'

Fidelma did not respond. She walked to the apothecary's door and tapped sharply on it. There was only a little pause before there was a movement behind the door and it swung open. The old physician peered at them as the light from the lamp he held shone on them.

'You are abroad late,' he observed, before standing back to let them enter. When they did so, he closed the door behind them.

'And you are up late,' Fidelma replied, moving through the musty-smelling room to where she knew Brother Conchobhar had some chairs placed before his fire.

Brother Conchobhar shuffled after her, with Eadulf following.

'You know that it is my habit,' he said. 'Late to bed, late to rise.'

'You don't believe in the old saying then – *sero venientibus ossa*?' sighed Eadulf wistfully, thinking of his own bed. It literally meant 'for the latecomer the bones' but implied that the person who rose early succeeded in life.

Brother Conchobhar regarded him with an expression of amusement.

'I spend hours on my little roof above watching the movement of the heavens, seeing the bright lights in the night sky moving here and there, and charting the course of our fortunes against the darkness of the canopy. It is not an occupation one can do in the daylight.'

Eadulf had forgotten that the other man was a student of the stars and their motions.

'And what did you see tonight, old friend?' asked Fidelma, as she sank down into a chair. The apothecary moved to a table and began to pour them drinks.

'Mostly the signs show a calm night with the moon in balance and no less than four planets floating on water, including the planet of knowledge. It is from water that we gain knowledge, according to the ancients. Therefore from tonight's actions much can be learned. That does not mean all is tranquil, for the defending planet stirs to action.'

Eadulf, who half-understood the symbolism, grimaced, saying: 'Did you see in the skies tonight a flying demon ready to attack Fidelma and myself?'

Brother Conchobhar turned to him with an expression of alarm. 'Are you joking with me, friend Eadulf?' he demanded.

'Alas, he is not, old friend,' Fidelma said, casting a look of disapproval at Eadulf. 'But tell me first, what was the cause of your earlier argument with Deogaire?'

Brother Conchobhar did not appear surprised at being asked.

'I hope he has not been causing problems,' he muttered. 'But relative or not, I confess I found myself losing my temper with him. I have accepted his strange views for the sake of my poor sister and our common ancestors, but there are limits to what I should have to put up with. We did, indeed, have a quarrel earlier today. We exchanged some sharp words over our respective beliefs. It came to the point where I could not restrain my temper, for which I am truly sorry. I told him to leave my house and not to return. So he left.'

Fidelma nodded slowly. 'Who, between you, would you say provoked his leaving?'

'*Mea culpa*. It was my fault and I am heartily ashamed that, even at my age and with my experience, this young man could provoke me into losing my temper. I was made even more ashamed and angry because Abbot Ségdae's steward was a witness. Brother Madagan had come to get some wild garlic for a distemper he had. But why do you ask this? What has happened to him? What has this to do with flying demons?'

Fidelma explained about the attack on them, quickly and succinctly. 'He will be all right under guard,' she added, patting the old man's hand. 'Tomorrow we will get down to the truth.'

Brother Conchobhar looked at her sorrowfully. 'I can believe many things but I can't believe that my nephew is guilty of an attack on you and Eadulf. For all his mistaken arrogance, he is right in one thing. There is evil here, if it is not among us already. Perhaps we should be fearful. We should fear what is coming from the east.'

'All we know is that it is supposed to be a peaceful deputation of members of the Faith. There should be no need to fear them.'

'You choose your words carefully, Fidelma. There *should* be no need to fear them. That means you have not discounted any such fear.'

Fidelma made a 'tut-tut' sound with her tongue. 'You have a sharp ear, Brother Conchobhar.'

'I need two sharp ears and sometimes a sharper mind,' replied the old man. 'Tell me, Deogaire was not the only one in the guest house, was he – the only one with access to the roof at the moment the statue crashed down on you?'

'He was not,' Fidelma nodded.

'And have you eliminated all the others from any possible involvement?'

'I have not,' she replied, much to Eadulf's surprise.

'You haven't questioned the others yet?' asked Brother Conchobhar.

'Not yet,' she confirmed. 'They are not likely to go far, all being safely abed in the guest chambers. You seem to have something on your mind, old friend.'

'Wasn't Brother Madagan there to support my nephew's claim that Deogaire and I had quarrelled?'

Fidelma realised that it was true: Brother Madagan had remained silent.

'How much did he hear?' she asked. 'Did he hear you telling Deogaire to leave?'

Brother Conchobhar was hesitant. 'Perhaps not,' he admitted. 'But he would have heard our voices raised.'

'That might not signify anything.'

'Brother Madagan speaks some of your language, Eadulf,' the apothecary told him.

'And fairly well, too,' agreed Eadulf. 'I know that, and he told us that he learned the language while in Láirge, the harbour township.'

'He was quite open about that,' Fidelma added. 'He told us that he spent two summers there teaching students from the Saxon kingdoms before they passed on to our colleges. Láirge is a favourite port where ships come from the lands beyond the seas.'

'Did he say whose school he was teaching at?' the apothecary wanted to know.

Fidelma glanced at Eadulf and then shook her head.

'It was his sister's school,' Brother Conchobhar said. He saw that they were waiting for him to explain further, so went on: 'Mella, his sister, had a little school on the right bank of the Siúr not far from the port. She knew your language well, Eadulf, for she had been in the kingdom of Cenwealh and his wife Seaxburh.'

'That is the Kingdom of the West Saxons,' Eadulf said immediately. 'How do you know this?'

'Because Brother Madagan once told me. That was some time ago. His sister had been a missionary there for a while and then, with her knowledge of the language, she returned to teach our language to those Saxons coming to this land. He went there to help her and thus he also acquired the Saxon tongue.'

'I did not know he had a sister there,' Fidelma said, surprised.

'No longer. Mella is dead.'

'How did it happen? Was it the Yellow Plague? As I recall, many died in that area during the years it ravaged this land.'

Brother Conchobhar shook his head sadly. 'No, she was not carried off by plague. One of the Saxon foreigners killed her – after having had his way with her. It was soon after that, Brother Madagan decided to return to Imleach and became steward to Abbot Ségdae.'

'You learned all this from him?' Eadulf queried.

'There were also whispers at the time,' admitted Conchobhar. 'But it was several years ago now.'

'What made you think of this?' Fidelma enquired patiently.

'I was reminded of what he told me just the other day. Maybe I should have mentioned it before. Brother Madagan was helping me prepare the body of Brother Cerdic for the funeral rites. I had left him in order to fetch a sheet for the *racholl* to wind the body in. When I returned, I was shocked.'

'Shocked?'

'I have rarely seen a face filled with such malignancy as his, as he bent over the body. I heard him curse it and say that all Saxons should be consigned to *Ifrenn*, the infernal regions, and not be allowed redemption in the New Faith.'

'That doesn't sound like Brother Madagan,' Fidelma said.

'It was as if some serpent spoke from him in that moment. Then he turned and saw me staring in horror at him. His face was pale with hate and then he quickly composed himself. He reminded me about his sister; how she was violated and killed.'

'Was the culprit ever caught?' Fidelma asked.

Once again, Brother Conchobhar shook his head. 'Mella's body was not found until the next day,' he said heavily, 'and then it was presumed that the man responsible had sailed back to his own land on the morning tide.'

'Why was it presumed?'

'Brother Madagan knew that a man called Ceolwulf had been paying more than usual attention to his sister. A Brehon had the port of Láirge searched for this man. There was no sign of him, but that morning, a ship set sail from Láirge for a foreign port called Clifadun, in the northern part of the Kingdom of the West Saxons. There was nothing to be done, for the Brehon had no jurisdiction to follow the ship. I wondered if the death of his sister had left Brother Madagan bitter against all Saxons.'

'He has never shown any animosity to me,' Eadulf said thoughtfully.

Brother Conchobhar smiled without humour. 'He keeps his temper under control but I think he was named wisely, for at times he can be a snarling little dog.'

'It does give us some new thoughts about motives for the attack on Brother Cerdic,' Fidelma agreed slowly. 'But it gets confusing when we consider the death of Rudgal and the attack on us.'

'I know we speak of your relative, but were I to make a wager at the moment, it would be on Deogaire's guilt,' Eadulf declared. 'He had the opportunity and the motive – the motive being to fulfil his threat to Fidelma; to create some fear in this place in advance of the arrival of Bishop Arwald and his party.'

Fidelma was not so certain. 'But again, it lacks a connection with the deaths of the others. In fact, we can find suspects for each murder – but not one to whom we can attribute all the deaths.'

'So maybe we are looking for several killers,' Eadulf shrugged.

'And you think Deogaire simply acted to justify his prophecy?' she asked. 'It is true that he does not accept the New Faith, yet there are little isolated pockets, like Sliabh Luachra, where the old ways persist. But the Five Kingdoms are irrevocably committed to the New Faith. For the last several centuries we have become so much a part of it that we welcome others to our shores to educate them, and we send our missionaries over the seas to encourage the pagans beyond to leave the old ways.'

'I know this,' Eadulf replied gruffly, 'but—'

'It does not explain Deogaire's behaviour, even if he seeks to create fear at the arrival of Bishop Arwald and his deputation. Why emerge out of the mountain fastness of Sliabh Luachra into a world already set in the New Faith in an attempt to turn back an unstoppable tide?'

Eadulf lifted his arms slightly and let them fall, expressing that he had no answer.

Finally, he said, 'Well, if you are looking for suspects other than Deogaire, you might as well say that Brehon Aillín had motive and opportunity. He must dislike me intensely.'

Fidelma did not smile. 'I have not dismissed that possibility,' she replied.

Eadulf was slightly surprised at her ready acceptance of the idea. 'I know he doesn't like me, and he will not take kindly to your brother's defence of me, but a Chief Brehon of this kingdom attempting murder out of revenge . . .'

'All people have it in them to strike out in fury when they are pushed too far,' replied Fidelma. She had not told Eadulf that Brehon Aillín had threatened to take action against him and had only been prevented by Colgú's intervention. 'But you are right: I don't believe he was the person who pushed the statue down on us. He is a frail, elderly man. You saw the iron bar that was wielded as a lever to shift that statue. It's heavy. And the statue is large, the size of a child. It would have taken some strength to shift.'

Brother Conchobhar had been sitting listening attentively as they exchanged their ideas. Now he spoke up.

'Fidelma, as much as I argue with Deogaire, I cannot accept that one of my own family would attempt this deed. I will not believe that he is guilty.'

'Try not to worry, old friend,' she replied. 'He will not be accused without a thorough investigation.' Fidelma made to rise and then an after-thought came to her: 'Did you ask the librarian about that ritual wool collar?'

The apothecary paused for a moment. 'Oh yes. He confirmed that some generations ago, all the bishops wore something similar during the services as a mark of their rank. But he seems to think that this dress fell into disuse when a new design was ordered by Rome. He is going to look up some manuscripts in the archives which he thinks might explain more about it.'

'Let us know as soon as you hear, my friend.' She rose and turned for the door. 'It has been a long day and I, for one, am tired.'

Eadulf had wanted to discuss matters further. He felt irritated and nearly pointed out that he had been ready for bed some time ago. First thing in the morning, he'd be taking his son out riding. This didn't happen often because Eadulf was not fond of riding as a pastime, unlike Fidelma. He rode only when he was forced to do so, as a means of transport. The idea that one rode a horse for pleasure was beyond his comprehension.

'Very well,' he said stiffly, as he followed Fidelma's example. 'We will talk more about this in the morning. But as you said earlier, there will be little time to reach any solution before Bishop Arwald and his party arrives. I do not think we have to fear Bishop Arwald, however. It is the fact that he is accompanied by the Venerable Verax, brother of the Bishop of Rome, which gives me concern.'

They wished Brother Conchobhar good night and left him to his studies. It was as they were entering their chamber that Eadulf suddenly asked: 'Do you believe what Brother Conchobhar was saying about Brother Madagan?'

Fidelma stared at her husband in surprise. 'I have never known him to lie. Is there a reason why we should disbelieve him now?'

'I find it curious that he comes out with this suspicion about Brother Madagan killing Brother Cerdic at the very moment that he learns that his own nephew has been imprisoned as a suspect.'

CHAPTER ELEVEN

෨෨

T he morning was dry and the dark stormclouds had vanished, but with the clear blue skies had come a cold and chilly wind whipping across the plains from the north-east. Eadulf felt exhausted already; he had barely slept. But a promise to his son was a promise – and he felt the guilt of too many times when he had followed Fidelma on missions that had taken them to many distant places, so that they had barely seen the early months and years of their son's growth to boyhood.

At least the cold breath of the wind seemed to be easing his throbbing headache. He rode awkwardly on his sturdy cob, just in front of Alchú who followed on his small pony. Even at his young age the boy seemed totally at ease on his mount; the master of the animal. Eadulf envied him. Beside the boy came the watchful Luan, one of the King's warriors. Knowing Eadulf's limitations as an equestrian, Fidelma always insisted that Alchú be accompanied by one of her brother's bodyguards.

Eadulf had chosen the easy path from Colgú's fortress palace, moving south via a track that led through the forest that spread before them. Tall yews, birch and elm predominated among the trees. Apart from the evergreens, the forest still had its gaunt and withered winter look, although here and there along the track were clumps of snowdrops, whose appearance usually foretold the end of winter. Now and then they mingled with

159

the small white flowers of *lus an spáráin*, rising from their sprawling green leafy growth. What was it he had learned about those flowers while studying the art of apothecary? The juice of the flower dropped into the ear would ease earache and pain. He tried to remember what the plant was called in his own language – Shepherd's something? He gave up almost immediately. There was evidence of the gorse preparing for the day when it would burst into bright yellow flowers, but that day was several weeks away yet.

From the thickets he could hear the 'tit-tit-tit' explosive cry of the tiny and inconspicuous wren, and glimpse it briefly before it fell silent while a songthrush with its white speckled belly suddenly darted from one patch of undergrowth to another. Then the sudden silence, the abrupt quietness of the birds, caused him to look around for a reason. Not far away was a solitary bird of ill-omen – the black raven – but that was a scavenger and certainly not enough to threaten the small active birds. Then he caught sight of a pair of kestrels hovering in the sky above the path. There was the female, with her rusty brown-coloured tail, and the long pointed wings of the male, with chestnut-coloured back and grey tail with black band. No wonder the smaller birds had fallen silent, for the kestrels were deadly hunters – birds of prey. The black raven was waiting for the kestrels to make their kill and then, when they had fed, it would pick up what was left.

Eadulf shuddered, reminding himself that it was a cruel world and, try as he might to disassociate himself from the idea, man was part of it. Man could be just as cruel and unforgiving as the hovering kestrels, watching for a tiny wren or songthrush to make a mistake and then—

He glanced behind him and saw the grinning face of little Alchú, staring innocently up at the birds above him. He wondered whether the boy would ever see them as he did: recognise this scene for the unforgiving cruelty that it demonstrated. Or did he see it as simply a ride among the whispering trees, lit by a pale sun?

Eadulf did not intend to ride a long way; perhaps as far as Rath na Drinne where Ferloga and his wife Lassar ran an inn. He and Fidelma had often halted there. It was close by an ancient enclosure, converted into a fortified farm. Its name meant 'Fort of Contentions'. Ferloga had once told him that in ancient times it had been so called because it was there that great contests were held. Contests like *immán* or *camán*, with players driving a ball with sticks of ash, over the grassy field, trying to get the ball between two poles. Then there were athletic contests, foot racing, wrestling and disc throwing.

It was just beyond Rath na Drinne that the forest eventually ended on the edge of an extensive grassy plain – the Plain of Femen which reached all the way to the Field of Honey by the side of the River Siúr. It was why the Eóghanacht, centuries before, had chosen their capital overlooking the plain controlling the wealth and security of the kingdom. To the south-west on the horizon rose the Sliabh na gCoillte, the Forest Mountains, and among them the strange waters of the Lake of the Dragon's Mouth. It was here that the old God of Love, Aonghus Óg, found the tall maiden, Cáer, whom he had sought because she had appeared to him in a dream. On declaring their love, the pair had transformed into swans, circling the lake symbolically three times before disappearing off to the Land of Enchantment. Eadulf smiled. He had heard these tales many times from the old storytellers in Cashel. They were the legends of Fidelma's people – her ancestors.

Then the smile dropped from his face. Fidelma's people? Not his. He was suddenly aware of what his brother, Egric, had said. Was he simply a stranger in a strange land; a land in which he didn't belong? Why was he questioning himself after all these years? Had he deluded himself that he had been accepted into this new culture? Was it his brother's comments that had disturbed him? Or was it old Brehon Aillín's prejudice? Indeed, was it the newfound prejudice of Brother Madagan . . . Had people simply been tolerating him, smiling to his face and viewing him with dislike behind his back? Eadulf swallowed hard. This was not right, this stream of dark thoughts.

Everything had been peaceful until Egric appeared and started to question his motives. What right had Egric to do so? He had made his own life. The brothers had taken separate paths. Why had he emerged now, at such a time and at this place? He had appeared abruptly at Cashel and now, even more abruptly, had vanished on a hunting trip with Dego. Gone without taking leave; without a word of warning. It was curious. Eadulf trusted Dego. The warrior had accompanied Fidelma and himself on numerous trips; they had shared many dangers. Dego was reliable. Surely Dego respected Eadulf? He would not dismiss him as a stranger of no importance. He would never have been persuaded to take Egric hunting without being assured that Eadulf was aware of the trip. Ah, now those bleak thoughts came over him like a flood. Was he deluding himself that this was his home or . . . It was surely Egric who had conjured these cheerless, negative thoughts into his mind!

That was it; it *was* his brother reminding him of the ghosts of the past, his family and boyhood home. But Eadulf had never rejected them; he had never denied them. He had simply grown up and moved on. That was exactly what he had told his brother. *Vestigia nulla retrorsum* – no footsteps backwards. He experienced a curious thrill of hatred because his brother had disturbed his life. Then he rebuked himself sharply for this train of thought. What of Fidelma? What of their son Alchú? What of the times he had shared with them in their world? Was he now beginning to believe he was in the wrong place? Of course not! This was the world that he had wanted to share; it was *his* world, not an alien one.

His mind drifted back to that first encounter with Fidelma in the Abbey of Hilda at Streonshalh. He had gone there with no other purpose but to represent the new teachings from Rome; to argue against the old rites of the western churches, so fiercely represented by the religious representatives of the Five Kingdoms. He had been walking along a corridor in the abbey when she had come swiftly round a corner and collided with him, her mind clearly elsewhere. He had reached out and caught her, to save her stumbling backwards and falling. Some empathy had sparked from her green eyes as he gazed at her tumbled red hair, her pale skin and delicate sprinkling of freckles. She had spoken stiffly in Latin: 'Forgive me.' He politely replied that it had been his fault. They had stood there for a moment – a moment when pure chemistry had passed between them. Then they had continued on their separate ways.

It was a few days later, after her friend Abbess Étain had been murdered and the outcome of the debate between the two factions had been jeopardised by the suspicions of both parties, when King Oswy and Abbess Hilda had suggested that Fidelma and Eadulf jointly investigate the mystery, so that neither faction could claim bias. They had been thrown together, strangers to each other apart from that one accidental meeting. Now, six or seven years later, they were still working together and had produced a young son. Of course Eadulf was no alien to this land, he was no alien . . .

'Brother Eadulf!' a voice bellowed in his ear and a firm hand was clapped on his shoulder.

Eadulf blinked rapidly and found he was leaning dangerously off his horse; the only thing preventing him from falling was the steadying hand of the warrior, Luan. Eadulf righted himself in the saddle and raised a hand to rub his forehead.

'You were drifting, Brother Eadulf,' rebuked Luan. 'I saw you nodding off.'

'Were you falling asleep, *athair*?' Alchú, seated on his pony, was regarding him gravely.

Eadulf turned and smiled reassuringly at him. 'I was just thinking, little hound. Just thinking.'

'Are you well, friend Eadulf?' asked Luan anxiously. 'Perhaps we should return.'

'I was awake most of the night,' Eadulf confessed. Then, seeing the look of disappointment on his son's face, he went on: 'I'll be fine. Ferloga's inn is just a little way on. We'll go on and rest there before turning back.'

He turned his concentration to his horse, annoyed with himself for letting his brother's unexpected appearance have such an effect on him.

Earlier that morning, having seen Eadulf ride off with Alchú and Luan, Fidelma set out to find Gormán. She wanted to make sure that Deogaire had spent the night safely in restraint. Having been so assured, she asked Gormán to accompany her to the roof of the guest quarters, to re-examine it in daylight. Things missed in the darkness of night might reveal themselves more clearly in the daylight. She started with the place where the marble statue of Aoife had been and saw where the iron bar or lever had been placed to ease it forward, leaving score-marks on the parapet.

She turned and said, 'Gormán, one of your men found an iron bar on the roof last night. It was used to topple the statue. I think he might have abandoned it by the door over there when we chased down the other exit.'

Gormán went across to the door and immediately returned with the piece of iron, which measured over a metre in length. Both ends had been hammered flat, thus producing an ideal tool for the purpose it had been put to the previous night.

'This looks like a *forsua-fert*. It's a smithy's work to produce this,' Gormán commented.

Fidelma held out her hands and took it. A 'pole chisel' was usually used in digging roots of a tree, or moving blocks of masonry or objects long sunken in the soil. The iron was certainly heavy and would have had to be raised to shoulder height or a little higher, to dig at the base of the statue. It would need a person of strength and determination to do so. 'Could our smith identify it and perhaps lead us to its user?' she wondered aloud.

'It's a common enough tool,' Gormán replied. 'Come to think of it, some of the workmen repairing the wall at the south-east corner were using similar tools to shift the rockfall. However, the smithy might be worth questioning.'

Deogaire was certainly capable of wielding the instrument. But who else had such strength? Then she suddenly asked herself why she had this curious reticence about condemning him. Everything seemed to fit. His antipathy; his threat – or warning, as he would have it; the coincidence that he had been ejected from his relative's house, having provoked that action . . . she was not overlooking the fact that Deogaire had provoked the argument in spite of Brother Conchobhar's excuses.

'Bring it with you,' she smiled apologetically, handing the iron shaft back to him. 'We need it as evidence.' Then she turned and continued her examination of the wall, but nothing else seemed to present itself. She sighed and turned to the patient warrior. 'Let's go back down through the main building.'

They had come up through the guest quarters and now, as they turned to descend, she halted abruptly, nearly colliding with Gormán behind her. A figure was blocking the stairway. Brehon Aillín raised a pale, startled gaze to her.

She said nothing but merely stood regarding the old judge, whose chest was heaving.

'I was just coming to get some fresh air,' he gasped, as if he had run up the stairs.

'I trust you are in good health, Brehon Aillín? You seem out of breath.'

Brehon Aillín drew himself up, his old arrogant self reappearing. 'Very well,' he said. 'I will tell you the truth. Whether your brother likes it or not, I am Chief Brehon. I came to see if there was anything I could find that might be overlooked by a young, inexperienced *dálaigh*.'

For a moment Fidelma held back her reaction to smile. She wondered if the old man knew that Colgú had told her of his attempt to take legal action against Eadulf, and even against Colgú, having learned that he had asked the Council of Brehons to meet and elect a new Chief Brehon. Brehon Aillín was certainly his own worst advocate. She did feel sympathy for his age and experience, but there came a time when people should retire with dignity.

'You are welcome to examine the roof all you want,' she replied. 'We have already done so. I do not think there will be much that you will be able to find now.'

Brehon Aillín scowled, turned and continued to climb the stairs onto the roof. As he did so, Fidelma saw his eyes fall on the iron shaft that Gormán still held. She saw his eyes widen a fraction and his mouth open a little. It was only for a moment and then his features assumed their usual expression of disdain. Fidelma was sure the old man had recognised the iron tool. A series of thoughts registered. Could she have been entirely wrong? Did Aillín have strength enough that he could have levered the statue from its place to fall on her and Eadulf as they passed? Had he come to the roof because he remembered that he had dropped the iron bar as he fled and now sought to retrieve it? It seemed impossible. But what was the meaning of the expression when his eyes fell on the metal bar? Well, it was no use pursuing that line at the moment. It would have to wait until she could manipulate the right situation.

Gormán cleared his throat uneasily. 'Lady?' he prompted, wondering why she still stood in the stairway. She gave him a quick smile and continued down the stairs. The guest chambers seemed to be deserted. An attendant was cleaning the rooms and so they passed on by. At the bottom of the stairway they met a troubled-looking Dar Luga, the housekeeper.

'Good morning, lady,' she greeted nervously. 'Is everything all right? Is there anything I can do?'

Fidelma reached forward and patted the woman's arm.

'Do not worry yourself, Dar Luga. There was nothing you could have done about last night. I presume all the guests have risen?'

'They have, lady.'

'Where are they now?'

'Brehon Aillín is still in the rooms above . . .'

'We saw him,' Fidelma acknowledged.

'The abbess and her steward have gone to the library. So has Brother Madagan. The abbot is in the council chamber with your brother.'

Fidelma turned and pointed to the iron lever that Gormán held. 'Have you ever seen this before?'

The woman took a step forward to peer at it. Then she stood back with a shake of her head, saying, 'It looks like a tool of some description.'

'We think that it might be a builder's tool of some sort,' Fidelma agreed.

'Perhaps you could ask the *rathbuigé*, the builder in charge of the repair work on the wall,' Dar Luga suggested. 'He might be able to tell you what it is.'

'Just to clarify: have you ever seen such an instrument in this building before?'

'Never.'

Fidelma allowed the housekeeper to continue on to the kitchens while she and Gormán went out of the main doors and into the courtyard.

'If it is a tool from the site, the would-be assassin must have carried it into the guest quarters,' mused Fidelma as she crossed the courtyard with the warrior. 'He waited until he knew we were leaving the feasting hall, then went up to the roof, knowing that Eadulf and I would take the narrow passage to our own quarters, and worked swiftly to push the statue down on us.' She frowned, halting suddenly in the middle of the courtyard. 'That requires an awful lot of effort and luck.'

Gormán regarded her for a moment. 'You don't think it worked like that?'

'It throws up too many questions.'

'I don't follow, lady.'

'To carry the iron bar, which is difficult – even impossible – to conceal, the would-be assassin could not have done so on the spur of the moment.

It was carefully planned beforehand. They would have had to take it to their room or the roof when there was no one who might encounter them. Do the guards come on duty just before the guests retire, or afterwards?'

'Just afterwards, lady. As soon as it is known the guests have retired for the night.'

'There would not have been time for any guest to leave the feasting hall, find the metal bar and take it up to their rooms. No, this bar was carried up there *before* the meal started.'

'Unless they had not attended the meal, such as Deogaire.'

'Or Brehon Aillín,' countered Fidelma. 'Even so, I don't like it. Even if the iron bar was carried up earlier, the right statue still had to be selected – one overlooking the narrow passage. The would-be assassin had to know the precise time Eadulf and I left the feasting hall; had to know which of the two ways back to our chambers we might choose. And finally, they must have known exactly how long it would take to dislodge the statue and judge the time from the moment it was known we entered the passage to where we would be when the statue fell. In short, the would-be assassin, acting alone, must have been a miracle worker.'

Gormán gave an involuntary shiver. 'You mean that there are evil spirits at work here?' His voice dropped to an awed whisper.

'Shame on you, Gormán!' Fidelma stamped her foot. 'No, I do not mean that at all! There is an answer to this and I will find it. Logic, in the very act of finding solutions, always throws up more questions.'

The young warrior was not really persuaded but he asked: 'So, what next, lady?'

Fidelma glanced up at the sky to judge the time. Although she was pretending that the late night had not affected her, she felt drowsy and realised that she had to give into it.

'I think I shall retire to my chambers for a while and wait until Eadulf returns with our son. That should be about midday. Then we shall question

Deogaire. He will have had enough time to think about his position to realise he must give us honest answers.'

Gormán gestured to the iron bar in his hand. 'What shall I do with this?'

'Put it somewhere safe in the *Laochtech* for the time being. We'll see what Deogaire has to say about it later.'

Fidelma had barely entered her chamber, sat down on the bed and closed her eyes when the next thing she was aware of was Eadulf coming into the room. Guiltily, she sat up, rubbing her eyes.

'You've been a very short time,' she said accusingly.

Eadulf regarded her with a tired smile. 'We've been quite a long while. It's well after midday and we went as far as Rath na Drinne, where we stopped a while at Ferloga's inn. I swear, our young son has more energy than any of your brother's warriors; certainly, he has more than I have. I am exhausted.'

'It's after midday?' Fidelma was aghast, and felt twice as guilty for being asleep so long. 'Where is Alchú?'

'I gave him back to the care of Muirgen.' Eadulf looked longingly at the bed. 'I am going to miss the midday meal and have a nap,' he decided. 'I'll get something to eat later.'

Fidelma rose. 'I was going to question Deogaire.'

Eadulf was stretching out on the bed. 'Can't it be done later?'

'I promised Gormán that I would meet him at midday. I'll tell you all I have discovered later.'

But Eadulf was already asleep and, with a shrug, Fidelma left him and went first to check all was well with Alchú, who was being washed by Muirgen the nurse. Having satisfied herself, she hurried on to the Heroes' Hall to find Gormán. The warrior was just eating a hurried midday meal. Strangely, Fidelma did not feel hungry at all. While he was finishing, she asked if he had any word of Beccan's return to the palace. Gormán assured her that he had not; nor had he been able to learn anything about the steward having a sick relative in the township. Finally, bringing the iron bar on her instructions, he led her to the room at the back of the warriors' quarters where Deogaire had been placed. This had been deemed safer than putting him in the outside storeroom where Rudgal had been murdered.

There was eagerness on the prisoner's face as Fidelma entered the tiny chamber in which he had been held since the previous night. He rose from the makeshift cot, asking, 'Has Beccan returned yet? Has he confirmed what I have said?'

Fidelma regarded him in silence for a moment and then sat on the single stool in the room. Gormán followed her inside; taking a stance in the doorway, still holding the iron bar. Deogaire suddenly saw it in his hands and took a step backward.

'You don't mean to use that?' There was a tremulous note in his voice.

Fidelma looked at him crossly. 'Don't be ridiculous,' she snapped. 'What backwoods do you think we live in?'

Deogaire spread his arms expressively. 'All I know is that I am being accused of something I did not do, and in a place where there have been two deaths already. What am I to believe? You imprison me and now you come in here with an iron bar. For what purpose?'

'To ask you if you recognise it, of course,' Fidelma replied grimly. 'Now, take a look at it – carefully. Have you seen it before?'

'One iron bar looks like another,' Deogaire replied nervously.

'Not exactly. I am told that this is a tool often used by builders.'

'I am no builder, lady.'

'So you have not seen it or a tool like it?'

'I have seen tools like it used for shifting rocks embedded in the soil or to prepare the ground for planting; maybe even used for moving stones into place when buildings are constructed.'

'Have you seen it specifically here in Cashel?'

Deogaire shook his head stubbornly. 'I have no use for tools and weapons. I am a philosopher.'

Fidelma told Gormán to set down the tool outside before turning back to the prisoner. 'Now, tell me again, how you came to be in the guest quarters.'

'But I told you last night,' protested Deogaire.

'You said you were thrown out of Brother Conchobhar's house and then went to ask Beccan, the King's steward, for a room to sleep in – a room in the King's own guest quarters; in fact, rooms reserved for special guests. Is that the truth?'

'More or less,' admitted the man.

Gormán grinned sceptically. 'How much more?'

'It is the truth!' Deogaire said. 'I was thrown out of Conchobhar's apothecary, the silly old fool; he was lecturing me on this new morality from the east. I told you that was what we were arguing over. We always argue over it, but last evening, my uncle really lost his temper.'

Fidelma did not volunteer that Brother Conchobhar had confirmed the story.

'Arguing about what, for example?' she asked.

'I told him that at least the old gods, the Children of Danú, made no pretence to omnipotence. They aspired to justice but had all the traits, failings and good points of mortals.'

'I don't see your point,' Gormán intervened. 'That is not something to lose one's temper over.'

'I said that this new God from the east is purported to be the one and only God. Omnipotent, all-seeing, all-knowing. He knows everything that has happened, is happening and is about to happen. It is claimed that He has all the power.'

'That is according to the Faith,' agreed Fidelma.

'So, having the power to prevent war, He permits it. Being able to prevent disease, He promotes it. I asked how people can believe in the goodness of such a God Who permits these things when He could stop them? I said that there is no logic in this eastern faith unless this God is evil or possessed of a sadistic sense of humour. That was when Conchobhar fell into a rage. I had never seen him so angry! He warned me that any attempt to reason along those lines would lead me to eternal damnation: I could end up in this place of eternal punishment – *Ifrenn* – that has become part of your religion.'

'Did you know Brother Madagan was witness to your argument?'

'I know he came to collect something from Conchobhar, but he left immediately.'

'So having quit Brother Conchobhar's apothecary, you went to see Beccan?'

'Not exactly. I was wondering what to do when I met Beccan crossing the courtyard. He saw how upset I was and asked me what was wrong. I told him that I had just been thrown out by Conchobhar and would prob-ably have to set out for Sliabh Luachra. He replied that it was late and not the best time to start out on the road. I said there was no alternative as I had no bed for the night. He told me that he could help me – but on certain conditions. If I could return to the apothecary and get some remedies for a sick relative of his – he told me what he wanted – he would find me somewhere to sleep. He asked if I could do this without Conchobhar knowing. I said yes.'

Fidelma hid her surprise. 'Did Beccan know the names of the medications he wanted? What sort were they?'

'They were remedies for fever and colds. There was nothing that was harmful, if that is what you are thinking.'

'And when you had "acquired" them, what then?'

'He said that if I came around to the kitchen door at the time when the King and his guests were sitting down to the evening meal, he would take me to a room in the guest quarters that was not being used that night. All I had to do was stay in the room until after the guests broke their fast the following morning. That was the time when the King's bodyguards would disperse. He explained that they usually stood sentinel in stairwells and at the doors of the palace. When it was daylight, I could then sneak out and be on my way.'

'And all this was in exchange for some medication which you provided?'

'It was.'

'And after you had left the palace, where were you going?'

'I intended to return to my home in Sliabh Luchra.'

'A further question: where were the kitchen servants at this time?' asked Fidelma. 'I mean, the time when Beccan let you in?'

'There was no one in the kitchens when Beccan took me through them.'

'Isn't that curious?' Fidelma mused.

'I don't like any of this story,' Gormán interrupted. 'Beccan should know more than anyone else that the King's security is paramount, especially after the attempted assassination of Colgú a few months ago. For that reason, the guest quarters are closely guarded.'

Deogaire bridled, his head rising belligerently. 'It is not in my philosophy to wish harm to anyone.'

'That we must prove,' Fidelma said.

'You doubt me?'

'I would doubt even myself until a solution is found,' Fidelma replied calmly. 'Beccan will have to explain several things, including his behaviour, which is not consistent with the standard expected of a steward in my brother's household.'

Deogaire glared at her. 'I am no liar, lady. I have told you the truth.'

'Then the lie will pass away and the truth will remain,' she said confidently, rising from her seat.

Deogaire gritted his teeth for a moment. 'Isn't it said that lies often go further than the truth?'

'Lies only run a short course,' Fidelma assured him. 'Truth is great and will prevail.'

'I wish I had your faith in the truth, lady,' he replied bitterly. 'Two deaths in this place already, and you and your man have escaped death by a miracle. No one knows who is responsible. Where has the truth been hiding these last days?'

Gormán said stalwartly, 'Truth will emerge, count on it.'

'We will wait until Beccan returns,' confirmed Fidelma. 'That means that you must remain here in the *Laochtech* until he does.'

Deogaire seemed about to make an angry retort, but then he sighed philosophically. 'At least it provides me with a dry bed and food.'

They left Deogaire and, in spite of his being locked in the room, Fidelma insisted that a guard should continue to remain close by.

Gormán cast a questioning glance at her. 'You still doubt that he is the guilty one, lady, and fear that someone might attempt to harm him?'

'Rudgal was certainly guilty of the attack on Brother Egric and the Venerable Victricius. He was under the protection of your warriors, Gormán, and yet he was killed because we were not watchful enough. What if Deogaire is telling the truth – although his story sounds unlikely – and someone else is responsible? He might be in harm's way. Better we ensure against that possibility.'

Gormán was about to reply when the sound of a warning horn caused them to hurry outside towards the gates.

One of the warriors called down to them from the watchtower: 'A small party is approaching from the east, lady. Four warriors and three clerics. One of the warriors carries the tree banner of the Clan Baiscne.'

Gormán turned to Fidelma in dismay. 'The Baiscne, lady – the body-guard of the King of Laighin! This must be the party of Saxon religious that the King is expecting. And Beccan is not here to perform the ritual welcome and arrange matters.'

chapter twelve

⊘

I n view of the distinguished rank of the leaders of the deputation, Colgú
received them in his council chamber in the presence of selected
members of his household. Fidelma and Eadulf were requested to attend.
Fidelma had just time enough to return to their chambers and rouse Eadulf
from his nap, and while he was refreshing himself, tell him of her
discoveries that morning and the results of her questions.

In the council chamber, they were joined by Abbot Ségdae and his
steward, Brother Madagan, Brehon Aillín was already there because he
had insisted that his presence was required by protocol as he had not been
officially dismissed by the Council of Brehons. It was a fact that Colgú
could not refute. Because of the peculiar circumstances in which Abbess
Líoch and her steward, Sister Dianaimh, had been summoned by Brother
Cerdic before his death, they were also invited to be present.

There was an uncomfortable wait, while Gormán, as Commander of
the King's Bodyguard, received the visitors at the gates of the palace and
the usual ritual welcome was enacted before he led them to the council
chamber. In view of Beccan's absence, Gormán also took on the role of
the King's steward in officially announcing the visitors.

Bishop Arwald of Magonsaete strode forward as his name was called.
'Arrogant' was the first word that came into Eadulf's mind. The man was

exactly as he had predicted him to be. He was tall, with thin, almost emaciated features, to which was added a disdainful look that appeared to be his natural expression. The dark eyes were set close together under thick brows that almost met across the bridge of his nose. He had a slightly protruding forehead. He halted before Colgú, who was preparing to rise from his chair of office as a gesture of welcome and friendship. But when Bishop Arwald made no indication that he was going to greet the King with the usual respect – not even an inclination of his head, a bow, or even dropping to one knee in token of the rank that divided them – King Colgú decided to remain seated.

Instead, he looked beyond Bishop Arwald to the shorter, grey-haired man who, at first glance, resembled a kindly, elderly uncle. He was almost cherub-like, with olive skin that showed his origins were further south. In spite of the baby-like quality of his face, something unpitying and harsh came through. The corners of the fleshy mouth were stern, revealing a ruthless streak in the elderly, white-haired man. Light-coloured eyes glinted like ice from under shaggy brows. He halted a pace behind and to the side of Bishop Arwald, and gave a slight jerk of his head when Gormán announced the name of the Venerable Verax.

Both Bishop Arwald and the Venerable Verax were clad in rich robes, and there was no disguising the fact that they were men of rank and importance. At the moment, their richly embroidered cloaks bore a film of dust from their journey but the quality of them was evident. Bishop Arwald wore a cross of silver around his neck and the Venerable Verax a cross of gold, which was more elaborately ornamented. Eadulf glanced towards Colgú and hoped he remembered that it was the Venerable Verax who was the real leader of the deputation. The question arose: why did Verax pretend that Bishop Arwald was the senior of the group?

Behind the two men, at a respectful distance of two paces, stood a nondescript young man. Clad in a simple dyed-brown woollen robe, with what appeared to be a bronze cross, he kept his head and gaze lowered, even when Gormán announced him as Brother Bosa, a scribe. To Eadulf's eye, he looked anything but a scribe. He was muscular, and moved with the precision of a warrior. The more he tried to make himself invisible, the more incongruous he appeared.

There was a momentary silence after Gormán finished introducing the deputation. Bishop Arwald had still made no move to acknowledge the King and so Gormán cleared his throat and declared: 'You stand in the presence of Colgú, son of Failbhe Flann, King of Muman, scion of the Eóghanacht of Cashel, Lord of Tuadmuma, Aurmuma, Desmuma and Iarmuma . . .'

Ordinarily, Colgú would have told him to cut the ritual short but he let it run on as it gave him the opportunity to inspect his guests more closely. Finally, however, he raised his hand to indicate that Gormán should bring his listing of his ancestry and territories to a close.

As Gormán was giving his recitation, the young scribe came forward and was whispering to Bishop Arwald and the Venerable Verax. It was clear that he was not only acting as scribe but as translator. Colgú finally realised that the scribe was translating into Latin.

'Most of us here speak Latin,' he interrupted. 'We may continue in this language.' The young scribe stepped back at a gesture from the Venerable Verax. Colgú continued: 'You are welcome here.'

It was Bishop Arwald who then spoke. 'I trust we are so.' His voice was brittle. 'Have your slaves bring chairs for us, for our journey through this savage land has been arduous.'

There were gasps of astonishment from the assembly, and even Colgú's eyes widened in spite of the years he had been taught to control his feelings when in council.

Gormán stepped forward nervously, a hand dropping automatically to the hilt of his sword. His tone was sharp and emphatic.

'I remind you that you stand in the presence of Colgú, King of Muman, who is the fifty-ninth direct descendant of Eibhear Fionn, the son of Golamh, who led the children of Gaedheal Glas to this land in the time before time; Eibhear Fionn, who was given this land to rule by the . . .'

Colgú raised a hand and motioned him to silence. His eyes had not wandered from the face of Bishop Arwald since the man had spoken.

'Our guests are strangers, and perhaps they have no understanding of the protocol that prevails in this place.' He spoke softly, as if addressing Gormán but looking directly at Bishop Arwald. 'In our uncivilised ways, we still place great store in courtesy and the observance of rules. It is custom to acknowledge the King when you are brought before him. If a King invites you, then you may sit in his presence. It is also important to learn that we have no slaves here. The only people you will find who have restrictions on their freedom are criminals of various classes, and hostages.'

Bishop Arwald's sallow skin had taken on a paler hue. His thin red lips seemed to disappear entirely in a slit. The muscles in his jaw were working, as if he were trying to find expression for his rage. But Colgú was now looking at the Venerable Verax.

'In view of your exhaustion, having been forced to travel through our uncivilised countryside, we invite you, Venerable Verax and your companion, Bishop Arwald, to be seated while we speak of what brings you to face the hardships and difficulties that obviously beset your journey.'

The Venerable Verax took a step forward, his features formed into a masklike smile.

'It will not be necessary, Colgú of Muman. You will excuse us for our lack of knowledge of your customs.'

'Yet they are the same customs that prevail in the Kingdom of Laighin, where you surely must have been guests of Fianamail the King?' It was Fidelma who, in her irritation, could not suppress the observation.

Bishop Arwald turned swiftly, eyes narrowed as if noticing her for the first time.

'And who are you?' The tone was almost a sneer.

'This is the lady Fidelma, my sister,' Colgú replied in an icy tone. Clearly, Bishop Arwald was not one to be immediately cowed. 'Beside her is Brother Eadulf, who is from your own country but who has made his home here, having married my sister. He is a respected friend and adviser of this court.'

'Eadulf – from my country?' queried Bishop Arwald. He looked at Eadulf with great suspicion, then glanced at the Venerable Verax with a look that seemed full of meaning.

'Not exactly your country, Arwald of the Magonsaete,' Eadulf replied. 'I am from Seaxmund's Ham, in the Land of the South Folk, of the Kingdom of the East Angles.'

'Eadulf of Seaxmund's Ham?' Bishop Arwald examined him carefully. 'I believe that you have only recently arrived here.'

Eadulf wondered at the sinister tone in the other's voice. 'I have not. Why do you ask?'

'Were you not in Canterbury only a short while ago?'

'You are mistaken,' Eadulf replied. 'The last time I was in the Kingdom of Kent was during the winter of five years ago.'

Bishop Arwald did not seem satisfied. 'Yet I heard a story that you departed Canterbury in the company of an elderly man only a few weeks ago. In Laighin we were told that you were seen landing in the country with that same man at one of the southern ports.'

Eadulf blinked in astonishment and exchanged a look with Fidelma. Was Bishop Arwald mistaking him for his brother? If so, what was the meaning of that undertone in the bishop's voice? He was about to put the question when Colgú, oblivious to the tension, interrupted.

'I can assure you that our friend Eadulf has been here these many years and, with my sister, has carried out many missions for me.'

The dark eyes of Bishop Arwald swivelled to him. 'Missions? What missions – and why with a woman?'

It was the second time that a general feeling of astonishment spread, that this stranger should dare to question the King in such a tone. Once more Colgú decided to answer, overlooking the breach of protocol.

'Is it possible that you have not heard of my sister, the lady Fidelma who, with her husband, Eadulf, has represented my interests in many parts of the Five Kingdoms and beyond? My sister is a *dálaigh*, a legal advocate and adviser in law to me.'

This time the information had an effect on the Venerable Verax. He turned to look at Fidelma more closely and exclaimed: 'Of course! I have heard the Venerable Gelasius extolling her wisdom. Did she not perform valuable service in Rome when Wighard, the Archbishop Designate of Canterbury, was murdered in the Lateran Palace? Oh yes, now I have it. The same Fidelma was part of the delegation arguing against the changes made by His Holiness which were debated at Streonshalh and later at the council in Autun. Oh yes, we have heard of *her*.'

Eadulf picked up a warning note in the last sentence, but was unsure whether it was aimed at Bishop Arwald or at Fidelma.

Colgú relaxed back in his chair. 'Well, let us hope you will hear many tales from my bards of their deeds while you are here. But now . . . we hope that your immediate needs after your journey have been met?'

Bishop Arwald was still staring at Eadulf and seemed reluctant to change the subject of the conversation but at a look from his companion, he addressed Colgú with his customary belligerence.

'We have an escort of four warriors provided for our personal protection by King Fianamail and the Abbot of Fearna. Your own warriors refused them entrance into this place.'

Gormán coughed to attract the attention of the King. 'Four warriors of the Clan Baiscne escorted the religious here. I have issued instructions that they be given quarters in Rumann's tavern in the town below.'

'That is so,' Bishop Arwald confirmed, obviously annoyed. 'I strongly protest. The warriors should be quartered here so that I can call when they are needed.'

'I trust you do not imply that you will need protection while guests under the King's roof?' Abbot Ségdae could not restrain himself from speaking. He had already taken exception to the man's arrogance.

Bishop Arwald glanced angrily at him. 'When we arrived, I was told that my emissary, Brother Cerdic, not only came into danger within these walls but has been murdered. I do not think I need *imply* anything.'

'We are investigating that matter,' Colgú assured him quickly.

'What?' Bishop Arwald feigned surprise. 'Has no one been seized and executed for this outrage? Then the murderer is still at large – and yet you say there is no cause for alarm! I am most displeased, for Brother Cerdic was but newly joined to the . . . to my group of pilgrims. He had volunteered to come here alone to prepare you for our arrival. Why was he killed?'

'Investigations take time.' Colgú was irritated that he had been put on the defensive. 'Here we are governed by our ancient laws and so do not seize and execute people without just cause. I have appointed my sister and her husband to investigate.'

The sneer broadened in the voice of the bishop. 'Ah! Then it is under-stood why there has been no resolution.'

Colgú raised his eyes at Fidelma, signalling to her not to react to the provocation, before he began to address the newcomers in a severe tone: 'Since you are strangers, we will explain why your armed escort are not allowed within the confines of this palace. Relations between the Kingdoms of Muman and Laighin have not been of the closest. Sometimes, warfare can be the result of mistakes or arrogance, leading to quickening tempers. It is a custom now, between us, that no armed warriors of Laighin may be admitted within the walls of this palace of Cashel, especially none of the Baiscne, who are Fianamail's élite bodyguards, just as the Nasc Niadh are mine. Nor would I expect any of my warriors to be admitted with their arms into the Laighin fortress at Dinn Ríg or even Fearna.'

Once again, as it seemed Bishop Arwald was about to respond angrily, it was the Venerable Verax who spoke in a conciliatory tone.

'Then we would not wish to interfere with this custom and provoke any antagonism.'

'My guard will always be at hand during your stay, so that you need have no fear,' Gormán added coldly.

'There are quarters for special guests here in my palace and these have been provided for you,' Colgú went on.

Abbot Ségdae leaned close to Colgú and whispered into his ear in their common language: 'Let us find out what these arrogant prelates want before we are all too exasperated to even speak with them.'

Thankfully, Brother Bosa did not appear to hear the remark. Colgú inclined his head in agreement. 'Now, we are sure you will want to rest from your long journey. However, before you do so, and so that our Chief Bishop, Abbot Ségdae, may be prepared for the coming discussions, perhaps you can indicate to us the reason of your coming. What is it that you wish to discuss?'

The Venerable Verax turned to examine the abbot. 'We have heard much about Abbot Ségdae. By accounts given to us he is an influential and powerful ecclesiastic. Why is he content to be merely an abbot?'

Receiving a nod from Colgú, Abbot Ségdae replied: 'I am afraid that, once again, you are not aware of the customs of this country. Here, we deem an abbot of *higher rank* than a bishop.' He stared directly at Bishop Arwald as he spoke, ignoring the man's angry gaze.

'Yet there is much talk about a primacy among bishops among your people. There is a bishop – or is it abbot? – at a place called Ard Macha, who claims that it was there that Patricius the Briton first taught the Faith in this land, and thereby this abbot should be appointed Archbishop, chief of all the bishops and abbots on this island.'

'We will disagree on many points, Venerable Verax,' replied Abbot Ségdae. 'This will be one of them. Is it to discuss this that you have come all this way?'

The Venerable Verax was silent for a moment. 'Perhaps it is one point where we might usefully exchange views,' he conceded.

Abbot Ségdae shook his head. 'Poor Brother Cerdic made no mention of the subject that has caused your visit. He merely summoned me from my abbey at Imleach and, it seems, he summoned Abbess Líoch from Cill Náile, who also stands before you. Naturally, we are all curious to learn what brings such distinguished prelates into this kingdom.'

The Venerable Verax turned with interest to examine Abbess Líoch.

'Do you also refute the claims of this Abbot of Ard Macha and make claim for your own abbey?' he asked.

'My abbey was established only a few years ago,' replied the abbess. 'I make no such claims.'

Brother Bosa had moved forward and whispered in the prelate's ear. The Venerable Verax nodded slowly and continued to address the abbess. 'I am told that you were some years in Oswy's Kingdom?'

'Were you there?' returned Abbess Líoch, speaking directly to the scribe. 'I do not know you.'

Brother Bosa obviously felt that he should answer. 'I have not been there but am told that you were once spoken of as having spent time in the Abbey of Laestingau.'

A flush came to the abbess' cheeks. 'Then perhaps *you* can tell me why Brother Cerdic summoned me to this curious meeting?' she said impatiently.

The Venerable Verax intervened. 'Perhaps we will be able to discuss matters later? We have only just arrived and need some time to recover from our wearisome journey. We will resume the discussion when we are rested.'

'So the purpose of your coming here remains obscure?' Colgú replied in annoyance.

'Let it remain so until we can sit relaxed and discuss it in more detail,' the Venerable Verax said smoothly – but there was no questioning the determination in his voice.

Colgú could see there was little point in pressing the matter. He looked at Gormán, who anticipated his orders. 'Dar Luga is waiting outside to escort our guests to their chambers.'

He opened the door and the plump housekeeper entered.

'This is our *airnbetach*, the housekeeper, who will take you to your rooms. Any requests that you may have, please make them known to her. This evening, there will be a small feast to welcome you, and then perhaps you will reveal the purpose of your visit here, which is a matter we all look forward to with great curiosity.'

This time, the Venerable Verax took the lead in bowing stiffly, and after a slight hesitation, Bishop Arwald followed his example. Then they turned, with Brother Bosa behind them, and followed Dar Luga from the room. Gormán closed the door after they had left and stood waiting expectantly.

Colgú sat back as the others gathered around him. He had a wry smile on his features.

'Well, friend Eadulf, you warned me and Ségdae what manner of man we might expect this Arwald to be. I could scarce believe that he is so untutored in the arts of diplomacy.'

'Diplomacy?' Eadulf grunted sarcastically. 'That is just the typical bad manners of Mercia. For too long they have conducted diplomacy at the point of their swords. I wonder that you kept your temper.'

Brehon Aillín had remained quiet the whole time, and now he burst out: 'If I were still respected enough to advise you, I would say that it is a legal matter. Their arrogance is breaking our laws and putting your honour price in danger.'

They turned to look at the old disgraced Brehon in surprise.

'How so?' Colgú demanded, intrigued in spite of himself.

'The law texts, the wisdom texts, all stress the importance of the respect that must be shown to a king. They state that he is no king to whom royal tribute is withheld. The *Crith Gablach* insists that he is no king who, not being treated with respect due to his office, overlooks any such offence. A king is expected to demand respect by force from those who are impertinent and do not bend the knee, otherwise he loses his honour price and thereby his kingship. Likewise, if he does not ensure that his household are shown respect, he loses his honour price and his kingship.'

They heard the words of the old judge and understood that his angry challenge had more to do with his earlier dismissal by Colgú than for any precise advice on law.

Fidelma stepped to her brother's side. 'Brehon Aillín,' she said softly, 'I am, as you know, not as accomplished as you and do not hold the office of Brehon. I am merely a *dálaigh*, pleading in the courts and being allowed to judge only in minor cases.'

Suspecting sarcasm, Brehon Aillín turned to her, his brows compressed in a frown. 'And I suppose you are going to tell me that my interpretation of the law is wrong?' he sneered.

'You have quoted the text correctly,' she replied. Colgú looked nervously at her. But before a triumphant smile had fully formed on Brehon Aillín's face, she continued: 'All those here were witnesses to the lack of respect these strangers showed to my brother. All those here heard my brother rebuke them for their disrespect, but a king, according to the text you quote, is supposed to be just and take cognisance of the facts and circumstance. My brother took the attitude that, being strangers, they did not know our law as intimately as you do, Brehon Aillín. And finally, all those heard the Venerable Verax admit that, as strangers, they were unaware of it. We all saw them show respect as they left by bending their head to the King.' She paused. 'If I had need to defend the King against a charge that he had allowed disrespect to go unheeded, then I would say, as I am sure all here would agree, that he did not.'

Brehon Aillín stood for a moment, blinking. His jaw clenched to hide his anger. Colgú was trying not to show his amusement that the irritating fellow had been bested. He said gently: 'You may retire, Brehon Aillín. I do not need to consult further with you at this time.'

The old man wheeled about with surprising dexterity for his age and stomped out of the council chamber.

Colgú's features broke into a grin, and he said to his sister, 'If looks could kill, Fidelma . . .' He left the rest unsaid.

'I would watch Brehon Aillín, lady,' Gormán muttered, unamused. 'Enemies such as he can develop their grudges into blood feuds.'

Abbess Líoch now caught their attention. She was clearly irritated. 'When are we ever going to know why these people have come here?' she demanded. 'They seemed to be speaking in riddles.'

'Let us hope that their objectives will be made clear this evening,' Colgú replied. 'I too am tired of these mysteries.'

'Speaking of this evening,' Fidelma asked, 'is there any news of Beccan's return?'

Colgú sighed. 'I was relying on Beccan to return to take charge of the welcoming feast this evening. Dusk is already approaching now, so it's too late to send someone searching for him.'

'Since he has not returned, who will take charge?' Fidelma asked.

'Gormán will have to take over ceremonial duties during the feast. The lot of overseeing the preparation and serving of the food will fall to Dar Luga. There must be music and some entertainment. We would not want to show our guests that we do not know how to entertain strangers.'

'Of course, we must show hospitality according to law,' Fidelma agreed. In the household of every king and prince within the Five Kingdoms was a band of musicians who were assigned to provide entertainment, especially for feasting. And among them were trumpeters, who would play on their assortment of horns and trumpets as a mark of honour for distinguished visitors.

'When our guests enter,' said the King, 'the trumpeters must be ready to greet them in traditional form.'

'What of the music to be played during the feast?' asked Gormán, taking his duties seriously.

'I'll leave you to speak to the musicians, Gormán,' Colgú said. 'The music must not be raucous, nor should it be of the kind that sends one to sleep. Tell them to play pieces in the *gan-traige* style.'

Gan-traige was a form of music that incited merriment and laughter

– infectious, happy melodies that would hopefully counter-balance the unfriendly atmosphere that the visitors had so far provoked.

'We should also have a few ballads after the meal,' Abbot Ségdae suggested. 'That will prevent the conversation from becoming too introspective. I heard your bard – what's his name? – playing his *cruit* the other day and singing the praises of your victory at Cnoc Áine over the Uí Fidgente.'

The *cruit* was a small eight-stringed harp on which poets would accompany themselves as they sang their poems and ballads.

Colgú met Gormán's eye. 'See to it, but suggest a subject less controversial than the Uí Fidgente plot. What of the one about the Blessed Ailbhe? There is a ballad about him being saved by a she-wolf when he was abandoned as a baby by his father. That will surely appeal to our distinguished religious guests.'

'It is certainly a good ballad to distract our guests with,' Abbot Ségdae said approvingly.

Abbess Líoch was still looking unhappy, as were both Sister Dianaimh and Brother Madagan. It was the abbess who brought them back to the main subject.

'It's all very well to divert these people with entertainment – but what do they *want*? They have not even indicated why they have come here. And why here, out of all the Five Kingdoms? That's what I'd like to know.'

'Líoch does have a point,' Fidelma told her brother. 'Since we have heard of their coming, we have witnessed many inexplicable happenings. Are those events connected with the purpose of their visit?'

'I cannot extract information if the strangers are not willing to give it,' Colgú replied defensively. 'Tell me a means of doing so, and I will do it.'

'The means will present itself tonight,' Abbot Ségdae said in a positive voice. There was a sceptical silence and so he continued: 'I will be the spear-point in the coming conflict. As *comarb*, the successor to the Blessed Ailbhe, therefore abbot and senior bishop in this kingdom, I shall *demand* answers!'

'And if the answers are not supplied?' There was a slight note of derision in Abbess Líoch's voice.

The abbot made an eloquent gesture with his hand. 'Then we have recourse to the law.'

Even Fidelma was confused at this remark. 'I think you had best explain that.'

'There is a movement among some clerics, especially those influenced by Rome, to reject our system of law and replace it with what they call the "Penitentials". A few of our abbeys are introducing them. They are a foreign abomination and I am against them.'

'We can agree in that, but what are you saying?' asked Fidelma.

'In our society, an abbot or bishop has no more rights under our law than a secular lord. He is constrained by the law. If he misbehaves, his *tuath*, the people, can impeach him. He must be heard before a gathering of the *derbhfhine* of the abbey, who are considered his family. If found guilty of misconduct under the law, they can dismiss him and elect a new abbot or bishop.' He addressed Abbess Líoch: 'And of course, the same law applies to the abbesses and their houses.'

He paused again for a moment, in order to gather up his arguments. 'All clerics of high rank have equal rights to provincial kings and are treated equally. I am an Eóghanacht and my honour price under law is fourteen *cumals*.'

Fidelma was shaking her head. 'I still do not understand. How does this mean that we might be able to force the strangers to tell us why they are here? What recourse to law are you suggesting?'

'There is a text in the *Bretha Nemed toísech* pointing out that a cleric is called upon to give *dagfolad* or consideration to society. If he refuses consideration, then he must face the consequences.'

Fidelma's eyes suddenly lit up as she began to see the point he was developing.

'The *Córus Béscnai* speaks of the consequences of the wrongdoing of clerics, even abbots and bishops. They can be treated like any other wrong-doer,' she said slowly.

Abbot Ségdae was smiling triumphantly. 'Do not the ancient annals tell us that even high-ranking churchmen can be taken as hostages and have their rights stripped from them, be confined to the territory and made to work for the good of the community?'

Colgú leaned forward nervously in his chair.

'Now wait. Are you suggesting that we have Gormán and his warriors here take Verax and Arwald as prisoners? Surely that would produce outrage in their own lands, and the next thing would be that foreign armies would land on our shores and we would have to contend with them. That is something I do *not* want to see!'

Fidelma was chuckling reassuringly. 'With God's help, neither shall you, brother. What Abbot Ségdae is talking about is only the *threat* that this could be done – while not making the threat a reality. It is a bluff that, should there be further prevarication, we can use by simply pointing out our system of law. Why,' she warmed to the idea, 'a few years ago, the Council of Brehons even passed an amendment to the laws, speaking of the punishment which should be imposed on a bishop who stumbles in the performance of his duties and obligations to the community.'

'Very well, how do we confront people like the Venerable Verax and Bishop Arwald?' Colgú wanted to know. 'How do you wrap up in diplomatic language the threat that either they tell us what they are doing here or we will simply reduce them to what they call slaves in their own country?'

'I would suggest that the Venerable Verax would be the one to approach in the matter,' advised Fidelma. 'What he decrees, Bishop Arwald, in spite of his arrogance, will obey. So with that in mind, let us wait and see what this evening will bring. Meanwhile, Eadulf and I will retire, for we have much to talk about.'

CHAPTER THIRTEEN

⚭

They were walking back to their chambers across the courtyard when Fidelma stopped abruptly in mid-stride. Eadulf immediately glanced nervously up at the surrounding walls, even though they were some way from the nearest one, in case there was a threat. However, Fidelma had halted because a thought, not a missile, had struck her.

'It just occurred to me that there is an easier way than confrontation to find out what this deputation is really about.'

Eadulf turned to her. 'I thought your original suggestion was the best. The Venerable Verax is the man with authority and he would be the best person to respond to reason.'

'But there might be another way. If you get a chance, have words with the young scribe who accompanies them . . . what's his name?'

'Brother Bosa?'

'Brother Bosa,' confirmed Fidelma. 'He has been keeping very quiet so far. As scribe to Bishop Arwald, he should be able to tell us what is going on.'

Eadulf was doubtful. 'He will obey his masters. If they have told him to say nothing, then doubtless he will say nothing. Anyway, I don't like him.'

'Why not?' Fidelma asked.

'There is something furtive about him.'

To his surprise, Fidelma laughed. 'I swear, husband, you are getting suspicious of religious; first your brother and now this scribe. Religious are not born. They enter the life from all manner of previous lives – even from the role of warrior. Anyway, his response will no doubt depend on the way he is questioned. I feel that he might provide the breach in the wall put up by Verax and Arwald. After all, you are a fellow countryman of his. You still wear the Roman tonsure, for you have not yet completely accepted the rites of our church.'

Eadulf was intrigued in spite of his reservations. 'It might well be a path,' he admitted. 'Do you remember how Arwald thought he recognised me as being at Canterbury a short time ago?'

'We know that was a mistake.'

'It was obvious that he mistook me for my brother, Egric. Superficially, there are similarities. At least it tells us that Arwald knows that Egric came to this kingdom. But why did he say, "in the company of an elderly man", and not the Venerable Victricius?'

'We must keep an open mind and . . .' Fidelma fell silent as she glanced towards the far side of the courtyard. The very person they had been talking about had emerged and was speaking to one of the guards. The warrior was pointing to the chapel, as if to give directions, and Brother Bosa began walking towards it.

'The ideal opportunity, Eadulf.' Fidelma smiled grimly. 'I suggest you follow Brother Bosa to the chapel while I return to our chambers. See what you can find out.'

Eadulf walked slowly towards the chapel and entered. A few lamps shed a shadowy light inside. He paused at the door, peering round in the gloom, trying to locate the figure of the Saxon. He saw him at last at the back of the chapel, kneeling in prayer.

Eadulf waited until it looked as if Brother Bosa had finished his devotions and then made his way towards him. Brother Bosa saw him coming and rose from his knees.

'You looking for me, Brother?' he asked brusquely in their common language.

'I could not help but notice that you act as both translator as well as scribe to this deputation,' Eadulf replied in as friendly tone as he could muster. 'I was wondering how you had such a good command of the language of the Five Kingdoms.'

'I make no secret of it,' replied the other with a shrug. 'I studied at the Abbey of Darú where many of our countrymen have studied. I was there for two years before returning home.'

'And where is home?'

The young scribe did not reply but changed the subject. 'I heard you say that you were from the Kingdom of the East Angles. Do you not find it difficult to live among these strange people? Look at the way the servants seem to think themselves equal to their King. We would have them flogged for such pretensions.'

'It is not the custom here to flog those who attend to our needs.' Eadulf felt his hackles rise. 'Rather, we reward them for their service to us. You should know that, if you have studied here for two years.'

'I did not concern myself with the lives of those outside the abbey. I concentrated on my studies and was glad to leave the country,' replied the other rudely.

'I presume that you are from Magonsaete?' Eadulf asked, trying to keep a calm voice and pursue the information he sought.

'Magonsaete? That backwater? Not I,' declared Brother Bosa, much to Eadulf's surprise. 'I am from the Kingdom of Kent. I am a direct descendant of Wecta, son of Woden. My father was Octha, brother to Eorcenbert.'

Eadulf was even more surprised. Eorcenbert had been a King of Kent and married to Seaxburh, daughter of Anna, King of his own people, the East Angles. Importantly, Eorcenbert was the first king to have been raised as a Christian, and when he had come to power in Kent, he had ordered the destruction of all the ancient gods and goddesses and their priests. He had appointed the first Jutish Archbishop of Canterbury. That had been Frithuwine, who took the Latin name Deusdedit, but who had died of the Yellow Plague.

Brother Bosa obviously took Eadulf's silence for awe and smiled indulgently. 'I am the son of kings and of the oldest kingdom among our people. My father, a pious man, sent me first to Rome for my education and then to Darú, so that I might learn the ways of the barbarians that surround our country.'

Eadulf regarded the young man thoughtfully, ignoring the slight. 'Bishop Arwald is from Magonsaete,' he pointed out.

Brother Bosa flushed in annoyance. 'I have never been to that place,' he said haughtily.

'But you serve Bishop Arwald. Why . . .?' Eadulf was frowning.

'I am of Kent,' snapped Brother Bosa. 'I am from Canterbury and serving in the household of Theodore, the Archbishop, who is also served by Arwald. I serve the Bishop because . . .' He suddenly caught himself as if he was about to reveal something he should not.

'Your master, Bishop Arwald, thought he had seen me before. In fact, he thought he had seen me in Canterbury only a short time ago in the company of an elderly man. Whoever he mistook me for, he said that he had come to this country and was known to have landed at one of the ports in the south.'

When Eadulf paused to allow a comment, Brother Bosa made no response.

'I was wondering why Bishop Arwald thought it was me and how he knew that this person and his elderly companion had come to the Five Kingdoms.'

Brother Bosa hesitated a moment and then, obviously unable to think up some prevarication, he said: 'I also glimpsed this person. He was remarkably like you but, now I look closely at you, he was much younger. While we were at this abbey called Fearna, Bishop Arwald made some enquiries of local merchants, and was told that two people answering the descriptions of those we sought had landed at a sea port to the south not so long ago.'

'So you seek these people!' Eadulf exclaimed. 'Why?'

Brother Bosa seemed hesitant again. 'I could answer, why should that be of interest to you?' he countered.

'If one of these persons looks so like me,' replied Eadulf 'then it is surely of interest.'

'I suppose it would be,' the scribe reflected. 'I cannot enlighten you, however. I can only say that Bishop Arwald was much concerned about them.'

'I suppose you know that the Venerable Verax is brother to the Holy Father?'

Brother Bosa seemed surprised that Eadulf knew, and confined himself to a nod of acknowledgement, before adding: 'I serve Canterbury and Rome, and therefore it distresses me to be among barbarians who have not accepted the True Faith. You yourself, Brother Eadulf, wear a tonsure of Rome, yet you live among these barbarians and have even married the sister of the King.'

Eadulf's eyes narrowed for a moment. 'And you disapprove?'

Brother Bosa did not appear perturbed at the frowning countenance of Eadulf. If anything, he was growing assertive, leaning forward to tap the other man on the chest with a forefinger.

'You are a religieux, and in spite of conversion to the Faith by clerics from this country, we are told that you went to Rome and declared for her teachings as decided at innumerable councils of her bishops. You represented the true path of Rome at the Great Council of Streonshalh against the false doctrines of the Church of Columba.'

'Therefore?' Eadulf's voice was quietly ominous.

'You have been seduced; married to a foreigner. A religieux should be celibate.'

Eadulf raised an eyebrow. 'Ah, so you are an advocate of celibacy among the religious?'

'There is no other path to follow but that of the True Faith. It is wrong for anyone in the religious to marry and have children.'

Smiling complacently, the young scribe did not notice the tightening of the muscles of Eadulf's features.

Eadulf completely forgot that the scribe had neatly deflected him from the purpose of his questions. He said icily, 'You are now in the Kingdom of Muman, Brother Bosa; in the Land of the Five Kingdoms which hold an allegiance to a High King who resides in the Middle Kingdom. All the kingdoms follow the same laws and practices and religious concepts. You would be well advised not to express the opinion that their liturgy is a false doctrine. Remember, it is Rome which, through its many councils and debates, has departed from what was originally taught when the Faith first came to this land. Here, they regard the liturgy and doctrines now followed in Rome as the deviant ones; ones rejecting the original teachings of the Faith.'

'That is nonsense!'

'Nonsense or not, not even the Bishop of Rome and his council have declared against marriage among the religious. So be aware of where you are.'

'What do you mean?'

'Have you ever read the works of Aurelius Ambrosius, a man from Gaul who became Bishop of Mediolanum, a city situated, so I am told, to the north of Rome?'

Brother Bosa was puzzled. 'I have never read his work.'

'There are two lines of advice given by him that you may well consider. *Quando hic sum, non jejuno Sabbato; quando Romae sum, jejuno Sabboto.*'

Brother Bosa thought for a moment and then translated: 'When I'm here, I do not fast on Saturday; when I'm in Rome, I fast on Saturday. What does that mean?'

'In other words, Brother Bosa, follow the customs of where you are and do not try to impose your own.'

'What if I know that I speak the truth? Am I to remain silent?'

'Ensure that your truth will not offend another's truth before uttering it!'

'And you take offence because I do not believe that you have followed the right path of the Faith in marrying yourself to a foreigner in order to gain favour with these people?'

Eadulf fought once more to restrain a surge of angry emotion. He was thinking of the attitude of his brother, Egric. 'It did not happen like that. Besides, nowhere in Christendom is this idea of celibacy mandatory for those in religious life. Even the apostles were married, for did not Christ cure the mother of Peter's wife? Did not Paul write to Timothy at Ephesus, accepting marriage among the church fathers but saying that bishops should only take one wife for there are some societies where there can be a plurality of wives?'

Brother Bosa bent forward, eyes fierce. 'Paul also wrote to the Christians at Corinth pointing out that the unmarried religious care for the Lord's business and devote their life to pleasing the Lord; but the married men and women care only for worldly things, aiming to please their wives or husbands and gain security through personal wealth.'

'Indeed, he did,' agreed Eadulf. 'He also explained that this was his personal view – which he did not impose on anyone else. There was no compulsion and people were in complete control of their own choices.'

'I have read, in the sacred texts, that the disciples asked Christ if it was better not to marry, and He said that His followers should renounce marriage for the sake of achieving the Kingdom of Heaven.'

'Return to the text, Brother Bosa, which is in the Gospel of Matthew,' Eadulf counselled. 'The words of Christ are very clear. He was speaking generally when he said some are incapable of marriage because they are born so. Others might decide to renounce marriage to devote their time to the sake of the Kingdom of Heaven. Nowhere does the Christ say that they *must* do so.'

'More and more, the churches are realising that you cannot serve the needs of the faithful while being distracted by the needs of your own family. It was one of the canons agreed by the bishops and priests meeting at the Great Council of Elvira,' Brother Bosa argued stubbornly.

'The Council of Elvira, three centuries ago, was the first Christian council in Iberia, limited only to a few local bishops and priests. Their declaration had no authority anywhere else. And don't tell me that the first council of bishops in western Christendom – that of Arles in Gaul – also declared for celibacy a few years after Elvira!'

'They did so,' affirmed the young scribe enthusiastically. 'Over forty-three bishops from churches in the west of the Roman Empire confirmed the decisions made at Elvira, including celibacy. We should stand by the edicts of Elvira.'

'Then, dear Brother Bosa,' Eadulf said coldly, 'I suggest that your party, being here, stand in peril of breaking those very edicts.'

Brother Bosa stared at him without comprehension.

'Canon nineteen of Elvira states that bishops, priests and deacons must not leave their churches to engage in other business, and must not go into foreign provinces.' Eadulf wasn't sure he had the detail correct but it was a vague memory. Brother Bosa's expression was suddenly nervous.

'We did not come here to . . .' he began, and then suddenly paused.

'Why did you come?' Eadulf tried to press the point. 'None of you appear willing to tell us.'

'It was not to be persuaded by outdated concepts already overturned at the Council of Arles,' snapped the young scribe.

'Arles was called by Constantine, the Roman Emperor, only to deal with the Donatists who were opposed to state interference in religious affairs. And many of the decisions at Arles were never accepted throughout Christendom,' sighed Eadulf, aware that he had missed the opportunity to press for the motive behind the deputation.

'But Pope Siricius declared that bishops and priests should no longer be cohabiting with their wives,' the scribe droned on.

'Dear Brother Bosa.' Eadulf smiled wearily. 'I can see that you have been converted to this concept. Thankfully, such an unnatural course between men and women is certainly not doctrine. The idea that you cannot involve yourself in the New Faith without becoming a self-imposed eunuch goes against creation, which surely must be an insult to the Godhead Whom we accept as creating it. It is not marriage that is an anathema to the Faith, but gratuitous sexual congress. It is this which breeds abuse among people. Comfort and support of men and women in vows of fidelity with one another is the natural succession of God's principle of human creation. And now,' he turned abruptly, 'I think we have spent enough time on this matter.'

He was frustrated at being led aside from his purpose by a debate on celibacy. He had come no nearer to finding out the purpose of this curious deputation at Cashel except . . . except that he was certain that there was a connection with his brother's unexpected arrival and the murder of the Venerable Victricius. He suddenly decided to test whether the name would provoke a reaction from the young scribe. He turned back.

'One more question, since you come from Canterbury. Did you ever meet the Venerable Victricius of Palestrina there?'

Brother Bosa's reaction was immediate. 'The *Venerable* Victricius?' he gasped.

'So you do know him?'

Brother Bosa was staring at him with suspicion moulding his features. 'Is he here?' he demanded slowly, adding: 'He was the elderly man mentioned by Bishop Arwald.'

Eadulf decided to stick to the truth. 'We had a report that such a man was attacked and killed on the river just south of here.'

'Who attacked him?' demanded the scribe in a fierce tone.

'Bandits,' replied Eadulf.

'Bandits?' There was dismay in his expression. 'He was robbed? Were his belongings taken?'

'The bandits took what they did not destroy,' Eadulf said, being frugal with the truth. 'You knew him then? We understood he was a senior cleric from Canterbury.'

Eadulf was not prepared for the man's next response. Brother Bosa began to chuckle and then quickly regained his composure. 'I knew of a man named Victricius in Canterbury, but he was neither a senior cleric nor anyone who would be entitled to such a prefix to his name. I am not even sure he was entitled to the name Victricius either.'

Eadulf tried to suppress the uneasiness that was welling in him. 'Who was he then, this Venerable Victricius?' he asked quietly.

'I suppose he could pass as a "venerable",' sneered Brother Bosa. 'He was old enough. When I saw him in Canterbury, he was tied to a whipping post and being flogged.'

'What had he done?' Eadulf closed his eyes for a moment, remembering Gormán's description of the healed lacerations on the back of the corpse.

'When I saw him he also wore a tonsure – the tonsure of Rome. He was passing himself off as a religious. I doubt that he was one. He was certainly a thief. He had stolen gold and silver plate from the new Abbey of Menstre – and was lucky not to be hanged. He was saved because he managed to convince the Princess that he was a Roman.'

'Menstre? Princess?' Eadulf was unable to hide his ignorance.

'Last year, the Princess Domneva, of the Royal House of Kent, became abbess of a foundation that she set up near Ypwines fleot, which is now called Menstre, the monastery. She caught this thief and sent him to Egbert at Canterbury for punishment. He was a thief, not a "venerable" of the Church. Are you sure that he and his party are dead? Are you quite certain that his belongings were stolen?'

The eagerness in the scribe's voice put Eadulf on the alert.

'I am told that a band of outlaws attacked the boat he had hired to bring him upriver. His boatmen were killed and his belongings were taken or destroyed.' Eadulf made no reference to Egric.

* * *

Returning to his chambers, Eadulf had barely finished relating the conversation to Fidelma when there was a tap on their door and one of the King's young attendants stood framed quivering in the portal.

'The King requests your immediate attendance in his council chamber,' the young boy intoned breathlessly to Fidelma.

'My attendance?' asked Fidelma.

'Both of you, lady, if it please you,' the boy stammered, before turning and hurrying off.

Fidelma and Eadulf exchanged a glance.

'Now what?' Eadulf wondered.

When they reached Colgú's council chamber, they found not only the King but Abbot Ségdae with Brother Madagan. Gormán was on guard outside the doors and showed them in.

Colgú glanced up with relief as they entered. 'I have need of both your talents,' he greeted them shortly.

'What has suddenly caused this?' Fidelma asked, taking the seat her brother had indicated.

'It seems our friend Eadulf has spoken to Brother Bosa and prompted a response from the Venerable Verax.'

'I have?' Eadulf was startled.

'As I understand it, you were trying to find out some information from Brother Bosa.' Colgú raised his hand as Eadulf was about to justify himself. 'Brother Bosa must have passed this on to his masters. So I think your questions have produced a result.'

Fidelma bent close to Eadulf: 'I suspect it was your news about Victricius,' she whispered.

'The Venerable Verax has sent a message to me saying he now appreciates our concerns at wanting to know the purpose of this visit,' Colgú said. 'He is prepared to explain things.'

'He is *prepared*?' Abbot Ségdae echoed disdainfully.

'He has offered to go through it before the meal begins, for a welcome feast would not be the correct place to discuss such matters. He has said that he personally will explain it to me and my bishop, meaning Ségdae here and his steward. I have said that I cannot accept this unless my legal adviser and my adviser on the Saxon matters are also in attendance. That is you, Fidelma, and Eadulf.'

'He agreed?' asked Fidelma with surprise.

'He agreed,' confirmed her brother.

'Then by all means, let us hear what the Venerable Verax has to say,' Fidelma urged. 'Then we can alleviate some of the tension for tonight.'

Gormán was sent to inform the Venerable Verax that they were ready. The warrior left and returned in hardly any time, escorting the austere figure of the Venerable Verax of Segni. The prelate's glance encompassed the assembly before coming to rest on the face of the King.

'You may be seated, Venerable Verax.' Colgú motioned to a chair. 'You have come to volunteer the reasons why your party has come here to Cashel?'

'I have, and you will pardon our initial reticence as we are strangers in a strange land and were much perturbed by the killing of our emissary, Brother Cerdic, while under your protection in this palace.'

Colgú shifted uncomfortably. 'I have assured you that this death is being investigated and when the culprit is found, they will be subject to our laws and punishment.'

'I now understand this.'

'So, what is the purpose of your coming here?'

The Venerable Verax considered for a moment. 'Let me tell you in my own way.'

'Then let us all be seated,' the King invited with a gesture of his hand.

After everyone was seated, the Venerable Verax leaned back and cleared his throat for a moment. 'There have, as you know, been many problems in Christendom. One of these problems concerns the spreading of the true word of the Faith to the far reaches of the earth. Certain people believe that they alone have the true interpretation of that word.'

Abbot Sédgae spoke up at this point to say: 'So far as we know, Rome has held many councils at which new interpretations of the Faith and new teachings have been offered. We here, in the west, maintain the Faith as it was originally brought to us.'

The Venerable Verax was equal to this. 'The Faith was first brought to you by whom? I can name a dozen different interpretations that were being taught – Donatism, Pelagianism, Iconoclasm, Priscillianism, Arianism . . . Oh, the list is endless. It is Rome's ambition that all these different interpretations may one day be united.'

'Under Rome,' muttered Abbot Ségdae, quietly but audibly, 'And how will Rome succeed in this? There are many who claim to be of the Faith, who believe in the teachings of Jesus. Yet some say he was just a man who adopted the title "Son of God", meaning that we are *all* the children of God.'

'That teaching was condemned by the Council of Antioch many years ago,' stated the Venerable Verax.

'Then there are many who say that they believe Jesus was a man – but that his soul was divine.'

'And *that* was condemned by the Council at Constantinople.'

'Arius claimed that the title "Son of God" was merely a courtesy.'

'Arian has also been condemned,' sighed the Venerable Verax. 'Many coming to the Faith have not been able to understand how Jesus could be both human *and* divine.'

'At the moment, Rome accepts that Jesus had two natures but one will.' Abbot Ségdae spoke out clearly.

'My brother, the Bishop of Rome, like many of us, is working towards changing that mistaken teaching as well.'

'With respect, these arguments are subjects for the scholars of the Faith to debate,' Colgú intervened. 'Such arguments are surely not your purpose in coming here. Let it suffice to acknowledge that the Faith is not united and never has been. When it was first brought to this island, we were told that Jesus was fully divine; soon afterwards, we began to hear that not everyone – even in Rome – accepted that. Such debates are held regularly to consider this interpretation or another one.'

'And now we must change,' Venerable Verax said aloofly.

'And you are here to preach that new change?' Colgú asked, perplexed.

The elderly prelate hesitated and shook his head.

'We are informed that this island contains Five Kingdoms. In these kingdoms, I am told, are many bishops. Bishops like yourself, Ségdae of Imleach. Each bishop seeks power over his territory.'

Abbot Ségdae glanced at Colgú before responding. 'We do not see it in those terms,' he said. 'I have already told you that abbots are more powerful than a bishop, for the kings and princes of the territory grant lands to the abbeys, and the abbots and abbesses are often of the same royal blood as those kings and princes. The abbots and abbesses are elected to their office by their *derbhfine* – that is, the family within the abbeys. Among us, sons often succeed family members, but *only* if they are worthy. Daughters become abbesses in place of their mothers. We believe in the family.'

The Venerable Verax grimaced, not trying to hide his distaste. 'Many of us believe that only in celibacy can we of the Faith serve God completely and without distraction.'

'A curious notion, but we will not debate it. We find Rome often preaches many notions that are alien to our understanding of life,' Fidelma said briskly. 'I believe Brother Eadulf has discussed that very topic with your Brother Bosa.'

Abbot Ségdae saw an opportunity to speak on a favourite subject. 'Here, we believe that men and woman are responsible for all their acts – whether they be good or evil. We are all capable of redemption. Yet I have heard that Rome now believes in the teaching of Augustine of Hippo, who declared that the original sin of Adam and Eve, at the beginning of time, tainted human nature, and from that time we were all condemned, each and every one of us. Only God knew who He would consign to Heaven or to Hell. Rome believes that no matter what a person does in their life, no matter how good *or* how evil, they are already condemned. We find that a curious and disturbing belief.'

The Venerable Verax's face had become blotched with red. 'We know that you are misled by the teachings of Pelagius. His heresy has long been declared at Rome.'

'Pelagius, in stating that we are all capable of choosing between good and evil and saving our own souls, was merely echoing what we all believe. Augustine's teaching imperils moral law, and, above all things, we believe in law in this land. If we follow his logic then we have permission to indulge freely in evil because, whatever crimes we commit, Augustine says that we have no chance of redemption, or choice between Heaven and Hell. It has already been decided.'

'God has infinite knowledge. Whatever we do, our future is ordained. Pelagius has been condemned,' burst out the Venerable Verax.

'Zosimus, Bishop of Rome, supported Pelagius – but when Augustine and his friends applied political pressure, he was *forced* to declare Pelagius' teachings heretical,' Abbot Ségdae replied steadily.

'Indeed, his teachings were declared heretical – but here in these western fastnesses you still cling to his heresy!' The elderly prelate was getting really angry now.

Colgú himself was also clearly annoyed with the direction of the exchange. 'I was not aware that I had called another council to discuss aspects of the Faith. I repeat: is this why you are here, Venerable Verax? If so, a proper council should have been summoned by the abbots and bishops involved. This is a matter for ecclesiastics and not for kings.'

Venerable Verax collected himself and said more calmly, 'My apologies. The Bishop of Rome is concerned that these western reaches are without a strong guidance as to the Faith. He was inclined to support the argument that the Archbishop of Canterbury might extend his authority over all the abbots and bishops of this island in order to secure some form of religious conformity. The reason we are here is to gather information as to whether that would be acceptable, or whether there is some alternative.'

The silent response was one of astonishment at the suggestion. Then Abbot Ségdae said slowly: 'There are too many differences in the paths chosen by our churches and among our people to take that proposition seriously.'

Even Eadulf was utterly surprised at the suggestion and felt he should contribute. 'Canterbury does not even exert religious authority over all the kingdoms of the Angles and Saxons,' he spoke up, 'let alone the kingdoms of the Britons in the west and the kingdoms of the Cruthin and Dál Riadans in the north. The Bishop of Rome is either not well informed or has been misled by his advisers.'

A look of annoyance crossed the Venerable Verax's features. He seemed about to say something in retort but then smiled thinly and said, 'What is the purpose of seeking information, other than to see how such a proposal would be received?'

'And this is why you are here?' Colgú demanded, still disbelieving. 'To see how we would react to such a proposal? Then you can be assured that we, in the Kingdom of Muman, would be united *against* any such idea. I am sure that you will have heard similar opposition when you were in the Kingdom of Laighin.'

'Yet we have also heard that there are some prelates of these kingdoms who wish to see an Archbishop preside over all the abbots and bishops here,' replied Venerable Verax.

Abbot Ségdae grunted, and said dismissively, 'We are aware that for some time the abbots at Ard Macha have tried to claim themselves to be the heirs of Patricius, and further, claim that he was the first to preach the Faith among the Five Kingdoms. Therefore, they argue they should be senior in rank to all other cleries on this island.'

'And you disagree with that?'

'As we told you before, you will find few who agree. It is a fact that the Bishop of Rome sent Patricius here as his bishop to those who had *already* been converted to the Faith. Moreover, he was sent here to argue against what Rome saw as the heretical teachings of Pelagius, which we had accepted. There were many teachers of the Faith here before Patricius the Briton – even the emissary from Rome, Palladius, who our friends in Ard Macha would prefer to wipe out of history.'

'So you would not agree that the abbots or bishops of Ard Macha have an historic right to be Archbishops over all these kingdoms?'

'Certainly not. Ségéne, the current Abbot of Ard Macha,' Abbot Ségdae carefully emphasised the correct title, 'is even opposed by the Abbot of Dún Lethglaisse, for it was there that the same Patricius the Briton lived, died and is buried.'

'So who would you claim to be senior among the churches?' pressed the Venerable Verax.

'Here in Muman we have had several teachers of the Faith who taught and established their abbeys in the south before Patricius the Briton arrived in the northern kingdoms. I, for example, am the *comarb*, the successor of the Blessed Ailbhe of Imleach; then there was Ciarán of Saighir; Declán of Ard Mór; Abbán of Magh Arnaide; Fiacc established the abbey of Slèibhte before Patricius visited him there; even Ibar set up his community on the island of Beg Ériu in Laighin long before Patricius.'

'Are you saying that these abbeys would claim precedence over Ard Macha?'

'It is long known that Imleach has been regarded as the first and most senior abbey in the south of this island. It is accepted in our Kingdom of Muman.' Colgú spoke deliberately in support of his Chief Bishop as it seemed that Abbot Ségdae was taking the brunt of the debate with the Roman prelate.

'If you had asked these same questions in the Kingdom of Laighin, on your way here, I think you would have received similar answers,' confirmed Fidelma.

The Venerable Verax turned to her. 'Ah yes . . ., you were formerly

Sister Fidelma and dwelled some time among the religious at Cill Dara. I am told that is in the Kingdom of Laighin?'

'I was there until I decided to serve my brother in my capacity as an advocate of our laws.'

'I heard that you left the abbey, after having disagreed with the abbess? Abbess Ita, wasn't it?' mused the Venerable Verax.

Fidelma made no reply, remembering the crimes of the abbess from which she had walked away, rather than expose her as a thief and murderess. Soon after, Abbess Ita had left and disappeared on some missionary cause beyond the shores of Laighin.

'Abbot Moling, who is Chief Bishop of Laighin, told me Cill Dara also claims to have precedence over all the other religious houses because it was established by the Blessed Brigit,' went on the Venerable Verax. 'That would never be countenanced by Rome.'

'Why so?' Fidelma asked.

'Because Cill Dara is a . . . what do you call a mixed house of men and women and their children? There is both an abbess and an abbot. I am told that Abbot Máel Dobarchon is currently answerable to Abbess Gnáthnat who is regarded as the true successor of the Blessed Brigit. Now that would make the senior cleric in these kingdoms a woman. That is a preposterous idea!'

'To your way of thinking,' Fidelma responded spiritedly.

'So who else could come forward to claim the Archbishop's title in the Five Kingdoms?' the Venerable Verax asked.

Abbot Ségdae turned to his steward, Brother Madagan, who had been silent. The steward cleared his throat as he realised he was expected to answer the question.

'I would presume that Abbot Colmán Cass of Cluain Mic Nois, where many of the kings of that place are buried. They would have as much right as any. But if you are here to discover who has the better claim to be Archbishop over all the Five Kingdoms, then you will have a hard task.

In spite of what the abbots of Ard Macha have written to Rome – for we know they have already done so – there are many among all Five Kingdoms who would dispute their claim.'

The Venerable Verax considered the matter. 'But rising from such disputes, you might say that there are some bishops or abbots here who would give much to show that they were endowed with the blessing of such an office by the Bishop of Rome himself?' The question was directed at Abbot Ségdae.

'I am not sure that any abbot of the Five Kingdoms would consider it necessary,' Abbot Ségdae replied with a brief smile. 'The Bishop of Rome is recognised as senior bishop of the Faith as a courtesy, for it was in Rome, so we are told, that the foundations of the Faith were laid and from where the teachings spread through the world.'

'But you would agree that such recognition by Rome would be valuable to support such a claim?'

Abbot Ségdae shrugged. 'I suppose it would be considered worth something. However, at the moment it is only Abbot Ségéne of Ard Macha who seems intent on getting recognition from Rome of such a title. For the rest of us, what is more meaningful is being *comarb* – successor – to the first of our blessed teachers.'

The Venerable Verax sat back, nodding thoughtfully. 'But still valuable?' he asked softly.

'Such recognition would influence some,' conceded the abbot.

There was a silence and then the Venerable Verax stood up and inclined his head towards the King. 'The day grows late and I must prepare for this feast and entertainment that you are so kindly providing for our poor inquisitive deputation. Do I have your permission to retire?'

Colgú was looking bewildered. 'So this was the purpose of your delegation? You have come to enquire about our views on whether we would accept an Archbishop from Canterbury or support the establishment of our own Chief Bishop over all the Five Kingdoms?'

'That is our purpose,' agreed the Venerable Verax solemnly.

Colgú waited until the doors had closed behind the prelate before turning to Abbot Ségdae and expressing his mystification. 'I have little under-standing of these arguments, but it seems that these people have made a very long journey simply to engage in an exercise of pointless speculation and argument.'

Eadulf added: 'I am afraid that most of the countless councils summoned by the Church are about silly, small and trivial details. Why, we might even hear of a council meeting to discuss whether Christ owned His own sandals.'

'Well, I for one am glad that the speculation about this strange deputation is over,' Abbot Ségdae commented.

As a murmur of agreement began, it was Fidelma's quiet voice that suddenly caused them to fall silent.

'You forget that one member of this strange deputation was murdered in our chapel here. Was he really killed merely because he was enquiring whether the clergy of the Five Kingdoms wanted a Chief Bishop over them?'

As she and Eadulf crossed the courtyard a short time later, Fidelma was even more forthcoming.

'The Venerable Verax made no mention of Victricius,' she pointed out. 'Yet it was your mention of Victricius that drew him out to make some explan-ation to us. Why? That explanation is not good enough. I believe the Venerable Verax was lying about the purpose of his mission here.'

chapter fourteen

ↄ⌒ↄ

The traditional welcome feast for distinguished guests had been hastily arranged. Dar Luga, the housekeeper, took over the management of the meal while Gormán attended to the protocols of the feasting hall. By the time Fidelma and Eadulf came into the hall, the guests were already arriving and being shown to their places. At a formal meal, everyone was assigned positions according to their rank. The tables were arranged along the walls, with the table for the guests of highest rank placed at the head of the chamber on a raised dais. Here would be seated King Colgú, and, usually, his heir-apparent and his Chief Brehon. However, Finguine, the *tánaiste* or heir-apparent, was absent gathering tributes from outlying territories, and Brehon Aillín had sent a message to the King excusing himself from attending in the circumstances. So Abbot Ségdae, as Chief Bishop of Muman, would sit next to the King on his right side while Fidelma and Eadulf would sit on his left.

Usually Gormán, as commander of the élite bodyguard, would also be seated – but since he had taken on Beccan's role to oversee the feasting, he would have to stand behind the King's chair. Because of his rank and position, he would be the only person allowed in the feasting hall to bear weapons. Ancient law and custom prohibited any other weapons to be carried within.

The visiting guests, the Venerable Verax and Bishop Arwald, were seated at the right hand nearest the top table. Seated behind them, but not at the table, was Brother Bosa who was to act as translator, as neither Verax nor Arwald spoke the language of the country, although they could both converse easily in Latin.

Because of the hurried arrangements, only a few local princes of the kingdom and their ladies were attending. These were princes of the branches of the Eóghanacht families such as Áine, Airthir Chliach, Glendamnach and the Chief of the Múscraige Breogan. They sat with their wives, each before their shields, hung on the wall behind them, and attended by their shield-bearers, who stood respectfully at their left shoulder. There was also a mix of religious: the Abbess Líoch, for example, and some of the local clerics, including old Brother Conchobhar, ranging along the tables to Sister Dianaimh who sat with Brother Madagan. Only one side of the long tables was occupied, for it was a tradition that no one sat directly opposite one another.

Fidelma breathed a sigh of relief as it seemed that Gormán had been able to get the seating protocols right, for any error could lead to a dispute which would be unseemly in front of foreign guests.

There was a sudden blast, followed by two more, as the *fear-stuic*, the trumpeter, blew the traditional signal for the arrival of the King. As the assembly rose, Colgú entered through a curtained portal behind his chair. Gormán, who had no staff of office to thump on the floor, merely stepped forward and called in stentorian tones: 'Give welcome to Colgú, son of Failbhe Flann son of Áedo Dubh, fifty-ninth in generation descent to Eibhear Fionn, son of Milidh, Milesius the warrior, who brought the Children of the Gael to this land and who subdued the Goddesses of Sovereignty – Éire, Banba and Fodhla. Colgú, descendant of Eóghan Mór, the progenitor of the great clan of the Eóghanacht, whose descendant Corc set up his citadel on this blessed Rock, the fortress of this Kingdom of Muman. Give welcome to Colgú, undisputed King of the Five Territories of Muman.'

Eadulf cast a surprised glance at Fidelma because usually Colgú had little time for such ritual and had been known several times to stop his steward from reciting the full rite. He had even known Colgú to halt the bards singing the traditional *forsundud* or ancestral praise poems in his presence. 'It is no use praising me for my ancestors,' he would say. 'I would rather the bards recognise me for what I do rather than what my fathers did.' However, Fidelma, who usually shared her brother's irritation on such matters, was sitting with a solemn expression. Looking across to where the Venerable Verax and Bishop Arwald were seated, Eadulf realised that Colgú was allowing this ritual for their benefit. He could see Brother Bosa struggling to explain what was going on.

When it was over, Colgú raised his goblet. 'I bid you all welcome this night. Health to the men – and may the women live forever!' It was the ancient toast, and those of the assembly who understood it responded in kind.

At the end of the hall, at a signal from Gormán, a group of musicians began to play soft music while the doors opened and a line of attendants entered with a variety of freshly cooked dishes, from venison and mutton to roasted boar; to dishes of goose eggs, sausages, and assorted vegetables: from cabbages spiced with wild garlic to leeks and onions cooked in butter – all served with an assortment of drinks: some wines imported from Gaul, but mainly cider, especially *nenadmin*, made from wild crabapples.

As feastings went, it was not one of the best Eadulf had attended. Even Fidelma was subdued and when he looked, Eadulf saw her gaze was fastened moodily on their guests. The table conversation was sporadic. There seemed no lightness to it, in spite of the best efforts of the musicians to introduce some note of levity by the choice of their compositions. Matters eased somewhat when Colgú rose and indicated that the guests should circulate and chat to one another. Eadulf suddenly found himself being confronted by Bishop Arwald.

'Well, Brother Eadulf, it seems I was misinformed about you being in Canterbury recently. I apologise.'

'As I told you, it is many years since I was there.'

'I believe that you know much about this kingdom?'

'As much as a foreigner can learn in the years that I have been here,' Eadulf conceded.

'Yet you have a unique role, being related by marriage to the King.'

'It has led to certain privileges,' Eadulf acknowledged diffidently. 'As well as certain disadvantages.'

'But you have come to know the leading members of the nobility here?'

'Some of them. Why do you ask?'

'For example, you must know Abbot Ségdae well?'

'Of course.'

'I am told that he maintains that his church was founded before the Blessed Patricius brought the Faith here.'

'That is the history among the people here. The Abbey at Imleach was founded by Ailbhe, son of Olcnais of the Araid Cliach. It is said that a bishop from Rome named Palladius was sent to propagate the Faith here, and it was he who baptised Ailbhe into the New Faith – and that was many years before Patricius arrived. Ségdae is Ailbhe's successor, chosen and elected by the people of the abbey who are regarded in legal terms as his family.'

'But I am told that he is also related to the ruling family – so is he related to King Colgú?' asked Bishop Arwald.

'He is. That is usually the way it works in this country,' said Eadulf.

'So there would be resentment in this kingdom against the claims of Ard Macha to be the senior church here, on the basis that it is in a different kingdom?'

'Naturally. It is not the first time that such resentment has boiled over among the leading churches of each of the Five Kingdoms.'

'But there is a High King who rules over all the Five Kingdoms. Doesn't he control the petty-kings?'

'The High King is High King mainly out of courtesy. Governing power is retained by the provincial Kings, who then agree who will be High King.'

'But the son of a High King becomes High King, surely?'

'Kingship does not work here like it does among your people. Here, a King is elected by three generations of his family – the *derbhfine* – and chosen because he is best qualified to undertake the task.'

Bishop Arwald gave a puzzled shake of his head. 'A strange custom. But I was wondering whether Abbot Ségdae had ever thought to make representations to Rome for recognition of his abbey, as he says it pre-dates that of Ard Macha?'

Eadulf was amused. 'You should ask Abbot Ségdae, as he stands but a short distance away,' he said, nodding to where the abbot stood in the feasting hall. 'But I would doubt that he is interested in what Rome thinks.'

'Why would that be?' Bishop Arwald reared up.

'Most of the churches of the Five Kingdoms see themselves as independent of any distant authority, either from Rome, Constantinople, or Alexandria. People here are not concerned with this idea of having a Chief Bishop.'

Bishop Arwald raised his eyebrows. 'But I know even the Britons and the Irish have recognised the authority of Rome.'

Eadulf found it interesting that Bishop Arwald was going over the same ground as the Venerable Verax.

'There is a difference between recognising Rome as having a special place in the propagation of the Faith and in accepting that it has authority over all things. You already know that the Five Kingdoms have often rejected the attempts by Rome to dictate rules and even laws; these laws are called Penitentials. Now some of the short-sighted abbots are accepting them and coming into conflict with the native laws here . . .'

'Ah yes. I believe that you can talk of these laws from knowledge. I find it amazing – as should you, being from the Kingdom of the East Angles – that a mere woman can go around questioning, judging and pronouncing the law.'

Eadulf's eyes narrowed. 'You mean my wife?'

'I mean any woman who is a lawgiver in this strange land. However, let us return to our friend Abbot Ségdae. Do you maintain that he would not wish to seek Rome's favour to be considered as Senior Bishop in all these kingdoms?'

'I cannot speak for Abbot Ségdae, but I would find it unlikely.'

'You don't think he would be interested in achieving the rank of Archbishop – Senior Bishop over all the bishops of these kingdoms – and acquiring some symbol to show it? Perhaps he might even *pay* for such a token . . . even from Rome?'

Eadulf examined Bishop Arwald suspiciously. 'What are you suggesting?'

Bishop Arwald immediately backed down. 'I suggest nothing. I am trying to ascertain how serious the bishops in this land are about this matter of the role of an Archbishop.'

'I think that if you wish to seek any more information, you should put your questions directly to Abbot Ségdae,' Eadulf replied coldly.

'I do not wish to offend you, Brother. As an Angle in this strange kingdom you have a unique position to tell me what people feel without my confronting them and causing them insult where no insult was intended. Please accept my apologies if you felt otherwise.'

Eadulf hesitated; being apologetic was not a natural trait of this man. Then he shrugged. 'So long as you understand that people set high store by frankness.'

'Then I thank you for *your* frankness, Brother Eadulf.'

Bishop Arwald turned and made his way towards a group surrounding Abbess Líoch. Eadulf stared after him for a moment before finding

Sister Dianaimh at his elbow. She was also staring bleakly after the bishop.

'You don't like our guest?' Eadulf ventured, interpreting her scowl.

The girl started. 'Does it show that much?'

'It does.'

Sister Dianaimh sighed. 'Then there is no use denying it.'

'Any particular reason?'

'I did not enjoy my time in the Abbey of Laestingau. I don't like the men of Mercia that I encountered.'

'Is that all?'

'What else should there be?'

'Why did you go to Oswy's Kingdom? Were you Abbess Líoch's companion then?'

The girl shook her head. 'I only met her when I went to Laestingau. That was after the Great Debate at Streonshalh at which I understand you and Fidelma were present.'

'What made you go to Laestingau?'

'In spite of the decision of Oswy to follow Rome, which caused many of the missionaries of our land to return home, small bands of teachers continued to go to the kingdoms of the Angles and Saxons, to convert and teach. I was one of a small band.'

'From what abbey did you join them?'

'I served at the Abbey of Sléibhte.'

'Ah yes, I remember. That is beyond Osraige Territory, isn't it?'

'It is in Uí Dróna territory,' confirmed the girl. 'Fiacc, son of MacDara, Prince of the Uí Bairrche, being converted to the New Faith before Patricius came to this land, founded it. The Uí Bairrche once ruled Laighin before the Uí Cennselaig overthrew them.'

'Who is the abbot there now?'

'Aéd of the Uí Bairrche. The abbey is regarded as an Uí Bairrche stronghold; it gets scant recognition from King Fianamail of Laighin who, of course, is descended from the Uí Cennselaig. Therefore, there were tensions there. That was when I decided to join the small band of pilgrims going to Laestingau.'

'And is that where you met Abbess Líoch?'

'Yes, although she was not an abbess then. It was after she returned here and went to Cill Náile that she became Abbess. She asked me to join her and I became her *bann-mhaor*, her female steward.'

Eadulf decided to seize the opportunity to press the question that still puzzled him and Fidelma. 'What I cannot understand is why Brother Cerdic especially asked for Abbess Líoch to attend here. The Venerable Verax tells us that they are only investigating claims for recognition of an Archbishop over the Five Kingdoms. If so, what role would the Abbess of Cill Náile play?'

'I would not know.' The girl looked uncomfortable.

'I presume Cill Náile isn't claiming to be regarded as a primacy?' he joked.

Sister Dainaimh looked startled for a moment and then realised that Eadulf was not serious so did not reply.

At that moment Brother Madagan joined them and made an excuse to draw Sister Dainaimh aside to talk to her while Eadulf went to look for Fidelma. She was seated talking with Abbess Líoch. He wondered if they had made up after their previous argument. Fidelma welcomed him with a smile.

'We were just talking about Brother Cerdic,' she commented, as he obeyed her gesture to sit down.

'What about him?'

'I was telling Fidelma that I am still no wiser as to why he wanted me to come here,' the abbess explained. 'There is nothing that these visitors have raised which is of any interest to me.'

'I must admit that it is strange, if we are to believe what the Venerable Verax tells us is the purpose of this deputation,' Fidelma agreed.

'You have reason not to believe it?' asked the abbess.

'When Brother Cerdic came to Cill Náile to ask you to come here, how exactly did he phrase the request?' Fidelma enquired, ignoring her question.

'Just as I have told you. He said it would "be in my interest" to come.'

'And that was it?'

'Yes. But as I said, I have heard nothing that is in my interest so far.'

'I was speaking to Sister Dianaimh a moment ago,' Eadulf said. 'I had not realised that she had been at Laestingau with you. I wondered whether she had encountered Brother Cerdic before?'

The abbess shook her head quickly. 'No – she would have told me. She came to Laestingau some time after the attack on that abbey. I had not known her before. I think you are aware that she came from the Abbey of Sléibhte?'

Fidelma sighed deeply. 'It is just hard to understand why Brother Cerdic would ask you to come here.'

Eadulf chuckled. 'Well, as I said to Sister Dainaimh, it is not as if Cill Náile would be one of those places to claim authority over all the other abbeys in the Five Kingdoms.'

'A silly idea,' the abbess replied, taking him seriously. 'Our churches are independent; they look to the protection of the kings and princes of the territory, and not to some over-lordship within the religious. Why, that would mean the religious themselves would be creating bishops and abbots who saw themselves as temporal princes. Next thing, they would be raising their own armies to protect their abbeys, which then became fortresses. We would have to start paying tribute to bishops instead of to kings.'

The abbess then excused herself, rose and moved off. Eadulf watched her go with a troubled expression. 'There must have been *some* purpose in the mind of Brother Cerdic,' he observed quietly.

'I saw you talking with Bishop Arwald,' Fidelma remarked. 'Did he say anything further that might cast a light on the matter?'

'He did not. He seemed to want reassurance that Abbot Ségdae was not interested in obtaining approval from Rome for claiming the primacy for Imleach.'

'How curious. I thought Abbot Ségdae had made himself clear earlier.'

'Do I hear my name mentioned?'

They turned to find Abbot Ségdae about to join them. He sat down.

'We were speaking about our strange visitors and their purpose,' explained Fidelma.

'A strange deputation, indeed,' confirmed the abbot. 'I would feel better if I could understand why their emissary, Brother Cerdic, had been killed. That alone makes their mission perplexing.'

Eadulf glanced at Fidelma, wondering whether to mention the links with the attack on the Venerable Victricius and his brother. She had obviously decided the time was not right.

'If I had been charged with such a mission,' continued the abbot, 'I would have gone first to the Kingdom of Midhe, to the seat of the High King himself, and then called a council of the chief bishops of all the Five Kingdoms and let each put forward their arguments. But this seems such a surreptitious means of sounding us all out. First to Laighin, then to Muman – and then where? Presumably to Connachta?'

Eadulf saw a certain expression on Fidelma's face which meant that the abbot had said something of importance. It was a fleeting expression that Eadulf knew well and which perhaps only he could interpret: the droop of the eye, the muscle twitching at the corner of her mouth.

'Deogaire did warn us,' Eadulf smiled, thinking to deflect the topic. 'Remember the night of Cerdic's funeral? You said something to Brother Madagan about the dangers of prophecy.'

Abbot Ségdae actually chuckled. 'My steward claimed to be having dreams. Some silly notion of digging up the tomb of the Blessed Ailbhe who founded our abbey.'

'Brother Madgan is usually such a phlegmatic person,' observed Fidelma. 'For what purpose does he dream of digging up Ailbhe's tomb?

'He said, in his dream, the tomb would reveal that the Abbey of Imleach's destiny was to become the greatest centre of the Faith in the Five Kingdoms. He believed it was a prophecy. After Deogaire's outburst, I remarked to Madagan that soothsayers and prophets are not taken seriously. Ah, I want a word with Bishop Arwald. Excuse me.'

Fidelma turned to Eadulf and motioned him aside, then murmured, 'Talk to the Venerable Verax and try to ask him why he was in Canterbury and what the purpose of his journey was. Would the Bishop of Rome really send his own brother on such a journey to our kingdom, merely to hear gossip? I believe there is a deeper purpose at work and that it has something to do with Canterbury.'

Eadulf raised his eyebrows a little. 'He did start off by asking us what we thought about Theodore of Canterbury extending his religious authority over the Five Kingdoms.'

'That answer would surely be known before the question was asked.'

Eadulf rose and examined the company. The Venerable Verax was in the company of Brother Conchobhar. He grimaced at Fidelma, before making his way over to them. The old physician looked almost relieved as Eadulf approached and it was clear that he was not happy with the conversation he was having with the Roman prelate. As he drew nearer, Eadulf understood why.

'Let now the astrologers, the stargazers, the prognosticators, stand up and save themselves from those things that shall come upon them,' thundered the Venerable Verax, obviously quoting from something. 'That is what is written in the scripture of Isaiah. Behold they shall be as stubble, the fire shall burn them and they shall not deliver themselves from the pain of the flames.'

Eadulf felt sorry for the old physician who, indeed, practised divination from the stars as was common among the people. But Eadulf knew that some in the New Faith were against the ancient science even though the birth of the Christ, according to the scriptures, was foretold by astrologers who then came to pay homage to Him. Eadulf glanced with sympathy at Brother Conchobhar, who mumbled some excuse and left them. Then Eadulf smiled at the Roman cleric.

'And are you finding your visit to this land enlightening, Venerable Verax?'

The old man sniffed disparagingly. 'What went you into the wilderness to see? A man dressed in fine clothes?' he replied, misquoting the text of Matthew. 'I did not expect to find more than I have.'

Eadulf blinked in surprise. 'Do you consider this a wilderness?' he asked, trying to keep the astonishment from his voice.

'Do you not find it so? Oh, I know you have formed an attachment here, but you have been to Rome, lived and studied there. This is a desert by comparison.'

'We could discuss such points but, I hope, with more retention of diplomacy than Bishop Arwald uses,' Eadulf commented.

'I come to bring the Faith and civilisation,' replied the other, oblivious to his tone. 'Diplomacy is a tool to gain trust. I can speak to you, Eadulf, for you are intelligent. I see from your tonsure that you support Rome.'

Eadulf was about to correct Verax's view of him but then he realised the display of good fellowship might be a means to getting the information he was after.

'Rome is certainly a different world,' he agreed.

'I have no illusions when I come among the barbarians,' went on the Venerable Verax affably. 'Do I not remember how the great historian Strabo described how these people were cannibals who thought it an honourable thing to eat their dead fathers. He also wrote that they openly had intercourse with their mothers and sisters.'

Eadulf could not help grinning at this.

'You disagree?' snapped Venerable Verax, seeing his reaction.

'I think you will find that Strabo was misinformed,' Eadulf replied diplomatically. 'Have you seen any such proof of this since you have been here?'

The Venerable Verax shrugged. 'Because I have seen no such proof, it does not mean that such proof does not exist.'

'And you have been here . . . how long?' Eadulf seized the chance.

'We arrived on the half moon of the first quarter – our boatmen took advantage of the neap tide. So now we are in the third quarter.'

'You landed in Laighin, of course. I have been there,' Eadulf confided. 'At which port did you land?'

'It was a port called the height of something or other. I cannot recall.'

'Ard Ladrann,' supplied Eadulf. 'That is a port on the eastern coast of the kingdom. I suppose you travelled directly west to Fearna?'

'We were greeted by the bishop of that place, Bishop Moling, who then escorted us to the King. He is a man much given to airs and graces, as also is the King of this place.'

Eadulf thought he would overlook that remark but come nearer to the point.

'From Canterbury to Ard Ladrann is a long journey,' he said sympathetically. 'You must have been exhausted!'

'Indeed, it was nearly seven days' ride from Canterbury to where we embarked by ship for this country. Truly, it was tiring – but each time we had to stop, members of the brethren gave us hospitality.'

'And before that, it seems you came all the way from Rome! The journey from Rome to Canterbury is not without fatigue and also dangers,' went on Eadulf, dropping his voice. 'I myself have made that very journey to and from Rome twice.'

'Many people have made it,' the Venerable Verax replied airily. 'How much more dangerous was it centuries ago, when Rome's great generals marched their armies to take possession of the island of Britain? They had hostile armies of barbarians to face.'

'I made the journey with Theodore after he was appointed Archbishop by your brother. Then he asked me to come here as an emissary and here I have remained, more or less. How is Archbishop Theodore?'

The Venerable Verax became confidential. 'In health, he is hearty. But many problems oppress him in dealing with the politics of the kingdoms that fall under his authority. That was why—' The old man suddenly pressed his lips together as if he had said too much.

'Was Brother Cerdic in your party when you travelled from Canterbury to Ard Ladrann?' Eadulf asked, pretending not to notice the awkward moment.

The Venerable Verax's eyes narrowed. 'Why do you ask about him?'

'Colgú explained to you that I and Fidelma are trying to resolve the matter of his death. Brother Cerdic arrived here with someone called Brother Rónán, who has now returned to Laighin. I was wondering at what stage he left your party to come on here alone in order to warn us of your arrival?'

The prelate considered the question for a moment. 'Brother Cerdic accompanied Bishop Arwald and myself from Canterbury; so did Brother Bosa. When we arrived in Laighin, we stayed for a time at the Abbey of Fearna and then for a few days at King Fianamail's fortress . . . a place called Dinn Ríg. Brother Cerdic volunteered to come here and prepare the way for us. Brother Rónán was appointed by Bishop Moling to accompany him as his translator and guide.'

'So he was asked to go to Imleach and ask Abbot Ségdae to come here. But why meet here?'

'I was told that Cashel was the seat of the King. It was King Fianamail of Laighin who felt that our enquiries were better discussed in front of the King of each territory.'

'I suppose that there is logic in that,' agreed Eadulf. 'Yet I am told Brother Cerdic also called at the Abbey of Cill Náile and suggested to the abbess that *her* presence was required.'

The Venerable Verax smiled softly. 'Hardly required. But you surprise me. Of course, Bishop Arwald knew that the abbess had been in Oswy's Kingdom for a while and maybe she was known to Brother Cerdic. But we certainly did not *require* her presence.'

'That's interesting. So Brother Cerdic might have known her?'

'That knowledge is beyond me. Why is it of importance?'

'Anything which might help with solving Brother Cerdic's death is worth considering,' Eadulf told him. 'However, I am sorry that this long journey that you have made has been so fruitless and has cost the life of one of your deputation. We will do our best to discover why he met his death, and by whose hand, before you depart.'

'You will have our gratitude, Brother Eadulf,' acknowledged the cleric. 'Well, I have told you all I know. Brother Cerdic left us at Dinn Ríg, the fortress of the King of Laighin, went to Sléibhte and came on here. That's all I can tell you.'

Eadulf had been about to turn away when he realised the extra information that the Venerable Verax had added. 'Did you say that Brother Cerdic went to Sléibhte?'

'I am told there is an old abbey there which he wanted to visit,' agreed the Venerable Verax before giving a nod of his head and moving away.

Eadulf remained a moment or two, locked in thought. Then he returned to Fidelma, who was now in conversation with her brother.

'I was just saying to Fidelma,' Colgú greeted him, 'that after all our expectations, we have found the matter exceedingly boring. I have suggested that our guests rest here another day and then, if they wish to persist with what I believe is a pointless enquiry, they should take the road for the Abbey of Cluain Mic Noise.' He shrugged. 'However, they will be told the same story there as we have told them here. Ard Macha's claims are not recognised by the bishops of the Five Kingdoms. As for accepting the religious jurisdiction of Theodore of Canterbury . . .' He ended in a bark of laughter.

'There is still the matter of the death of Brother Cerdic to be resolved,' Fidelma pointed out.

'Are you still holding Deogaire for the attempt on your lives?' her brother asked. 'Surely we can get a confession from him. Isn't his guilt obvious?'

'That is what is troubling me,' Fidelma said. 'Surely a guilty person would be able to come forward with a better excuse than the one he gave us?'

'The facts should speak for themselves,' her brother maintained.

'But often facts can be seen from a distorted perspective so that they appear entirely contrary to what they really are.'

'I don't quite see what you mean.'

'Perhaps I shall be able to demonstrate the point as time progresses.'

'But there is not too much time, Fidelma. Remember, Brother Cerdic's death occurred in my palace and I am responsible for that death under the law. I will have to pay the Venerable Verax compensation and receive the judgement of fines. That would be a mark against my character. There are many who would be willing to use that against me. Some would even claim that I am not worthy of kingship, and try to unseat me from the throne.'

'You have in mind Brehon Aillín,' Eadulf observed. 'That man could do much to stir malcontents who would use such methods.'

'Just find the killer of Brother Cerdic before the Venerable Verax departs and all else will follow for the good,' Colgú said tightly. 'And now it grows late. I see the Venerable Verax coming this way and I suspect he will be offering his excuses so that he might retire for the night.'

Fidelma drew Eadulf aside as Colgú went to speak with the Roman prelate. 'Did you learn anything from Verax?'

Eadulf shook his head. 'Nothing we did not already know. Although I did gather that Brother Cerdic had been to the Abbey of Sléibhte before he went to Cill Náile and then on to Imleach.'

'Why on earth would he go to Sleibhte?'

'Venerable Verax told me that Brother Cerdic had heard that it was an ancient abbey and simply wanted to take a look at it. The interesting thing is that at Sleibhte they have a claim to be older than Ard Macha, and Sister Dianaimh once studied there.'

Fidelma gave a brief sigh of frustration. 'I wonder if it is true, after all, that this is a means of testing whether Theodore of Canterbury could claim ecclesiastical jurisdiction over these kingdoms as well as the Saxon kingdoms? It just does not feel right.'

'I agree that it seems odd that such a high-ranking person as the Venerable Verax, brother of the Bishop of Rome, should then be sent all this way to test the views of these kingdoms which have already been made perfectly clear to Rome.'

'I cannot help feeling that there are lies being told,' Fidelma said.

'Everywhere there seems to be a wall in front of us.'

'But on a practical level, there is still Beccan to question about Deogaire's story,' Eadulf reminded her. 'Afterwards, I am not sure where we should turn from there. One thing I do agree with you about is that I don't believe this suave prelate from Rome – even if he is the brother to Pope Vitalian.'

CHAPTER FIFTEEN

~꩜~

The morning was dry but a blustery wind and heavy dark clouds promised wet weather to come. Fidelma and Eadulf were taking their morning meal, scarcely speaking to one another as each engaged with their own reflections about the previous evening. When Muirgen entered to clear the table, she said: 'I hear Beccan has returned this morning.'

The announcement caused both of them to look up.

'This morning?' Fidelma glanced towards the window. 'He must have arrived early.'

'I went down to the kitchens to get hot bread and saw him coming through the main gates,' confirmed the elderly nurse.

Fidelma was already rising from the table. 'We should have a word with him at once.' She was at the door when Eadulf, snatching a last piece of bread which he had coated liberally in honey, joined her. They reached the courtyard and were crossing it towards the main building when they encountered Abbess Líoch, hurrying towards the chapel.

'Have you seen my steward?' she asked Fidelma as they came abreast of one another.

'Sister Dianaimh?' Fidelma shook her head. 'We have only just arisen. I am afraid we are up late today.' She peered more closely at the other woman. 'You look worried.'

'It is only that I needed to consult her on something,' the abbess said distractedly. 'She is nowhere to be found.'

'She has probably risen early and is about the palace somewhere. If not, then the guard would tell you whether she has passed through the gates,' Eadulf offered.

'I have already spoken to the guard. She has not left the palace grounds.'

'There are few places in the palace she can have gone,' Fidelma assured her. 'You were on your way to the chapel, weren't you? She might well be there.'

Abbess Líoch did not seem convinced but continued on her way towards the chapel.

'Now,' Eadulf said tightly, 'let's see whether Beccan supports this strange story that Deogaire would have us believe.'

They found the steward, looking contrite, in the palace kitchens. He was speaking with Dar Luga. On seeing them, he immediately approached, wringing his hands.

'I have heard the news, lady. It's my fault. All my fault.' His voice was almost like a child's wail. 'Luan told me – he was on guard at the gates when I arrived.'

Fidelma and Eadulf exchanged a puzzled glance.

'What is your fault, Beccan?' Fidelma asked calmly.

'Being absent at the very time important guests arrive.' He was practically in tears. 'I have told the King that I am ready to take the consequence. I should never have—'

'And have you been told about Deogaire?' interrupted Eadulf. Seeing the steward's baffled look, Fidelma swiftly enlightened him.

'My fault again,' he bleated. 'I should never have allowed Deogaire to use a room in the guest chambers.'

'Calm yourself, Beccan,' Fidelma said, as the man seemed on the verge of hysteria. 'Just tell us – slowly – what happened in relation to Deogaire.'

The punctilious little steward rubbed his face with one hand and paused as if to gather his thoughts. 'Deogaire came to the door of the kitchen last night and asked to see me. He was aware of my position as steward.'

'Of course. You knew him?'

'I knew of his relationship with Brother Conchobhar, the apothecary. And I had seen him about the palace during his current visit.'

'Go on.'

'He told me that he had argued with his uncle and now lacked a bed in the palace. It was too late for him to leave to commence his journey home, so he asked me . . .'

'One moment. Why did he come to you if you did not know him? Why did he not ask anyone else for a place to sleep? Why not go to the inn in the town below or find a corner in the stables from the stable-master? He could also have sought a corner in the *Laochtech*, with the warriors. Why come to the King's house to ask his steward?'

'As King's steward he probably realised my importance in running the household,' Beccan replied with an ill-concealed pride.

'So he appeared at the door of the kitchen and asked you for a bed?'

'That is as it happened,' the steward assured her.

It was certainly not the account given by Deogaire.

'You then took him to the King's guest quarters and showed him into an unoccupied room?' she asked.

Beccan nodded shamefacedly. 'I did not realise that he would use it as the base for an attack on you and Brother Eadulf,' he mumbled.

'That is yet to be proven,' Fidelma replied. 'You confirm, however, that you acceded to his request to be allowed to stay in the empty guest chamber? Did you tell him that he must remain there until first light and not venture out?'

Beccan thought for a moment. 'I expect I did. I explained that it was the custom of the King's bodyguard, the warriors of the Golden Collar, to be stationed at the doors and on the stairs during the hours of darkness.

The King never liked the arrangement, but after the attempt on his life . . .' he ended with a shrug.

'So Deogaire knew it was impossible to move from the floor of the guest quarters without being challenged?'

'Especially after the guests retired. Yes, I told him so.'

'Did you also tell him that he could exit onto the roof, cross it and take the second stairway down to the side to leave the building?'

Beccan dredged his memory. 'I usually insist that the guests know of that exit, in case of fire. The guests, especially after a feast, could have an accident with their lamp or even candle. Thankfully, it has never happened in my time, but I am told there was one such fire when Máenach Mac Fingín was King here. Tragically, two guests choked to death on the fumes.'

Fidelma had heard of that fire. It had happened about the same time she had left Brehon Morann's law school, and joined the Abbey of Kildare on the advice of her cousin, Abbot Laisran of Darú. There had been nothing for her at Cashel after the death of her father, King Failbhe Flann. Her father's nephew Máenach had become King. After him, a distant cousin, Cathal, ruled but he had died of the Yellow Plague at the very time he had invited her back to Cashel to advise him. It was only then that her brother Colgú had been elected as King and her world had stabilised. She had met Eadulf, was gaining a reputation as a *dálaigh* and felt no need to seek the security of a religious house.

She shook herself slightly and returned her thoughts to the matter in hand.

'So Deogaire knew the way up onto the roof and across to the other stairway?'

'Probably.'

'Very well, Beccan. So you left him in the empty room and returned to your duties?'

'I did.'

'I remember that you greeted the guests at the evening meal before you left.'

'There were few guests that evening.'

'But then you left, handing over your duties as steward to Dar Luga, the housekeeper.'

'I sought permission of the King to absent myself for two days. It was only a small intimate gathering that first night,' Beccan said with a note of protest in his voice. 'I was not needed to relay the protocols. I left instructions. Dar Luga said she locked the kitchen door and replaced the key on the hook. That would have been my last duty anyway.'

'Where did you go?' Fidelma asked. 'Two days is a long time to absent oneself, especially in view of the imminent arrival of important guests.'

'It was a private matter, lady,' he responded defensively. 'I told the King.'

'You know well enough, Beccan, that when a *dálaigh* asks a question relating to a serious crime, there is no such thing as privacy.' She used the old legal term *derritius*. 'I am told you went to nurse someone.'

'I went to the township to nurse a . . . close friend.'

'Be more specific.'

'A woman,' the rotund steward said shortly. 'A woman friend.'

'You must tell me her name,' Fidelma insisted.

He hesitated a moment and then answered: 'Maon.'

'I know no one of that name in the town, so you must explain a little more about her and your visit last night. I will need to question her if you are not specific.'

Beccan seemed agitated. It was some time before he managed to answer. 'Maon was ill. That's why I had to see her and take remedies to help her.'

'I am sorry to hear it,' replied Fidelma. 'Do you know what is wrong?'

'She was suffering from fever. I had to leave here to nurse her.'

'But there is a physician in the township and our apothecary Brother Conchobhar here in the palace. Why not summon one of them to examine the lady?'

'I sent for the physician in the township but was told that he had been called to the Ford of the Ass and was not expected back for two days. I did not know what to do.'

'So whose idea was it that Deogaire could provide you with medicine taken from Brother Conchobhar's apothecary in exchange for a bed and your silence?'

She delivered the question in an even tone and for a moment Beccan seemed not to understand it.

'He offered it as recompense,' he replied.

'But how did he come to know your troubles?'

'I had seen my friend earlier in the day. Thus I knew her to be ill and that was when I found the physician had left the township. I was coming back to the palace, sick at heart, for I knew the King expected my services. I had no idea how to help her. It was then I encountered Deogaire in the courtyard and he asked me what was wrong. I told him. He said he would appear at the kitchen door later and bring with him some potions; if I took them to Maon and made her drink them, it would help her. He assured me that the fever would break. He was right.'

'You trusted him?'

'He said he would bring the potions from his uncle and I knew Brother Conchobhar to be a respected apothecary.'

'And the fever broke?'

'It did. She is now almost recovered. In fact, I left her quite well, having nursed her these last two days.'

'I am confused. Why didn't you go to Brother Conchobhar directly? Why didn't you tell *him* the story and let *him* attend to this Maon?'

'My thoughts were in turmoil. I met Deogaire on coming back here and so the need to see Brother Conchobhar no longer occurred to me.'

'And when you met Deogaire in the courtyard, was this before or after his argument with Brother Conchobhar and his need to find a room?'

'It was after. We arranged that he come to the kitchen door with the medicine.'

Fidelma paused for a moment before continuing, 'Well, it is best that Brother Conchobhar be told this story now. He should know that some of his remedies may be missing. But he should also visit Maon and ensure all is well with her, to check that she was given the correct potions. Fevers have a habit of recurring.'

'Do you think he would want to see her?' asked the round-faced steward. 'After all, she appears recovered.'

'I will ask him. But why have you been so secretive about this Maon? I can't seem to place her in this township.'

Beccan spread his arms, seeming to grow in confidence now that he had explained. 'I am of the Déisi, south of the River Siúr, as you know, lady. She is from my home village, which is just by the Church of the Blessed Míodán. She ran away from her family several days ago to join me. I managed to find a small cabin on the forest track beyond the Road of Rocks. She had only been there a few days, when this fever took her. I was hoping to find her a job in the kitchens here. I think she caught a chill because of the hardship of her journey on foot across the mountains amidst the cold rains and winds. She was not well when she arrived here.'

Fidelma made a sympathetic sound with her tongue. 'Unfortunately, today you are needed in the palace. If only it were otherwise, because I would advise my brother to send you back to look after Maon for the next few days. However, I shall ensure that Brother Conchobhar visits her.'

It was Dar Luga, working nearby, who coughed to attract attention. 'I know the cabin beyond the Road of Rocks, lady. It is not far from Della's place.'

'Della would welcome the opportunity to help her,' Eadulf added.

'I came by there a few days ago, after visiting my sister Lassar, Ferloga's wife, at Rath na Drinne,' went on Dar Luga. 'I was wondering why there were signs of occupation at that old cabin.' She shook her head disapprovingly at Beccan. 'It is not exactly in suitable condition for someone suffering from the fever. You should bring the poor girl to the palace; there is room for a bed among the attendants' quarters. Strange though . . .' She paused as if at a sudden memory.

'Strange?' prompted Fidelma.

Dar Luga glanced at Beccan. 'You said your friend travelled there on foot, but when I was passing, I thought I saw a horse tethered outside.'

Beccan immediately shook his head. 'I know nothing of that. Perhaps it was a passing rider who stopped to make enquiries.'

'Well, no matter,' Fidelma continued. 'You may leave the matter in our hands. Thank you for answering our questions.'

Outside, Eadulf was thoughtful. 'The story is too glib. I find it hard to believe. If it is true, then we have much to ask of Deogaire who tells a contradictory tale.'

'You are right. However, I shall not press Beccan for the moment,' Fidelma agreed.

'We can be sure of one thing at least.'

'Which is?'

'We know that Beccan left the palace gates while we were feasting with your brother and did not return until this morning. He was certainly not on the roof when the statue was toppled onto us. So why would he be lying about the other details?'

'Why, indeed?' Fidelma said grimly.

They were crossing the courtyard towards the *Laochtech*. Fidelma suggested they see Deogaire first before going to old Brother Conchobhar's apothecary and telling him about the sick woman. As they walked, they suddenly heard the sound of a child's voice blending with the stern tones of a guard at the gate.

Fidelma halted and glanced in the direction of the altercation. A small boy of ten or so was standing defiantly in front of one of the guards who was obviously trying to refuse him admittance.

'I *must* see the King's Brehon!' the lad yelled.

They did not hear the gruff response of the guard but saw his finger pointing as if to bid the boy to go away.

Fidelma hurried across to the gate followed by Eadulf.

'What is this?' she asked.

The warrior straightened and raised a hand in salutation.

'A boy obviously playing some prank, lady. I've told him to clear off.'

Fidelma turned to the sullen-faced child. 'What is it, boy?' she asked in a kindly tone.

'My father says I must see the King's Brehon.'

'Your father? I seem to recognise you, lad. Aren't you Rumann's son? Why do you need to see the King's Brehon?'

'Because . . . because . . .' The boy's brow puckered as if trying to remember some message. 'Because my father has found a body in his ale-making house.'

Then, seemingly relieved to have delivered this message, he turned and ran off down the hill, back towards the township.

Eadulf exchanged a startled glance with Fidelma. 'Did you say that he was Rumann's son?' he gasped. 'Rumann the innkeeper?'

Fidelma nodded assent.

Eadulf's face was suddenly white. 'But . . . my brother! Egric, my brother! It must be his body!' He turned and was running off down the hill in the wake of the boy.

Fidelma spun around to the startled guard. 'Tell Gormán of this news and inform him that we shall be at Rumann's inn.' Then she, too, was moving rapidly down the hill towards the township. It was some distance but it was pointless waiting while horses were saddled.

Rumann's inn lay on the far side of the town square. It was a large enough establishment; more substantial than any other set of buildings among the farms and houses that spread themselves under the shadow of the Eóghanacht citadel on the ancient rock towering above it. As well as the *bruden* or inn itself, with its adjacent accommodation for travellers, there were stables for guests' horses, grounds beyond for a small group of animals such as pigs and poultry and then, beyond that was land cultivated for various vegetables and fruits. All in all, Rumann's inn was self-sufficient in many things, not least in the brewing of ale, mead and *nenadmin*, which was a cider made from crabapples.

At the side of the inn was the small group of buildings where Rumann managed the brewing of the beverages that he sold, for as well as being an innkeeper he was also a *scoaire* – a professional brewer licensed under the law. According to the law, the most prestigious ale-making houses were accorded 'lawful' status, being *dligtech* or legalised houses. The local Brehon would examine them and give them certification. Other places, which were deemed not lawful, were not penalised – but the important difference was that if the ale produced there was bad, then the inn was forfeited to the local prince and the innkeeper had to pay compensation to all who had drunk the bad ale.

Of course, owners of legal inns and ale-making houses tended to take advantage of their status by charging higher prices, but it was often wiser to pay and feel confident of the quality of the drink consumed. Rumann was proud of the status of his business as a licensed inn and ale-making house. It was his privilege to accommodate those visitors to the King's palace who could not be found rooms in the royal guest quarters. Indeed, he was now housing the warrior escort from Laighin which had accompanied the Venerable Verax and Bishop Arwald.

As Eadulf and Fidelma hurried across the square to the inn, they noticed the Laighin warriors sitting under a thatched shelter in front of the inn playing *dísle* – an ancient dice game that was popular among warriors. They seemed preoccupied and it was clear they knew some-thing was amiss as they cast some nervous glances at the newcomers.

Rumann was standing agitatedly in the doorway and came quickly to greet them. As they reached him, he said nothing but motioned them to follow.

'Who is it?' demanded Eadulf as he entered the inn hot on Rumann's heels. 'Whose body have you discovered?'

The innkeeper half-turned: 'The fellow is a stranger to me,' he muttered.

Eadulf actually seized him by the arm, almost swinging him round. 'Was it Egric? The man who was in here the other day with Dego, the warrior?'

To his relief the innkeeper immediately shook his head. 'Not him. I haven't seen hide nor hair of him or Dego since they left for the mountains the other day.'

'Then who is it?' Eadulf asked, relief making him sound brusque.

Fidelma moved forward to take matters in hand. 'You had better show us this body then, Rumann,' she said calmly. 'Kindly show us where and in what circumstances it was found.'

Rumann led the way through the inn and out of a back door, talking as he did so.

'We had to cater for the Laighin warriors last night, as well as several others who came for food and drink. So it was not until a short time ago that I and my assistant decided to start the fermenting process of the *bracat*.'

Bracat was ale fermented from barley or rye but taking its name from *bracha*, malt.

'The grain had already been dried in the kiln and was ready mashed to be placed into the vat for boiling, straining and fermentation. As I was about to start cleaning the vat, I peered down . . . and there was a body at the bottom of it!'

They had crossed the outside yard where three men were waiting – Rumann's brewers. One of them was standing nervously near a great wooden vat. At his feet was something covered in sackcloth.

Rumann gave a quick nod to the man, who bent down and pulled off the covering. In spite of the coating of drying mash that covered the body, it was easy to recognise the corpse as that of Sister Dianaimh of Cill Náile.

Chapter Sixteen

Eadulf's expression was grim. 'Do you have water to wash the mash off so that I can examine her?' he asked Rumann.

The innkeeper relayed the instruction to one of his workers, who hurriedly brought over a bucket of water. Eadulf poured some of its contents over the head and neck of the dead girl. Then he bent down beside the body and made a cursory examination.

'It seems that she was strangled.' He glanced up at Fidelma. 'See there, the mark of a cord of some description which has cut and bruised her neck.' He bent further in his examination. 'To achieve this, the killer must have approached from behind, put the cord around her neck and twisted it with some force. She might have had time to cry out, but perhaps the surprise was so complete that she did not.'

Fidelma looked at Rumann. 'I suppose no one heard any cry during the night?'

'Not I, lady.'

'I shall need to ask your family, workers and guests in a moment.'

'Very well. The only permanent guests are the warriors of Clan Baiscne from Laighin. Apart from myself there was just my son in the inn. As you know, my wife died from the Yellow Plague some years ago. I closed up before midnight and went to bed and slept soundly. My boy had gone to bed before me and he was asleep when I went up.'

'And your guests? The warriors?'

'Most of them had retired, although I left two downstairs with a lamp playing a game of *búanbach*.'

'Lasting victory' was another favourite board game among warriors.

'And what of your brewers?' She turned inquisitively to the three men.

'We all live on the far side of the square, lady,' one of them volunteered as spokesman for all three. 'We left the brewery just after sundown, having finished our day's work. We returned this morning and started to prepare the brew, and that's when Rumann found . . .' He swallowed and indicated the body with his head. 'Rumann immediately sent his son to the palace to fetch a Brehon.'

Fidelma glanced at the body and then back to the three brewers. 'May I make a request? Would you wrap the girl's body and carry it to Brother Conchobhar in the palace? You would act under my authority and be rewarded for your trouble.'

The spokesman glanced at his companions, before turning back and raising a knuckled hand to his forehead.

'We will do so and willingly, lady.'

Fidelma led the way to the front of the tavern where the Laighin warriors still sat at their dice game. It was clear that their concentration was not on their game. As Fidelma approached, they all rose to their feet immediately.

'What is it, lady?' asked one nervously. 'Is something amiss?'

'There has been a murder here,' she replied. 'Who is in charge among you?'

One of them took a step forward. 'I am Muiredach, lady. I command these men.'

'I am Fidelma of Cashel and a *dálaigh*.'

Muiredach inclined his head in acknowledgement. 'How may we help?'

'Did any of you see or hear anything during the night?'

There was a shuffling of feet and shaking of heads.

'What time did you retire?'

One young man coughed with apparent embarrassment. 'We went abed before the tavern-keeper. I am afraid some of us had indulged too freely in his liquor.'

Another of the younger warriors added defensively: 'It is boring, simply waiting for the religious who we are escorting. We have to hang around for them to finish their business before we can move on. There is nothing to do here except play dice and drink.'

Fidelma felt a momentary sympathy with the young man and made a mental note to raise the subject with her brother. Members of his bodyguard could surely arrange hunting expeditions or indulge in contests with these men in order to distract them from their boredom. But at the moment, there were more important matters to consider. She was aware of the commander, Muiredach, looking displeased with his subordinate.

'I can understand your boredom,' she said briskly, 'but for the moment, some questions. Who went to bed early? I am told at least two of you stayed up playing a game of *búanbach*.'

Two of the warriors indicated self-consciously that they had imbibed too much and gone to bed before the others. It was Muiredach and another man who admitted to being the game players.

'We were playing a tough game, lady,' Muiredach confessed. 'Rumann had left us with a lamp and we played on until the pieces resolved themselves on the board.'

'I was the victor,' the other man smirked, with an obvious pride that he had bested his commander.

'How long did the game last?'

'Not very long,' affirmed Muiredach. 'But everyone was asleep when we retired to our beds. You could be deafened by their snores. Neither of us heard anything else and it was only after we awoke this morning that we learned that something had happened. It was a murder, you say?'

'A young religieuse was strangled among the brewery vats,' Eadulf explained in a heavy tone.

Muiredach and his companions looked shocked.

At that moment the brewery workers came by the front of the tavern. They had constructed a makeshift stretcher on which they had placed the body.

'Perhaps you should look upon her face and see if anyone recognises her,' Fidelma suggested, and she instructed the men to halt and put down the stretcher. Eadulf bent and gently removed the piece of sackcloth from the young woman's face.

The warriors moved forward and glanced down. Muiredach's expression immediately revealed that he recognised the victim.

'Where have you seen Sister Dianaimh before?' Fidelma asked, at the same time indicating to the brewers to continue carrying the body to the palace.

'I do not know her name, but I have seen her before we came to Cashel,' the warrior said.

'*Before* you came to Cashel?' Fidelma was puzzled.

'A few weeks ago, in Sléibhte.'

Fidelma gazed at him astounded, wondering if she had heard correctly. 'Where did you say?'

'At the Abbey of Sléibhte. I was sent to escort Brother Rónán and one of the foreigners to the abbey. That girl was there. I have no doubt it is the same one.'

'Can you remember the circumstances?'

Muiredach pursed his lips for a moment. 'There is not much to say. I escorted Brother Rónán and the foreigner from Dinn Ríg to the Abbey at Sléibhte. We stayed two days. Then Brother Rónán said that they would not require my services further, so I rejoined my companions at Dinn Rig. Then I was informed that I must escort the other three foreigners to Cashel and should choose a few of my fellow warriors for the journey.'

'Yes, yes.' Fidelma was impatient. 'But what of the girl, Sister Dianaimh?

You saw that she was at the Abbey of Sléibhte? Exactly where and when did you see her?'

'On the day after we arrived at Sléibhte, I was sent back to Dinn Ríg. I was preparing my horse for the journey when, in the stableyard, I saw a girl mounting a horse also ready to leave the abbey. It was this girl. What is more, Abbot Aéd himself came into the stableyard to bid her farewell.'

'Abbot Aéd?' Eadulf questioned.

'The abbot and Bishop of Sléibhte,' Muiredach confirmed. 'I remember now. Something was passed between them as she sat on her horse and I heard him saying "God's speed. If you are able to acquire it, it will be a great support for our cause." I did not hear her response but then she rode off. That is all I heard. It comes back to me now that I think on her dead features.'

Fidelma was silent, considering what the warrior had told her.

'So you never saw her again until this moment?'

'Never, lady. I don't think that I can help further.'

'You have helped more than I can say.' Fidelma turned to Rumann. 'I'll send back your brewers immediately and keep you informed of the investigation.'

As they walked slowly back to the palace, Eadulf asked: 'What next?'

'Next, we must discover how Sister Dianaimh left the palace and went to Rumann's brewery if she did not pass through the gates by the guard.'

Gormán was standing waiting for them at the gates. His expression was grave.

'They've taken the body to Brother Conchobhar's apothecary, lady. This looks very bad. I am afraid Deogaire's prophecy is coming true.'

'Who was on duty at the gates throughout the night?' Fidelma asked, ignoring his gloomy tone. She knew that Gormán feared no mortal thing but now the idea of something supernatural, the prophecy of Deogaire, was beginning to prey on his imagination.

'Enda, lady,' he replied.

'Where is he now?'

'Asleep in the *Laochtech*, if he has any sense.'

'Then I am afraid we must wake him.'

Fidelma and Eadulf remained in the antechamber while Gormán went into the sleeping quarters and returned soon afterwards with a slightly dishevelled and hastily dressed Enda.

'I am sorry,' Fidelma told the warrior, 'but I do need this information quickly.'

'Gormán has told me that Sister Dianaimh was found murdered in Rumann's tavern,' Enda said gruffly. 'How can I help?'

'What time did you come to watch the gates?'

'The King's feast was just finishing towards midnight. The musicians were still playing their last tune. That was when I commenced my guard.'

'But you were not on duty all night?'

'Of course not, lady. I was relieved by Bríon.'

'I'll get him,' Gormán said hurriedly. 'He's asleep too.'

'A simple question. When did Sister Dianaimh leave the palace?'

'Not on my watch, lady,' Enda said immediately. 'Abbess Líoch already asked the same question of both me and Bríon.'

Fidelma recalled that the abbess had been searching for Sister Dianaimh earlier. 'There is no way you would have missed her leaving?'

'There is only one exit and entrance. Young Bríon took over from me for the second *cadar*. It was a clear night so we can be precise.'

Clear nights were important, for the most intelligent measured time throughout the night by rough estimates according to the position of the stars; exactly as the farmers had done since time immemorial.

Bríon, who was hardly more than a youth, came blinking into the room, rubbing his eyes.

'I am sorry to disturb you, Bríon,' Fidelma said again. 'What time did Sister Dianaimh pass through the gates here this morning?'

The young man stared at her for a moment and then stifled a yawn. 'As

I told Abbess Líoch, lady, she did not pass through while I was here. I finished my watch just after sunrise.'

Fidelma expected no other answer but she had to be sure. 'So your watches spanned the entire night from the ending of the feast and until sunrise, and yet you say that Sister Dianaimh did not pass through? Were the gates shut and bolted from midnight, as is the custom?'

'Only once was it opened,' Enda confirmed, 'and that was shortly after the feast ended, when the musicians left to return to their homes in the township. But I knew every one of them. Sister Dianaimh was certainly not among them, I can assure you of that.'

There was silence for a while and then Fidelma told them to return to their interrupted sleep.

'That confirms that Sister Dianaimh did not leave by the main gate.' She added: 'So now we have to find out how she did so.'

'There is no way, unless she flew,' Eadulf replied in a dour tone. 'I cannot see her climbing the walls and scrambling down the rocky slopes. I would not like to try that even in the daylight, let alone the dark.'

'The fact is that she did so,' insisted Fidelma. 'But how? The answer will come to us eventually.'

Gormán was listening to them with a frown. 'I don't know if it is worthy of repeating, but I did hear some words that passed between her and that Saxon – your pardon, friend Eadulf – Brother Bosa.'

'Let us judge whether the words are worth repeating,' Fidelma said quickly.

'Well, I was passing by them last night at the meal. It was when the guests were mingling with one another. I was pausing to look round to make sure all was in order and did not hear the opening of the conversation. But I will try to reconstruct it exactly as I heard it.'

He then closed his eyes and recited the following dialogue.

Brother Bosa said: 'But your abbot is not interested?'

'He is not my abbot any more,' Sister Dianaimh replied sharply.

'But you continue to visit the abbey.'

To which she answered: 'I have often carried messages for Abbot Aéd, that is true. But I can assure you that Aéd has already pledged his loyalty to Abbot Ségéne of Ard Macha.'

'Wouldn't that be contrary to the wishes of King Fianamail, who supports Cill Dara as the prime church of this island?' asked Brother Bosa.

'Aéd is of the Uí Barraiche. Fianamail is of the Uí Cennselaigh.'

Gormán added that Brother Bosa did not understand the enmity between the rival families of Laighin nor, it seemed, did Sister Dianaimh take the trouble to enlighten him.

'So,' went on Brother Bosa, 'it is not true that Aéd would not be interested in the market?'

Gormán said that at this point, the girl turned away and left the scribe.

'Not interested in the market?' Fidelma exchanged a thoughtful glance with Eadulf. 'So Brother Bosa was aware that Sister Dianaimh had recently been at Sléibhte. We'd best visit her room in the guest quarters.'

The girl had shared a room with Abbess Líoch. The abbess was now sitting on her bed, head in hands in a state of distress. The news of Sister Dianaimh's murder had spread swiftly.

'I don't understand it!' she cried, raising a tear-stained face to them as they entered. 'Who would want to kill that innocent girl, Fidelma?'

'While she was undoubtedly innocent of many things, she must also have been guilty of something,' Fidelma replied grimly. 'What she was guilty *of* is for me to find out. I would like to have a look at her personal belongings, if you have no objection? I presume that no one else has searched through her possessions since her death?'

'Who would want to?' the abbess rejoined sadly. 'She had little enough.' She nodded to the spare bed with a single woollen cloak spread across the bottom of it. There was a *srathar* or saddlebag hung nearby, and a *ciorbhog* hanging up behind the bed. This was the inevitable comb bag, which women of all ranks and offices carried. There was the usual change of clothes in the saddlebag. Fidelma took down the comb bag, sat on the edge of the cot and searched through it. She then set it aside with a sigh. There was little of value in it; it contained only the usual items. She shifted her weight to replace it and caught her breath as she felt something hard beneath her thigh.

She stood up and lifted the straw-filled mattress. A leather bag was concealed underneath. Fidelma lifted it up.

'Heavy,' she muttered.

With the mattress back in place, she reseated herself, put the bag beside her and untied the leather thongs that held it together. Then she widened the neck of the bag to look at the contents.

Eadulf, who had come to peer over her shoulder, exhaled through his teeth, a curious whistling sound to denote his astonishment.

'What is it?' demanded Abbess Líoch, rising from her bed and moving towards them.

'Did you know Sister Dianaimh was carrying these coins?' asked Fidelma.

'Coins? What coins?' Abbess Líoch saw – and gasped.

The bag was filled with gold and silver coins – a mixture of Roman, Gaulish and coins of the early Britons among them.

'Why, there must be . . .' Eadulf was trying to calculate the value.

'Enough to pay the honour price of any one of the Kings of the Five Kingdoms,' Fidelma concluded.

'Enough to buy a herd of nearly fifty milch cows,' breathed Abbess Líoch, having seated herself again. She was in a state of shock.

Fidelma retied the bag, saying to the abbess, 'I presume that you had no idea your steward carried such a sum?'

The abbess shook her head slowly. 'None at all. But why?'

'We must take this into safekeeping until the matter can be resolved,' Fidelma declared. 'Meanwhile, you must not breathe a word to anyone about this.'

Abbess Líoch, beyond speech, could only give an assenting gesture.

'Do you think we have found the motive for her murder?' Eadulf asked. 'Perhaps the murderer knew she would be carrying the sum and killed her for it?'

'I would have thought even someone with impaired vision would see that she was not carrying the coins on her. If they knew she was the bearer of such wealth, they would be aware that she would never carry it on her person but would place it somewhere for safety – somewhere like this hiding-place we have found. So if she was killed for this, why did they not enter here and search for it?'

Abbess Líoch glanced nervously at her. 'But I was asleep here all night, and only this morning did I find Sister Dianaimh missing.'

Fidelma made no reply but stood and picked up the bag, handing it to Eadulf. It was quite heavy.

'Where to now?' he asked.

'Now we shall place the money in the safekeeping of my brother,' Fidelma said. 'I have an idea.'

'I am getting more confused as time goes by,' Eadulf sighed as they went towards Colgú's apartments. 'We start with the murder of a Saxon cleric. Then there is an attack on my brother and his companion on the river. We think they are attacked by robbers from the Déisi. The robbers are captured and killed, except for their leader. He is brought here because he says he has something which he will use as a bargain to save himself from punishment. *He* is then murdered. We are told a deputation from Canterbury is coming here. Then someone tries to kill us. Then we are told my brother's companion is no religious but a thief. And now Abbess Líoch's *bann-mhaor*, her young steward, is murdered. She has been carrying a fortune with her. What can we make of all this?'

'A tangled skein can be untangled if one has patience,' observed Fidelma.

'But if it is true that this Venerable Victricius was a thief, what was he doing on his way here? Is that why he did not tell my brother what his purpose was?'

'After we have deposited these coins with Colgú, we will search out Brother Bosa and see if he can add anything more to this matter.'

Brother Bosa was on the walkway of the fortress walls when they found him, leaning against the parapet and gazing towards the distant mountains in the north-west.

'Not my sort of country,' he greeted them as they approached. 'There are mountains in every direction. Give me the low hills or flatlands, the sky and the sea.'

'I have been once in the Kingdom of Kent,' Fidelma offered. 'We were in Canterbury for a short time before going to Aldred's Abbey. I do remember the low hills and rivers and no sign of any mountains. I suppose each to their own. We have a saying here, there is no hearth like your own hearth.'

Brother Bosa sighed and seemed almost vulnerable compared to the arrogance he usually displayed.

'We wanted to ask a few questions,' Eadulf volunteered.

In a moment the man's affable expression became guarded. 'About what?'

'You will have heard that Sister Dianaimh has been murdered?'

'I am told that she was found in a tavern. It's hardly a place for a moral religieuse.'

'Being murdered, she might not have been able to protest about where her body was placed after her death,' Eadulf replied sharply.

'You will understand my position as a *dálaigh*,' Fidelma went on smoothly, giving Eadulf a reproving glance. 'I need to ask some questions.'

'Why of me?' asked the scribe.

'You were talking to her during the meal last night. I just wondered if she said anything that might have indicated whether she was afraid of anyone?'

Brother Bosa shrugged carelessly. 'I did not speak to her for long.'

'What did you talk about?'

The scribe said reluctantly, 'You know by now that our mission here is to gather information about claims for a primacy in this island.'

'And that is what you were asking her about?'

'My understanding was that she had been trained at an abbey called Sléibhte which was already in existence when Patricius came to administer to the faithful here. While we were in Laighin, we heard a rumour that they might contend for the primacy against Ard Macha. King Fianamail of Laighin supported another abbey called Cill Dara, which would certainly not be considered by the Holy Father because its abbot was subservient to an abbess.'

'So you were asking Sister Dianaimh if the Abbot of Sléibhte, Abbot Aéd, was pressing his own case to be regarded as a primacy?' clarified Fidelma.

'The Venerable Verax wanted an assurance, so I thought that I would ask her.'

'And did you get the information you wished?'

'Not really.'

'So why did you think that Sister Dianaimh, who was *bann-mhaor* to Abbess Líoch of Cill Náile, would have any particular information about Sléibhte?' Fidelma asked.

'As I said, I was told she had links with the Abbey of Sléibhte,' muttered Brother Bosa.

'Could it have been that she had recently been observed at Sléibhte by Brother Cerdic? And would *that* have been the reason why she was invited especially to Cashel to meet with your deputation?'

'I don't know what you mean.'

'We have been trying to understand why Abbess Líoch and her steward Sister Dianaimh had been invited by Brother Cerdic to attend here. It was pointed out to the abbess that it was in her interest to do so. If the purpose of your deputation was merely to gather such information – as could have been obtained by other simple means – why invite the abbess of a new and small community that would not rank in such research?'

'We did not know Brother Cerdic had extended such an invitation,' protested the scribe.

'But he did. Apparently he went to Sléibhte and saw Sister Dianaimh there. It occurs to me that he, or your deputation, needed Sister Dianaimh at this meeting in Cashel. He could not openly invite her as an individual, but if he invited Abbess Líoch, then she would naturally bring her steward.'

Brother Bosa was looking blank. 'You have lost me, lady,' he said.

'The mystery is,' Fidelma was reflective, 'why go to all that trouble, simply to get such information? Had your deputation gone to the High King's palace at Tara and sat with Cenn Faelad and his Brehon Sedna, you would have learned all this, without the necessity of a journey to each kingdom. It makes me wonder if there is some other, hidden purpose to your deputation.'

Brother Bosa flushed. 'What other purpose could there be?' he blustered.

'Are you selling anything?' Eadulf blurted out, even surprising Fidelma.

'Selling . . .? What do you mean?' demanded the scribe, startled.

'I had the impression last evening that I was being asked if Abbot Ségdae would give something – presumably pay out for some sort of approval if he made a claim for the primacy. I am told you appeared to be asking the same question of Sister Dianaimh about Abbot Aéd.'

'King Fianamail had already told us that Abbot Aéd was supporting the claims of Abbot Ségéne of Ard Macha,' replied Brother Bosa angrily, then realised he had confirmed his interest.

'So is *that* why you are here?' smiled Eadulf. 'You are here to find the highest bidder among the abbots of these kingdoms for the recognition of the primacy by Rome?'

The muscles in Brother Bosa's face had tightened. 'What nonsense is this?' he spluttered. 'Do you really think the Holy Father would countenance the buying and selling of such office?'

'Why not?' replied Eadulf easily. 'Buying favours seems a natural human failing.'

'Absolute nonsense,' snapped Brother Bosa. 'Now, if you will excuse me!' He pushed roughly past them and headed to the steps leading down into the courtyard.

'Well, well,' breathed Eadulf after he had gone. 'That seemed to upset him. But I cannot understand why Abbot Aéd would support Ard Macha, if his abbey has a prior claim of seniority.'

'Simple enough,' returned Fidelma. 'It is a matter of politics rather than religion. The first Bishop and Abbot of Sléibhte, Fiacc, was a prince of the Uí Bairrche. They were once the ruling clan of Laighin. But Fiacc's brother, Prince Oénghus, slew Crimmthan, a prince of the Uí Cennselaigh. And so the Uí Cennselaigh have gradually erased the power of the Uí Bairrche from all their strongholds in Laighin in retribution. Abbot Aéd is of the Uí Bairrche and he knows that ecclesiastical and political overlord-ship work in tandem. He doubtless fears that the Uí Cennselaigh will take over his great abbey. If he has agreed to recognise Ard Macha as having primacy over his abbey, and thereby receive its protection, then he has obviously been moved by the politics of power.'

For a moment or two, Eadulf stood digesting this information.

'But that doesn't seem to fit with what the warrior, Muiredach, told us he saw at Sléibhte. What was it that Sister Dianaimh was meant to acquire – and was her bag of valuable coins to be used to purchase it?'

Fidelma leaned against the wall, her hands clasped before her as she gazed out at the green swathe below. Eadulf waited nervously, in case he had said the wrong thing.

'It is an interesting point,' he added in justification.

Fidelma finally turned to him. 'Interesting? It is a very important question that needs an answer.'

'Do you really think that Vitalian would give the primacy to someone who offered him money?'

'No, I don't,' replied Fidelma, to his immediate disappointment. 'Nevertheless, it still remains a good question. Why *did* Sister Dianaimh carry all that money? What did she hope to achieve with it? To buy something? But what?'

Eadulf uttered a sigh. 'I am beginning to think that our friend Deogaire was right.'

'How so?'

'That this deputation – and he did describe it as a deputation from the east – has been sent by the devil. So far, it has brought four deaths, including this mysterious Victricius – eight if you count the boatmen.'

'Plus an attempt to kill us,' Fidelma reminded him with a wry smile.

She pushed herself away from the wall and stretched. There were clouds in the sky but it was still dry and not too cold for the time of year. She examined the wall where it ran towards the south of the fortress complex.

'I have an idea,' she said suddenly, starting to move along the walkway. Eadulf trotted after her. There were one or two sentinels on the walkway who stood back respectfully as they passed. One of them, however, called a warning.

'Be careful of the south-west corner, lady. That's where the stones crumbled. The builders are still at work there with their scaffolding.'

She raised her hand in acknowledgement. It was precisely to that point she was heading, cursing herself for not having remembered it before.

A mason was at work dressing a stone down on the scaffolding as they came up. Seeing them approaching, he stopped working with his hammer and chisel and saluted them.

'Have a care, lady,' he said politely. 'It is dangerous here.'

'I shall be careful,' Fidelma assured him. She leaned forward cautiously and peered down through the wooden structure that went all the way to the ground. There were several workmen below, cutting and hoisting stones to repair the wall which had been damaged in a rock-slip.

'Is it easy to come up and down that way?' she asked.

'Bless you, lady, it's very easy to the trained. That is our job.'

'What if one was not skilled – could it still be done? I see ladders in place. Are they always there?'

'The ladders are lashed to the structure, lady, for security. It would be time-wasting to keep removing them and replacing them each day. Already the steward of your household is chiding us about the length of time it is taking to finish. But we are working as quickly as we can.'

'So they are there during the night?'

'They are so. But you need have no fear of an enemy attack from here, lady.' The man chuckled at the idea. 'The structure is easily defended from the wall.'

'But anyone could climb up or down without any skill?'

'There's no skill in climbing a ladder, lady.'

Fidelma turned to Eadulf with a smile. 'I think we might have resolved one more question,' she said in an undertone before turning back to the stonemason. 'I am going to climb down,' she announced. 'I want to test how easy it is.'

The man was astounded. 'But, lady, we cannot afford it if you slip or have some accident.'

'If anything happens, Eadulf is witness that I make this climb of my own volition and you are absolved from making any recompense if I injure myself.'

Without a further word, she swung over the wall and, gripping the wooden supports of the structure, lowered herself to the first platform where the stonemason was working. With the astonished man still mumbling protests, she trod carefully over to the first ladder. Eadulf, having stifled his own protests, gave a groan and he, too, swung after her. At the third ladder, she paused and reached forward to where the wood was splintered. Several strands of dyed wool had been caught on the jagged edge. She picked them off carefully. They were of the same material as might be used in a religious robe.

It was a quick and easy descent, from each ladder to each platform and so on, until they had reached the bottom and were gazing up towards the towering walls of her brother's fortress. As Eadulf, sweating and nervous, joined her, Fidelma was standing with a satisfied smile on her face. Puzzled workmen were standing nearby, gazing astonished at their unexpected descent.

'So now we know how Sister Dianaimh could have secretly left the fortress without the necessity of coming through the gates!' she exclaimed in triumph. She showed the strands of wool to Eadulf. 'I will wager with you that when we examine the robe that Sister Dianaimh was wearing, we will find a match.'

'I would have believed you without the need for a practical demonstration,' Eadulf replied glumly. Then he glanced over his shoulder. 'It is certainly an easy walk from here to Rumann's inn. But that would mean she was going to meet someone there.'

'I believe she *was* going to meet someone,' Fidelma agreed. 'Someone she knew and with whom she was—'

'Going to negotiate a payment with the sack of coins?' Eadulf interrupted.

'Well, she did not carry them with her,' Fidelma pointed out, 'but I think I am beginning to see some light in this dark matter.' And before Eadulf could say anything further, she added brightly: 'Well, do you prefer to walk round to the main gate and surprise our guards, or would you like to climb back up?'

Eadulf screwed up his face as if in agony. 'I would willingly walk three times around The Rock than climb back up those ladders,' he replied in a tone of fervour.

They turned and began to walk along in the shadow of the citadel towards the main gate.

'Having discovered how Sister Dianaimh could leave the palace without being seen,' Eadulf speculated, 'there is another thought that occurs to me.'

'Which is?' Fidelma asked in high good humour.

'If it was easy for her to leave, it was just as easy for someone else to gain entrance.'

It was a thought that had already occurred to Fidelma but she gave a quick nod. 'I will tell my brother that he should have a guard permanently mounted there,' she said quietly.

ChAPTER SEVENTEEN

ॐ

B rother Conchobhar was working in his apothecary and looked up with a welcoming smile as Fidelma and Eadulf entered.

'I received your message,' he greeted them. 'I've checked my missing medications and it seems that Deogaire took the correct ones for the conditions you described. I plan to check on her condition as soon as I can.'

'Then Eadulf and I will join you,' Fidelma told himself, 'as it will be interesting to see this woman.'

'Meanwhile, I have some news for you – so I am glad you came by,' went on the old man. They detected a suppressed excitement in his tone. 'It is about that band of lambswool. The Keeper of Books finally found a reference to it which confirmed what we had thought: a generation or more ago, it was worn by all the bishops when they performed the rites of the Mass. It then dropped out of use in the churches of the Five Kingdoms as we set more store by our abbots.'

Fidelma's face fell. 'Nothing more?'

Brother Conchobhar's smile broadened. 'He also told me that it was called a *pallium* but that its symbolism has changed in the last hundred years or so. The Bishop of Rome, the one they called Gregory, ordered that it could only be worn by bishops of special rank. He wrote to Bishop

John of Ravenna nearly a century ago about pastoral rules and mentioned what it symbolised. It is now a symbol given by the Bishop of Rome only to those appointed as Chief Bishops or Archbishops. Its use is limited. No one else is allowed to wear it without the approval of the Bishop of Rome.'

'You mean that it was used only by an Archbishop such as Theodore of Canterbury?' asked Eadulf in astonishment.

'It is apparently the symbol of the new Roman power, to be worn as a liturgical vestment only in the church and during the Divine Mass unless otherwise authorised by the Bishop of Rome,' confirmed the old apothecary. 'Our Keeper of Books remembered that he had seen some such reference to its change of use. Apparently we have a copy of that book of pastoral rules in our *tech screpta*.'

'So this *pallium* is a symbol of an Archbishop . . .' Fidelma considered the implications.

'If Rudgal had stolen it in the attack on the river, what does it mean?' Brother Conchobhar asked. 'Was it being brought to a bishop here? The churches of the Five Kingdoms recognise no Chief Bishop over them. Bishops are subordinate to abbots among our churches.'

'This is what the Venerable Verax's deputation is discussing,' Eadulf explained. 'Apparently, Abbot Ségéne of Ard Macha has petitioned Rome, making the claim for Ard Macha to be the primacy of all the churches in the Five Kingdoms because the abbey was founded by Patricius. This deputation must have come to ask the views of the abbots and bishops before Ségéne was presented with this *pallium*.'

'Hardly likely,' Fidelma declared.

'Patricius preferred to work at the Abbey of Dún Phádraig, the Fortress of Patricius, where he died and is buried,' pointed out Brother Conchobhar. 'Even by citing Patricius, their claim falls.'

'If Rome has sent the *pallium* into the Five Kingdoms as the answer to the claim of Ard Macha, why would an emissary from the Bishop of

Rome come to Cashel bearing this symbol of authority? Why not travel directly to Ard Macha?' Fidelma asked.

'Could this *pallium* be meant for Abbot Ségdae? That Imleach and not Ard Macha was to be recognised?' Brother Conchobhar wondered.

Fidelma regarded both men with an expression akin to sadness. 'I am afraid that you are overlooking several important facts. Firstly, how did we come by this *pallium*?'

'It was hidden on the body of Rudgal, a robber, who knew its value because he was going to use it to bargain for his freedom,' Eadulf replied promptly.

'And how did Rudgal acquire it?'

'Why, from the Venerable Victricius when Rudgal and his robbers attacked their boat and—'

'And who *was* Victricius? Brother Bosa claims he was a thief without any right to be called a priest of any sort.'

Eadulf thought about it. 'If so, was Egric his accomplice – or was he duped? My brother said he met Victricius in Canterbury and was employed by him as a translator and companion. He says he was informed that Victricius was on a mission from Theodore, but was never told what it was. Who should I believe?'

'If we do not believe what Brother Bosa says, then we must assume that he – indeed, this entire Saxon deputation – are not who they say they are.'

Eadulf was silent as he considered the alternatives.

'Another point,' went on Fidelma. 'Why would Rudgal know the symbolism of this item when we did not? To most people, it is merely a piece of lambswool, a band or even a scarf. Only certain people would recognise the importance of the *pallium*. To those few, this piece of lambswool might well seem valuable enough to make a man rich – if he knew how to trade for it. Do you really think that Rudgal would have such knowledge?'

Just at that moment, the door of the apothecary opened abruptly and
Enda came in. The warrior's face was tense.

'Forgive me,' he said to them. 'I was told Eadulf was here.'

'I am here. What is it, Enda?' Eadulf said, turning towards him.

'Brother Berrihert from Eatharlach is at the gates and demands to see
you immediately.'

Eadulf was surprised. Three years ago, he had helped Berrihert and his
two brothers, Pecanum and Naovan – all brothers in blood as well as
in religion – settle in the great Valley of Eatharlach among the Uí
Cuileann clan. He had known Berrihert at Streonshalh. After Oswy's
fateful decision to follow Roman rites, Bishop Colmán, rather than
change his religious allegiance, had gathered all those who continued to
adhere to the teachings of Colmcille, and taken them, first to the kingdom
of the Britons called Rheged, then on to his own land of Connachta. Berrihert,
with his two brothers, eventually sought out the peace and tranquillity of
Eatharlach where Miach, chieftain of the Uí Cuileann, had accepted them
into the valley after Eadulf had vouched for them.

'What does *he* want?' Eadulf asked in surprise. 'He and his brothers
hardly ever leave the valley.'

Enda's voice was troubled. 'Whatever it is, I think it bodes ill. He came
on horseback.'

'Is it so unusual to see a religieux on horseback?' Fidelma wondered
at the comment.

'The horse that he is riding is the same one which Dego was riding the
other day,' Enda replied grimly. 'I recognised it. I asked him how he came
by it, but he just demanded that I fetch you at once.'

Eadulf was already out of the door. After swiftly advising Brother
Conchobhar to keep the *pallium* hidden in a secure place, Fidelma hurried
after him. They found Brother Berrihert, still covered in dust from his
journey, standing by Dego's horse in the courtyard. He lost no time in
polite salutations.

'I have ridden without stop from Eatharlach, Brother Eadulf, with news that you and your friends here should know.' The man paused to clear his throat as his voice was cracking with dryness. Enda immediately fetched the man a beaker of water; Brother Berrihert drained it in gigantic gulps before handing the vessel back. 'Sorry, lady,' he said to Fidelma. 'I am unused to such exertions.' Then, before she could reply, he hastened on: 'Yesterday, I found this horse wandering loose. It was still saddled and was grazing on the lower slopes of An Starracín.'

'An Starracín?' Eadulf gave a puzzled glance in Enda's direction.

'It is called the Pointed Peak – is one of the peaks of the Sliabh na gCoillte,' Enda explained.

Brother Berrihert continued, 'I began to examine the area. It was not long before I found the rider . . . he was a warrior and he had been badly injured. It seemed that he had camped by a stream. There were signs that he had been fishing. I brought him and the horse to my cabin; the one which my brothers and I also use as a chapel. We are nursing him there. I recognised him as a warrior of Cashel since he wore a golden torc around his neck.'

'He's badly hurt, you say?' Fidelma asked.

'He had wounds to the back of his skull, but the worst wound was in his arm for he had lost blood as if gushing from a fountain. He had also been stabbed in the back – but that was no more than a flesh wound. He managed a period of lucidity, enough to tell me to search out Brother Eadulf.'

'Dego!' exclaimed Enda, having his fear confirmed. 'It must be him.'

'Dego was hunting in that area in the company of my brother,' Eadulf burst out. 'What of Egric? Where is he?'

Fidelma reached out a hand and placed it on Eadulf's arm to steady him.

'I saw no other person,' Brother Berrihert said. 'The warrior was alone and hardly able to speak. His wounds were grievous. I have left my brothers tending to him. But he was adamant, that I should come to find you, Eadulf.'

'What did he say?' Eadulf asked urgently.

'All he could manage was "tell Eadulf, tell Eadulf". Nothing else. So I took his horse and rode here straightway. There was no mention of any companion called Egric.'

'Dego is at your cabin, you say?'

'Yes, being nursed by my brothers, Pecanum and Naovan,' the man repeated. 'But nothing compares to his agitation in wanting you to be informed.'

Fidelma turned to Enda. 'See that Brother Berrihert is given refreshment, and can you provide him with a fresh horse? He and Eadulf will return immediately to An Starracín.' Eadulf regarded Fidelma in surprise but she went on: 'You must go at once. You'll be there before nightfall if you maintain a good pace. I think that you should also take Gormán and Aidan with you. Aidan is an excellent tracker and this could be invaluable if you need to search for Egric.' She added this for Enda's benefit because he was looking disappointed at not being included. 'Enda, you must stay here to be in charge of the guard; you are senior in rank after Gormán. Now find Gormán and Aidan, and tell them what they must do.'

It was not long before Fidelma was watching the band of horsemen as they swept down from The Rock and through the township, south-west towards the distant glen of Eatharlach. Then she returned to her chambers to get ready to accompany Brother Conchobhar to the cabin where Beccan had said he had left his woman friend, Maon. Fidelma had barely entered the chamber when Muirgen, the nurse, knocked and entered.

'Little Alchú is ready for his morning ride,' she announced

Fidelma flushed. Events had been moving so fast that she had forgotten all about it. Muirgen pursed her lips reprovingly as she read Fidelma's expression.

'He likes his morning ride with one or other of you,' she observed. 'Brother Eadulf rode with him yesterday, so it is your turn today, lady.'

'I know, I know,' replied Fidelma testily. 'But there is so much to do at the moment.' Then she sighed. 'Bring the boy in here.'

A moment later, Muirgen led the little boy in. '*Muimme* says you are busy, so I can't go riding,' he said accusingly. The intimate form *muimme* or 'mummy' was always used for a nurse or fosterer, whereas *mathair*, the more formal 'mother', was used for one's birth mother.

Fidelma bent down to the child. 'She didn't really mean that,' she told her son with a forced smile. 'I have some terribly important things to do for King Am-Nar so we have a little surprise for you.'

The word for a maternal uncle was *amnair* which Alchú had not been able to pronounce and so Fidelma's brother, Colgú, was always simply 'King Am-Nar'. The boy frowned slightly at her statement, wondering what the surprise could be.

'I am going to take you to see your Aunt Della and ask her if you can ride in her paddock. She can show you many tricks with horses. You know just how well she feeds you when you visit.'

A broad smile wreathed the child's mouth and he clapped his hands. 'Aunt Della! Aunt Della!'

Fidelma looked relieved at his reaction.

In the stables, their horses were waiting and saddled. Fidelma and Alchu were joined moments later by Brother Conchobhar, with his *lés* or medical bag slung across his back. The rank of a physician entitled him to travel on a good horse, and the symbol of his status as a physician was the *echlaisc* – a riding whip. It was not for use but carried as a token and valued as part of a physician's honour price which could be confiscated by law if he was found guilty of misconduct. Brother Conchobar might be aged but he was a good horseman and, indeed, he had often ridden with Fidelma when she was a little girl.

'It will be good to call on your friend, Della,' he said when she explained

Alchú's presence. 'I need to collect some herbs that she has been gathering for me. The cabin that Beccan described to you lies not far up the hill from her place.'

'It shouldn't be too difficult to find,' agreed Fidelma. 'It is always a pleasure to see Della and find out how that girl Aibell is settling in.'

'I hear that Gormán is much attracted to her,' beamed Brother Conchobhar.

Fidelma smiled back. 'He has been attracted to her ever since we found her hiding out in a woodsman's hut near Della's paddock. You may recall that we thought she might have had a hand in the attempted assassination of my brother.'

'I heard she had a sad life as a bondservant among the Sliabh Luachra. I should have asked Deogaire if he had encountered her in that dark inhospitable country.'

It had never occurred to Fidelma to ask Deogaire about that connection. Now she was reminded that it would be a good opportunity to reassure the girl in case she encountered Deogaire and recognised him as being from the clan – the clan that had once held her as a bondservant after her father had illegally sold her to Fidaig, the Chief of the Luachra.

Mounted on her stallion, Aonbharr, with little Alchú on his pony at her side, and followed by Brother Conchobhar, the three set off at a sedate pace. Fidelma was keeping the pace slow not only because of her young son, but in order not to tax the old physician. While he was a good horseman, she knew that his age wearied him. Even so, it was not long before they crossed the main square of the township where, she could see, the warrior escort of the curious deputation were still passing the time with their dice games.

Della's house was on the very outskirts. At the gate to her paddock, Fidelma slid from her horse and helped Alchú dismount. A large dog came bounding towards them, keeping up a series of yelps which Fidelma recognised as being those of recognition and not warning. Della had kept the dog for some time. It was called a *leth-choin* or 'half-dog' – a cross between a wolfhound and a terrier.

She had barely called a friendly greeting when a young woman came running from the house. She wore her hair loose, a blue-black mane which surrounded her symmetrical, attractive features, with their splash of freckles on the cheeks. Her dark eyes flashed and the red lips were parted to show a very white set of teeth.

'Aibell!' called Fidelma. 'Best hold onto the dog lest he knock Alchú over with enthusiasm.'

The girl bent down to catch the dog by its collar and ordered it to sit. The dog obeyed, thumping its tail on the ground.

Aibell then turned to Brother Conchobhar who was still seated on his horse. There was a faint look of disappointment on her face which Fidelma noticed.

'Gormán has gone with Eadulf to the glen at Eatharlach,' Fidelma explained with a gentle smile. 'So I am afraid that he will not return for a while.'

'You are very welcome here, Brother Conchobhar,' the girl called to hide her embarrassment, adding: 'I knew Brother Conchobhar was expected, to collect some herbs . . .'

'We are going to leave Alchú with you and Della, if we may,' Fidelma said. 'It is only for a short while. We have a call to make first, and then we will be back. Please explain to Della our discourtesy in not staying to greet her.'

Aibell was surprised but agreed, and came forward with a smile to take the boy by the hand while Fidelma remounted.

With a quick wave, Fidelma and Brother Conchobhar moved around the paddock at the back of Della's homestead and joined the track leading south up the hillside which, because of its stony nature, was called the Road of Rocks. The road would eventually lead on to Rath na Drinne, where Ferloga kept his tavern, but before that, almost at the edge of the township, the forests and woodlands started. Further to the south stretched the famous Plain of Femen. Fidelma took the lead along the narrowing track through the tall trees.

'It's a curious place for Beccan to allow this girl to stay if she was so ill,' Brother Conchobhar remarked, as the surrounding trees seemed to increase the chilly atmosphere.

'I expect she was too unwell for him to move her to the town,' Fidelma replied. However, she was not entirely convinced of her own arguments and it was one of the questions that had already passed through her mind.

'I think that might be it, just ahead,' called the physician.

The place was much smaller than Fidelma had remembered. However, she had not been in this area of the woods for many years, and memory often distorted the size of things. In fact, it was hardly larger than the woodsman's hut where they had found Aibell.

As if reading her thoughts, Brother Conchobhar said: 'As I recall, it was used as a cabin where the woodsman lived. It must have been deserted for many years. Have you noticed that there is no sign of smoke from a fire, nor a horse or wagon here? In fact, it looks deserted still.'

Fidelma had been thinking the same thing. Beccan had already explained the lack of a horse, even though Dar Luga had suggested that she had once seen a horse outside. Fidelma was more concerned by the lack of smoke, showing there was no fire in the cabin on this winter's day.

She halted a little distance from the cabin and raised her voice: 'Maon! Do not be alarmed! It is a physician come to see you. Beccan sent us.'

The only response to her shout was a cacophony of birds rising in alarm into the sky.

They dismounted, tethered their horses to some nearby bushes and walked slowly towards the door of the hut. As Fidelma tapped on it, the rough wooden door, not being latched, merely swung open.

It was very dark inside, but it was immediately obvious that the place was not occupied. The first thing that registered with Fidelma was the stale aroma of alcohol. Looking over her shoulder, to see Brother Conchobhar staring around in disapproval, Fidelma took a hesitant step inside and pulled down a piece of sackcloth which covered a window so that a little more light could creep in.

'Well, someone has been staying here,' she observed, pointing to the rough straw mattress that lay in one corner. She bent down and felt it with her hands. 'But not for some time. The straw is damp and cold.'

'Then how do you know someone has been here?' asked Brother Conchobhar.

She pointed to the table on which there were two empty earthenware mugs and, on its side, what was called a *lestar*, or container for alcohol.

'If those had been there longer than a week, there would have been some dust across the table. See how the dust accumulates on those shelves.'

Brother Conchobhar sighed. 'There are no other huts that I know of in this forest. If Beccan was not nursing the girl here, then where?'

Fidelma did not reply but went outside the hut and stood looking about her. Then she made her way around the side of the hut to where there was a level patch of grass. Perhaps it had once been used by the woodsman as a space for his cart or his horse. Fidelma noticed that it had not been overgrown but trampled – and that had occurred fairly recently. An old bucket was standing nearby, against the wall: it still had some water in it. She bent down and immersed her finger in it, drew it out and placed it in her mouth. The water was fairly fresh. Nearby were several ears of oats, spread in a loose pattern. It was obvious that a horse had been stood, watered and fed here. She turned and her sharp eyes examined the surrounding trees. She did not have to look far before she saw what she was looking for. One tree had score-marks on its trunk a few feet from the ground. A rope had obviously been tied around it, and the marks were caused by a restless horse moving at the other end of it.

She returned to the front of the hut where Brother Conchobhar was waiting.

'We've had a wasted journey, I'm afraid,' she said.

'Did Beccan mistake the location of the hut?' asked the old physician.

'I think not,' she said dryly. 'Alas, it is not the first untruth that has been told to me in recent days. Well, there is nothing else to do for the moment but return to Della's homestead.'

They remounted and made their way back through the woods to the Road of Rocks and came slowly down the hill on the western side of the township. They crossed a field before arriving back at Della's paddock and outhouses. In the paddock was Alchú, astride his pony, riding in a circle and jumping over small obstacles placed at intervals. The little boy was clearly enjoying himself, shouting with glee at each jump. Keeping a wary eye on him, balanced on top of the surrounding fence, was Aibell.

In a corner of the paddock, Della's workhorse was munching peacefully at the grass. Usually, Della's son Gormán, as Commander of the King's Bodyguard, kept his warhorse there when his duties did not keep him in the palace. Beyond the paddock was Della's cabin. The boy saw them first and, with a 'whoop', Alchú halted his pony, turned it and came trotting across.

'Hello, *mathair*. We can't go home yet. Aunt Della is making cakes. We must eat those first.'

Fidelma smiled. 'Don't worry, little hound,' she told him. 'There is plenty of time to have your cake before we go.'

Aibell climbed down from her perch and helped Alchú dismount.

Della suddenly appeared on the porch wiping her hands on an apron. She was about forty years of age, of short stature but the years had not diminished her youthfulness or the golden sheen of her hair.

'Fidelma, have you come to collect the child already? I was just about to serve some hot cakes. Ah, and Brother Conchobhar is with you. Welcome, Brother. I have all your herbs ready. So come in, come in. Taste some of the cakes I have just taken from the oven and I have good cider to wash them down with.'

Like a mother shepherding her young, she drew everyone into the house. Aibell had calmed the dog, once more excited by the arrival of visitors. It took its impatient post just outside the door. Alchú was placed at the table with a cake and a beaker of the crushed juice of apples.

After the formalities of tasting the delicious cakes and sipping strong apple cider, Fidelma asked: 'Have you seen Beccan in these parts recently?'

'Beccan? I don't really know him,' Della replied with a shake of her head. 'He's the new steward at your brother's palace, isn't he? A strange little man, I am told. I gather he's very proper, very courteous, but he surrounds himself with a wall so no one ever gets to know him.'

'Ah, I thought you might have known Beccan and seen him passing here.' Fidelma was disappointed.

'Dar Luga told me that Beccan was given a job in your brother's kitchens and then, scarcely a full moon or two went by before he rose to become steward of the King's household.'

'That was because of the unexpected death of the previous steward,' Fidelma pointed out.

'I thought it strange that your brother did not choose a steward from one of the Eóghanacht clans rather than a man of the Déisi. At least, Dar Luga *said* he was from that clan.'

Fidelma's head jerked upwards. 'The Déisi?' Of course, she had been overlooking the fact that Beccan came from that territory.

'Now why would you think Beccan would be coming around here?' Della asked comfortably.

Fidelma explained the story Beccan had told her about Maon, and where she and Brother Conchobhar had been and what they had seen.

'Odd you should mention that hut,' Della commented. 'The other day, Gormán had an errand which took him through the woods, along that very path. When he came back, he asked me about the woodsman's cabin and whether it was used. I said it had not been used, so far as I could recall, since I was a young girl – and that is certainly not yesterday. When I asked my lad why he was enquiring, he said he had seen a horse tethered outside.'

Fidelma sighed. 'Dar Luga said the same to me. She had also passed along that path.'

'Shame on Beccan if he took a poor sick girl to nurse her there,' Della sniffed. 'There was room enough here, had he sought my hospitality.'

Fidelma exchanged a meaningful glance with Brother Conchobhar. 'Somehow, I do not think that we need fear for her health just yet,' she said dryly. 'Anyway, we must return to the palace and have a further word with Beccan to find out where the girl has gone.'

'It seems strange that she should have gone anywhere, immediately after a fever. It usually takes a few days to recover one's strength,' Brother Conchobhar observed.

Fidelma silently agreed with him. Then she remembered the other matter she wanted to raise with Aibell.

'Aibell, I need to prepare you . . . Brother Conchobhar here has a relative who has been staying at the palace. He is of the Luachra and from Sliabh Luachra.'

A scowl formed on the girl's face. 'I hoped never to hear the name of those people and that place again.' She looked accusingly at the old physician. 'I did not know you were from Sliabh Luachra?'

'I am not,' replied the old man. 'But I had a sister who married a man of the Luachra. She died many years ago, but now and then her son passes through Cashel and insists on visiting me.'

Despite being of the age of choice, Aibell had been sold to Fidaig, the chief of the Luachra, as a bondservant in an act of petty revenge. Her father had been an evil lout and wife-beater, and when his wife had fled from his home, he had carried out the illegal transaction of selling his own daughter into bondage. She had remained trapped in that position among the Luachra until she had seized a chance to escape.

'I thought I should mention this to you in case you encountered the man and recognised him, or he recognised you,' Fidelma said gently. 'At the moment, he is under guard as a suspect in the deaths that have occurred. But I thought it best to forewarn you.'

'I shall do my best to avoid any member of the Luachra,' the girl shuddered.

'Indeed. Anyway, you have nothing to fear now from any member of the clan Luachra.'

'We have heard gossip of deaths in the palace,' interposed Della. 'Is this man responsible?'

Brother Conchobhar broke in here, on the defensive. 'I refuse to believe it. Even though I disagree with my nephew's views and way of life, I know he would never raise a hand in anger to anyone.'

'Who is this relative of yours, Brother Conchobhar?' asked Aibell. 'Would I have known him in Sliabh Luachra?'

'Perhaps not. His name is Deogaire.'

The effect on the girl was remarkable. Her mouth opened with a loud gasp and her eyes widened.

'Do you mean Deogaire the soothsayer?' she breathed.

'Indeed, I do. Deogaire is my sister's son.'

The girl took a pace backwards and sat down abruptly.

CHAPTER EIGHTEEN

❧

'So you do know him?' Fidelma observed quietly.

To her surprise, a happy smile spread over Aibell's features. 'Yes, I know him. Where may I see him? Is he at the palace?'

A feeling of disquiet came over Fidelma at the girl's enthusiastic response.

'What is he to you?' she enquired.

'He was someone who was very kind to me.'

'Deogaire was kind to you?' Brother Conchobhar looked even more surprised. 'How so, child?'

'Without Deogaire's help I would not have been able to escape from the household of Fidaig, where I was confined as a bondservant against all law and morals,' the girl said firmly.

'You have never told us the story of your escape from the mountain fastness of the Luachra,' Fidelma said now. 'I know only that you escaped; that you reached the Ass's Ford at the River Siúr and managed to get a ride on the wagon of the merchant Ordan of Rathordan. He brought you to Cashel where we found you in the woodsman's hut across the paddock there.'

'There was little enough to tell,' the girl shrugged.

'Tell us that little, so that we might understand,' coaxed Fidelma.

'For a long time I was forced to serve in the house of Fidaig of Sliabh Luachra. I was ill-treated and could confide my anguish to no one. Hope was beyond my thoughts until . . . until one day, Deogaire came to the fortress of Fidaig. He was treated with respect because the Luachra are very superstitious; many believe in the old gods, even though some, like Artgal and Gláed, the sons of Fidaig, seem to follow the New Faith. You know how remote the territory is, surrounded by many mountains and set in impenetrable marshes. Don't they call the twin peaks that rise there the Breasts of Danu? She was pagan Mother Goddess of our people.'

Aibell paused for a moment and then continued: 'Whenever there were guests at Fidaig's fortress, which was not often, I was forced to serve them and thus I served Deogaire. He was truly in tune with the spirits, for he saw at once how unhappy I was; how desperate I had become. For the first time since I was taken by Fidaig, I found I had someone to talk to. All my anguish poured forth with his encouragement. At last, he said that his heart went out to me. He taught me that even a barren wood can eventually renew its foliage. He gave me hope for the future. He helped me flee from the fastnesses of that terrible place.'

'He helped you escape from Fidaig?' Fidelma was surprised.

'One night he took me on his horse. We avoided the guards and rode off into the mountains. Fidaig sent his warriors after us. Once or twice they nearly caught us. Then we were sheltering in the Glen of Ravens – a grim solitude in which, Deogaire told me, the old Goddess of Death and Battles dwelled. From our hiding place, we saw Fidaig's men searching for us and realised that it would not be long before they discovered us.

'Deogaire said we would have to part company. If we both fled on our single horse, we would soon be overtaken and captured. If he fled using my cloak, he might be able to convince them that I was clinging to his back. He could then lead them away from the Glen of Ravens. He told me that as soon as he drew them off, I should make my way out of the mountains and go eastward, where he would try to join me. It happened as he said. I saw him galloping down the valley and, in hue and cry after him, rode a score of Fidaig's warriors. As soon as they were out of sight, I set off on the route he had instructed me to follow.' She looked at Fidelma. 'I never saw him again.'

'And you eventually reached the Ford of the Ass where Ordan the merchant picked you up,' Fidelma repeated. 'And you have not heard of Deogaire since your escape?'

'Alas, I have not heard of him again – that is, until now.'

Brother Conchobhar seemed cheered by her story. 'Then there must be some good in him, after all.'

'Good? How could you doubt it?' demanded the girl, showing a touch of her old aggressiveness. Then before Brother Conchobhar could answer, she went on: 'I suppose it is because he will not give up the old religion of our people that others condemn him? Why should he accept the New Faith from the east? Because someone does not agree with you, it does not make them bad. I would rather have Deogaire's friendship and support than someone like my father, who claimed all his life to uphold the New Faith.'

Brother Conchobhar shifted uneasily. 'I would hope that Deogaire is not beyond redemption,' he muttered piously.

'Redemption? Does he need to be delivered from what you see as a corrupted state? When we hear of the quarrels among those professing the New Faith, arguments of whether this interpretation or that is right or wrong – arguments which have often led to bloodshed – who has the right to judge that someone like Deogaire stands in need of being saved from his beliefs? Is there something better to be offered by this New Faith?'

Della looked unhappy, glancing towards young Alchú who was sitting in wide-eyed solemnity at the passionate-sounding adult discussion. 'Aibell, we are all of the New Faith here,' she chided gently. 'Surely you are not saying that you uphold the old ways?'

Aibell flushed and then seemed to calm herself. 'I am sorry, Della. I do not mean to sound insulting. I am not sure *what* I believe after the way my father treated me. I simply cannot abide someone like Deogaire being criticised because his beliefs are different. They were the beliefs of our people a thousand years before the coming of those new ideas from the east. They were the beliefs of the time before time. Surely he is entitled to them?'

There was a silence and then Fidelma leaned forward and patted the girl's arm. Secretly, she felt sympathy with the logic of her arguments. 'No one will condemn a person for their beliefs,' she said. 'Everyone is entitled to their own views, so long as those views do no harm to anyone else.'

'Deogaire is up at the palace?' Aibell was still animated. 'I must come up and see him.'

Fidelma said uncomfortably, 'I have told you that it will not be possible immediately. He is being held under guard while an investigation into several deaths is being conducted.'

The girl's expression was shocked. 'Are you serious? He is being accused of involvement in these deaths?'

'Among other things,' confirmed Fidelma.

'Then . . . then you must defend him,' Aibell burst out. 'You are a *dálaigh*. You will clear him.'

Fidelma hesitated a moment or two. What was the old saying? *Even truth may be bitter.* 'I am the one doing the investigating, Aibell,' she said quietly. 'It is I who have ordered his incarceration because of the evidence so far.'

The hope seemed to die from Aibell's face. Then she said in a fierce but respectful tone: 'I will not accept that Deogaire has harmed anyone. I *refuse* to believe it.'

'Then let us hope that we can support your belief.' Fidelma rose. 'Come, Alchú. We must be getting back now.' She turned to the girl. 'I will keep you informed, and as soon as it is possible to see Deogaire, I will send for you, Aibell. You have my word.'

She then thanked Della for her hospitality. Her friend looked troubled as she handed the bags of herbs to Brother Conchobhar and bade them all farewell. Aibell sat silently at the table, staring unseeingly before her and forgot to even say goodbye to Alchú.

After they had ridden a little way, Brother Conchobhar ventured a look at Fidelma. 'You are worried,' he commented.

Fidelma glanced quickly at little Alchú on his pony. His mind seemed occupied with his mount at that moment so she replied in an undertone: 'I *am* worried. This is a new development. Has Deogaire ever spoken to you of Aibell?'

'He keeps many things secret,' sighed the old apothecary. 'I suppose there is no reason why he should have mentioned her. He probably did not even know that she was in the township.'

'Aibell seems to have a very high regard for him,' Fidelma said. 'That is quite apparent.'

The old man nodded slowly. 'You mean that she is enamoured of him? Well, there is no denying it. I too can see the signs. I think that you are now worried about young Gormán?'

'I knew Gormán and liked him even before I found out that my old friend Della was actually his mother. Remember how that was hidden until they were accused of both murder and incest – and then the truth emerged?'

'At least *that* truth emerged,' Brother Conchobhar replied. 'And you were the instrument of it coming to light.'

'I saw that Gormán was stricken with Aibell from the first moment he saw her. I have heard tales of what they call the *teinntide* but did not really know it existed until I saw Gormán's reaction to her.'

'*Teinntide* – the lightning bolt.' Brother Conchobhar gave a deep chuckle. 'It is the thing that all the bards rhapsodise over. When young lovers are smitten at first sight and—'

'Gormán suffered that malady,' interrupted Fidelma stiffly. 'I had believed that there was some reciprocation from Aibell, but seeing and hearing her speak about Deogaire just now, well . . . I think there is another vying for her affections.'

'That is hard,' agreed the old physician. 'I think a lot of people "suffer the malady" as you call it. Didn't you, when you first met Eadulf?'

Fidelma fell silent. She was not thinking of Eadulf but of earlier days, when she was a young student at the law school of Brehon Morann and had experienced the *teinntide*. A young warrior named Cian stole her heart and then went off with another, leaving her desolate. She had not been able to overcome the effects of the affair until, many years later, she re-encountered Cian on the pilgrim voyage. She had recognised Cian for the vain and self-centred personality that he was and always had been. Her feelings for him had been no more than an infatuation and not an emotion that would have grown and strengthened through the years. She had to say that she had never felt that way with Eadulf. It was merely a friendship that had grown until such time when it was impossible to turn back. They had become inseparable, even though she had tried several times to break the bond between them. Now she acknowledged that it was real love and not the *teinntide*, although Eadulf had always claimed that he had known his feelings from the moment they had first bumped into each other, hurrying from opposite directions around the corner of a corridor in Hilda's Abbey in Streonshalh.

'You are silent, my dear,' interrupted the voice of Brother Conchobhar. She started from her reverie. 'I am sorry. What were you saying?'

'I was asking if you felt this lightning bolt when you first met our friend Eadulf?'

'This love at first sight is not to be trusted,' she said impatiently. 'Love is knowing someone. You cannot know someone with the first look. Loving is knowing the faults as well as the good qualities.'

Brother Conchobhar disguised his surprise. He had always understood from Eadulf that his had been a matter of the *teinntide* and thought it had been reciprocated by Fidelma.

'I am afraid for young Gormán,' Fidelma was continuing sadly. 'The fact that Aibell is living with Della, Gormán's mother, and already becoming part of the family . . . that will lead to difficulties. I was expecting to hear an announcement of the intentions of Aibell and Gormán soon.'

'It will become even more difficult if Deogaire is indeed the person who attempted to kill you and Eadulf,' the old man dryly observed.

They were crossing over the town square by now. Fidelma glanced towards Rumann's tavern. The Laighin warriors were still there and seemed to be paying court to a couple of local girls from the township who were obviously enjoying their attentions.

'Somehow I do not believe that Deogaire will be found guilty for everything,' she replied absently.

'I hope not, if only for the fact that I, as his only kinsman here, would be responsible for paying his fines, compensation and honour price.'

Fidelma whipped round – and then saw that the old physician's eyes were twinkling. She chuckled. Brother Conchobhar was known for his oblique sense of humour. 'I think your money will be perfectly safe, Brother Conchobhar,' she said. 'Oh yes, I'm sure of that.'

Gormán had led the way at a brisk pace, with Eadulf, clinging precariously to his speeding mount, alongside Brother Berrihert, while Aidan brought up the rear, keeping a watchful eye on the unskilled riders. They paused only once to allow the horses to water, and thereby made good time across the low-lying country towards the mountains that marked the beginning of the wide pass into the great glen through which the broad River Eatharlach flowed.

As Eadulf had estimated, the sun had already lowered behind the mountains as they turned into the mouth of the valley which ran east to west. They forded the river across to the south side of the valley, which brought them into the foothills of the range called the Forest Mountains. Some dozen peaks emerged from the great spread of trees which covered their slopes. A little way from the river, but near one of the myriad streams that fed it, Brother Berrihert and his two brothers had built a little wooden hut and had started work on erecting a chapel in which they could tend to the spiritual needs of the local Uí Cuileann clan. Dusk had not entirely encompassed the mountains but they could see a flickering fire through the trees from some distance before they came into the clearing where the buildings were. The reason the fire had been built outside was so as not to present any danger to the wooden buildings while they were under construction.

Brother Berrihert gave a cry of reassurance as they were challenged.

One of his brothers emerged to greet them from the wooden hut as they came into the clearing. Eadulf was already dismounting from his horse and recognised Brother Pecanum.

'He has grown worse,' Brother Pecanum said without preamble. His features were set in a mask of concern. 'I thought we had managed to control the wound but I fear corruption has taken hold of his arm. I have seen the like before. I fear that the arm may have to be removed.'

Eadulf was horrified. 'Is Dego's wound that bad?'

'We are at fault. We thought it was a clean wound, but since Berrihert left for Cashel, the cuts have worsened. He was stabbed in the arm – his sword arm,' Brother Pecanum replied contritely. 'We cleaned it as best we could, but now there is much putrescent, foul-smelling odour from the wound.'

There was a sharp intake of breath from Gormán. As commander of the King's bodyguard he knew what it meant to a warrior to have his right arm amputated, even if he survived the surgery.

A cry of pain came from within the hut and Eadulf asked: 'Have you given him anything to ease the suffering?'

'He has insisted nothing be done until he has seen you, Brother Eadulf,' was the reply. 'He is a determined man.'

Eadulf turned to Gormán and Aidan. 'Wait outside while I go and examine him.' He paused, swallowed as if preparing himself, then he entered the hut. The interior was lit by a couple of lamps. Naovan, the third brother, was squatting by the side of a palliasse, dabbing with a damp cloth at the brow of the figure that lay writhing on it. Brother Naovan glanced up, giving no more than a quick look of recognition, before leaning close to the figure and saying, 'Brother Eadulf is here.'

The warrior's face was bathed in sweat in spite of being almost sickly pale in complexion. The eyes were barely open and seemed unable to focus. There was little of the handsome young man that Eadulf had last seen at Cashel, only a few days before.

'Friend . . . friend Eadulf?' the voice croaked. 'Are you there?'

Eadulf crouched beside the palliasse. He could already smell the odour of decay from the arm. 'I am here, Dego.'

'I am . . . am truly sorry.'

Eadulf ran a tongue around his dry lips. 'Sorry for what?'

'We were fishing, Egric and I . . . fishing. Leaning over water . . . stream. Something hit me . . . hit me from behind. Sharp blow. They . . . someone . . . Egric disappeared. Whoever attacked me must have dealt with him. Heard horses. Sorry I . . . I didn't . . . didn't protect your brother.'

He was agitated and Eadulf told him to relax, but even as he did so, Dego fell back into semi-consciousness and started to mutter incoherently.

Brother Naovan reached forward, feeling his forehead. Then he said: 'Berrihert saw no sign of any companion with the warrior. Someone had attacked him from behind. There is a small flesh wound in his shoulder but a jagged dagger wound in the arm. I think the attacker was aiming for his back, but then Dego moved and the knife struck into the arm. Before he could turn to defend himself, he was also hit across the back of his head. The head wound was not so bad and could be treated. So could the smaller wound. But the one in the arm . . .' He ended with a shrug.

'Let me see this arm,' Eadulf muttered, trying not to think about his brother for the moment. He peered down at the tortured face of the warrior with whom he and Fidelma had shared so many adventures. His first duty was to do what he could for the young man.

Brother Naovan moved aside the coverings and exposed the right arm. Eadulf's mouth tightened as he saw the condition of the swollen tissue and smelled the curious foetid odour like a rotting cheese. Whatever knife had been used, it had not been clean nor was it sharp. The infection had spread rapidly. Brother Pecanum was right, the area was blackening. Eadulf had not wasted his time in the period that he had studied the apothecary's art at Tuam Brecain. He knew the signs.

'We must amputate the arm immediately if he is to have any chance at all of surviving,' he announced.

'So we thought,' agreed Brother Naovan. 'But we lack any skill. Simple things we can do – administer potions, make salves . . . but to take a knife to the flesh, muscle and bone – that requires knowledge.'

'Yet it must be done,' Eadulf replied roughly. He rose and went outside to where the others were waiting and looked around grimly. He had been speaking in his own language to Brother Naovan: now he sought for the right words so that Gormán and Aidan could also understand what was to be done. He settled on *trochugad*, a cutting-off of the limb.

'His arm needs amputation and it must be done now,' he said. 'Does anyone know the art? You must have seen it done in battle.'

They mumbled negatively. Eadulf gritted his teeth and stated: 'Then I must attempt it.'

Fidelma had left Brother Conchobhar at the stables and made her way to the *Laochtech* where she founded Enda and Luan relaxing. They rose uncertainly as she entered.

'I have come to see our prisoner,' she announced.

'I shan't be sorry when we can release that one,' Enda said, reaching for the keys.

'Why? Is Deogaire giving you trouble?'

'You might call it that,' Enda sighed. 'He's been constantly calling out, asking if Beccan has returned. When I said he had, he kept demanding that Beccan be brought here so he could confront him with the truth.'

'I presume that you did not comply with that request?' Fidelma asked anxiously.

Enda looked offended. 'Of course not, lady. Gormán left strict instructions and these could only be contradicted by you. I even ignored the demands of Brehon Aillín.'

'Brehon Aillín? she exclaimed. 'Has he tried to interfere?'

'He came and asked to see the prisoner. When I told him my orders, he was quite upset. He pointed out that he was Chief Brehon but I said that the orders of my commander could only be countermanded by the King or someone delegated by him. If the King summoned me to do so, I would let him see Deogaire.'

'That's interesting,' Fidelma said thoughtfully, almost to herself. 'When was Brehon Aillín here?'

'Some time after you and Brother Conchobhar left the palace.'

'And he went away when you refused him?'

'He did so, lady. But not in the best of moods.'

'Very well. Unlock the door and then wait outside while I have a word with Deogaire.'

'Is that wise, lady?'

'I deem it so.'

Enda unlocked the door and opened it, allowing Fidelma to pass into the small room beyond before closing it. Deogaire leaped up from the cot on which he had been sitting when she entered.

'Has Beccan returned?' he demanded excitedly. 'Has he told the truth?'

'He has returned.'

'Then I am free?'

'Sit down, Deogaire.' She pointed to the cot. Without waiting for him to obey, she sank onto the only stool in the room, then said: 'Why do you think Brehon Aillín wanted to see you this afternoon?'

'Did he? Was that what the fuss was about?' Deogaire sat down. 'I heard some shouting earlier. Look, lady, I am not privy to the old man's thoughts,' he went on. 'If you didn't send him, maybe he wanted to question me himself. You must ask *him*.'

'Perhaps.'

'If Beccan is back, then why am I not released?' he then demanded.

Fidelma looked at him levelly. 'Because your truth is different from his truth. His account and your account do not entirely tally.'

Deogaire blinked for a moment. 'I don't understand.'

'There is no question that your relative, Brother Conchobhar, and you had a row and that you left his house. But you said that Beccan suggested to you that you could stay in the guest quarters. However, Beccan says that *you* sought him out and suggested it to him! He says that you offered to pay with herbal remedies taken from Brother Conchobhar's store, after Beccan had mentioned his sick friend.'

Deogaire stared at her in incomprehension.

'Don't you see?' went on Fidelma patiently. 'If you told Beccan that you would give him these medicines in return for a room in the guest quarters, then it places a different complexion on matters. It would imply that you wanted to stay in the guest quarters for a specific purpose.'

'I just needed a bed for the night! I could have gone to the stables, curled up in the chapel, or even gone down into the town where there is an inn. I did not want to start out for Sliabh Luachra in the dark.'

'But you didn't stay in any of those places. You stayed in the guest quarters that night. While you were there, there was an attempt on the lives of Eadulf and myself.' She paused. '*Now* do you see the question of logic that arises as to how you came there? Am I to believe you or Beccan, my brother's steward?'

Deogaire was shaking his head. 'Question of logic or not, I tell you it was no doing of mine. Beccan suggested the solution to me and not I to him.'

'And what logical purpose would it serve Beccan?'

Deogaire raised his hands in the air in a gesture of helpless mystification.

'I have no understanding of it,' he said. 'All I know is that I have spoken the truth.'

Fidelma sighed. 'Then you can only wait until I have investigated further. I need to have another word with Beccan. But here you are and here you must remain until things become clearer.'

'And if they don't?' snapped Deogaire. 'Am I to be a victim of Beccan's lies?'

'Every tide has its ebb, Deogaire,' Fidelma assured him as she rose. 'Isn't that in your philosophy?'

The young man scowled but made no reply. Fidelma felt instinctively sorry for Deogaire. She leaned forward and touched his shoulder.

'You once taught a young girl that even a barren wood will renew its foliage. In her case, it came true. Take note of your own advice.'

He glanced up, his brows drawn together, trying to read a meaning behind her words.

'At least you have one friend in the vicinity,' Fidelma amplified. 'One who believes that you could never do what is now suspected of you. A young girl whom you helped set free from Fidaig's bondage.'

'Aibell?' Deogaire rose from his seat. 'Is she here? Did she escape from the Valley of Ravens? Where is she?'

Fidelma raised a hand to calm him. 'All in good time. You see, sunshine follows dark clouds. At least, Aibell sees you for what you are and not the person people think you are. You will see her later when this matter is sorted out.'

'When will that be?' he asked hopefully.

'All I can say is that I hope it is not long. You have been used for a purpose, but I am not sure what. This is why you must remain here, because I think it is the one place that you will be safe.'

Back outside, after Enda had locked the door, she said quietly, 'I want your most trusted warriors to guard the prisoner; trusted men to keep awake in this corridor all night as well as day.'

'It shall be done, lady,' Enda replied, a note of excitement in his voice. 'Do you think that he will try to break out then? Try to escape?'

She shook her head with a soft smile. 'Oh no, my friend. I think someone might try to break *in* – and kill him.'

Eadulf was regarding his companions in the firelight with a grim countenance. 'I will have to carry out the amputation. At least I have seen it performed by a physician.'

'What about your brother, friend Eadulf?' demanded Gormán hesitantly. 'Should we not try to find him first?'

'Dego might well be dead before this night is out. He is our first priority. Besides, there is nothing we can do about Egric before first light. We can't go hunting for him in darkness.'

Eadulf looked around. Near the fire was a rough wooden table at which the three religious no doubt prepared their food and took their meals.

'Have you several lanterns?' he demanded of Brother Berrihert. Receiving the affirmative, he pointed to the table. 'I need you to wash that table down with water and hang the lanterns around it so that it is well illuminated.'

Berrihert and Pecanum immediately bent to their task. Eadulf then turned to Gormán and Aidan.

'Your task will be distasteful, my friends. You will have to hold Dego down while I work on him.'

'Understood,' grunted Gormán. 'I have a *lestar* of *laith*; it is intoxicating liquor that might help him.'

'I have another,' Aidan said. 'It is very strong.'

Eadulf approved. A *lestar* was a container for carrying liquids. 'The stronger the alcohol, the better. It will help both as a means of easing the pain and for dressing the wound to prevent infection. Also, cut a couple of stout twigs and strip the bark – he will need something to bite on and I will need something to use to twist cloth to make a band to encircle his arm, which will control bleeding.'

While these tasks were being done, Eadulf went to his horse and untied the leather bag that he always carried. It was called a *lés* – a small medical bag; it had become his habit to carry it with him. Several times he had had recourse to it during his travels with Fidelma, and he always tried to keep its contents in good order. Inside were some surgical instruments and some small containers, *soithech*, for herbal infusions, among which were antiseptics and sedatives. He took the bag and returned to where Brother Pecanum was finishing dousing the table with water. Brother Berrihert had lit and hung the lanterns.

'Very well.' Eadulf viewed the preparations with satisfaction. He took a stool and, putting his *lés* upon it, took the containers of alcohol offered by the warriors. 'We will have to work fast. Very fast. You need to understand that I cannot guarantee that I will save him, but if nothing is done he will be dead by morning anyway.'

They stood silently before him. Eadulf was thankful for the distorting shadows of the lanterns, for he hoped they disguised his pallor and nervous expression. The other men looked to him for confidence and leadership now.

'Gormán, take one of the containers of alcohol and get Dego to swallow as much he can take. After that, you and Aidan will lift him from inside and place him on this table. You, Aidan, will hold his legs still while Gormán restrains his left arm and shoulder. I will be attending to his right. I am hoping the alcohol will make it easy.' Eadulf took a deep breath. 'Berrihert, I want you at my side all the time, holding one of the lamps as I instruct you. Pecanum, you will have to be my assistant and pass me whatever tools I want. I shall show you the items beforehand that I shall need.'

He looked around. They did not have any questions.

'When we start, I shall need to work quickly. So, let us begin. Gormán, off you go, and see how much you and Naovan can get Dego to take. With luck, he will pass out. Pecanum, come, and I will run through the items that I shall need from this bag.'

A few minutes later, Dego was carried out and laid on the table. He was muttering restlessly, in a semi-conscious state, the alcohol mixing with his fever. Eadulf, grim faced, glanced at his companions.

'Ready in positions?' he asked tersely. Then he placed a piece of cloth around the top of the warrior's right arm, inserted a small twig and twisted it until he could turn it no more. Then he passed another twig to Gormán, who took it, prised open Dego's mouth and placed it so that his teeth would clamp down on it.

'Now!' Eadulf grunted.

Gormán and Aidan pushed their weight down on Dego to hold him still. Brother Berrihert moved forward with a lamp.

Eadulf had already taken the razor-like *altan* – a surgical knife – in his hand. He worked as quickly as he dared. Only moments later, he called for Brother Pecanum to pass him the *rodb* – a sharp-edged surgical saw. That was when Dego began to scream, and Gormán and Aidan had to use their full weight to contain his threshing body. The arm came away, leaving a bloody stump above the elbow. Then, mercifully, Dego sank into unconsciousness. Quickly again, with Brother Pecanum's help, Eadulf poured the *laith* generously over the bloodied stump. Then he took the clean tissue and flap of skin he had left and drew it over the end of the stump, taking the needle, already threaded with gut, and sewed it into place. Once more he poured the alcohol over it.

'You can all relax now,' he sighed, glancing round at his companions.

Dego was lying unconscious on the table. Eadulf leaned forward, placing his hand on the warrior's forehead. It was clammy. He bent forward, placing an ear to the man's chest, just above his heart. There was a heartbeat, rapid but regular. He stepped back to his *lés* and extracted a roll of fresh white linen and then one of the small containers. He poured the liquid contents over the linen and then proceeded to bandage the stump of Dego's arm with it. Finally, he stood back again, breathing heavily after his exertions.

Brother Berrihert was standing next to him and proffering a cup of something. 'You need it,' he said.

Eadulf did not argue but took a swallow. He had not expected the strength of the fiery liquid and coughed several times.

Brother Berrihert grinned. 'It's brewed from bog berries – you know, the red flowers of some heather and who knows what else. Pretty powerful, eh?'

Eadulf simply nodded and wiped his stinging lips.

'You can carry Dego back to the bed,' he instructed Brother Berrihert and Aidan. As they lifted the unconscious man, something fell out of Dego's clothing. Eadulf caught sight of a glint in the torchlight. He bent forward and felt for it, thinking it might be a coin. However, the item was too heavy and soft for a piece of bronze, silver or gold. He took it to the lamplight and held it up, turning it over and over between thumb and finger.

He had seen something similar enough times to recognise it. He whistled in surprise.

'What is it, friend Eadulf?' asked Gormán.

'Just a piece of lead. It dropped from Dego's clothing.'

'Oh, that.'

Eadulf glanced questioningly at Gormán. 'Have you seen it before?'

'It was something Dego was going to use as a weight for his fishing line.'

'But where did he get it?'

Gormán paused to think and then remembered. 'Oh, it was among the debris left when the Déisi thugs attacked your brother and his companion at the river.'

Eadulf felt his heart pounding more rapidly. 'Tell me, Gormán – was anything attached to it?'

'Attached?' Gormán was puzzled. 'It's just a lump of metal with a pile of burned documents.'

'Documents? It wasn't attached to any parchment with a piece of ribbon?'

'The documents had been burned. I can't remember if they were vellum, parchment or papyrus. They were all too damaged to make anything of them. That slug of lead was lying among them, as I recall. Dego picked it up and, realising it was worth nothing, said he would use it as a weight for his fishing line.'

'Worth nothing,' muttered Eadulf, regarding it thoughtfully.

'Well, it can't be a coin. It's lead. Maybe it's a good luck amulet because it has the Latin word for "life" on one side. See there – v. i. t. a. – life.'

Eadulf smiled gently and shook his head. 'Not "life", Gormán, but a name – Vitalian.'

'Why would someone inscribe their name on a piece of lead?' wondered the puzzled warrior.

'I'll keep this by me for the time being,' Eadulf replied, without answering. 'Don't worry. I'll compensate Dego for it.' He suddenly glanced at the makeshift operating table and the limb that had been left on it.

'Someone had better bury that,' he instructed quietly. 'And also thoroughly scrub down that table with hot water.'

Gormán immediately set to work with Brother Pecanum.

Brother Berrihert re-emerged from the hut. 'Naovan is sitting with him,' he reported. 'Is there nothing else we can do?'

'Nothing now except say a prayer. We will know more by daylight.'

'Well, whatever happens now,' called Gormán, looking up from his task, 'I hope the bards sing your praises, friend Eadulf. I have never seen such skill before. Come the day when I am bested in battle and in danger of losing an arm or leg, I trust you will be there for me. You are even greater than Fingín Faithliáig.'

Eadulf gazed incomprehendingly at the warrior, knowing he was paying him a compliment. 'Who?'

'He was the greatest physician in all Muman,' declared Gormán. 'Have you not heard of the Battle of Crinna that took place up in Midhe, the Middle Kingdom?'

Eadulf shook his head. Exhaustion was beginning to catch up with him. His thoughts were becoming jumbled. A horse blanket lay near the fire and he went across and sat down on it. He could hear Gormán's voice without really understanding the words.

'Crinna was fought over four centuries ago, even before the Eóghanacht established Cashel as the centre of their kingdom. Tadg son of Cian was King in those far-off days. Fingín was his chief physician. The story is that a king from Ulaidh, one Fergus son of Imchadh, marched his army into Midhe in an attempt to overthrow the High King, Cormac son of Art. Cormac called upon those provincial kings who were loyal to him to come to his aid. Only Tadg and his warriors marched from Muman to help him. There was a great battle at Crinna in which Fergus was defeated and killed. But in the battle, Tadg was badly wounded; some say his skull was split open. His physician Fingín went to his aid and healed him. He was hailed as the greatest of all physicians.'

Eadulf tried to smile but could not summon the energy.

'The time to comment on my competence, Gormán,' he tried to say, wondering why a fog seemed to be welling out of the surrounding forests, 'will be in the morning and . . .' He was falling . . .

He felt the strong arms of Gormán catching him. Someone cried out in alarm and he heard Gormán say: 'It's exhaustion, that's all. He . . .'

The voice receded into the distance and Eadulf seemed to be swimming in a dark pool with no sense of space or time.

CHAPTER NINETEEN

❧

Fidelma came awake with someone shaking her shoulder. She was sitting up in a moment, ready to defend herself. However, it was only Muirgen, the nurse. The sky was light but grey, and it must be well after dawn. She had slept long and deeply. She was about to apologise when it became obvious that Muirgen was waking her for a purpose.

'What is it?' Her first thought was of her husband. 'Is Eadulf back?'

Muirgen shook her head. 'No, lady, it is Enda who asks you to go to the gates immediately.'

'Immediately? I am not up yet, not washed or dressed.'

'He said it is most urgent, lady. Another body has been found.'

It took a second for the news to register before Fidelma swung quickly out of bed and was frantically seeking her clothes. She began hurriedly dressing with the aid of Muirgen.

'It is not Deogaire who has been found?' It was the first thought that came to her.

'He did not say, lady.' Muirgen pushed Fidelma onto a stool and began to tidy her hair with the means of a comb. Fidelma fretted, moving impatiently while the old nurse attended to her toilette. Finally free, she raced out of the chamber, across the courtyard and towards the gates, where Enda and another warrior stood with a man who looked familiar: it was the stonemason she had spoken with earlier. Fidelma gave an inward groan. She had meant to ask her brother to place a guard on the scaffolding, but had forgotten all about it.

'What is it?' she asked breathlessly, glancing from Enda to the stonemason.

The warrior indicated that the stonemason should speak first.

'Me and my lads were coming to start this morning's work, lady,' the man began nervously. 'It was just getting light. We found a body at the base of the scaffolding. It was obvious from the way it lay that the man had fallen from the top to the bottom. He was quite dead.'

Fidelma's mouth felt dry with fear. 'You didn't by any chance recognise him?'

'Sadly, we did.'

'Why sadly?'

'Sadly, because he was the man who employed us to do the building work.'

'I don't understand. The work is done on behalf of my brother . . .'

'His steward, lady. Beccan. He was the man we dealt with.'

She stared at him, so intensely that he dropped his gaze and shuffled unhappily before her.

'You mean that the body is that of Beccan?' she repeated, as though she had not understood the first time.

'That is so, lady. It was the body of Beccan the steward.'

Several thoughts were going round in her mind, most of them spurred by guilt. Having found out that Beccan had lied about the woman who was supposed to be ill in the hut in the woods, his story contradicted by Deogaire, she had been determined to confront him. But she had decided to let a night pass; lull Beccan into a false sense of security before tackling him head on. If she was right, and Beccan *was* involved, then this death could be blamed on her inaction. She had even hoped that Eadulf might have returned with further information by now, because the key to the whole series of deaths, she now saw clearly, lay with what had happened on the River Siúr. Eadulf's brother Egric was an important link to that.

Enda asked respectfully: 'Shall I order the body to be brought around to Brother Conchobhar's apothecary, lady?'

But the stonemason was talking. 'It is hard to see how anyone could fall accidentally,' he told Fidelma. 'As you well know, there are plenty of ladders and platforms. To miss the ladders or fall off a platform . . . well, it doesn't seem likely. Me and my men have been working on such scaffolding for years without a single mishap.'

'So you think he was helped to fall?' she asked. 'Or jumped?'

The man shrugged. 'It is not my place to say. I am responsible for the scaffolding, and if any accident happens, I would have to pay compensation. My opinion therefore must be biased, lady.'

Fidelma turned to Enda. 'Is Deogaire still safe in the *Laochtech*?'

'As you instructed, lady. He has been guarded night and day.'

'Then let us look at this scaffolding first before we remove the body,' Fidelma said. She led the way up the steps onto the wall which surrounded the palace complex. It was a short walk to the south-west corner of the ramparts. She was still silently cursing herself that she had not carried out her intention to have her brother post a sentinel by the scaffold. The stonemason and Enda watched her as she made a quick examination of the wall and the scaffolding. Her eye caught a large piece of dressed stone, not quite fitting correctly on the wall. As the wall was being rebuilt, that would not have been a matter of particular interest. What caused her to prise it loose and examine the underside of it was the sight of dark staining on the bottom. She placed the stone to one side on the top of the wall before leaning forward and peering downwards across the parapet.

'I presume that you found the body just to the side of the scaffolding?' she asked the stonemason.

The man gave a nod. 'Aye, lady.'

'There was blood on the head?'

'Of course, lady. After such a fall . . .'

'Blood on the *back* of the head?'

'He must have hit the back of his head hard. I noticed a great wound on that part of the skull.'

Fidelma turned to the others with a grim face. 'Beccan was murdered: he did not fall from the scaffolding by accident.'

The stonemason's mouth gaped stupidly. Enda whistled softly. 'How can you tell, lady?' he asked.

Fidelma lifted the piece of masonry she had taken from the wall and showed them the blood. 'Beccan had injuries to the back of the head. I take the stonemason's word for it, although we shall shortly confirm it when I view the body. It seems that this rock was used to inflict those injuries by his killer. The blood is still fresh on the underside.'

'How can we be sure that it was no accident?' Enda pressed.

'It seems unlikely that Beccan hit himself on the head, replaced the stone in this wall, then started to climb down the scaffolding, slipped and fell,' she replied. Her sarcasm was a disguise for her own self-blame. She turned and pointed across the parapet. 'Had he fallen from the scaffolding, he would not have fallen to the side where our stonemason friend here says that he was found. The position he was found in meant that he fell straight down from this spot. Someone knocked him on the head and pushed him over.'

There was a silence as they considered what she had said. The stonemason, with justification, was looking relieved at her conclusion that his equipment was not at fault.

'Now, am I right that you believe your scaffolding is still safe?'

'I say it is, since you agree that the steward did not fall from it,' the stonemason said stoutly.

'I only ask,' she told him, 'because we shall use it to climb down and view the body, rather than go all the way round through to the gate.'

Before the men could protest, she had climbed over the parapet and begun the descent. Having done it before, she found it quite easy. As she climbed down, she was thinking furiously.

She had been coming to the conclusion that Beccan was the culprit. Now he was dead. It was true that she had not entirely worked out his motive. He had been near the chapel when the body of Brother Cerdic was found; he could have easily had access to the barn where Rudgal was being held; he had lied about Deogaire and about going to see a woman called Maon at the woodman's hut; he could have returned unseen to the guest chambers that night to push the statue off the roof in an attempt to kill them. He must have used the scaffolding for access and exit without being seen; in the same way, he could have met Sister Dianaimh in the darkness and killed her. And although it could be argued as prejudice, he was of the Déisi and of the same area where Rudgal and his robber band had come from. It had all seemed to fit although she had been unable to collect the strands into one final knot. It was the motive that eluded and frustrated her.

There was more to this matter than she had thought. She must be missing something – something that would tie it all together. But what?

When Eadulf awoke he was aware of a strong, flickering light. It was the sun shining through the rustling leaves of the trees above. Then he became aware of the cacophony of birdsong. It was well past dawn. He was lying near the fire outside the wooden hut. Someone must have covered him against the cold of the night for there was a heavy blanket over him. Just then, a dark shadow intervened between him and the sun. He looked up into the smiling face of Gormán.

'Rest, friend Eadulf. All is well.' He held out a beaker of water.

Eadulf rubbed his head and tried to collect his thoughts. 'What happened?' he asked, realising that his throat was very dry. He took the beaker and sipped at the water; it was fresh and cold from the stream.

'You were exhausted,' Gormán said simply. 'You had a long ride here and then the task you had to perform at the end of it . . . well, I could not have done it. So, when you had finished, you fell into a deep sleep, which is natural.'

'Did Dego . . . has he . . .?' Eadulf began uncertainly.

'Dego lives. According to Brother Berrihert, he went into a natural sleep and slept for most of the night.'

Eadulf breathed a sigh of relief and swallowed the rest of the water in large mouthfuls.

'Sleep is the great healer,' he said. 'He should sleep as much as he can for the next few days to regain his strength.' He rose and handed the beaker back to Gormán. 'I'll go and check the wound.'

Dego was lying still on the cot. Eadulf was amazed to see that his eyes were open, although he seemed very drowsy. He even forced a faint smile as Eadulf bent over him.

'How are you feeling?' Eadulf asked.

'I've been better,' replied the warrior with a touch of humour.

Eadulf nodded sympathetically and gently unwrapped the arm. There was no foul odour and the wound was clean. Unless there were any mishaps, the stump should heal nicely without further infection. He glanced up to Brother Pecanum, who was standing by.

'The wound must be regularly washed and bathed. I shall leave some of the herbal infusion to pour onto it from time to time. It is important that it is freshly dressed to keep infection at bay. But in a few days . . . he should be healing well.'

He turned back to Dego. 'We'll soon have you up and active again.'

A dark cloud crossed the young warrior's face. His voice was bitter.

'I've been a warrior all my life. I've known nothing else but service in the Nasc Niadh. With my right arm gone, what is left for me now?'

'Come, my friend. Wasn't I told by your bards that Elatha had one hand and one eye, yet he was able to seduce the Goddess Ériu?'

'Ancient legends,' grunted the young warrior. 'He was King of the Fomorii – the undersea dwellers – who were all disfigured.'

'Well, there's many a truth in legend. Anyway, what's your left hand for? I've seen warriors fighting with their sword in their left hand.' While he was speaking, Eadulf was redressing the wound. 'We are going to leave you in the care of Berrihert and his brothers while we go in search of Egric and whoever did this to you.'

'I am sorry that I was unable to protect him. We were fishing and I heard nothing before I was knocked unconscious, although I seem to recall the movement of horses as I lay, so I must have had moments of consciousness.'

'Don't worry,' Eadulf assured him. 'Concentrate on getting well.'

Dego gave a slight movement of his head in acknowledgement but did not reply. It was clear that he was suddenly contemplating the enormity of this change in his circumstances and what it meant for his future. Outside, Eadulf had a quick exchange with Berrihert and Naovan.

'Look after him, my friends. But as well as keeping watch on that wound, keep a watch on his spirits. He is young; a warrior. So now he is thinking of what his life will become with only one hand – and his left hand at that. He may become morose, and those feelings are not conducive to heal the body.'

Brother Berrihert reached forward and took Eadulf's hand in his.

'Don't worry. We shall take especial care of him. You are truly a physician of renown, Brother Eadulf. I have never seen such work.'

'Thanks be that God guided my fingers,' muttered Eadulf. 'Thanks be that everyone was here to help. But it is early days yet. So be vigilant.'

'We understand,' replied Brother Naovan. 'He must rest as much as possible and we must keep a sharp eye on the wound lest infection occurs.'

'I shall now take you to the spot where I found Dego,' said Brother Berrihert. 'It would be difficult to find it without guidance. My brothers will look after Dego until I return.'

'Then we welcome your company, Berrihert.' Eadulf went to his bag and took from it three baked clay *lestar* sealed with *farcan* or cork imported from Iberia, reinforced with *cáir*, a malleable wax-like substance. These he showed to Pecanum and Naovan, explaining the purposes of the mixtures. 'I need you to remember the mark I have put on each container. This one is a distillation of the stalk, leaves and flowers of goldenrod, *stat óir*. It is an antiseptic and astringent that usually prevents infection, and arrests bleeding. Should you see any infection in the wound, bathe it in this.'

The two brothers nodded.

'This other one is a strong sedative which can be given as a drink. It's made from what they call *goimín serraigh*, a wild pansy. The third is a similar sedative, inducing sleep and easing headache; it's a distillation of cinquefoil, what is called here *tor cúigmhéarach*. Is that clear?'

'It is clear, Brother Eadulf. We will keep vigil over Dego and pray he grows stronger.'

Eadulf turned back to Gormán. 'Now . . . let us try to find my brother.'

Within a short time, Brother Berrihert was leading Eadulf and his companions up the mountainside. He remained on foot, while the others walked their horses. The elevation of the hill path made it difficult to ride up the slopes but Brother Berrihert had assured them that they would be needing a horse once they passed through the high valleys. It seemed that they would not be ascending any of the higher peaks of the mountains. They began to climb beyond the treelines and crossed the hill called the Pointed Peak before dropping southwards along a track that led through a valley, with one peak rising to the west and another to the east. Here they began to descend more rapidly as the path followed what was, at first, a gushing stream. It grew in strength and pace, rushing towards the plains below.

Gormán smiled. 'I recognise it. That stream will become what is called the River of Ducks: it feeds the River Siúr further across the plain there.'

'So you know this area?' Eadulf asked in surprise. In truth, he had become disorientated.

Gormán raised his hand to point to an obscure track across the southern shoulder of the mountains. 'That is called the track of Maranáin. He was an Uí Fidgente rebel who was trying to escape after the Great Uprising which ended at Cnoc Áine a few years ago. And that is where he is buried.' The young warrior's tone was that of grim approval.

'And it was just by those tracks on the east side of the river that I discovered your companion, Dego,' interrupted Brother Berrihert.

'You said that when you found him, there was no sign of my brother not even his horse?' queried Eadulf.

'As I have said, there was no other living creature nearby *except* his horse. The signs were that Dego had been fishing there when he was attacked. All I could do was set him on his horse and take him back over the eastern path.'

'You crossed the mountain with Dego and his horse from here?' Eadulf asked in astonishment.

Brother Berrihert pointed to the east. 'I brought you here by the quick route. I took him by a longer route but an easier one. It leads through that area of the forest called the Thicket of Gloiairn and there is a narrow pass between An Starraicín and Sliabh an Aird. It may be longer but far less taxing for a wounded man and his horse.'

'Well, let us see what we can pick up from the place where you found Dego.'

They reached the site identified by Brother Berrihert. Some bags and what was probably Dego's fishing tackle were still strewn about near a long-dead campfire. Aidan was already crouching on the ground and examining the area with keen, experienced eyes. He rose and trotted along the bank of the stream a little way before giving a grunt of satisfaction. Then he disappeared off towards a small copse. They waited in silence until he reappeared.

'Horses,' the warrior said laconically. 'Two horses were tied there behind the camp. There are plenty of marks indicating that two people had dismounted here and were making camp. That was Dego and Egric. But then two other horses came from the east and halted in that wood. Two men dismounted. They must have moved quietly. They crept up on the encampment. See the dried blood on that rock? I think that is where Dego was attacked.'

'And Egric?' Eadulf asked.

'There are signs of a struggle, but no blood. I think he was simply overpowered. There are marks on the ground as if he were dragged still struggling to his horse . . . there. Then there are tracks of a horse being led back to the copse where the others had left their mounts. The tracks show that three horses moved off to the east.'

'Are you saying that Egric was taken as a prisoner?' Eadulf said, impressed by Aidan's skill despite his worries. 'He was not killed?'

'It would seem that he was taken as a captive, friend Eadulf,' agreed Aidan. 'That is how I interpret the signs.'

Gormán pulled thoughtfully at his lower lip. 'What now? Who could these people be?'

'We must follow them,' Eadulf decided. 'I know the tracks are at least two days old, but we must see if they lead us anywhere. I need to find my brother and those responsible for what happened to Dego.'

It was decided that Brother Berrihert could contribute no more than he had already done. So he departed back on foot across the mountains, leaving the three grimly determined riders to follow the tracks to the east.

Colgú was pacing up and down. Now and then he cast a worried glance at his sister. They were alone in his private chamber and Fidelma was sitting relaxed in a chair before him. Finally, he halted and ran a hand distractedly through his fiery red hair.

'I have no understanding of these happenings, Fidelma. Is there some personal danger to us? After all, you and Eadulf were attacked and almost killed.'

'I do not think so,' she replied with a shake of her head. 'I believe the attack on us was done merely as a distraction; an attempt to lead us off on a wrong path. I think this affair is far more complicated than a threat to the kingship.'

'Is this some curious conspiracy of the religious then?' he demanded.

'In a way,' she conceded.

'A threat from Deogaire and the supporters of the old ways trying to stem the tide of the New Faith?'

'I am fairly sure that Deogaire was used simply as part of a diversion. I think his role is an innocent one. It is frustrating, however, that Beccan, who was my main suspect, met with his own death before I could confront him. That was a miscalculation on my part.'

'But Beccan . . . it seems impossible that he was involved! Do you have other suspects?' asked her brother.

'A lack of suspects is not the problem,' she assured him.

'Then is there any news from Eadulf yet?'

'Not yet.'

'Dego was one of my most trustworthy warriors. I pray that his wounds are not grievous. If only Gormán were here to advise me. Should I raise a *catha* of my warriors in case of trouble?' Colgú seemed distracted. Gormán had recently been promoted to a *cath-mhilidh*, the commander of a battalion of the élite warriors.

A *catha* or battalion of warriors consisted of three thousand men; it was sub-divided into companies of one hundred, platoons of fifty men and squads of nine men. Of these trained warriors, the élite were the order known as the Nasc Niadh, warriors of the Golden Collar and chosen as bodyguards to the King. Usually, only a company was permanently quartered in the place, while the rest were encamped nearby where instruction in military sciences, practice with weapons and other modes of training occupied their time. But they were always close enough to come forward in time of need.

'I don't think the danger will come from armies but from something far more dangerous,' Fidelma replied. 'Ideologies are far more dangerous to deal with than men with weapons.'

Colgú sat down and reached for a drink. 'What had Beccan to do with this religious business? I don't understand.'

'I have not pieced everything together yet. There is something I am overlooking, a single strand which leads to the centre of the knot.'

'Does that piece reside with Eadulf's brother, Egric?'

Fidelma shook her head. 'I worked out his role some time ago. I have not mentioned this to Eadulf for I think it is going to be difficult for him to accept it. Didn't Cicero refer to *bellum domesticum* – family strife? It is nothing new, but I do not think that Eadulf was expecting to be confronted by it.'

Colgú looked troubled. 'For a stranger to this land, Eadulf has given unsparingly of himself to help our people. I hope he is not in any danger?'

'There is always danger of some sort. That is why I suggested that he take Gormán and Aidan as his companions. They are two warriors in whom I place my greatest trust.'

'I hope that you will not put yourself in danger,' Colgú said anxiously. 'Are you sure that I do not need to increase the guard?'

'I have told Enda to be vigilant. It was my fault that Beccan was killed for I had fully intended to make sure of a guard at that scaffolding. I just did not think his own partner in this affair would turn on him.'

Colgú stared at her in surprise. 'So you know that Beccan had a partner?'

'Oh yes,' she replied enigmatically. 'But I am only just beginning to work out the identity of that person.'

It seemed to Eadulf that they had been following the tracks of the three horses for a long time. However, the position of the pale sun in the sky told him that it was not even midday. Aidan rode in front, leaning across the shoulder of his horse from time to time, eyes on the ground to watch the path unfolding.

'The tracks are still clear – three horses. The tracks are evenly spaced so they are not hurrying themselves.'

'Where do you think they are heading?' Eadulf asked, not for the first time.

'South-east,' replied Gormán. 'Towards the River Siúr at any rate.'

'I don't suppose there is any chance of overtaking them?'

Gormán could not lie to him. 'Let's face it, friend Eadulf,' he said. 'Dego was attacked and your brother taken two whole days ago. Even if they make leisurely camp during the nights, then they are still well ahead of us. Our only hope is that they are making for a specific place. If they stop, then we shall overtake them.'

Eadulf fell silent. It had crossed his mind earlier to ask why they themselves were travelling at such an easy pace. Surely if they increased their speed, they would overtake their quarry all the sooner? The answer came to him almost immediately. He could even hear Fidelma explaining that to do so would tire the horses, and a tired horse when they might need its strength and mobility was no use to anyone.

They were heading towards a large wooded area and Eadulf knew the River Siúr must lie beyond it. They had been travelling along a track through this forest for some time. He barely registered the different trees that made the woodland almost impenetrable except for the small path that they were following. Every so often, Aidan paused to check the trail and then signalled them onwards.

It was while Eadulf was almost dozing, so tedious was the journey becoming, and the gentle jogging of his cob allowing him to rock back and forth . . . that a sudden terrible scream shattered the air nearby. Then before the cry died away, it was followed by another.

At once, Gormán and Aidan had their swords in their hands, peering around them to identify the danger. Then, seeing nothing immediately threatening, Gormán made a motion for them to dismount, placing a finger on his lips. He gestured to Aidan who seemed to understand what he wanted, for the warrior took the reins of Gormán's horse, while Gormán moved forward in a crouching position along the path ahead of them. It twisted and turned out of sight around a bend. He was not gone for long for he soon reappeared, but approached Eadulf and Aidan with his finger once more to his lips.

'We are in luck,' he whispered. 'Those we pursue have made some permanent camp just around the bend in those trees. There seems to be an old disused cattle-pen there and a hut beside it. I presume that this is some hideout.'

The word he used was *fochlach* which Eadulf had not heard before, but supposed it meant a hiding place or den.

'Was it Egric who cried out?' he whispered back, fearing the worst.

'He is a prisoner,' confirmed the other. 'Easy, friend,' he warned as Eadulf began to move. 'They are questioning him – and none too gently.'

Eadulf stiffened but made an effort to control his emotions. 'What are we to do?'

'Egric seems to be tied to an old cattle ring on the wall. There are two captors, no more. I don't think we will have any trouble. They don't look much like warriors. We'll leave the horses here. Aidan,' he hissed 'you are good with a bow. Make your way to the far side of the cattle-pen. There is some high ground there, but plenty of cover from trees and bushes. You can see down into the pen. I will approach from this path . . .'

'I must come with you,' Eadulf said.

Gormán was about to argue but saw the determined look on his face. 'Very well, but keep behind me and in cover. I will call on the two men to surrender. Let us hope they do so. If they don't, Aidan will take care of the one who offers an immediate danger. Understood?'

Aidan took his bow and quiver of arrows from his horse and slid with astonishing quiet and ease into the undergrowth in the direction Gormán indicated.

Gormán waited for a moment, estimating the time it would take for

Aidan to get into position and then, unsheathing his sword, he motioned to
Eadulf to follow, indicating that he should do so stealthily and quietly. As
Gormán had said, it was not far before they rounded a bend which broadened
into a clearing, in which there were the remains of a circular, drystone wall
cattle-pen. The walls that came up to waist-level were crumbling and almost
overgrown with moss and tufts of grasses. To one side was a hut, perhaps
where the cattle-drover stayed when tending his herd.

Gormán reached out the flat of his hand, with a backward gesture to
Eadulf to keep behind him.

There were two men standing upright in the enclosure. One of them
had his sword in his hand and seemed to be staring down at something
before him. Eadulf could not see what it was as it lay out of sight below
the stone wall. Another man was taking a drink from an earthenware jug.
There was no sign of Egric. Close by the hut, three horses were tethered.
Smoke rose from a fire before the hut and other indications showed that
the men had been encamped there some time.

Gormán glanced across the clearing to where the trees followed the rise
of a small hillock. If was as if he were trying to see if Aidan was in place
among the green foliage and bushes. His sharp eyes must have seen
something that Eadulf could not, for he nodded to Eadulf, rose to his full
height and cried: 'Throw down your weapons! You are surrounded!'

The man with the flagon in his hand threw it away, staring in the direction
of Gormán, and shouted to his companion: 'Finish the bastard!'

The man with the sword was raising it as if to plunge it into something
at his feet – but as he did so, he suddenly gave a coughing sound and fell
forward. Eadulf just had time to see the arrow in the man's back.

Gormán was running towards the cattle-pen, sword in hand, as the other
man was turning to see what had happened to his companion, while at
the same time trying to withdraw his own sword. Gormán took the wall
in a gigantic leap. Eadulf was running after him. Gormán had a moment
to regain his balance but it was too late to stop the first man thrusting

with his sword at a figure that lay on the ground half underneath the body of the man with the arrow in his back. Then the killer wheeled round to defend himself, but the tip of Gormán's sword had entered under the breastbone. As Gormán removed his weapon, the man gave a choking cry and fell forward.

Eadulf, with a cry of anguish, had recognised the figure on the ground. Egric lay with his back propped against the stone wall. His wrists were tied by rope to an iron cow-ring set in the stone. There was blood staining his garments, covering his face and arms. It was clear that he had suffered torture. The fingers of one hand were broken and bent. Eadulf knelt towards him and one glance was enough to assess his brother's condition. He pulled the corpse of his erstwhile captor off his brother, drew his knife and severed the cords that bound Egric's wrists. The young man slumped forward with a groan.

Eadulf gently lifted him back into a semi-sitting position, legs splayed out on the ground before him. Eadulf then drew out a *lastar*, containing water, and allowed it to dribble against his young brother's mouth. Egric groaned and opened his eyes, trying to focus.

'Is it you, Eadulf?' The voice was the merest whisper.

'I am here, Egric.'

'Sorry . . . so sorry that it has turned out . . . like this.'

'Lie still and all will be well.'

'Don't try to lie to me. I know . . . I am not long for this world. Trouble is, I don't share the beliefs that you have adopted.' Egric started coughing blood. 'Must tell you . . .'

'I knew that you were no religious,' Eadulf replied tenderly. 'That doesn't matter now.'

'Never could fool you, even when we were young,' the dying man joked. 'But it was true I lived among the Cruthin. I was a warrior in Oswy's army. After the retreat . . . went to Canterbury. Nothing to do. Met old Victricius . . . a fine thief. We made a good pair . . .'

There was another bout of coughing and blood dribbled from the corner of his mouth.

'Going to leave you . . .' he whispered.

Eadulf forced a smile. 'Can't do that. You have only just found me. Anyway, who were these men? Who were they who tortured you?'

'Wanted to know where it was hidden . . . couldn't tell them.'

'Where what was hidden?'

Egric groaned and Eadulf allowed him a little more water. It didn't really matter now if it was the wrong thing to do.

'Leader . . . called Maon. Maybe same gang as attacked us on the river. Maon. Don't know.'

'What did he want?'

There was another bout of coughing. Egric's face was screwed up in pain.

'Who . . . who is Brother Docgan? Ask *custodes* . . . ask . . . Bosa! Bosa! No time now.' His face contorted again.

'We'll find out. Don't worry,' Eadulf promised.

Egric tried to shake his head. 'Not worried. I hear them coming – soon be off to Gladsheim.' Then an anxious look appeared on his face. 'It does exist, doesn't it, big brother?'

Eadulf swallowed hard. Gladsheim – Woden's Castle in Asgard. Thoughts of his youth, the time before he adopted the New Faith, flooded into his mind. Should he deny the Old Faith now? He realised that his younger brother's eyes were becoming dull and foggy. It would not be long now.

'If you truly believe in the House of Vali, you will speed yourself to Asgard, little brother,' he mumbled. 'Woden will be waiting for you in Gladsheim.'

A smile of contentment spread slowly across Egric's features and he closed his eyes for a moment. Then they were suddenly wide with anxiety again, and his eyes flickered from side to side as if seeking something.

'But I must go . . . weapon in hand! Can't enter without sword!' Some incredible power caused his hands to flail about as if searching.

Eadulf turned quickly to Gormán. 'Lend me your sword for a moment.'

Gormán did not question him but handed him his sword, hilt first. Eadulf took it and seized the uninjured hand of his brother, placing it around the hilt.

'Feel it, little brother? Feel it?' he whispered urgently. 'The sword – your sword – it is in your hand.'

Egric's eyes closed again, the smile once more on his face. His hand was clutching spasmodically at the hilt of the sword.

'Thank you, big brother.' His voice was no more than a sigh. 'I will see you again, one day, in the great city of Aesir. Live long and be well, before that day surely comes.'

A coughing fit came on him, and when it passed, a curious strength and purpose moulded his features. Slowly he raised the sword in his one good hand until the tip was pointing skyward. Then he gave a mighty shout. '*Woden!*' His voice was still echoing through the surrounding woods when he fell backwards, his eyes staring sightlessly up at the sky.

Eadulf felt the tears begin to stream from his eyes.

'God's speed, little brother,' he wept. 'May Woden be ready to greet you in Gladsheim. And may my God forgive me for helping you journey to him rather than to the Heaven of the Christians.'

After a few moments he realised that Gormán was standing nervously at his side. He took the sword from his brother's lifeless hand and, without wiping away the tears, handed it back to him hilt first.

'You have just seen the death of a warrior of my people,' he said. 'The death of a warrior, according to the rituals of the old gods of my race.'

Gormán said nothing but allowed Eadulf to continue to kneel in silence by the side of his brother and take his own time in saying his farewells.

Eventually, Eadulf drew himself together. He rose and looked around. Gormán and Aidan had searched the camp and placed the bodies of the two men side by side.

'I don't recognise them,' he said. Gormán and Aidan shook their heads at his unasked question. 'My brother mentioned the name of one of them. What was it? Maon.' He frowned suddenly: where had he heard that name before? Wasn't it the name of the girl that Beccan said he had taken medicines to? No, that was surely wrong. He turned to Gormán. 'What sort of name is Maon? I thought it was a girl's name, but my brother said it was the leader of these two men.'

'It can be either a male or female, friend Eadulf,' answered the warrior. 'It means the Silent One and was a by-name for one of the old pagan gods. The lady Fidelma would know it also, for Maon was the name of the daughter of her teacher, the Brehon Morann.'

Eadulf glanced around and then up at the sky. 'Can we get back to Cashel from here by nightfall? It is important.'

'Nightfall comes early at this time of year. But we could cross at Finnian's Height now that the brothers in the abbey there have built a new bridge across the Siúr, and there is, as you know, a good road from there. The last part of the journey could be made in safety even after nightfall.'

'Is Finnian's Abbey nearby?' Eadulf asked in surprise. 'I know that road well.'

'It is. What do you wish to do, Eadulf?'

'Put these bodies in that hut. We'll take their horses to the abbey and tell the brothers there that they can have them if they come and retrieve the bodies for burial or dispose of them as they will. We do not have the time. However, I shall take my brother's body back to Cashel.'

Gormán and Aidan exchanged a glance but said nothing. Gormán took a blanket and wrapped Egric's body carefully in it. As easily as if he were lifting a child, he picked it up and slung it over one of the horse's backs and secured it. While he was doing this, Aidan gathered some dead wood and branches and covered the two bodies.

'There was absolutely no means of identification on them?' Eadulf asked.

'None,' affirmed Gormán. 'They were certainly not warriors. Perhaps they were members of Rudgal's thugs. Didn't Cummasach say that two of them had escaped?'

Eadulf had forgotten. 'Let's get back to Cashel,' he said wearily.

With that, they mounted, with Gormán leading the horse bearing Egric's body. Eadulf followed while Aidan brought up the rear, leading the other two horses. Apart from their brief stop at the abbey in Finnian's Height, the journey back to Cashel was made in sombre silence.

chapter twenty

E adulf was gazing gloomily from the window, down towards the gates, as a group of horsemen entered the courtyard. They were warriors, led by Enda. After recent events, Colgú had decided to increase the number of patrols around Cashel.

'I hear the Council of Brehons have made up their minds,' Eadulf said, turning to where Fidelma was sitting before the fire.

'I can't help feeling sorry for old Aillín,' she replied. 'He leaves tomorrow for his retirement, but does so unwillingly. I agree that he should have stood down from the office voluntarily. It's a bad end to a long career.'

'Do you know this new Chief Brehon – what's his name . . . Fíthel?'

'I met him only once at a gathering of the Council of the Brehons, but our paths have never really crossed. He is from the Corco Mruad in the north-west of the kingdom and I have had no cause to spend time there. He is quite young and has a reputation as one who has never made false judgements. I am told he arrives later today.'

She rose and began pacing the floor of their chamber deep in thought, and now she came across to join him at the window.

'Are you *sure* your brother used the word *custodes*?' It was not the first time she had asked the question.

'I have told you exactly what he said,' Eadulf replied patiently. 'Why do you refuse to let me challenge Brother Bosa? Didn't Egric indicate he was at the bottom of this entire affair?'

'Your brother also asked who Brother Docgan was.'

'That was the person Egric told Gormán he and Victricius were due to meet in Cluain Meala. We now know there is no such person.'

'It is a Saxon name, you said, and it means "little dog".'

'Knowing the meaning doesn't help.'

Fidelma whirled around and immediately continued her pacing.

'You will wear a groove in the floor soon,' Eadulf said in exasperation. 'Look – my brother identified Bosa with his dying breath. There is no need to delay – we should challenge him immediately!'

Fidelma's features were like the onset of a thunderstorm as she halted and turned to face him. Then she caught herself. Her features softened in sympathy and she placed a hand on his arm.

'It's hard, Eadulf, I know. You had not seen Egric in ten years, and just when you thought you had found him again, he was snatched away by death. But you must not let emotion cloud your vision.'

'He said . . .'

'I know what he said, and it confirms what I have been thinking. I believe that I know who is behind these killings . . . *all* these killings . . . and I am now trying to work out a means of ensnaring that person.'

'Maybe if you shared your knowledge with me, we could find some way,' retorted Eadulf dryly.

'When you cast your mind over everything that has happened, you will realise that there is no witness to any of the murders apart from the killer or killers. It is difficult to go to law without witnesses. We have none to the attack on Victricius now that Egric is dead; no witness to the murders of Brother Cerdic, Rudgal, Sister Dianaimh and of Beccan. We do not even have a witness to the attempt on *our* lives.'

'And you really believe that they are all linked?'

'Oh yes, they are. And one by one, the people who could have provided witness have been eliminated. Sadly, even this man Maon and his companion are now dead – but that cannot be helped.'

'You believe that Beccan was referring to Maon when he talked about taking medicine to someone in the woodman's hut?'

'Beccan was not good at remembering names. My brother once commented on it, if you recall. He suspected that because Beccan was no good at remembering names, he had to write them down. Beccan needed a fictitious woman's name to cover the fact that he was actually meeting Maon. As Maon could be used for either a man or a woman, he decided to stick with the real name so that he could remember it.'

'That is a circumstantial deduction,' Eadulf argued.

'This whole affair rests on circumstances. What we call "indirect evidence under the law". But while the law acknowledges ground for suspicion, even the accusation of guilt cannot be made without what we call the "*arrae cuir*" – a number of reputable people who individually make accusation. Even then, it is not valid if the accused can demonstrate some innocent reason to explain that these suspicions are not justified. That is the frustration.'

'So you know who is at the centre of these mysteries, but you can't accuse them because you don't have the evidence?'

'Correct. I have no conclusive proof with which I could demonstrate that guilt before Chief Brehon Fíthel, who must now judge the matter.'

'In some ways your law system here is good, Fidelma. In other ways, I prefer that of my own people. If there are grounds for suspicion, the person is charged and it is up to him or her to show their innocence.'

'Let us stick to the law as it applies here,' Fidelma replied. 'You said that Maon and his companion tortured Egric to make him reveal . . . reveal what? Where something was hidden? We both know what that something is, and I think you now understand how it came into the hands of Victricius and your brother.'

Eadulf gave an unwilling gesture of affirmation.

Suddenly, Fidelma was smiling. 'Eadulf, I think I have finally found a way to get the evidence. In fact, I am ashamed that I did not think of it before. Let us find Gormán.'

Puzzled, Eadulf hurried after Fidelma as she set off in search of the Commander of the Warriors of the Golden Collar.

He was at the *Laochtech* and greeted Fidelma with a tired smile.

'I hope you are here to tell me to release Deogaire, lady,' he asked hopefully. 'I am not only getting problems from him, but now I have to put up with criticism from Aibell. I didn't know that she knew him.'

'Has Aibell been here?' Fidelma was annoyed. 'I told her I would inform her when she would be allowed to see him.'

'You may recall that she was never any good at accepting orders, lady,' Gormán replied glumly. 'She's been here several times, demanding to see Deogaire. Of course, I am following your orders, but you would think from her manner that I had turned into some kind of ravening monster.'

'I am sorry that this has become a problem between you both.' Fidelma was contrite. 'However, I think we must hold him one more day. At the moment, there is a task I want you to undertake. I want you to seek out some people, but in a manner whereby they will think that they are meeting you by accident. Above all, they must not know that you have spoken to any of the others.'

Gormán's eyes brightened. 'Is this a secret task, lady?'

'Something like that,' smiled Fidelma. 'What I want you to do is spread some gossip. Have you talked to anyone in depth since you came back with Eadulf after the attempted rescue of his brother?'

'We reported to you and to the King, of course.'

'But to no one else?'

He shook his head. 'My duties have kept me busy, lady. But I should think that the King might have told people like Abbot Ségdae what happened.'

'What happened, yes – but now I want you to remark casually that Eadulf brought back a small leather box. Egric had hidden it but Eadulf recovered it – and being anxious about it, took it straight to Brother Conchobhar who has placed it securely in his apothecary.'

Not only did Gormán look startled, but Eadulf as well.

'A leather box?' Gormán ran a hand through his hair trying to understand.

'It is a ruse,' Fidelma explained patiently to them. 'The people you tell must know that the box is in safekeeping with Brother Conchobhar; that it had been in the possession of Eadulf's brother and that Eadulf is worried about the safety of its contents. Is that understood? Above all, it must appear as if you were confiding only in the individual you speak to.'

'I don't understand it, lady.' But Gormán shrugged and grinned, 'However, I shall ensure the message is passed on in the form of gossip, as only a warrior sometimes knows how to gossip about things he doesn't understand. Now, who are the people you want this information to be made known to?'

Brother Eadulf shifted uncomfortably in his seat on the cold floor in the corner of Brother Conchobhar's apothecary, wishing he could get up and stretch to ease his cramped limbs. Fidelma was similarly seated on the opposite side of the room. He wondered whether old Brother Conchobhar had fallen asleep in his little back room. Then he spared a thought for Gormán, hiding in the shadows of the chapel's side entrance across the small courtyard that separated the two buildings. It was the only place where he could view the door of the apothecary. It was a night without stars and no trace of moonlight penetrated through the clouds. Eadulf had no conception of the passing of time but was sure it was well after midnight. He was pessimistic that this so-called ruse of Fidelma's would work.

Time passed. He was just beginning to drift off as natural tiredness overcame him, when he heard a noise and was suddenly wide awake. There was a movement at the side window. He pressed back into the shadows. There was a faint tinkle of breaking glass and the squeak of a catch. He felt the cold night air as the window was opened. Heavy breathing followed, and a grunt, as someone hauled themselves through the opening which, he recalled, was not large but just big enough to take a human.

Now the figure was in the apothecary, standing upright and trying to adjust to the darkness.

'I was hoping that you would be the first to arrive, Brother Bosa,' Fidelma's clear voice rang out.

The man whirled round with a gasp. 'I am—' he began.

'Stay still, do not speak,' Fidelma ordered in an even voice before calling: 'Conchobhar!'

The adjoining door at the rear of the apothecary opened and Brother Conchobhar's voice whispered: 'Do we have him?'

'We have our first visitor,' Fidelma confirmed. 'Brother Bosa, go with Brother Conchobhar and wait with him quietly until I say so. Oh, and be careful. Brother Conchobhar has in his hand an *altan* – what you would call a sharp surgical knife. Its cut can be painful. So I suggest that you say and do nothing.'

Eadulf was starting to crawl from his hiding place but her voice ordered him to stay where he was. Time passed and he was getting restless again when he heard another sound. Fidelma had insisted that the door of the apothecary be shut and locked to avoid any suspicion, for she had estimated that her adversary would realise the door would be locked. If it had been left unlocked, then it would have looked suspicious – like a trap. There was a scraping of metal on metal, followed by a snapping sound. Eadulf was feeling tense now, peering forward in the darkness.

In spite of the depth of the night, he could make out from the difference in tone when the door opened. Something dark appeared – and then there was complete blackness again. Eadulf presumed that the door had swung shut behind the intruder. There was silence for a moment and then the soft sound of stone on metal as the newcomer tried to light a lamp in the darkness. Then came a flame – and suddenly there was illumination.

Eadulf heard Fidelma rising on the other side of the room and he too stood up, staring with amazement at the figure revealed by the light. Shock registered on their features. This was the last person he had expected to respond to Fidelma's ruse.

The figure dropped the lamp, which was immediately extinguished, but the door swung open and a tall shadow was blocking it. Gormán's voice was sharp.

'There is no escape, so just relax.'

At that moment, the interior door opened and the place was flooded with light again as Brother Conchobhar came in holding high a lantern with one hand and his knife in the other. Briefly, the figure seemed to be trying to decide whether to put up some resistance. Then there came a deep sigh and the shoulders slumped in resignation.

It was mid-morning when King Colgú, on Fidelma's advice, summoned all those concerned to attend in his council chamber. He sat with the newly appointed young Chief Brehon Fíthel. The latter was gaunt in appearance with sandy, almost frizzy hair and elfin-like features. Yet the first thing one noticed about him was the icy-blue eyes that fixed one with an almost unblinking stare and seemed to penetrate to the very soul. He sat on Colgú's right side on the dais.

Before them, to the right of the council chamber, sat Fidelma and Eadulf, and beyond them Abbot Ségdae, Abbess Líoch, Brother Madagan and Brother Conchobhar. On the left side of the council chamber, directly opposite them, were the Venerable Verax, Bishop Arwald and Brother Bosa.

Deogaire had been brought from his place of imprisonment and Muiredach, the warrior of Clan Baiscne, had been summoned from Rumann's inn. They were seated at the far end of the chamber facing the King and Brehon Fíthel. Placed strategically around the chamber were Gormán, Enda, Aidan and Luan, the senior warriors of the King's bodyguard.

The air of expectancy was palpable.

Having ascertained that everyone was in their correct places, as Fidelma had advised, Colgú addressed them all.

'It is usual for my steward to commence these proceedings,' Colgú began. 'But as he is no longer of this world, I shall take this task upon myself and be advised by my new Chief Brehon, who will be sole judge in this matter. As I understand that Latin is common to all the participants, excepting some of my guards, the proceedings shall be in that language unless there are difficulties in comprehension. Is it agreed?'

There was a mumbling of agreement from the gathering. Colgú then glanced to Brehon Fíthel, who cleared his throat and asked if Fidelma was ready.

Fidelma rose from her seat, inclined her head quickly to her brother and the Chief Brehon, before walking to the centre of the chamber.

'I have often had difficult matters to deal with in my years as a *dálaigh*,' she began. 'For an advocate of the courts of this kingdom, no matter is more frustrating than when there are no witnesses to the actual crimes; when we have to rely on piecing together the events by conjecture and then making deductions. This was the problem I was faced with in this matter. Because no one seemed willing to tell us the truth, we had to create a picture from odds and ends of evidence. That led me to devise a ruse so that the person I had begun to suspect would declare their own guilt.

'I submit that, after I make my arguments, this ruse should be regarded in law as a method of obtaining the perpetrator's *coibsena* or confession, and under that they are self-declared *bibamnacht* . . . guilty of the crimes.'

She paused for a moment to glance at Brehon Fithel, who nodded to show that he did not disagree with her opening submission.

'So now, let us proceed and piece together this sad story.' She swung round to the Venerable Verax. 'Tell us how the theft took place of those items that you had brought from your brother, Vitalian, the Bishop of Rome, to give to Archbishop Theodore of Canterbury?'

The Venerable Verax started in surprise at the direct question. He glanced at Brother Bosa who was seated nearby but simply shrugged indifferently. The Venerable Verax turned back to Fidelma, his eyes narrowed.

'Are you clever, Fidelma of Cashel, or are you just guessing?'

Fidelma shook her head with a sad smile. 'You should have learned one thing about me from the *nomenclator* of the Lateran Palace, the Venerable Gelasius, whom I was proud to have called a friend in Rome. I *never* guess.'

The Venerable Verax paused for a moment, as if undecided. Then he replied: 'Then you will know that I set out from Rome on a mission to Theodore of Canterbury, bearing with me certain items that were given by the Holy Father and intended for Theodore and none other.'

'I presume that you had but recently arrived in Canterbury when the theft occurred?' she prompted. 'But I should like to know the exact circumstances.'

'I had brought with me certain holy objects. These I carried with me in a chest which was never out of my sight nor that of my personal servant.'

'Except at the time when they were stolen?' she pointed out with dry humour.

'I thought them to be safe in the chest in my residence whilst I was in discussion with Archbishop Theodore. I returned to my chamber late one night, however, and found that my servant had been attacked, the chest had been forced open, and these items and papers removed. Enquiries were made. At this time Bishop Arwald was serving Archbishop Theodore as the head of his *custodes*. He undertook the task of helping to track down the thief or thieves.'

Fidelma turned to Bishop Arwald. 'Archbishop Theodore had decided to copy the Lateran Palace and set up a group called the *custodia* which took care of the security and valuables of the church at Canterbury. Is that so?'

'He had.'

'And you were placed in charge of them?'

'I was.'

'And they included Brother Bosa and Brother Cerdic?'

'They did.'

'So, you undertook to discover the thief. When did you learn that a thief, passing himself as a priest called Victricius, was responsible for the theft of these objects?'

'It did not take long. There is no honour among thieves, and Victricius was a known thief. Witnesses saw him at the Archbishop's residence and leaving the quarters used by distinguished guests. He was later observed at various taverns meeting with a young man – a warrior from the descriptions. This young man had previously been seen by both Bishop Arwald and Brother Bosa, but it was only later that a connection was made. The young man resembled Brother Eadulf there, as had already been pointed out. It was not long before their hiding place was betrayed by other thieves. One of the *custodes* went there to investigate but the two had already fled, leaving behind, I should say, some inconsequential documents from their theft, which evidence confirmed their guilt.'

'Was it Brother Cerdic who was sent to investigate their hiding place?'

Bishop Arwald seemed surprised but nodded. 'He was but newly joined in our *custodia*. He had impressed me with his enthusiasm.'

'He reported back that the thieves had fled?'

'When thieves fall out, truth is to be found,' replied the Bishop Arwald. 'I afterwards questioned the innkeeper where they had been hiding and learned that they had set off for the coast north of Canterbury. Riders went after them but found they had embarked on a merchant ship heading for this kingdom. We realised they would doubtless find buyers for those items they stole here.'

'What made you believe that?'

It was the Venerable Verax who answered. 'I knew from my brother and in our archives that Ard Macha had already petitioned to be recognised as a primacy here. Obviously there would be interest in these objects.'

'Are we to be told what these objects are?' asked Chief Brehon Frithel.

'Yes; we will come to them in a moment,' Fidelma replied. She turned back to the Venerable Verax. 'So you decided to follow the thieves here?'

'There was no option but to make an attempt to retrieve the items.'

'It puzzles me that you did not follow by the same sea route,' Fidelma commented.

'Storms were coming up and we were told it might be several days before we could find a ship. We took advice from Brother Bosa, who had been here before, and it was decided that we ride for a harbour in the land of the West Saxons and take ship from there. Brother Bosa had studied here in Darú and knew the route well. He felt that we might even land in advance of the merchant ship because of the long voyage it had before it.'

'A question!' It was Eadulf who interrupted, and receiving permission of the Brehon Fíthel, he asked: 'I can understand the *custodes* giving chase in this fashion, but why was the presence of the Venerable Verax necessary? He was a distinguished visitor from Rome.'

'I was given a commission by the Holy Father,' explained the elderly prelate. 'It was my task to see it carried out. Anyway, I alone knew what these items were and could identify them.'

'Well, the thieves could identify them as well,' Eadulf replied pointedly.

Brehon Fíthel leaned forward and declared: 'I must now insist that we are told exactly what these valuable items were.'

'Items of extreme value to certain people within these kingdoms wishing to show authority from Rome,' Venerable Verax prevaricated.

'Certain people?' Fidelma smiled indulgently. 'To be succinct, those who wanted to be recognised as Chief Abbot or Bishop of the religious over all these kingdoms. That, of course, is why you were so interested in finding out which of our abbots and bishops would want to claim this primacy. The intention of Victricius and his companion was clearly to sell these items to the highest bidder, as they would seemingly confer the authority of the Bishop of Rome on whoever owned them.'

Abbot Ségdae now intervened with a frown. 'Surely, it must have occurred to the thieves that such a transaction would be as illegal as it would be invalid?'

'Invalid because the items would not have the authority of the Bishop of Rome and because they were presumably intended for another,' agreed Fidelma.

The Venerable Verax smiled tightly. 'Unfortunately, the declaration of the name and office on the parchment, given under the Holy Father's own seal, was left to be filled in later by a scribe.'

'I thought that you said these items were sent to and intended for, Theodore, Archbishop of Canterbury?' Eadulf said sharply.

'Theodore was already Archbishop,' agreed the Venerable Verax. 'He needed no such authority. But he was finding it hard to control all the kingdoms of the Angles and Saxons. He had sent an emissary to Rome with the request that he be allowed to elevate a bishop called Wilfrid as Archbishop of Northumbria, with his cathedral in a town called York. This Wilfrid would therefore become the second Chief Bishop among the kingdoms of the Angles and Saxons. However, Theodore wanted the power to do this without Wilfrid being specifically named, until such time as Theodore was certain of his ability, since there were still some matters of contention between them. My task was to take the *pallium* and the declaration, given under the Holy Father's seal, to Canterbury. As I said before, the name and bishop's see, the official centre and jurisdiction of the bishop, was left for one of Theodore's scribes to fill in.'

'In other words,' Eadulf summed up, 'someone could purchase these items from the thieves and then append their own name? Rome might deny it, but the claim could be announced and could convince enough people to cause a schism that might last for generations.'

'Exactly so,' confirmed the Venerable Verax.

'Well, I would have had nothing to do with such false baubles,' Abbot Ségdae declared immediately.

'But there may be others who have no such scruples,' Fidelma pointed out. 'I have attended councils at Streonshalh and at Autun; I have seen how bishops and abbots are no better than temporal princes in their quest for power. No doubt there would be many who would pay a king's honour price for such items. Fortunately, some of these items were destroyed.'

The Venerable Verax leaned forward with a gasp. 'I hear they were stolen from the thieves – but do you know for certain that they were destroyed?'

'Having come thus far, let us finish.' Fidelma ignored his question. 'You landed in the Kingdom of Laighin. You told people there you were on a deputation to learn the views of the abbots and bishops. But you also asked questions of merchants and travellers to see whether your thieves had reached there. In fact, they had landed in a port further south but not in Laighin. It was a port in this Kingdom of Muman called Láirge. They had hired a river boat to take them here.'

Brehon Fíthel interrupted. 'One of these thieves you say was someone who called himself Victricius?'

'He called himself the Venerable Victricius of Palestrina, passing himself off as an elder of the religious,' Fidelma confirmed. 'He had already been caught stealing and was flogged in Canterbury.'

'I am afraid that his companion was my own brother, Egric,' Eadulf added stiffly. 'My young brother, who by the strangest coincidence of fate survived the attack and was brought to Cashel. He tried to keep up the disguise that he was a religious, travelling with this Venerable Victricius on some religious mission. I felt he was lying but could not accept it.'

'So Victricius and Egric were the thieves who stole the items from Canterbury and brought them to Port Láirge?' Colgú concluded.

'Indeed,' Fidelma nodded. 'Victricius and the boatmen were attacked and killed on the river. Egric survived. The items were initially thought to have been stolen or destroyed.'

Everyone was tense now, looking towards her. She turned and motioned to Eadulf, who produced something wrapped in a cloth, which they had brought into the council chamber.

'Unfortunately, when the thieves arrived at the harbour of Láirge, they met the person who was to set in motion the events that led to all the deaths here. Until he makes a full confession, we can only surmise the details. He met Victricius and Egric at Láirge. He discovered what they had to trade. He saw the tremendous value of the items and knew that, with them, he could acquire rank and power. There was just one problem: he personally could not afford to purchase them.

'So he told Victricius and Egric to take a boat up the River Siúr, to head for Cluain Meala, the Field of Honey, where they would be contacted. Of course, he had no intention of them ever reaching that township. He arranged with a small band of outlaws, led by Rudgal, to ambush them. They were to steal what they could, but ensure that certain items were taken and brought to him. As we know, Rudgal and his companions killed Victricius and the two boatmen, and also believed they had killed Egric.'

'But you said some items were saved?' the Venerable Verax pressed anxiously.

Fidelma gestured to Eadulf, who unwrapped the cloth he had before him. From it, he produced the embroidered lambswool band that Brother Conchobhar had found wrapped around the waist of Rudgal. The Venerable Verax rose and took the item from Eadulf, his eyes wide and hands trembling.

'It is the *pallium*!' he gasped. 'The same *pallium* blessed by the Holy Father.'

'Unfortunately,' continued Fidelma, 'Rudgal and his gang of cut-throats were not too mindful either of life or the value of the written word. Rudgal found and kept the *pallium*, but his companions simply ransacked and destroyed the papers, including the document given under the Bishop of Rome's seal. Rudgal and his attackers took what items they deemed of immediate value and set fire to the rest.'

'How can we be sure that the document with the Holy Father's seal was destroyed?' demanded Venerable Verax.

Eadulf reached into his robe and drew out the small lead fragment that looked like a coin.

'It is lucky that when I was in Rome, I had seen similar items,' he said. 'Here is the lead seal with the letters V.I.T.A. inscribed on it and an emblem. When our warriors came across the scene of the attack by the river, one of them, Dego, spotted this lead token on the ground. It was among the burned papers. He picked it up, thinking it was merely a worthless coin, and decided he would use it as a weight for his fishing line. So this was the only other item that survived.'

He dropped it into the Venerable Verax's outstretched hand. The man glanced at it and uttered a deep sigh. 'It is indeed the Holy Father's *bullae* – his seal – which is attached on all official documents from his hand.'

Brehon Fíthel asked to see the item, turning it over between his fingers. 'Curious, indeed,' he remarked. 'I would have thought such an important seal would have been made of a metal of finer quality than mere lead. What do you call it? A bull?'

'The word *bullae* means a seal,' explained the Venerable Verax, taking it back from the Chief Brehon before glancing at Fidelma. 'So this is all that has survived? No other documents?'

'It is all,' confirmed Fidelma.

'Then it seems that our journey has been wasted.' Bishop Arwald was clearly disappointed.

'Wasted?' rebuked Fidelma. 'Is any journey wasted? I hope not. You have the *pallium* and you have the *bullae*. And perhaps you and your party may have learned something about our kingdoms.' She looked the Venerable Verax straight in the eye and added, without a change of expression, 'You may even inform people that Strabo was in error when he told the world that we were cannibals. Learning that fact, surely, was no waste of a journey!'

'I mean that our fear of these items falling into the wrong hands was no fear at all,' Bishop Arwald replied stiffly.

'On the contrary,' Fidelma returned, 'there *was* a fear – and that fear has engendered the deaths of eight people! In addition, a young warrior is now disabled for life and, had Eadulf and I not been lucky, it might have meant our deaths or injury as well.'

'Eight deaths?' The Venerable Verax frowned.

'Your thief and his companion, Egric, two innocent boatmen, Brother Cerdic, Rudgal, Sister Dianaimh, Beccan the steward . . . I am not even counting the gang of outlaws led by Rudgal.'

'Are you saying that all these deaths were caused by the same event – all came about through the robbery of these items in Canterbury?' It was the Chief Brehon Fíthel who asked the question.

'I do.'

'*Post hoc, ergo propter hoc,*' Bishop Arwald commented sarcastically. 'As these events happened after the first event, so you claim that they must have been caused by that event. Well, it does not follow.'

'On the contrary, I have already said that when the theft took place in Canterbury, the thieves came to this kingdom, and landed in Láirge's harbour, where they met the person who was determined to get what they carried by any means. So their fate was sealed – and that action had a series of reactions.'

'And who was this someone?' asked Chief Brehon Fíthel. 'Are you going to identify him?'

'Of course. Some here already know his identity. However, let me lead you through the morass of deceptions, so you will understand the logic. After the attack by the Déisi outlaws, and the report of the incident to the Brehon at Cluan Meala, Cummasach, the Prince of the Déisi, set out to find the band of outlaws to track them down. They put up a fight and most of the band perished. There were three exceptions. Two men escaped – Maon and his companion, who are now dead. But their leader, Rudgal, was taken captive. He had been told the value of the cloth. He wrapped it around his waist and intended to bargain it for his freedom.

'The conceiver of the murderous plot could not allow that. There was a crude attempt to make Rudgal's death look like suicide, but what his killer did not realise was that Rudgal actually had the *pallium* wrapped around his waist. It was found when the body was prepared for burial and has been hidden in Brother Conchobhar's apothecary ever since.'

'But what of the other deaths?' Brehon Fíthel asked. 'Are you saying the same person – one person – was responsible for *all* of them? If so, I have been told that some of them took place while Deogaire was being held as a prisoner. If he was not responsible for the attempt on your lives, who was?'

'Deogaire is most assuredly innocent – but I had to hold him to allay the suspicions of the killer and later to protect his life in case he too was attacked. For I have to say, this killer has no compunction about sacrificing the innocent.'

Brother Conchobhar leaned towards his nephew and clapped him on the shoulder in congratulation. Deogaire was looking relieved.

'But then it means that Beccan was the guilty person,' Colgú concluded. 'But how . . .? He was also murdered, and so was Sister Dianaimh.'

'We have a saying that whether it is black, dun or white, it is its own kid that the goat loves,' Fidelma suddenly said.

'And so?' Brehon Fíthel was clearly puzzled and he was not alone.

'I think everyone will recall that Beccan was of the Déisi. They are the people who live south of the River Siúr,' she added for the benefit of the Venerable Verax and his companions. 'When Beccan spun the false story about seeing a woman named Maon – who actually turned out to be a man called Maon who was one of Rudgal's outlaws – he let slip that his home was at Míodán. Prince Cummasach, when he brought Rudgal as prisoner here, told us that Rudgal and his band had been caught near their home at Míodán.'

'Are you saying that Beccan was one of them?' demanded Brehon Fíthel.

'Beccan did not have that capability,' Fidelma responded. 'It was his inability even to remember names that almost caused his downfall but has led to another confirmation of the plot. Beccan was afraid of forgetting a fictitious name. It had been observed here that whenever my brother had guests, Beccan had to write them down. So he decided to stick to the real name of the person he was to meet because he knew him well from his own village. Beccan was forced into this conspiracy by his very own family and was used to draw a false trail when the person concerned mistakenly thought I was getting too close to them. Sadly I was not, otherwise . . .' She shrugged.

'How was he persuaded?' questioned Colgú. 'I still don't see.'

'Because I think we will discover that he was related to the main deviser of this murderous conspiracy and also to Rudgal and his outlaws at Míodán.'

'You said Beccan was told to lead a false trail,' Brehon Fíthel frowned. 'By whom and how?'

'Beccan was told to implicate Deogaire in this matter. Unfortunately, honesty of thought often leads to a bad reputation. Deogaire made no secret that he did not share the Faith and so we, in our prejudice, could believe anything about him. So if Deogaire was made to appear guilty – guilty of something – it could direct us away from the truly guilty. It was a complicated plot.

'Someone knew about Deogaire's argument with his uncle. There had been a witness. That person instructed Beccan to do the following: he suggested to Deogaire that he could stay in the guest quarters that night. The idea of it being done in exchange of some medicines was firstly to allay any suspicion that Deogaire might have as to why Beccan had suddenly become friendly enough to make the offer, and secondly to give

Beccan an excuse to leave the palace that night. You see, Maon and his companion had to be alerted to the news that Eadulf's brother Egric had survived the attack on the Siúr and that he had gone to Eatharlach with Dego. The murderer had come to the wrong conclusion – that Egric must have saved the *pallium* and the *bullae* and hidden them. He had to instruct Maon to chase Egric. Why didn't the murderer go himself? Because there was no way he could leave the palace without being missed and giving rise to questions.

'All went as it was meant to. The real killer levered one of the statues so that it would fall. I don't think it was meant to kill us because there was no guarantee that it would do so. I believe it was simply part of a general plan of distraction. We were meant to find Deogaire in the guest quarters and jump to the conclusion that he was responsible. In retrospect, it was a foolish idea because, while we imprisoned Deogaire, once Beccan reappeared, his story would clearly be contradictory. Did the killer think we would simply believe Beccan instead of Deogaire and that would be an end to it? Did this person think that we would not check out Beccan's story about Maon – the so-called ill woman? Or did they think that we might then place the entire blame on Beccan? I confess that I did so, at first.'

'Was it Beccan's death that caused you to change your mind?' asked Colgú.

'I had found out that anyone could exit and gain entrance by way of the scaffolding without being seen at the gates. So at first I was convinced that Beccan had probably done so.' Fidelma sighed. 'The biggest mistake of all was when the initiator of the plot killed Beccan. I can only conclude that he feared that Beccan, when confronted, would immediately reveal all under questioning.'

'So how did you proceed?' Brehon Fíthel asked.

'As I said, there were no witnesses to any of the murders so there was nothing to do but concentrate on the facts as I knew them. It was by a process of elimination that I came to my suspicion. There was now only one person around at the times of all the murders; this same person also had a connection with the village of Míodán and had been in Láirge's harbour when Victricius and Egric landed there.'

She paused for a moment and the gathering leaned forward on the edge of their seats. If anything, Fidelma in her career as *dálaigh* had acquired the use of a dramatic pause in the courts.

'What I did, therefore, was set a trap – a ruse by which the guilty person would reveal themselves. A ruse to obtain the *coibsena* or confession, as I have explained before. Certain people here were told that Egric had, indeed, been keeping in his possession a box which he had been hiding. A rumour was spread that Eadulf had brought that box back to Cashel and placed it for safekeeping in Brother Conchobhar's apothecary. On hearing this, the guilty person would, we hoped, break in and try to steal it.'

She paused again and looked at their expectant faces.

'Our trap worked. Last night, two people broke into the apothecary of Brother Conchobhar.'

ChAPTER TWENTY-ONE

Fidelma now had their complete attention. 'The first person to break in', she told them, 'was Brother Bosa.'

When the ensuing hubbub had died down, Bishop Arwald was on his feet, his face contorted in anger.

'Are you claiming that Brother Bosa is guilty of these crimes? I have known him as a loyal servant of the *custodia* of Canterbury for these last five years. Why, he was not even here when—'

'Sit down!' Brehon Fíthel ordered sharply. 'Brother Bosa, did you break into the apothecary of Brother Conchobhar last night?'

Brother Bosa rose. 'I do not deny it.'

'For what purpose?'

'To retrieve the items exactly as has been claimed.'

'You need to explain the motive,' Fidelma told him above the loud exclamations.

'I am a member of the *custodia* of Canterbury. As a *custodes* it was my *duty* to retrieve these stolen items and return them to the rightful owner once I discovered where they were.'

'I would ask you another question, Brother Bosa. Bishop Arwald has mentioned that Brother Cerdic was a newcomer to the *custodes*. Is that correct?'

'It is.'

'Can you also confirm that it was Brother Cerdic who was sent to the place where the *custodes* learned that Victricius and his confederate were hiding?'

'That is so.'

'He reported that he reached there too late to apprehend them, for they had conveniently fled?'

'What are you implying?' Bishop Arwald intervened, catching the intonation in Fidelma's voice.

'I never imply,' returned Fidelma solemnly. 'But now some questions for you. Did Brother Cerdic specifically ask to accompany you on this pursuit of the thieves?'

'He was not my first choice, but he was very eager to be a member of our party,' the bishop agreed.

'When you arrived in Laighin and heard that Victricius and Egric had landed at Láirge, it was reported that they had started upriver, along the Siúr, making for this kingdom. Whose idea was it to send Brother Cerdic to advise us of the coming of your party? He did not speak our language, whereas Brother Bosa did. Surely Bosa would have been a better choice as emissary?'

'Brother Cerdic was also keen to fulfil that task,' the bishop replied quietly.

Fidelma paused for a moment. 'There are two possibilities for what happened. Firstly, that Brother Cerdic was part of Victricius and Egric's plan from the first, or secondly, that having discovered them in Canterbury, they persuaded him to let them escape in return for a share in the proceeds.'

The Venerable Verax looked shocked. 'How do you know this?'

'By deduction. Muiredach, one of the warriors who escorted you here, escorted Brother Cerdic and Brother Rónán to the Abbey of Sléibhte. Whether by coincidence or design, Sister Dianaimh was at the abbey.'

Abbess Líoch, who had not spoken during the hearing, gave a gasping sob.

'Brother Cerdic went first to the Abbey of Sléibhte because we were told that it was one of the earliest abbeys,' Bishop Arwald explained. 'We thought it might be interested in claiming the primacy.'

'What you did not know was that Abbot Aéd had, for political reasons, decided to support the claim of Ard Macha. We all know that the abbot is a descendant from the ancient royal princes of Uí Bairrche, and they resent King Fianamail's family. So Aéd, by supporting Ard Macha as primacy, would be defending himself against any ambitions of the current King of Laighin. However, there was a twist.'

Brehon Fíthel shifted his weight in his chair. 'A twist? Explain.'

'Sister Dianaimh had lived in the Kingdom of Oswy, at Laestingau, and so spoke Brother Cerdic's language well,' went on Fidelma. 'He did not need an interpreter to speak with her. In fact, he managed to talk to her privately outside of Brother Rónán's hearing, and suggest a transaction. Dianaimh felt a loyalty to Abbot Aéd and told him what Cerdic was planning. I suggest the abbot decided to give his new protector Ard Macha a gift. He gave Sister Dianaimh coins to purchase those sacred items. She would, of course, have to come with that money to Cashel, where Brother Cerdic expected Victricius and Egric would meet.'

'But Sister Dianaimh only came here because she was my female steward,' protested Abbess Lioch. 'I knew she had a fondness for the Sléibhte, where she had trained, but she was my *bann-mhaor*.'

'One of the matters we could not understand was why Brother Cerdic arrived at your abbey requesting your presence to attend this deputation. You had no interest in their purpose. But Brother Cerdic knew very well that you, as abbess, would not attend alone but insist on bringing your *bann-mhaor* with you. Thus he and Sister Dianaimh could ensure her presence here with the money when the items were ready to be purchased.'

'So this Brother Cerdic was working *with* Victricius and Egric?' Brehon Fíthel asked.

'I suspect that he was doing so from the very beginning,' replied Fidelma. 'Though that cannot be proved now.'

'You said *two* people broke into Brother Conchobhar's apothecary last night,' Brehon Fíthel reminded her.

'Let us return to last night when Brother Bosa broke into the apothecary to get those items he had been informed were there. You entered, Brother Bosa: what then?'

'You and your companions were there, having laid a trap,' confirmed the *custodes*. 'You told me to remain quiet and we waited until—'

'Until the second intruder came,' Fidelma finished. She turned to where Brother Madagan had been sitting with a face of stone. It was only now that the others gathered in the chamber realised that Gormán and Aidan had positioned themselves very near to the steward of Imleach. Brother Madagan raised his head and a sneer formed on his features.

'I cannot deny that I came to Brother Conchobhar's shop last night. But as to the rest, you have no evidence, no witnesses, only your theory. I might well have come to Brother Conchobhar's to collect the items to safeguard them for the abbey.'

'Which would mean you knew what they were and their value,' Fidelma smiled.

'Or perhaps I had a toothache and sought a remedy from old Conchobhar.'

'By breaking in through a locked door?'

'Anyway, you have failed to present evidence,' he went on. 'You argue that I was in Láirge, that I am a Déisi from Míodán – but of the rest, where is your proof?'

'If you are to accuse him, you must present something substantial,' Brehon Fíthel pointed out.

'Remember how Abbot Ségdae told us that Brother Madagan had just arrived back at the abbey from Láirge's harbour? He was there when Victricius and Egric landed, and somehow they confided in him what they had for sale. Maybe because he boasted that he was steward of one of the oldest abbeys in the Five Kingdoms.

'He told Victricius and Egric to hire a boat and go upriver to Cluain Meala, the Field of Honey, where a contact named Brother Docgan would meet them with the money they were asking. But Brother Madagan, of course had no intention of paying. He simply arranged for members of his clan, the Déisi, who dwelled at Míodán, to attack them on the river and steal the items.

'But when he returned to Imleach, there were complications. Brother Cerdic had arrived and identified himself as part of the group of thieves. More importantly, he revealed that he had another buyer for the items. That was Sister Dianaimh. Brother Madagan had to get rid of Cerdic. Then Sister Dianaimh had to be eliminated, although he did not manage to discover where she kept the money that she was going to pay for the items. Don't forget, Brother Madagan could not and had no intention of buying them.

'Brother Madagan was horrified when he heard that Egric had survived the attack on the river. I wondered why he seemed to be avoiding Egric. He had to be at the funeral of Cerdic that night, but wore a cowl which hid his face, since Egric would have been able to identify him. Once Egric knew that his confederate Cerdic was also dead and members of the Canterbury *custodia* were about to arrive, he contrived to leave Cashel, using a fishing trip with Dego as an excuse.

'The question Madagan now had to ask was – *where were the items*? When he confronted Rudgal in the barn, Rudgal was intent on using the *pallium* to buy his own freedom, so refused to tell him. He did tell Madagan that, once he was free, he would be rejoining Maon, who was waiting at a hut in the woods. Madagan killed Rudgal, not realising he had the *pallium* concealed on his body. Madagan thought Egric still had the items. That led to the convoluted method of getting Beccan to pass that information on to Maon while, at the same time, thinking to distract us by placing the blame on Deogaire for a silly attack on us. As I say, that attempted distraction was the biggest mistake he made.'

'But who was this other conspirator?' Brehon Frithel asked. 'Brother Docgan, I think you said?'

'Brother Docgan is a Saxon name. That was quite a wry touch. It means "little dog". Brother Madagan, would you like to tell our visitors what the name Madagan means?' Brother Madagan simply glowered at her. 'No? Well, it means . . .'

'It means "little dog",' interrupted Brother Conchobhar in a triumphant voice.

As she sat down, having finished her summation, Abbot Ségdae stared horror-struck at his steward.

'Can all this be true?' he uttered in a strangled voice. 'Madagan had often said that Imleach should be recognised as a great abbey but . . .'

Brother Madagan turned an angry expression on him mingled with something else; something akin to pity. 'Imleach is older than Ard Macha. Ailbhe converted this kingdom long before Patricius set foot on Sliabh Mís to preach the New Faith. You should have claimed what is rightfully yours many years ago. To Imleach belongs the primacy of all the Five Kingdoms. Respect and power would be given to it through all the Five Kingdoms, and Imleach would be recognised even as far as Rome. That is what you have lost.'

Brehon Fíthel sat back in his seat, nodding slowly in satisfaction. 'There is your *bibamnacht* – the expression of the guilty.'

The Venerable Verax shook his head sadly. 'I cannot see how you came to suspect this man in the first place, Fidelma. It could not have been the similarity of the meanings of the names. It is such a complicated plot that he seemed to have blocked all possibilities of discovery.'

'When all the possibilities have been eliminated, that which remains must be the solution,' she replied gravely. 'But I was subconsciously alerted when Deogaire foretold doom and gloom coming from the East at the funeral of Brother Cerdic. Abbot Ségdae turned and made a curious remark to Brother Madagan about prophets not being respected. I wondered what this referred to. Some time later, when I asked the abbot, he told me that Brother Madagan had started to recount a dream whereby he had dug up the Blessed Ailbhe's tomb and in it found some items which would indicate that Imleach would be chosen as the principal abbey in all the Five Kingdoms.'

'A silly dream,' added Abbot Ségdae in a bitter tone.

'Not so silly,' she replied. 'Brother Madagan was preparing you for the stage when he had the *pallium* and seal in his hands. He doubtless planned to bury them in Ailbhe's tomb and then, acting on his dream, have them dug up and a miracle proclaimed.'

There was no need to confront Brother Madagan to verify whether this was the truth or not.

'But this man was only my steward,' objected Abbot Ségdae. 'What profit would the elevation of the abbey be to him?'

'He would become steward in a powerful abbey,' replied Eadulf. 'So he, too, would be reflected in its power. He might even have thought that he would eventually replace you as abbot.'

'Why?' demanded Abbot Ségdae, shaking his head sadly as he stared at his steward. '*Why?*'

Brother Madagan merely smiled with an air of disdain. 'It is better to be the object of envy than of one of pity.'

Some days had passed when Fidelma and Eadulf sat before the fire in their chambers, warming themselves for the day was cold and there had been a light dusting of snow earlier that morning.

'It seems so peaceful now that the Venerable Verax and his companions have set off east again,' Fidelma sighed.

'I think my compatriots were all astonished that Brother Madagan was not immediately put to death,' Eadulf remarked. 'Sometimes I do find it hard to accept the different concepts of law and punishment between our people.'

'What does it benefit society to kill someone in vengeance? Instead, they should be made to compensate those whom they have wronged and through that work, rehabilitate themselves.'

'So what will happen to Brother Madagan?'

'Because his crimes were heinous, I am told that he is being escorted by Prince Finguine to one of the islands off the lands of the Corco Loígde. There are hundreds of islands and islets there. One will be chosen; then he will be left there with a few tools and his own devices. In a year or so, the island will be revisited to see if he had been able to survive. In that way, we will leave it to God to judge his fate.'

'Yet he still has a life,' Eadulf objected. 'He did not personally kill Egric and, of course, my brother was a thief but . . . Ah, maybe *I* was in the wrong? Maybe I should have kept a closer watch on Egric when he was growing up. I did leave him to pursue my own ambition.'

'You cannot be blamed for the path Egric chose,' Fidelma replied firmly. 'And who knows what other influences he encountered along the way.' There was a brief silence between them. Then she said: 'I hear that Dego has arrived back in Cashel this morning. I must visit him.'

'I saw Gormán a short while ago,' Eadulf told her. 'He tells me that Dego appeared in good spirits. His arm is healing nicely and he can already ride a horse. He rode all the way back from Eatharlach, albeit with some help from Brother Berrihert.'

Fidelma smiled, for Eadulf was not the best of horsemen. 'You don't need two hands to ride a horse. A good warrior can ride into battle with his sword in one hand and buckler in the other, guiding the animal by the squeeze of his thighs.'

'I wish Dego well. I did try to put cheer into him by telling him about the one-armed warrior of the Fomorii.'

Fidelma was not impressed. 'The Fomorii? Better that you should have reminded him of Nuada of the Silver Arm.'

Eadulf frowned. 'I haven't heard of him.'

'He was an ancient king, so it is said, and much associated with my own family, the Eóghanacht. Eóghan Mór, the progenitor of our house, was often called Mug Nuadat, the servant of Nuada. Nuada lost his arm in battle.'

'So what happened after he lost his arm? I thought that having a physical impairment excluded a person from kingship?'

'The story goes that the physician to the gods, Dian Cécht, made him a hand and arm of silver. That is how he became known as Nuada of the Silver Arm. But as time went on, Miach, the son of Dian Cécht, proved himself an even greater physician than his father. He made Nuada a hand and arm of flesh and blood again.'

Eadulf grimaced sceptically. 'Ah, the tales of gods and heroes of yesteryear. Well, no god or physician will appear to create a hand and arm of flesh and blood for poor Dego. Such stories must be confined to the fantasies of the mind.'

'But it is from the fantasies of our minds that the will to achieve is born. I am sure Dego will not be content to retire to a corner of an alehouse and simply bemoan his lot. I have no worries about his future . . .'

'But . . .?' prompted Eadulf, hearing the unfinished thought in her speech.

'There is one matter I *am* very worried about.'

'Only one?' Eadulf teased.

'An important one,' she confirmed seriously.

'Ah, you mean Aibell,' he said.

'Have you already noticed?'

'How could I not notice?'

'I have been wondering whether to advise Deogaire that he should set out for Sliabh Luachra immediately. Have you seen the way Gormán is glowering at him the whole time?'

'He has a right to glower,' Eadulf replied. 'Aibell has been constantly in Deogaire's company ever since he was released. Knowing the way Gormán feels about the young girl, I would not be surprised if there was some bloodshed before long.'

'Isn't that precisely what I was trying to tell you?' Fidelma frowned. 'That is why Deogaire should be told to leave here. I suppose I must be the one to tell him.'